Praise for the Honey Badger Chronicles

"There are no dull pages in *Breaking Badger* . . . Laurenston immerses readers in a world full of family, friends and shifter dynamics that never fail to amuse. Secondary characters with smart mouths and interesting abilities boost the high-octane entertainment. There's nonstop banter, plenty of blood and gore and flaming-hot lovemaking as the intrepid Mads battles her dangerous relatives while learning that teammates can be friends and that your true family is the one you choose." —***BookPage*** on *Breaking Badger*

"Laurenston expands her 'Honey Badger Chronicles' series to the friends of the MacKilligan sisters with her trademark snark and over-the-top humor. Fans will be screaming to read this entry . . . Laurenston should be a required purchase for public libraries." —***Library Journal*** on *Breaking Badger*

"A wild, brilliant ride." —***Kirkus Reviews*** on *Badger to the Bone*

"Fans of shifter romances will not want to miss the latest installment of the Honey Badger Chronicles." —***Bookish*** on *In a Badger Way*

"After reading *Hot and Badgered*, I asked myself in which areas of my life can I be more like the honey badgers. . . . Among my favorite things about Laurenston's writing is how very affirming and inspiring and a whole lot of fun it is, because angry, fearless women make room for themselves, they get shit done, and they're heroines. More honey badgers please." —***Smart Bitches, Trashy Books*** on *Hot and Badgered*

Turn the page for more

"Laurenston is a comic genius who understands that absurdity often lies at the heart of adventure and romance . . . Laurenston does it again with her newest book, *Hot and Badgered*, which is easily the top contender for Best Book Title of the Year."
—*The Amazon Book Review* on *Hot and Badgered*

"Shelly Laurenston's world of shape-shifters is hilarious, sexy, often casually violent and always absolutely fascinating. . . . The plot zips along with surprising twists, turns and fearless honey badger bravery. The non-stop action also allows for excellent character development and lots of snarky humor is a testament to Laurenston's skills." —*BookPage* on *Hot and Badgered*

"For all the joyful zaniness of her characters, Laurenston can also cover some heavy topics amid the hilarity and action. Mental health issues are addressed as Stevie works toward self-acceptance with the love and support of her sisters and Shen."
—*The Philadelphia Inquirer* on *In a Badger Way*

"Laurenston writes paranormal romance filled with offbeat humor and mayhem . . . Laurenston makes me laugh out loud. She has been known to make people laugh so hard they roll off their bed." —*Sunday Citizen-News* on *Badger to the Bone*

"Laurenston delivers all the dark, hilarious lunacy her fans expect. . . . Filled with familiar faces and more than a few kooky, delightful surprises, the plot neatly ties up loose ends while dangling tantalizing promises of things to come. Series readers will gobble this up."
—*Publishers Weekly* on *Badger to the Bone*

TO KILL
A BADGER

Also by Shelly Laurenston

The Pride Series

The Mane Event

The Beast in Him

The Mane Attraction

The Mane Squeeze

Beast Behaving Badly

Big Bad Beast

Bear Meets Girl

Howl for It

Wolf with Benefits

Bite Me

The Call of Crows Series

The Unleashing

The Undoing

The Unyielding

The Honey Badger Chronicles

Hot and Badgered

In a Badger Way

Badger to the Bone

Breaking Badger

Born to Be Badger

TO KILL A BADGER

SHELLY LAURENSTON

kensingtonbooks.com

KENSINGTON BOOKS are published by
Kensington Publishing Corp.
900 Third Avenue
New York, NY 10022

Copyright © 2025 by Shelly Laurenston

All rights reserved. No part of this book may be reproduced in any form or by any means without the prior written consent of the Publisher, excepting brief quotes used in reviews.

Without limiting the author's and publisher's exclusive rights, any unauthorized use of this publication to train generative artificial intelligence (AI) technologies is expressly prohibited.

All Kensington titles, imprints, and distributed lines are available at special quantity discounts for bulk purchases for sales promotion, premiums, fundraising, educational, or institutional use.

This book is a work of fiction. Names, characters, businesses, organizations, places, events, and incidents either are the product of the author's imagination or are used fictitiously. Any resemblance to actual persons, living or dead, events, or locales is entirely coincidental.

To the extent that the image or images on the cover of this book depict a person or persons, such person or persons are merely models, and are not intended to portray any character or characters featured in the book.

Special book excerpts or customized printings can also be created to fit specific needs. For details, write or phone the office of the Kensington Sales Manager: Kensington Publishing Corp., 900 Third Avenue, New York, NY 10022. Attn. Sales Department. Phone: 1-800-221-2647.

Kensington and the K logo Reg. U.S. Pat. & TM Off.

ISBN: 978-1-4967-3022-0 (ebook)

ISBN: 978-1-4967-3020-6

First Kensington Trade Paperback Printing: September 2025

10 9 8 7 6 5 4 3 2 1

Printed in the United States of America

The authorized representative in the EU for product safety and compliance
is eucomply OU, Parnu mnt 139b-14, Apt 123
Tallinn, Berlin 11317, hello@eucompliancepartner.com

This entire Honey Badger series is dedicated to all the educators/ teachers out there who see that weird kid in the back of the room, trying to blend into the woodwork. One was Mr. Lemos, my tenth grade English teacher and my homeroom teacher until I graduated high school. He always treated my writing seriously. Even when what I was writing was ludicrous, he gave me feedback like an editor. I didn't realize it at the time, but that supportive energy would stick with me and guide my work for ages.

Then there was Mrs. Kingsley. She wasn't my teacher, though. She was my best friend in high school. We met when she sat behind me in social studies. For decades, she's been flourishing in one of those brutal careers. Like Navy SEAL or CIA operative or battlefield nurse . . . she's been an elementary schoolteacher. And one of the best. She always supported me and my writing. And, to this day, she *still* has my back.

So, for all those amazing teachers out there, helping kids who are different, like I was—and still am—thank you. I will always be grateful.

Prologue

"I didn't sign up for this."

And he hadn't! Kevin really hadn't! He was head of security for his client; had been for three months. That meant he was supposed to protect the guy and manage his team. What it *didn't* mean was that he was supposed to stand by while his client tortured some rando for information.

"I'm letting him go," Kev informed everyone.

"No! The bastard has stolen from me and I will have it back!" his client yelled in that thick French accent that, after three months, was starting to wear on Kev's nerves.

He had told the Frenchman, when he applied for the job, that he didn't speak French. Nor did he speak any other language but English. But he got the feeling his client liked the idea of having an American security team. All those steroid-enhanced muscles seemed to make him feel more protected than some European security team. He probably watched way too many American action movies.

And maybe, after watching all that nonsense, his client thought security teams would start killing anyone, because that's what they do in the movies. In those movies, the teams always know the most ancient of martial arts, can use any weapon, can fly helicopters and, when it was all over, one of them got the girl. Sadly, real security wasn't like that at all. It could be tedious and boring and involve standing outside doorways for hours while your client either closed deals or fucked his latest girlfriend.

What it didn't involve, as far as Kev was concerned, was letting this man torture people while he watched.

"If he stole from you," Kev reasoned, "let's call the cops. We can let them deal with it. Legally."

"Are you stupid, eh? We cannot take him to police."

"Well, we're not keeping him!" Kev shot back.

"You work for me, yes? You do what I say." He gestured at the Asian man zip-tied to the chair. "Now break his fingers."

Startled, Kevin mutely stared at the Frenchman for a few seconds.

"What now?" Kev finally asked.

"Break his fingers. Now."

"I am not breaking the man's fingers. I'm just going to let him go."

"You are pathetic," his client snarled, before pointing at one of the other guys. "You. You break his fingers."

His teammate shrugged before stepping forward, reaching for one of the man's hands.

Kev raised his arm, blocking him. "What the fuck are you doing?"

"Gonna break this dude's hand."

"You're not breaking anything," Kev said between clenched teeth. "I'm not letting this happen."

"Oh?" his client asked, smug. "How will you stop this? We are in the middle of an ocean."

They'd anchored the yacht in the Singapore Strait, a few nautical miles from the port. He could maybe swim the distance back to safety, but not if he was carrying a captive with him.

It didn't matter. He wasn't going to let this happen. He'd managed to go through life without killing anyone; he wasn't about to start now. Not even if it meant pissing off a billionaire.

Kev took a moment to take a quick look around the cabin. He knew this ship better than anyone. He'd taken his time to explore every part of it so that if pirates ever made it onboard, he could get his client out. Now it looked like he'd be doing that exact thing, but with some calm Asian man who hadn't said a word since Kev had been here. He didn't look upset either. Even when Kev's teammate was reaching for a zip-tied hand. He simply sat there with curious brown eyes, watching everything unfold before him. It was strange, but Kev didn't have time to analyze any of that. Although he did hope *not* to find out that his captive was some kind of war criminal with a million deaths on his head. Then again, if he was, Kev was sure his client would have told him that by now to get him on his side.

Knowing he needed to move fast, Kev noted there were two doors into this particular cabin, on opposite sides of each other. He was glancing at the one on his right when he heard a dull thud outside the other. He had men in the hallway, so maybe one tripped or something.

Then again . . . Kev briefly studied how the Asian man was dressed. It suggested that he, too, came from money, like Kev's client. The cufflinks alone were worth a small fortune, and the tailored tux was designer. Then there was that watch. Worth about half a mil, easy. So the man probably had his own security team ready to die for him. Things were quickly spiraling, and Kev knew he had to be smart about all this.

With a hand signal, he silently told his men to draw their weapons and get ready. He pulled his own Glock and held it in one hand while yanking the door open with the other.

The small Asian girl standing outside that door—and she was a girl, maybe seventeen or so—was pulling herself onto the shoulder of one of his men; her small body clothed in a wetsuit, a harpoon gun strapped to her back. When her legs were around his man's neck, she placed the barrel of a Beretta against the top of his head and—dark brown gaze locking with Kev's—she pulled the trigger.

"Fuck!" Kev yelped in shock when the blood and brain splattered across his face and chest before slamming the door shut and turning to his men.

"Get him out! Get him out!"

Two of his men immediately went to their client to grab him, while a third opened the other door. He was a big man, so he completely filled the cabin doorway. But he still should have gotten through. Instead, he just stood there. Blocking the exit for the rest of them.

"What are you doing?" Kev demanded. "Move!"

He did move. He fell backward like a massive oak falling in the woods, a blade stuck in his throat, choking on his own blood until the weapon was pulled from flesh by another small female. She was in all black; multiple blades sheathed on her leggings, boots, and a corset wrapped around her waist.

Before Kev could give the next order, guns were raised and his men started shooting, but he immediately ordered them to stop. This new girl was young, too! She didn't seem older than Kev's own middle daughter.

Thankfully, his team still followed *his* orders and stopped firing. A few seconds later, the girl bounced back into the open doorway, unharmed, and . . . grinned. She grinned as if she were having the best time of her life. Kind of like the time his youngest daughter found a duck in the lake behind their house. Of course, that duck attacked her, and now she hated all birds . . .

Still grinning, the girl pointed at their client, and they all looked at him, wondering what the hell was happening.

Maybe the Frenchman deserved this. Kev had no idea what his current client had been up to before he'd taken this assignment. The man could have made his billions by selling girls just like this. Kev didn't know and he didn't care. He just knew he needed to get out and he needed to take the captive with him.

"*Kill her!*" his client yelled, pointing back at the girl. "*Kill them all!*"

Kev was not exactly shocked by such ridiculous orders, but he was surprised that his men followed them, again opening fire on the girl standing in the doorway.

Moving fast, Kev went to the captive.

"Don't worry," he told the man. "I'll get you out of here." The man silently gazed at him, and Kev realized that he may not understand a word Kev was saying. He had yet to react to anything that had happened to him in the last hour, so maybe Kev should just worry about getting him out of here rather than successfully communicating with the man. He didn't have time.

The gunfire abruptly stopped, and his men stared not at the dead body of a child, but an empty hallway. Somehow, his team had managed *not* to hit the girl with the knives. Again. And Kev had no idea what happened to the girl with the Beretta. He took the opportunity, however, with everyone's focus on something else, to use his tactical knife to release the man. He dropped to a crouch beside the chair and quickly cut the ties used on his legs. When he sat back on his haunches to tackle the man's hands, he discovered that the hands were already free, and the captive was busy rubbing feeling back into his wrists. How he'd done that, though . . .

That's when the man warmly smiled at him. And winked.

Before Kev could react to any of that, he heard screaming and lifted his gaze in time to see one of his men dragged up through an open emergency hatch and into the ceiling. The others stumbled back as a bleeding corpse was thrown back out a few seconds later. Another of his men screamed as the floor beneath him seemed to open up and he was dragged partially down. The remaining of his team grabbed his arms to hold him in place, but eventually he stopped fighting and just sort of died where he was stuck.

They'd just released his arms when the first girl, the one with the Beretta, reappeared, and before Kev could yell a warning, she used the harpoon gun she had strapped to her back to snag their client.

The spear slammed into his upper thigh, right through the bone. The Frenchman's screams of agony cut through everything else going on around them, and the girl yanked their client back the way she came. Reaching out, the Frenchman grabbed at one side of the doorway, holding on for his life.

Without really thinking, Kev started to move toward his client to help him. It was instinct more than a desire to help a man ready to torture some dude in an expensive tux, but a hand on his shoulder stopped him.

"I would not," a low, male voice said from behind him in what sounded like a British accent. "She is quite irritated."

Irritated? Kev wasn't exactly sure that's how he'd describe the girl dropping the harpoon gun long enough to reach over and grab Kev's client by the back of his designer suit and yank him into the hallway. The Frenchman had been holding on so tight to the wood, he'd actually taken some of the doorway with him, but that hadn't stopped her.

6   *Shelly Laurenston*

Once she had the client in the hallway, she picked up her harpoon gun and proceeded to drag the man away like she was dragging a shark from the ocean, a thick trail of blood and the Frenchman's screams following in their wake.

"No, no, Maxine. Not him."

Startled again, Kev turned to find the girl with the knives about to cut him across the throat. But the former captive had stopped her, for which he would be eternally grateful. At this point, he just wanted to get back home to his wife and girls alive.

"It's just Max, Mr. Zee," the bouncy young girl said, smiling. "And are you sure you don't want me to waste him?"

"Don't say 'waste him,' dear. You're not in a John Woo movie."

"I can make it painless," she insisted. "If you want. Or I can make him suffer. I can even make him cry or squeal like a pig. If that's your thing. I have discovered I am really good at torture, because I don't care what sounds people make when they're dying!"

The worst part of everything the girl had just said was that she said it all like one of his daughters talking about putting glitter on her favorite sneakers or something. It was just so cheery and happy. She was still smiling! It was fucking terrifying!

She continued on. "My older sister says I'm this way because I'm a sociopath. But my baby sister, who's studied this stuff, says I'm not a *full* sociopath. She thinks I'm just a *borderline* sociopath. But I'm pretty sure I'm completely normal!"

"You're not," the man said before Kev could. "But that's okay," the man went on. "You have other qualities that are to be appreciated."

"Awww. Thanks, Mr. Zee!" Her grin made Kev want to crawl into the ceiling.

"Are we ready?" a blonde white girl with a big machete resting on her shoulder asked, as she came to a stop in front of the door. Blood dripped from the head of that weapon, but Kev refused to focus on that—or the blood splattered across her face. He couldn't. "We should go. We've got that"—she glanced at Kev with narrowed eyes—"thing."

"Yes, yes. The *thing*. Of course," the man said. "Although I do think we have time to make a few stops before we get back."

"Oooh!" the girl with the knives cheered, clapping her hands together like an excited three-year-old. "Does that mean what I think it means, Mr. Zee?"

"No," the blonde said. "We're not doing that, because it's not necessary and we're not taking advantage."

"Why not?"

"Shut up," the blonde snapped before sweetly telling the man, "Thanks anyway, Mr. Zhao."

"I appreciate your concern, my dear Mads, but I think we *do* have to make those stops before returning home," the man insisted. "Since it looks like Max-a-lona here has lost dear Emily's watch."

"It's just Max, Mr. Zee. And no I didn't—oh, damn," she grumbled, while grabbing her empty wrist and suddenly studying the area beneath and around her feet.

"I warned Tock you were going to lose her watch," the blonde said.

"I didn't *lose* it. I *misplaced* it."

"What's the difference?"

"Semantics."

"Mr. Zhao!" Another girl—this one armed with guns *and* knives and, he was guessing, of South Asian descent—walked into the cabin. She had brown hair that reached down her back in one long braid, and she immediately went to Zhao and gave him a warm hug. "I'm so glad you're okay."

"Thank you, Cass."

"You owe me five bucks," the blonde told the long-haired girl.

"Max! You lost Tock's watch?"

"You guys took bets?"

"She's going to kick your ass."

"No, no," the man said. "Not if we move quickly. We can get some shopping done and get back in time for the . . . *thing*." Finally, he motioned to Kev. "But, first, I do need to deal with my friend here."

The long-haired girl studied Kev a moment before asking, "Do you want us to . . ." She drew her forefinger across her throat in as dramatic a fashion as humanly possible.

"No, no," Zhao said with a smile. "I just need to get him to safety."

"Ohhhh! That's not a problem. The yacht staff is getting on the barge right now. But he better move." She looked at the watch on her own wrist. "You know Tock and time. She's got all this scheduled down to the second."

"Of course." Zhao turned to Kev. "Thank you for your help today, Kevin."

Kev wasn't going to ask how the man knew his name. His client had never used any of their names. Just pointed and made demands.

"My pleasure, sir."

The long-haired girl stepped forward. "Okay"—she pointed left— "go that way. If you see Tock—tall girl with curls and a never-ending expression of terse misery on her face—just tell her Max lost her watch. Do it *before* she can put a bullet in your head, and she'll instantly know you're with us, and should not be put down like a dog."

"I didn't lose it," the other girl argued. "I *misplaced* it."

"Tock won't care." The long-haired girl gave Kev an award-winning smile. "It was lovely to meet you, Kevin."

Unable to speak at this point, he simply nodded and headed out. By the time he got to the deck—without being threatened by anyone else—the last of the staff was getting on the barge. They all looked terrified and confused. And since that's how Kev felt at the moment, he happily joined them.

Once the barge was a good distance from the yacht, Kev finally let out a relieved sigh.

"What do we say when we reach land?" the yacht captain asked Kev as they watched the vessel recede mile after nautical mile.

"Just say pirates."

"Pirates that let us go?"

Kev shook his head, still trying to understand what he'd just been through.

"Just say pirates," he repeated.

"What do we say happened to *Monsieur*—"

"He's gone."

As if to prove that point, the force from the explosion that took down the yacht sent such a strong shockwave through the ocean that for a long moment—holding onto the railing with one hand and grabbing hold of the yacht captain with the other—Kev was sure the barge would capsize. Thankfully, that didn't happen and, with people now desperately huddling together and either crying or simply shaking in silence, the barge continued on.

It was a minute or two later that a speedboat zipped from behind the mountain of still-falling yacht debris, heading back to shore. A lone Asian man in an expensive tux and a bright orange life jacket had the wheel while surrounded by five young girls, who were either laughing or bickering amongst one another. It looked like a rich father taking his daughter and her friends on a quick excursion before a family get-together rather than what it was, which he assumed was some kind of weird murder cult.

The boat took a quick turn around the barge, and that's when Kev noticed the girl with all the knives. She raised her hand and waved, that big, happy, *disturbing* grin on her face. Then, with her gaze locked with Kev's, she brought her hand to her mouth, raised her forefinger, and pressed it against her lips.

"Yeah," he reiterated to the yacht's former captain. "Pirates. We'll say pirates." And that's exactly what Kev would be repeating to the local government authorities and anyone else who asked him what happened on that yacht. In fact, that's all he'd ever say about any of what happened this day for the rest of his life.

Arthur Zhao took the open spot on the ancient football field benches, right next to his beautiful wife. The locals were cheering and applauding, but not his wife. Never his wife. She didn't believe in "vulgar displays." No matter the event. Instead, she sat there in her extremely expensive Chanel suit, shoes, and purse, with a light windbreaker folded beside her in case the Wisconsin weather decided to turn on them at the last minute.

"You took your time," she said without looking at him.

"We had to pick up a few things in Italy first."

"I see that," she noted, gaze locked on the five teens jumping into the line of gowned-and-capped students preparing to go up on stage for their awards and diplomas. "How much did you spend on those not related to us by blood?"

"They saved my life."

Her eye roll was epic. "You could have gotten yourself free at any time. You were testing her."

"Of course, I was. She's about to go out on her own. And how wonderfully she passed. They all did. A-pluses all around." He crossed one leg over the other; removed some lint from his pants that he was positive was there. "To be quite honest, I'm surprised you're here at all, my dove."

"Why?"

"Last we spoke, you were not wasting your time watching your daughter graduate from a lower-caste school that gave her nothing but an American education."

"It does seem like a waste of time. She could have graduated from here when she was fifteen."

"And leave all her friends behind?"

"Her *friends*?" she questioned. "You mean the junior spy, the minor Viking, the actress, and the useless half-Asian?"

"You do know we're sitting *right* here?" the "junior spy's" mother demanded from behind them. "And that you're both speaking English? At least have the decency to talk shit about our kids in Cantonese."

Arthur glanced at the three families surrounding them. "Junior Spy" Emily "Tock" Lepstein-Jackson's parents—the mother was Israeli, the father Jamaican; "the actress" Cass "Streep" Gonzalez's parents—Filipinos with a love of all things Catholic and ancient; and the two sisters of Maximus Dominus MacKilligan—that was her name, yes? She *insisted* on calling him Mr. Zee—or, as his wife insisted on calling her, "the half-Asian." The "junior Viking," Mads Galendotter, did have blood relations, but none who would actually attend an event that might show they cared. Over time, however, the three other families and the two sisters had quietly "adopted" the Viking, letting her stay over as much as she wanted with their daughters, making sure she got some dinner, and that she had somewhere to go every American holiday.

At first glance, these four sets of families had absolutely *nothing* in common, and he was certain his dear wife would say they were as different from them as apples from dead toads. But that wasn't true. They had much in common, because they were all honey badgers.

With nothing but a thought, any of them could shift from their human form into their honey badger one. Unlike the rest of the shifter community, though, his kind lived almost exclusively among the full-humans, who couldn't shift into anything. Why would they bother with these average people? Because they could. Because it was easy. Because, unlike the bears and cat shifters, honey badgers weren't giants among tiny full-humans. And because the full-humans were fun to toy with.

Over the centuries, honey badger shifters had started dynasties, destroyed despots, and instigated wars. They also stole royal jewels, smuggled ancient artifacts, and counterfeited endless works of art so they could have the real piece in their living rooms until it one day ended up in someone's garage sale for three dollars.

That was why Arthur had been completely unconcerned when he was grabbed off the streets of Singapore by full-humans. He could have gotten out of that situation long before they got him on that yacht, and with minimal damage to himself and the city streets. But for years, he had heard secondhand about what his youngest daughter and her friends were like when they worked together. He wanted to see them all in action.

He had not been disappointed.

He strongly felt it was good to have friends one could count on no matter how much time had passed since one had last seen said friends. He had friends like that from long before he met his wife. And so did his wife. Of course, both their friend groups came from families like theirs. Wealthy honey badgers who were born and raised in Hong Kong when it was still a British territory and had a very long

12   *Shelly Laurenston*

history dating from the Ming Dynasty. Lorraine's bloodline actually came from the Ming Dynasty's first emperor, due to one of his early concubines.

Sadly—for his wife—none of Nelle's current friends had that kind of lineage. Lorraine strongly believed their daughter's friends were "nobodies" who didn't deserve to be around a family as rich and powerful as theirs. Arthur, despite his own lineage, had never felt that way, but he didn't bother arguing with her on the subject, because it had never been necessary. By the time little Nelle could walk, she had made it clear she didn't need anyone to fight her battles for her. She did what she wanted, how she wanted, and was never, ever rude about it. Just like her mother.

Hoping to avoid a nasty badger fight between his wife and Tock's mother, Arthur turned to look at the parents of his daughter's friends and said, "I hope all of you are coming to our house for the celebration tonight. Our eldest has arranged a lovely evening for Nelle and your daughters, and it promises to be a delightful event."

"Hey!" a full-human parent Arthur didn't know, seated a couple of bleachers in front of them, piped up. "My hubby and I are having a big barbeque at our house, too! If y'all want to stop by. It's for the entire girls' basketball team! Gotta celebrate their amazing season, now don't we?"

Arthur wasn't sure any of their group but his wife *meant* to silently stare at the poor woman who'd opened her mouth during their loudly held private conversation. It wasn't anger or even annoyance that brought out all that silent gazing, though. No. They were merely . . . thinking. Debating whether it would be worth it to attend a full-human event at this person's house.

Specifically, the Gonzalezes were probably wondering what religious artifacts the full-human family had in their house that would be worth taking—probably nothing, since they all appeared rather "money light," as one of Arthur's sons liked to say, and the Gonzalez family was known among the art world's black-market buyers and sellers for their excellent taste in choosing, stealing, and recreating religious artifacts that they sold to the highest bidder.

The Lepstein-Jacksons were clearly sizing up the woman to see if she was possibly a foreign operative trying to lure them into a dangerous situation.

While his wife stared because she wondered why this "peasant" was speaking to her at all.

That sweet, welcoming smile on that poor full-human's face slowly faded and, after letting out a small throat-clearing, she turned back around and focused on the line of students beginning to go up and get their diplomas. Her husband quickly grabbed her hand and squeezed, while the other full-human parents moved in closer to the couple. For the rest of the event, she never turned around again.

"Did I approve this little soiree that's happening in my home?" his wife asked.

"*Our* home, Lorraine. And it's a gift from our eldest daughter to our youngest. She assumed you would approve."

"I did not." She gestured at the families of their daughter's friends with a dismissive hand. "Do you really think that I want these . . . *people* in my house. No offense," she casually added.

"Offense taken," Tock's mother shot back.

"We would *love* to attend," Streep Gonzalez's mother informed Lorraine with a cheery smile and hate in her eyes. Then she muttered "I hate that bitch" to her husband in Tagalog—the language of their Filipino homeland—and, with a quickly raised finger, Arthur silenced his wife's retort, since they both knew Tagalog as well.

"We will definitely be there, Mr. Zhao."

Uh-oh. Arthur had completely forgotten about the sisters of Duke Maximilian Joseph MacKilligan—that was her name, yes?

The eldest, Charlie, had a forced smile on her face that did nothing but worry Arthur, because she was so very protective of her siblings. All the MacKilligan sisters had different mothers but the same useless father who continued to bring danger and horror to their door. It had bonded the three together like war buddies.

"Is that necessary?" his wife asked Charlie. "You and your sisters attending? Can't you simply be there in spirit?"

"Is there a problem?" the eldest asked.

14   *Shelly Laurenston*

Arthur leaned forward, ready to intervene. "Of course n—"

"She won't take off her shoes," his wife announced.

Arthur blew out his breath and waited for this to go badly.

"Pardon?" the eldest asked politely.

"She won't take off her shoes when she enters our home."

Arthur was about to remind his wife about "cultural differences" when the youngest sister announced, "That's because of the fungus, Mrs. Zhao."

It took all of Arthur's strength not to scramble away from the two girls on his right, but then he saw Charlie drop her head and begin rubbing her nose with the back of her hand. An excellent way to prevent a smile or laugh.

"Excuse me?" his wife asked, already looking quite green.

"Foot fungus. Max has it *real* bad. And, as I'm sure you're aware, a fungus can spread to other things. Like furniture and bedding." She let the pause hang out there, her gaze locked on Lorraine's, before finally adding, "People."

"I—"

"Doctors have tried everything. *I've* tried everything. It's been quite the science experiment for me. You know how I love those. But absolutely nothing works. Her feet are just covered in that fungus. It's all flaky; the skin peels constantly. Her toenails are a nightmare. Just grotesque. It is, in a word, vile. My sister's really embarrassed about it, not surprisingly, so she never takes her shoes off. Ever."

Since Arthur had just been shopping with all of his daughter's friends, and they had all tried on expensive heels to go with their expensive graduation outfits, he could say with certainty that MaxVonda—that was her name, right?—did not have any kind of foot fungus. But why ruin this moment of firsts? When, for once, his wife had been stunned into silence by anyone, much less a thirteen-year-old prodigy about to go off to his Oxford alma mater while her nineteen-year-old sister currently worked at a nearby Dairy Queen?

The diplomas were finally handed out, the students making their way across the stage to varying degrees of applause, based on whether

TO KILL A BADGER   15

they were basketball champs or had wolves in their family. So. Much. Howling.

With the name Zhao, it seemed to take forever before his daughter finally made her way across the stage. Her graduation gown was open so everyone could see her designer dress, and her cap was tilted on her head just so, making it appear like she was about to walk a runway in Milan.

Strutting across that stage in the five-thousand-dollar shoes he'd bought her on their shopping spree and diamond earrings and a gold diamond necklace—he didn't know where she'd gotten any of that from, and he knew better than to ask—she went to the headmaster and accepted her diploma. As she turned for a picture from the school photographer, moving the tassel on her cap to the other side, Arthur and Lorraine politely clapped. He'd expected the same from the audience, of course.

Nelle was an immigrant, after all, who looked different from most of the children from this school; had what many considered a British accent but was, in fact, one of the typical Hong Kong accents for those who had studied at the British-run private schools; and her family was wildly rich. Something his daughter had never hid from anyone. So a few polite claps from these people was exactly what he and Lorraine had been expecting.

That's not what they got, though.

The screams, howls, and hysterical cheers from the MacKilligan sisters, the Gonzalez village of family direct from the Philippines, the Lepstein-Jackson clan discreetly inserted into the crowd, the entire basketball team and their families, as well as every male in a thirty-mile radius, rang out, drowning out any polite applause and sanity that Arthur and his wife were trying to invoke.

How wrong he'd been when it came to Nelle Zhao and her innate ability to charm. He would not make that mistake again.

"Are all these people going to be at our house tonight?" Lorraine demanded to know, not even attempting to keep the annoyance out of her voice.

16 *Shelly Laurenston*

"I don't—"

"Because we can't have scorpions and live cobras if these people will be wandering around. You know how they'll panic. Especially the wolves. All that howling."

"We should only have regular food at our event. Just in case."

"Fine." She stood and pulled out her Blackberry. "I'll let the servants know."

He caught her hand before she could walk through the still-cheering crowd and stared at her. He didn't have to say "thank you" for allowing their child to have this party with *these* people, because they knew how to read each other without saying a word.

Lorraine gave a short nod before moving down the line toward freedom. He was proud of his wife. She'd handled herself well, considering—

"*Owwwwwww!*"

"Oh, dear!" his wife said to Charlie MacKilligan, "did I *accidentally* stomp on your giant feet? Ever so sorry."

Lorraine wasn't sorry.

"Daddy?" Arthur looked to see his daughter waiting for him a few bleachers down, the cap and gown he'd made her promise she'd at least wear until she got her diploma held in her hand. "Everything okay?"

"Everything is fine."

He smiled at the child he adored, and she smiled back: a lovely moment shared between father and child.

And that moment lasted until a bouncy She-badger jumped in front of his child and cheered, "Hey, Mr. Zee! Enjoy the show?"

"I did, Max-Tina. It was wonderful. I'm so proud of all of you."

"It's just Max, Mr. Zee! So to your house for the party?"

"Yes. All of you can come with me in the limo, if you'd like."

"Ya! Limo ride!" The She-badger raised her leg and pointed at the Doc Marten boots she'd finally chosen for her graduation day ensemble while the others had purchased designer heels. "And I'm going to take my shoes off this time, Mr. Zee!"

"You! MacKilligan!" Lorraine suddenly yelled from the other

side of the bleachers, all of them looking toward her as she pointed a damning finger at Max. "You keep those fucking shoes on, peasant! I won't have you spreading that fungus all over my perfect home!"

Eyes wide in confusion, Max-Nancy—that was her name, wasn't it?—looked back at Arthur, but when she heard her baby sister giggle, those wide eyes narrowed in accusation, and the new graduate took off running after the younger girl.

The rest of the team and the eldest MacKilligan ran after them, except his dear Nelle. She didn't chase anyone. Instead, she held her hand out for him and waited until he reached her.

Arm in arm, father and daughter made their way back to their limo.

"Don't worry, Daddy."

"Worry?"

"That I'll be spending all my life with my teammates."

"I believe that's your mother's worry. Not mine."

"Well, it won't happen. All of us are off to different parts of the world to do different things, and my only concern right now is our little family vacation to San Francisco."

"Ahh, yes. That."

She stopped, forcing Arthur to stop, as well. "Is there a problem?"

"Well, as you know, my older brother is running this, uh—"

"Vacation."

"Yes. He's running our vacation, and he wants your sister handling . . . our vacation's events. You'll be backing her up."

Her expression unchanged, Nelle said, "Tell me you're joking." He simply stared back at her as a response. He knew that if he was speaking of his eldest daughter, none of this would be a problem. But this was Nelle's "other sister." Only two years apart, they did not get along. "And you're allowing this?"

"As you know, I am not in charge of this . . . vacation. Your uncle is."

"Uh-huh."

She turned to walk away, but Arthur caught her arm and gently forced her to face him.

"Do not throw your sister down the stairs."

"Of course not."

"Or tie her up and leave her to die in a closet."

"Never."

"You promise?"

"I promise."

He took her arm again, and they continued toward the limo.

"And," he said after a few moments of silence, "I doubt your friends will be out of your life for good."

"I'm sure I'll see them during holidays and visits home, but I doubt I'll be hanging out with them like I have for the last six years. We're adults now," she insisted. "We have to get serious. No time for any more insanity."

Chapter 1

Eleven years later . . .

Claws slashed by, missing her by no more than half an inch. Nelle ducked under the big fur-covered forearm swiping at her, and went back to work on the lock.

"Get him off me!" she yelled out when she felt another swipe near her spine. "Get him off!"

The full-humans trapped inside the cage she was working on continued to scream until she snapped, *"Quiet."*

They immediately did as ordered, giving her a few seconds of peace.

She worked the lock until it finally released. She yanked off the thick metal and pulled open the cage door.

"Out!" she ordered, the full-humans stumbling as they pushed and shoved one another to get free. She was about to roll her eyes at the pathetic way these people were acting when something grabbed her around the waist and yanked her off her feet.

The next second, Nelle was flying. Across the room and directly into a wall. She hit it hard, her nose crushed on impact, before she rebounded off and landed on the floor.

She laid her hands flat on the ground and pushed herself up until she was on all fours. But before she could stand, that forearm grabbed her again and threw her.

It was Nelle's back that hit the other wall this time before she slid down and landed on her ass. She lifted her gaze in time to see the thousand-pound grizzly charging toward her.

20 *Shelly Laurenston*

They'd been told that Lithuanian bears would be protecting this transport ship filled with full-human cargo, but no one had told them the Lithuanian bears would be drugged out of their minds. There was a combination of cocaine-infused honey that had been making the rounds with bear addicts, but whatever these bears were on was way stronger. Because no matter how many times they were getting stabbed or shot, they just kept fighting.

As the bear neared, it opened its maw and grabbed her leg. If she were another breed, it would have bitten her leg clean off, but she was badger. Made of tough bones and even tougher skin.

Frustrated she wasn't already bleeding out, the bear swung her around for a few seconds while Nelle reached over that giant head to tear out the bastard's eyes with her claws before bashing him, head-first, into the floor. But the doped-out-of-his-mind bastard still didn't release her.

Nelle grabbed at the gun holstered to her hip, yanking it out just when Max landed on the bear's back and stabbed at it with two tactical knives, hitting it in the neck and head.

It dropped Nelle, and she landed at its giant back paws, the front ones trying to slap Max off. Nelle put a round in the chamber of her Sig Sauer and, ignoring the blood pouring from her leg, proceeded to quickly climb the front of the bear while it tried to get Max off its back. She avoided its swinging forearms and snapping fangs, which allowed her to reach its shoulders. She moved to its right side and wrapped her legs around its neck, pressing the barrel of her gun against the top of its head. She pulled the trigger three times, and the bear dropped to its knees, then face-first to the floor.

Before it could hit the ground, though, she had already rolled clear.

Too bad there was another crazed bear just a few feet away. She only had a moment before that claw hit her right across the face and sent her flying again.

When she landed on the ground this time, she raised her weapon to start firing, hoping to at least get the bear to back off until she could shoot it directly in the head, but she never pulled the trigger. She was too busy staring at the older She-badger. It was Tracey Rutowski. Mads's aunt whom they'd only recently met. And the female had an axe. A big one, probably grabbed from somewhere on the ship. Holding the weapon with both hands, the She-badger lifted it above her head and, with a roar, swung it down. The axe head embedded into the middle of the bear's face. The crazed beast screamed in pain, blood spouting from the wound, but that didn't stop Rutowski. After a couple of hard tugs to dislodge the weapon from its skull, Rutowski kicked the bear in the chest, knocking it to the ground. Her sleek, gray bob—expertly cut in some exclusive Manhattan salon, no doubt—fell in front of her face as she swung that axe again. She hit the bear in the face, then the neck, the shoulder. She just kept swinging the axe again and again until the bear stopped moving and its face and head were nothing but hacked bone, muscle, and blood.

Panting a little, the She-badger stopped her assault and held out a blood-soaked hand; Nelle grabbed it and allowed the female to help her up.

Rutowski studied her for a moment. "Your nose. Here."

"No, n—" was all Nelle managed to get out before Rutowski viciously yanked the pieces of bone back into what probably looked like a nose. Maybe. Nelle felt less certain about that when the older badger cringed a bit after taking a look at her handiwork.

"You may still need a bit of plastic surgery there, kid," Rutowski told her, before gripping Nelle's jaw with her fingers and roughly turning her head to the right. "You may want to get this checked out, too. That bear got you good."

Nelle was aware of the bodily damage she'd already sustained. She didn't need this female tugging her face like a pimp checking out new product.

Instead of telling Mads's aunt to unhand her, Nelle instead informed her, "Behind you."

"Huh?"

"Behind—"

Rutowski didn't wait for her to finish a second time, probably sensing the bear charging toward them both. She simply swung that axe again, more blood hitting Nelle in her already wounded face.

22   *Shelly Laurenston*

Rutowski was now having trouble getting the axe out of the bear's shoulder, and this one was fighting back because his brain hadn't been damaged yet. The pair struggled away from her, and that allowed Nelle to see that this She-badger's middle-aged friends had also found their own axes and were finishing off the rest of the drugged-out bears. With axes. Because, clearly, none of them were part of a functioning society! *Who lived like this? Using axes in this way? What was the eighties like, exactly?* Nelle wondered. Did the Cold War make them like this? Just turning them into wild badgers with axes? Every last one of them had their own gun or tactical knife or bear-specific pepper spray! This sort of messy violence was unnecessary!

To be honest, though, the axes were only a small part of the problem. Because this was *not* how all this was supposed to be going. Nelle and her teammates had just done some necessary work in Italy, before doing a little shopping in Switzerland—then, on the way back to the States in one of her family's private jets, they'd gotten a message from Rutowski asking for help in raiding a transport ship outside Boston Harbor. Charlie MacKilligan, who had been with them, had headed home immediately to check on family and friends, but the rest of them had all shrugged at each other and said, "Sure. Why not?"

It wasn't until they'd invaded the ship and found the human cargo that Nelle realized she should have stayed on the jet and headed back to New York with Charlie. And, for once, Nelle couldn't even blame Max for this fiasco. Max was usually the source of all their crazy, but not today. Today it was Rutowski and her Old Crone Reading Club—as Max liked to call them—dragging them unprepared into a very bad situation. Nelle and her teammates were already exhausted from what they'd taken care of in Italy, and now they had to deal with all . . . *this.*

Mads ran up to Nelle, shooting a charging bear twice in the face before stopping in front of her. "Are you okay?"

"My face—"

"Will heal. What about the rest of you? Any broken bones? How are your shoulders? Knees?"

Nelle could only open one eye at the moment, but she narrowed

TO KILL A BADGER   23

it on her teammate. "You're not asking about this because you care. You're asking because of the championships . . . aren't you?"

"Of course, I care . . . about you . . . as a friend. My friend, I mean."

"You liar! I have a *crushed* face, and you just want to make sure I haven't broken my legs or arms because of that goddamn championship."

"You're our power forward!"

The five of them had been playing basketball since they were thirteen. After they'd graduated from high school, they'd gotten picked up by the Wisconsin pro shifter-only team. Most basketball teams were filled with big cats and bears. The occasional She-wolf. While the badgers would normally be considered too small to go up against a six-five She-grizzly with aggression issues, honey badgers were all about aggression. While others were running away from rampaging bears, honey badgers were running right at them.

Nelle and her teammates, though, were not simply vicious players. They were good. They worked together well and enjoyed taking other players' balls away. It amused them.

But of the five of them, Mads was the most competitive about the game. She'd loved basketball from when she was a toddler, according to her great-grandmother. So anything, absolutely *anything,* that got between Mads and a possible championship win made her intolerable.

Intolerable!

"Stop touching me!" Nelle snapped, slapping at Mads's groping hands on her shoulders.

"That bear tossed you around like a dog toy—"

"Thanks for intervening with that."

"—and if you get any bones or joints replaced with titanium, you're off the team, Nelle. *You're off the team!*"

Nelle lifted her hand, palm out, and turned her face to the side. "You're getting hysterical. I don't like it." She let out a small snarl before growling at Rutowski, "And would you stop hacking that bear! *It is definitely dead!*"

Max came across the room in her big combat boots, tiptoeing around all the blood and gore and bear bodies like an evil ballerina. It

24   *Shelly Laurenston*

was adorably ridiculous, which Nelle assumed was just Max's brand at this point. "Adorable Ridiculousness Designed by Max now available at your local Target."

She pirouetted to a stop in front of Nelle and Mads. "How are we all doing?" she asked with a big smile.

"The crone watched too many slasher movies, and Mads felt me up."

"I did not feel you up. I checked your bones."

"Did you just call me a crone?" Rutowski rested the blood-covered head of her axe on her shoulder like a lumberjack. "And after I fixed your nose, too."

"You didn't fix anything."

"She's right," Max agreed, leaning in close to study Nelle's nose. "You did not fix anything."

"At least she can breathe now."

"No. I can't."

"The American weakness of the young badgers sickens me."

Nelle glared at the Russian She-badger, Oksana "Ox" Lenkov. Tall, for a badger, Ox had been born and liberated from the Soviet Union when she was still a teen. How that happened, though, was something none of the older She-badgers would share with anyone. Which, of course, made Nelle wildly curious about the whole situation. Not enough to look into it or anything, but . . . yeah. Getting a teenager out of the Soviet Union during the Cold War without them being professional ballerinas on tours or gymnasts during the Olympics must have been . . . challenging.

"I am hardly American," Nelle reminded the Russian.

"She says with British accent," Rutowski muttered.

"My family has always gone to British-run private schools in Hong Kong. How do you expect me to sound? As if I'm from Brooklyn?"

"My cousins are from Brooklyn," Steph Yoon announced, prying her axe from some bear's spine.

"I don't care," Nelle shot back. "Look at my face! My beautiful, perfect face!"

TO KILL A BADGER 25

Max quickly put her hands on Nelle's shoulders and turned her away from the dismissive crones. At least she tried. Despite the pain coming from the wounds on her neck, Nelle kept her gaze locked on the three badgers while the rest of her body kept moving in the opposite direction. She also growled in annoyance so everyone knew how pissed off she was. Max finally took hold of her jaw and turned her head as well, so that Nelle was forced to look at her.

"There's my little baby girl," Max teased in a ridiculous "mom" voice. "There she is! Who's my baby girl? Who's my pretty baby girl?"

Nelle rolled her eyes and fought hard not to laugh. Max had been doing that to soothe Nelle's rage for years. The first time had been after a colossal fight with Nelle's mother. It was normal that a rage like that would stick with Nelle for days, even weeks. But when Max started saying such stupid things during the middle of a game, in front of both teams, coaches, an audience, *and* Nelle's mother, Nelle could do nothing but laugh. Laugh so hard she was benched for a bit until she could stop. It was when Nelle finally laughed this time that Max went ahead and broke Nelle's nose again—completely ignoring her snarl of pain—putting the pieces back together into something that, at the very least, allowed Nelle to breathe.

"This is your fault," Mads argued, pointing an accusing finger at her aunt.

"*Me?* What did I do?"

"You gave us no warning about—"

"Bears? We told you there were bears. We were very clear about the bears."

"You said we'd be in and out. More of a heist than a slam-and-slaughter combined with a rescue mission!"

Appearing genuinely confused, Rutowski asked, "Why are you so upset? You guys do this sort of thing all the time."

"*Not during championships!*" they all yelled in unison.

"Oh, my God . . . is this about baseball?"

"No, no, no," Yoon corrected. "Soccer. They play soccer."

"I thought bowling," Lenkov guessed.

26　Shelly Laurenston

Nelle's nose was completely forgotten as she and Max quickly grabbed Mads before she could get her hands around her aunt's throat and choke the very life from her.

The three older badgers stepped back in shock, eyes wide.

"*Basketball!*" Mads bellowed. "*We play basketball!*"

"Is it really that serious, sweetie?" Rutowski asked.

Nelle had to dig her heels in even harder, the muscles in Max's arm bulging as they both fought to restrain Mads.

"We're pros," Mads snarled between clenched fangs. "It's our *job* to *win*. And *you* are getting in my way."

Nelle and Max smirked at each other behind Mads's back. Because their teammate had gone from "our" to "my" really fast. But when it came to winning, it was always more Mads than the rest of them. They all enjoyed winning, but they would tank a game in a second if it would help them in a heist or some other thing they also enjoyed doing. But they'd learned very early on that was *not* an option for them. Not with Mads as part of any team they happened to be on. The girl liked to win, and anything that got in the way of that was nothing but an enemy that must be stomped out. Including even her newly found aunt, whom she really seemed to like.

"I don't understand," Yoon interjected. "You guys just came back from starting a war. This is part of that whole thing. How is any of what we've done in the last few hours a problem?"

Mads closed her eyes and took in a deep breath. She let it out. Then she calmly announced to Nelle and Max, "They're clearly going to get in the way of the championship. I say we kill them all now and be done with it."

While Rutowski and the others gasped in shock, and Max lowered her head so Mads didn't see her laugh, Nelle simply nodded and calmly replied back, "Completely rational response."

Mads shrugged. "I know."

Keane Malone walked down one of the long hallways toward the sports medical center. He was dressed in his practice uniform and

TO KILL A BADGER 27

equipment, except he hadn't put on his cleats or helmet. They were back at the practice field with the rest of his team.

He usually didn't leave practice. He liked to be there with everyone else, getting in his workout and cracking the whip on any of the losers who thought they could float through the time because they could naturally run over fifty miles an hour due to their freakish long legs and ability to lick their own asses. "Why do we need practice? We're cats! We're naturally gifted," they'd all say to him. At least the bears complained less, and the wolves didn't complain at all, because they needed to work off their extra energy anyway. They were like border collies left alone in a house . . . they became destructive if not given something constructive to do.

The complainers, though, were always cats. *His* people, yes, but they drove him nuts! The constant complaining. The constant grooming. The constant knocking stuff over for no reason. It was endless! And Keane had no patience for any of it.

Still, he had left practice because his shoulder had been bothering him for about a week, and his coach ordered him to see a doctor to make sure it wasn't a real problem. Keane didn't think it was, though. It was probably just sore from the last few days of drama he'd recently had in his life. Fighting lions and fellow tigers had probably done some temporary damage. He wasn't really that worried, because the season hadn't started yet, and the doctors working at the arena were all well-trained and fellow shifters. They knew how to care for their kind. Not only that, but it wasn't easy to permanently harm shifters. That's why their football league was way better than what the full-humans had. Full-humans were so brittle. Like porcelain on a high shelf.

Keane went around a corner, and that's when he saw a woman in four-wheel roller skates. She was leaning over at the waist and staring into the face of someone sitting on a bench across from the medical office. She reached out her hand and said to the one on the bench, "Now don't panic. I'm just going to take your arm and lead you into the office. You're going to be fine."

It took a moment for Keane to understand what was going on. The female sitting on the bench? That was Nelle Zhao. She hung around Max MacKilligan. They played basketball together on the women's pro team. She had amazing legs and lots of private jets. The other female was Blayne somebody. He found her annoying, but she wasn't the problem. The problem was Blayne somebody's husband. He was half-Amur tiger and half-something else. He played hockey. Keane hated him. The half-tiger, half-something else hated Keane. It was a mutual hatred that worked for both of them. What worried Keane was that the mixed-breed freak had fangs that no normal shifter should ever have. Two long ones that looked like something from a walrus. The pair of them avoided each other, because it would be a nasty fight and neither wanted to get so wounded they couldn't play for their next games or be forced to get replacement joints. A shifter couldn't continue on a pro team if they had any titanium in their body. It gave them too much of an edge during gameplay.

Like any decent cat, though, the half-tiger, half-something else was known to protect his mate, as any shifter would once they had a cub or two. Which meant that if Blayne somebody pissed off that honey badger, she was going to find herself mauled beyond recognition, and the half-tiger, half-something else would go on a vengeful rampage. A perfect example of a "violence circle." The kind of thing that Keane usually sat back and watched with feet up on his ottoman and a big bowl of popcorn in his lap.

But Mads was with Keane's brother now, and he didn't want to hear that idiot's whining because she was unhappy. Meaning Keane knew he had to step in.

Blayne somebody almost had her hand on Nelle's forearm when he caught hold of it and pushed her away. Not hard, though, since she was wearing skates and simply glided backward.

"Hey!" she exclaimed. "Get off."

"Leave her alone."

"I'm just trying to—"

"Help. Right. Nelle," he asked without looking at the badger, "do you need help?"

"No."

TO KILL A BADGER 29

"Do you want this woman to touch you?"

"No."

"Do you want her to go away?"

"Yes."

"See?" he asked Blayne somebody, releasing her arm. "She wants you to go away. So go away."

"She's bleeding."

Keane shrugged. "She's badger. She'll be fine." He motioned to Blayne somebody. "Go find someone else to help."

"Look at her face. She's sweaty and pasty. Having trouble breathing."

"And?"

"Her neck is wounded on the left, and the bleeding hasn't stopped since I've been standing here."

Keane looked Nelle over, trying not to focus too closely on Nelle's body in that basketball outfit. Tank top. Shorts. Her legs crossed at the knee. Sneakers with heels already built in, which was just weird and ridiculous. Then he moved up to her neck, leaning a bit so he could get a clearer look. And Blayne somebody was right.

"You *are* bleeding."

"I am?" Nelle put her hand to her neck and pulled back bloody fingers. "Huh."

He pointed at the medical office about fifty feet away. "So when you get a chance, go see one of the docs. Okay?"

"Sure."

"Great."

Keane turned and started off to get to his last-minute medical appointment.

"Is that it?" Blayne somebody yelled.

"Is what it?"

"You're just going to leave her?"

"She's a badger. She'll be fine." When the female's mouth opened, and her eyes went wide, and she shook her head back and forth at him like some kind of confused foxhound, he asked, "Don't you have some homeless people to help?"

30 **Shelly Laurenston**

"It's *unhoused*, and I do that on Sundays. Help her!"

"I've got an appointment right now, and also, I don't care." In shock, Keane took a quick step back and asked, "Are . . . are you *crying?*"

"I am about to get really mad with you. And sometimes that means tears. And when there are tears, I usually *lose my mind!*" she hysterically screeched. *"Help her!"*

Not sure what was happening, Keane went back to the bench and quickly grabbed Nelle's forearm. With his gaze locked on the insane mixed-breed canine snarling at him, he pulled the badger off the bench and dragged her across the floor toward the medical office.

"You can't pick her up?" the canine sobbed.

"She's *fine!*"

"You are a worthless human being!"

"That's because *I'm a cat!*" he yelled back before throwing open the medical office door and dragging the badger inside with him. He stopped long enough to close the door behind him, and then he turned the lock to keep the crazed canine out. She stood in front of the door, obviously seething, and he knew he'd done the right thing. Hopefully there wouldn't be any real emergencies that needed to get in before he got Nelle Zhao out of his life.

"Blayne giving you shit?" the receptionist asked with a laugh.

"Does she just sit outside forcing people to deal with bleeding badgers?"

"No. She's waiting for her husband and daughter. The kid is getting her shots for the upcoming kid's hockey season. You know . . . all the important ones. Measles, mumps, flu . . . canine flu, distemper, feline AIDS, parvo, plus flea and tick prevention."

"Are you supposed to tell me any of that?"

"Probably not. You know . . . the whole HIPAA thing, but they don't even know we exist so . . . who cares?"

Not in the mood to argue with a bobcat, Keane simply announced, "My trainer booked me in here to see the orthopedist about my shoulder. And the badger's bleeding from the neck."

"You sound like you really care," the bobcat teased.

"No, I don't. Because I *don't* care. I know it. The badger knows it—"

"I do," Nelle muttered. "I really do. And I'm okay with it."

"See? Completely rational." He pointed at the clear door the heaving mixed-breed canine was standing in front of. "But that female is insane."

"You afraid to take her on, Malone?" The bobcat laughed.

"No. But I can promise that none of you guys want me and her husband going crazed in your very nice offices here."

"That's true. But, uh . . . your little badger friend there—"

"She's not my badger friend. Simply a badger I know."

"Yeah, well, whatever she is to you . . . it looks like she's passed out. Or is dead. You know . . . from the bleeding."

Startled, Keane looked down at the female, whose arm he still held, and said the only thing he could think of . . .

"Oh, for fuck's sake!"

"Are you stabbing me in the neck?" Nelle asked whomever was poking at her throat.

"I'm trying to repair your carotid artery, but . . ." Dr. Jai Davis, doctor to the sports stars—at least the shifter ones—took a step back from the operating table and, slightly panting, asked, "Is your artery . . . *fighting* me?"

"Possibly."

"I . . . I think it keeps attacking my instruments," she noted, studying the tiny heads of the equipment she was currently using.

"Yes. That can happen."

"How is that normal?"

"Full-humans don't know we even exist. How is *that* normal?"

"Great," the doctor sighed out. "I get the philosopher."

"Just close up the wound, so I can go."

"I'm trying, but your arteries are fighting me, and you are supposed to be out. Why aren't you out? Or screaming in pain and panic now that you're awake?"

"Because I don't need you repairing my artery. It'll repair itself."

"You were bleeding out in our waiting room. You were clinically dead for at least three minutes when the tiger brought you in here."

"I only brought her in because of that crazed canine outside the office harassing me."

With the operating table tilted at a ninety-degree angle so the doctor didn't have to bend over to work on her neck, Nelle only had to move her gaze to the other side of the room to see Keane Malone sitting on a separate table, another doctor examining his shoulder.

"Why are you here?" she asked.

"My shoulder has been bothering me."

"I don't mean why are you seeing a doctor. I mean why are you *in* the operating room with me? This whole thing feels terribly unhygienic."

"Stop whining, you'll be fine," the doctor snapped, while still fighting whatever was going on inside Nelle's neck.

"I strongly suggested that she not work on a honey badger alone," the other doctor told Nelle. "The last time I did that, I nearly got my throat ripped out."

"You did go for the nurse's throat when we thought you were dead, Miss Zhao. Didn't she, Hugo?"

"She did!"

"Is that why I'm strapped to the table?" Nelle asked.

"Yes," the doctors said in unison.

"Mind if you unstrap me?"

"Are you going to act right?" Davis asked.

"I don't know what that means."

"Yes, that's the problem." But she undid the straps holding Nelle down anyway, before returning to her wounded neck.

The orthopedist working on Keane's shoulder abruptly walked out of the room, but returned a few minutes later with big goggles resting on his forehead and a giant sledgehammer.

"Well," he said to Keane, "let's get this done."

He lowered the goggles over his eyes and lifted the massive sledgehammer, resting the big head on his shoulder.

TO KILL A BADGER   33

Eyes wide, Malone blurted out, "What the fuck are you going to do with that thing?"

"I need to rebreak this shoulder. Sledgehammer is the easiest way."

"*Are you insane?* I'm not letting you do that!"

"Oh, come on! Don't be such a pussy!" Then the lion male laughed at his own joke. "Get it? Because we're all pus—"

"Yes. Yes. I get it. But if you try to hit me with a hammer, I'm going to beat what little brains you have right out of your giant lion head."

"I went to Princeton. Where did you go?"

"Long Island 'I will beat the shit out of you if you touch me with that hammer' University."

As entertained as Nelle was—and she was just so entertained right now!—she raised her hand to stop the escalating argument. You never know what could set two cats off, but she was pretty sure threatening one with a sledgehammer would do it.

"Everyone calm down; I can—" Nelle paused while her doctor struggled to pull something from her neck. She tugged and tugged, her mountain-lion fangs slipping from her gums, until she finally yanked something free. Holding up her blood-covered hand, she showed off what she held tightly with a pair of titanium needle-nose tweezers.

"Is this a bear claw?" she asked.

It wasn't the whole claw, but yes. That was a piece of bear claw she held.

"I had a feeling something was in there," Nelle explained. "I just didn't know what."

Davis leaned in closer. "It looks . . . gnawed upon."

"Just my blood fighting back."

"See what I mean? Even for shifters, *that's* weird. That is just so *weird.*"

Ignoring Davis's observations over her kind's blood cells, Nelle calmly told the orthopedist, "Don't break his shoulder. I'll take him to my guy. He can fix that shoulder without breaking anything."

"What?" the lion immediately sneered. "Some Eastern, hippy medicine crap, involving tea and prayers?"

Feeling much better now that the piece of bear claw was out of her neck, Nelle decided to have a little fun.

"Why would you ask that? Because I'm *Asian*. And because I'm *Asian*, I must be taking Malone to some old man from Shanghai who has a decrepit office somewhere in Chinatown, where he's doling out tiger dong tea to heal rashes and cancer?"

The lion blinked at her behind his goggles. "No, no. I didn't mean—"

"My people are just all the same to you, aren't we?"

"I just meant—"

"Ach!" she said, with a simple hand toss and shifting her gaze away from his stunned face.

The orthopedist stood in the middle of the room, stammering nonsensically for several seconds, until he finally walked out, taking his sledgehammer with him. A move that seemed to relieve Malone a great deal.

"Nicely handled," Davis chuckled, before quickly stepping back and announcing, "I'm disturbed by this, but your wound just healed up before I could even get in a stitch, so—"

Nelle slipped off the exam table. "Great. Thanks. I have to go shower off all this blood and get changed." She pointed at Malone. "I'll meet you after our practices end, and we can go see my specialist, yes?"

"Well, I wasn't really planning—"

"Excellent."

"Wait, wait, wait," Davis said, before Nelle could get out the door. "It's not normal your wound . . . abruptly healed. And we should ensure that it didn't just hide an infection or some other issue."

"It didn't."

"But—"

"Doctor, for more than a thousand years, the Zhao honey badger has been evolving into the being you see before you. And it'll be a cold day in some Christian's hell before an opened carotid artery takes my kind out. But thank you for doing an excellent job of digging out that bit of claw from my neck. This way, I won't miss practice today, and

I won't have to listen to my teammate bitch about it. Because she will. See you in a few hours, Malone."

The door closed behind the badger, and Keane was left alone with a stunned Jai Davis. She kept staring at the exit Nelle Zhao had gone out of and didn't move or speak.

So he decided to try distracting her with light conversation.

"So . . . how's your daughter?"

She blinked and her head snapped around, gold eyes glaring at him. "How do you know my daughter?" There was a ton of accusation in that one question. Accusation he did not like at all, but that wasn't the real insult.

"You don't remember me, do you?"

"Remember you? I've operated on you before? I mean, I have a lot of clients. Especially football players. You guys are *always* getting your arteries torn open, but—"

"I'm first cousin to your best friend, Cella Malone? I've met your parents? I remember when you were a teen mom?" When she continued just to stare at him, he brutally added, "My father was murdered and his brothers did absolutely *nothing* about it?"

"Ohhhh! Right. Keane. Keane Malone. Hi, Keane. You've . . . grown."

Disgusted, Keane stood and walked to the exit, not caring he was forced to push past the smaller cat in his way.

The last thing she said as he slammed the door shut behind him: "Glad to see you're still so very angry!"

Chapter 2

"Fuck off, fuck off, fuck off."

Max stopped dribbling the basketball in her hands and looked over at the chairs where the team had dumped most of their stuff. Towels, hairbrushes, phones, any sports creams with lidocaine. When anyone took a break, they went to sit in the chair with their stuff. But, at the moment, no one was sitting there. No one wanted to get yelled at if Mads saw anyone, "Being lazy!"

Max heard it again. "Fuck off, fuck off, fuck off."

A few seconds later, it was Nelle who walked over to a neatly folded pile of sweatpants, sweatshirt, and designer microfiber towel with a several-thousand-dollar designer handbag sitting on top of it all. She reached into that bag and took out her phone covered in a diamond-encrusted case. Nelle had that phone case specially made, because most cases didn't have actual diamonds on them. For very good reason, too. No one needed actual diamonds on a phone case that could easily be grabbed while riding the subway.

"Is that your ringtone?" Max asked.

"Only for my sister."

"Did you tie her up and leave her in the closet again?" Max shook her head. "You have to stop doing that. It's going to give her a complex."

"My sister *is* a complex, easily diagnosable by a good psychiatrist. And tying her up in a closet isn't why she's calling. Instead, I've decided not to involve myself in this travesty called her life any longer. Hence the ringtone."

Max loved that Nelle used words like *hence* and *notwithstanding*, and Max's personal favorite, *unbeknownst*. It was fun having a friend who could speak fancy words with the confidence of a nineteenth-century English earl. The only reason Max C'd her way through every English class in high school so she could graduate with her teammates was due to Nelle. "No teammate of mine is going to fail an *American* English class in an American public school," she'd say. And she said it in a way that suggested Max should be much more insulted for the nation of her birth, but she really couldn't be bothered.

Besides, Nelle made books fun. Well, more fun than anyone else ever had. Normally, Max liked comic books and magazines. Who had time to read thick tomes with vaguely sexual titles like *Moby-Dick* and *The Scarlet Letter* when the books themselves had absolutely nothing to do with anything as interesting as sex? But her friend always made sure Max got interesting books to read and write papers on, because their English teachers loved Nelle so much. And anything that kept Charlie MacKilligan away from their classrooms "to discuss Max's grades" was worth a change in the teaching plan.

"What travesty?"

"Her wedding." Nelle sighed, looking at texts on her phone. "It's happening in a few days."

"Your sister's getting married? That's why you've been locking her in the closet?"

"I thought she'd see how stupid she's being and end this nightmare. But she has not."

"Maybe she loves the guy."

"My sister only loves herself. And that lemon sponge cake from that Chinese bakery on Seventh. It's going to be her ten-tier wedding cake."

"Ten tiers? Isn't that a lot?"

"Not when you're having five hundred people at your wedding."

"Jeez. Are you going?"

"I've been told I have to. I'm supposedly her maid of honor."

Max glanced off before asking, "Didn't you throw her out a window just after high school?"

"I also threw her out a window a week ago during an argument, but we weren't that high up, so it didn't really do any damage." Nelle shut off her phone. "Look, the only reason she made me maid of honor was because our mother told her to. Trust me when I say she'd rather have one of her very, *very* blonde friends do it instead."

"It sounds like you're jealous," Max teased. But the look Nelle gave her had her changing to, "Or you'd rather set yourself on fire than be part of this wedding."

"She's marrying a full-human, Max. A full-human! He doesn't even know what she is. None of her so-called 'friends' do either," she added with air quotes.

Honey badgers were known to spend most of their lives around full-humans. They were small predators, and it was simply easier to deal with full-humans than it was to manage the obsessive nature of canines, the arrogance of cats, or the excessive food bills of bears. But badgers usually *married* their own. Who else but a fellow badger would understand that when you were out until five in the morning, you weren't cheating "with some whore," but were actually robbing a bank or toppling an empire or accidentally burning down London in 1666.

Before they could delve deeper into this conversation, Max heard the opening music to the original *The Omen* movie. She went to her pile of clothes and tossed them aside until she reached her black backpack, which she had bought on the street from some guy selling fake Chanel bags, and dug through it until she found her phone.

"I hate your ringtone!" one of her teammates yelled out.

"Sorry." Max dismissed the call before looking at the number. She smiled.

"Tell me that's not her," Nelle gasped. When Max only smiled wider, Nelle did something she rarely ever did . . . she threw herself at Max, desperately attempting to get her phone.

Nelle was doing her best to get Max's phone when that bitch called right back.

"Oh, my God!" one of their teammates yelled out when they heard that ridiculous ringtone again.

"Sorry! Sorry!" Max said with a laugh. She grabbed Nelle by the throat and pushed her back. Then she answered her phone! She answered it!

"Hello?"

Nelle couldn't exactly make out what her sister was saying, but she could sense the fake tears from where she was, as she desperately reached for that damn phone.

"Oh, I know, hon. I know," Max said in that soothing voice she used when she was starting shit.

"Give it!" Nelle barked, after punching Max's hand off her throat. It was like playing one-on-one, but instead of fighting over a ball, they were fighting over that goddamn phone.

"Of course your wedding is the most important thing ever!" Max lied. "Absolutely *everyone* is talking about it! And you know your baby sister. She's just jealous of the love you've found with your fiancée. You can understand that, can't you?"

Nelle stopped fighting long enough to stare at Max in open-mouthed shock.

"You lying little cun—" was all she got out before Max slapped her hand over Nelle's mouth.

"You know," Max continued on, "we can make sure she gets to your wedding. Me, and Mads and Streep and Tock. Especially Tock. You know how she is about being on time. We can make sure Nelle is totally involved, you know"—Max's smile turned so wicked, Nelle's knees almost buckled—"if the four of us are invited to the wedding and reception. We'll make sure she's there and ready to be involved. Not only as your maid of honor," she added with unbelievably fake sincerity, "but as your *sister*. A sister who loves you."

That's when Nelle snapped and she knocked Max's hand away, so she could wrap her arm around the badger's throat and drop both of them to the ground.

Somehow, Max kept up her side of the conversation while they struggled on the floor.

"Really?" Max went on. "Then it's a definite deal, sweetie! We'll take care of it. So stop crying and be happy! You're getting married to the man of your dreams! Okay, okay." Then the bitch had the nerve to add, *"Love you!"*

Livid beyond reason, Nelle rolled the pair so that Max was on her knees and Nelle was draped over her back. Holding her with one arm, she pulled the other back and started punching her best friend in the face and head. But before she could turn Max into a bloody mess, a big shadow covered them, and the size of it had both females pausing so they could look up until they saw Keane Malone's never-smiling face gazing down at them.

"What—" he began, but a woman wearing a baseball cap that had NEW YORK written across the front stepped in front of him, cutting his next words off. The hat's logo made it look like it represented the New York Yankees baseball team or the New York Giants football. But it was for the shifter-only New York football team. Nelle just never bothered to learn the team's name, mostly because she didn't care about their name. She had never understood America's love for their football. *Real* football was fabulous, but American football was just a chance for bear-like men—and actual bears on the shifter-only teams—to knock each other down for a few hours. She could watch that at any shifter bar.

The female, who smelled like feline, pointed at Nelle and Max. "Are one of you the badger that told him you had a doctor who could fix his shoulder?"

"That was me," Nelle said, tightening her arm around Max's throat in the hopes of choking her out.

"Well, I want you to take him to that doctor *now.*"

Not liking how this feline was speaking to her, Nelle didn't know whether to keep choking out her teammate or this woman. Right now . . . both were pissing her off.

Mads was about to start yelling at people to get back to work when she spotted Keane walking over to a battling Nelle and Max. He was with one of the football coaches—she didn't know which one . . . or care. It just seemed strange to see him here at all without one of his brothers. He didn't really bother to attend their basketball practices on his own. Mostly because he hated basketball as much as she loathed football. She did, however, hope he'd be the one to pull Nelle and Max apart, because she didn't really want to be bothered. Getting in the middle of a badger fight always left open wounds and damaged feelings. She simply wasn't in the mood for any of it. She had a team to pull together! At this very moment, she didn't feel they were ready to take on their Los Angeles enemies. Those trifling Southern California bitches. She was ready to wipe them from the map! To take all they love and turn it into nothing but ash and memories!

Shaking her head, Mads thought, *Okay. Wow. I went full-Viking there fast, didn't I?*

"What's Keane doing here?" Streep asked.

"No idea."

"Should we ask?" Tock questioned, glancing at her giant watch.

"Must we?"

Streep clasped her hands together. "I thought I heard the word *wed-ding!*" she annoyingly sang. "We should find out what that's about."

"We're not worrying about any weddings until we're done with the championship," Mads reminded them. "We don't have time for anything but that right now."

"Then maybe we shouldn't have started a war with cats," Tock pointed out.

"We didn't start anything," Mads reminded her. "They did."

"We always have time for weddings," Streep pushed. "All that love and romance and—"

"Jewelry," Mads and Tock said together.

"Insured jewelry," Streep said with a smile. "So no real moral issue."

"How do you get there?" Mads had to know.

"Easily."

With that, Streep happily skipped over to Max, Nelle, Keane, and that woman Mads didn't know.

Streep leaned close to Nelle and Max, still struggling on the floor, and asked, "Did I hear wedding?"

Streep had always been fast, so she quickly moved out of the way of Nelle's slashing claw.

42   *Shelly Laurenston*

"We are *not* going to that wedding!" She had Max by the throat again and had pinned her to the floor. "And you, Max, are going to call that idiot and tell her you're not involving any of us in this bullshit!"

"It's the wedding of the cent—*ack!*"

Finally fed up with getting choked to death—and probably coming to the realization that no one was going to help her—Max brought her knees up to her chest, then kicked them both out, sending Nelle slip-sliding across the court floor.

Free, Max sat up, coughed a few times, and rubbed her neck before turning to Streep and announcing, "We are *all* going to the wedding of the century!"

Streep squealed. Max cheered. Mads rolled her eyes. And Tock looked at her watch again.

"I am *not* going to that wedding," Nelle told them now that she had picked herself up off the floor. "I refuse."

"But—"

"Quiet," Nelle ordered before looking at Keane and the coach. "And what do you two want again?"

"Nothin'," the eldest Malone brother replied before turning to leave. Not that Mads blamed him. It was rare to see Nelle pissed off about anything. But, man, when she *was* pissed off, it was best to simply stay away.

Yet the football coach grabbed his arm, and easily yanked the much bigger cat back to her side. "You said you had a doctor that could help, since Mr. Weak Kitten here is afraid of a little sledgehammer."

"It wasn't little, and no one is hitting me with that thing!"

Rubbing her forehead with the back of her hand, Nelle replied, "Yes. I know someone."

"Then take him now."

"We're in the middle of practice," Mads was quick to remind the football coach before Nelle could say anything. "That may mean nothing to you, but—"

Mads halted her lecture when she realized that Nelle had Max

TO KILL A BADGER 43

pinned to the ground again and started to pummel the badger's face. At this rate, with all this drama over Nelle's sister, nothing would get done for the rest of the day. Streep was dancing in a circle about going to some fucking wedding, and Tock kept looking at her watch until she finally announced, "I have a date tonight."

That seemed to stop everyone.

"With who?" Mads asked.

Tock frowned. "Who do you think? Shay."

"Oh. Why?"

"What?"

"You're already fucking him. What do you need to date him for?"

"Okay. I'm walking away. But understand that in exactly three hours, I am out of here. I will not be late for my date."

"Fine." Mads motioned to the once-again fighting Nelle and Max. "Take her," she ordered Keane.

"I'm not getting in the middle of that."

"Oh, my God, Malone! Would you pussy up already and just grab her!" his coach yelled.

Apparently used to taking orders from coaches, Keane reached down and took hold of Nelle's arm, yanking Mads's teammate away from her prey. But he'd only gotten a few feet toward the exit before Nelle ordered Keane to put her down, which he immediately did.

Calmer now, Nelle took a moment to brush away the stray slashes of blood that had come from Max's nose. Although it didn't actually wipe anything away. Just spread the blood around.

Nelle pointed at Keane. "Go take a shower, change your clothes, and meet me outside, at the first-floor main entrance, in fifteen minutes."

"Why can't we just—"

"You smell. I'm not sitting in a car with you smelling like sweaty male."

"That's my musk."

"That's disgusting and *no*." She swung around, now pointing that damning finger at Max. "And you . . . fix what you have wrought."

"But—"

"I will destroy what you love!" Nelle warned as she marched toward the locker rooms.

Grinning, face bloody, Max looked up at Mads and the others. "This is going to be the best wedding *ever.*"

And Mads had to ask, "How are you not dead yet?"

"I don't know!" she replied, still smiling. "You'd think it would have happened by now! Because people shockingly hate me."

"Shockingly?" Tock repeated. "Are we sure that's the right word?"

Chapter 3

Nelle watched Keane Malone walk out of the massive double doors in the very front of the sports center. There were other entries that shifters used to enter the building that would take them directly to the elevators that went deep underground to their stadiums, arenas, skating rinks, and everything else they needed that full-humans should never know about. He exited exactly fifteen minutes from when she'd told him to meet her. Impressive. She usually only saw that kind of timeliness from Tock.

Full-humans instinctively moved out of the cat's way without even realizing what they were doing or why. It was always entertaining to watch full-humans react to the apex predators among them. Mothers pulled their children closer and scurried past Malone to get inside the building. Men kept their eyes lowered and held their breaths until they'd passed him. Children ignored him altogether because they were reaching out for the panda ice skater walking into the building. They wanted nothing more than to hug the woman loudly chewing on a bamboo stalk.

It was different for honey badgers, though. No one ever noticed them. It's what made their kind so dangerous. They could slip their way into and out of all sorts of situations. Entire empires had toppled because honey badgers had started some shit and then eased their way out. Not even caring about the nightmare they'd left behind. It was the giant apex predators that had created this whole "other" world that

46   *Shelly Laurenston*

kept them fed, protected, and entertained. Badgers didn't need that. They could fit in anywhere.

"What are you wearing?" the cat asked, once they were standing next to each other on the corner.

Deciding not to slap him based on his tone alone, Nelle questioned, "What's wrong with it?"

"It's a little fancy, isn't it? For going to the doctor, I mean. Can I even afford this guy?"

Ohhhh! He wasn't insulting her, per se. He was more freaking out about his obvious poverty. Okay. Fair enough.

Nelle glanced down at what she wore. Black jeans; dark red T-shirt; six-inched-heel, short, designer boots that cost thousands of euros; and gold-and-emerald jewelry around her neck, wrists, and dangling from her ears to really set the casual outfit off.

However, instead of earnestly explaining fashion to a male who would never understand it, she decided to be a little more flippant and said, "I dress for *my* mood. Today I felt very . . ."—she thought a moment before tossing off, "New York Swan off to see Truman at La Côte Basque."

Not surprisingly, the cat simply stared at her with that constant frown on his face, only now it was deeper and seemed more confused than usual. She didn't care. Poor thing. Not understanding literary references because he lived in a world of nothing but football and—

"Aren't you a little *young* to be a Swan?" he queried. "And borderline trashy."

"Excuse me?"

"They were all matrons with adult children. You're not even thirty."

Unable to hide her shock, Nelle gawked at Keane Malone. She didn't know whether to slap him for calling her "borderline trashy" or hugging him for understanding her reference. "You know who Truman Capote was?"

His frown got even deeper. But he looked less confused now and more pissed off. "What the fuck does that mean?"

"Uh . . . nothing. We should go."

TO KILL A BADGER 47

"I do *read*."

Did he? Or did he just read about Truman in an old *Vanity Fair* article while at the dentist's office?

"Yeah. Sure. Okay," she said to avoid a continuation of this conversation, since she didn't want to have him lambasting her for assuming he was a big, dumb jock. They both knew he was; why keep going until his feelings were really hurt?

Thankfully, he seemed to take her response at face value and, suddenly, raised his arm.

"What are you doing?"

"Hailing a cab. Why? Is the office near here, so we can walk? Or do you want me to call a car for Her Majesty, which I loathe on moral grounds. Yellow taxies are the backbone of Manhattan."

Nelle held her hand up to stop whatever speech he was about to give.

"I don't care," she told him honestly. "And it doesn't matter. I already have a car."

"You called a car?"

"No. I *have* a car."

Her driver had pulled up and, blocking the street, came around to open the door for her.

"Miss Zhao."

"Hello, Charles. This is Keane Malone. He likes taxies. We'll be going to see Dr. Weng-Lee."

"Of course."

"And," she said to Malone, "this is Charles. He's my driver and personal security."

"Why would *you* need security?"

"Just get in the car," she growled out between clenched fangs.

This cat was really starting to get on her nerves.

Personal security? This woman has personal security? Why? If he were to be honest, it was everyone else that needed personal security to protect them from her.

And while she sat in her personal car with a security guy she didn't

48 Shelly Laurenston

need, she was looking down her pug nose at him. He knew she saw him as nothing but some knuckle-dragger wandering around, drooling, trying to scare innocent schoolchildren, and afraid of fire.

Then again, who cared? This woman's life was none of his business. So he would just sit here and wait to arrive at the, he was sure, overpriced doctor's office.

Keane thought he wanted some fresh air, so he pushed a button on the door, and the window went down. The vehicle they were in was a hundred-thousand-dollar car, and the window made absolutely no sound when he lowered it, which fascinated him. His SUV—which the insurance company had just totaled out due to Mads landing on the front end after being thrown off a roof not too long ago—had made all sorts of weird noises and did not have this level of smooth ride. Wanting to hear the silence again, Keane closed the window, then opened it . . . then closed it . . . then opened it . . . then—

"What are you doing?"

The badger was glaring at him.

"Nothing."

"Stop playing with the window."

"It's not like you can hear it."

"I can hear you pushing the button, and it's driving me nuts!"

"Okay, fine."

He closed the window since the AC was on and went back to looking around the back of the car. That's when Keane noticed a line of water bottles sitting inside the door. They each had their own hole, snugly fitting inside. He studied them while the car sat in traffic until he picked one up by the top and dropped it. Then he grabbed the second one. Dropped it. Then the third. He liked the little "pop" sound the holder made when he pulled each bottle out. So once he'd taken them all out, he put them back and proceeded to pull each one out again.

"Now what are you doing?"

Keane looked at Nelle. "Huh?"

"What are you doing with my water bottles?"

He shrugged. "Nothin'."

"Stop playing with the water bottles," she growled through clenched teeth, her fangs now gone.

"Fine."

Now really bored, Keane looked out the window and resisted his urge to keep messing with the bottles. Comfortable in silence, Keane was surprised when he heard, "So what do you read?"

"Why are you asking?"

"Because I'm interested?"

"I doubt it."

"Uh-huh." She was quiet a moment before she asked, "Do you think I'm not interested because I don't care about other people?"

"That," he replied, his gaze focused on a naked man arguing with two cops on the street. "And because you're vapid."

Charles made an *ooooph* sound from the front.

"You think *I'm* vapid?"

"Yes."

"What makes you think I'm vapid?"

"Well"—he felt her small fist tap his chest, and he turned in time to see she was very close to him and taking a selfie of them with her camera—"just a guess."

The badger moved even closer until she could relax against him fully, then took another picture.

"You are extremely judgmental," she surmised, studying the pictures she'd taken before moving back to her spot on the other side of the car.

"I'm a *cat*. I judge all of you and, of course, find all of you lacking. Except my niece," he added. "Because she's amazing. And my sister and my mom, because I'm wisely afraid of my mom and adore my sister."

"As long as you know yourself," Nelle said, now completely immersed in whatever was on her phone.

"Are you ever *not* using your phone?"

"Why would I not use it? I have constant access to information, shopping, my friends."

"You have friends?"

50 *Shelly Laurenston*

"I have lots of friends."

"People you know in real life?"

She looked away from her phone and stared at him a moment before asking, "Why would I need to know them in real life?"

"How do you call someone a friend that you don't personally know?"

"It's easy." She held her phone up and pointed at some social media app. "See all these people replying to my recent comments on that new mobster TV show . . . all friends."

"How are they your friends?"

"We chat almost every day."

"Personally, I feel a friend is someone that, if you bump into them on the street, you would recognize them and say, 'Hi, Joe.' Not have to be reminded who they are and then say, 'Hi, love my kitty cat underscore lover thirty-nine.' "

She gazed at him a moment before asking, "Is that really your online name?"

"I do not have an online name, and never ask me that again."

"This is not a doctor's office," Keane announced when they walked through the front door of Dr. Weng-Lee's business, the *ting-ling* sound of the bells over the door nearly drowning him out.

"I never said I was taking you to a doctor's office," Nelle pointed out before nodding at Layla behind the counter.

"I'm leaving."

Christ! Cats were so moody! "Calm down. If anyone can help you, it's Dr. Weng-Lee."

"Licensed physicians do not have storefronts in Chinatown next to Shang Hai Hot Chicken franchises."

"I love their chicken."

Keane growled. "That's not the point."

"What is the point other than you are seriously uptight?"

"I am not uptight. This is my shoulder we are talking—*stop taking my picture!*"

"There's this guy I'm attempting to ward off before he asks me out,

TO KILL A BADGER   51

and I have to hurt his feelings, and I'm convinced your constant terrifying glare should do the trick."

Before the cat could complain more about Weng-Lee's space, the door in the back of the shop opened, and a woman wearing a gold necklace, gold bracelet, and gold diamond earrings from a Cartier collection Nelle had her eye on walked out, Weng-Lee right behind her.

"Thank you so much, Dr. Lee," the woman sighed out, moving her head from side to side. "You are an absolute miracle worker. I've already put appointments on the books for my sister and two of my girlfriends. I've told them all about you, and they can't wait to see you. They're in constant pain from yoga."

Weng-Lee, silent, put his hands together like he was praying, closed his eyes, and bowed his head the tiniest bit. It was a move that Nelle always enjoyed watching. The client mimicked the praying hands before bowing to him like this was an old black-and-white movie about that "Chinese" detective that was never played by someone who was actually of Chinese descent.

Weng-Lee gestured to the front door. The woman brushed past Nelle like she wasn't there and walked to the double-parked limo outside.

They all waited for the door to close before Nelle and Weng-Lee faced each other, put their hands in the praying position, and bowed to each other. When they were standing straight again, gazes locked, they both burst out laughing.

"She still does that?" Nelle asked.

"Every time. She must tell her friends to do it, too, because they all do," he said with his trademark eye roll. "These Anglos love it," he added, his true New York, private-school accent coming out. "So what's going on, beautiful?"

"Wait," Malone cut in. "I don't under—"

"Weng-Lee is from here."

"Bronx. Born and raised," Weng-Lee bragged with his big smile. "But these rich broads don't want their Eastern medicine provided by a guy who got a full scholarship ride to the High School for Math, Science and Engineering at The City College of New York, as well as

52   *Shelly Laurenston*

Stanford and Harvard, unless they also sound like they helped build the railroad in 1823. So I give 'em a little show."

"You don't find that demeaning?"

"Demeaning? That woman pays me fifteen-hundred *an hour* to help her with the migraines she gets from being in a loveless marriage. I mean, first I had her go to a neurologist to rule out a tumor, because you never know, but nope. Just a loveless marriage. So if she needs to believe the guy working out the kinks in her neck is just off the boat . . . how does it hurt me or the summer home I just bought out in the Hamptons for me, the wife, and the kids? Not only near the ocean, but also has a pool."

"Did you get your daughter that pony yet?" Nelle teased.

"I am *not* getting her a pony. And stop telling her to ask me for one. Now"—he let out a breath—"what do ya need today, beautiful?"

"It's him," Nelle told Weng-Lee, pointing at the cat with a jab of her thumb.

"Wait one minute," Malone quickly cut in, gaze searching the store as he spoke, lip curled in obvious disappointment. "I am not paying fifteen-hundred bucks for any of this weird shi— Oh, my God. You really do have tiger dong tea."

Weng-Lee hand-waved away the cat's concerns. "The fifteen hundred an hour isn't for us. It's for *them*."

"White people?" Malone asked solemnly.

"No. Full-humans. You guys get a discount. Nine hundred an hour."

"I am not *paying nine hundred—"*

"But for a friend of my dear, sweet Nelle, it's free."

Nelle turned her head, lifted her chin, and grinned at the big cat.

"Don't," Malone sneered back.

The Himalayan wolf opened the door to his back office and gestured them in before asking the woman at the front, "When's my next appointment, Layla?"

"Not until after two, doc."

"Great."

TO KILL A BADGER 53

Once inside the shockingly white but much more medical office–like room, the wolf went to the sink to wash his hands. A move that made Keane feel eternally grateful.

"So what's going on?" the wolf asked while he scrubbed away.

"Shoulder problems," Nelle replied before Keane could say anything.

"I can speak for myself."

"Can you?"

"I know you're used to running the lives of your friends, but we're not friends."

"Oooh," the wolf said, laughing. "Saucy!"

"I'm leaving," Malone announced.

"Oh, come on. I was just joking." His hands and arms washed and dried like he was going into surgery—again, Keane was quite happy about that—the wolf pulled on nitrile gloves and nodded at the medical table with a toss of his head. "Sit, sit. Let's see what we have before you run away screaming."

"I'd prefer to see a real doctor."

"I am a real doctor," the wolf lied.

"Right. A *doctor* that has his office out of a Chinatown storefront. And sells tiger dong tea."

"You are really focusing on that," Nelle noted.

"Do you have any idea how much rent is here?" Weng-Lee asked. "This isn't the seventies. Some Arab prince just bought a condo up the street. I doubt he'll ever live there, but he paid a fortune for it."

"Look, I'm sure you worked hard for your PhD in . . . voodoo, but—"

"I have a PhD in Eastern *medicine* from Stanford, a second PhD in East Asian Studies from Princeton, my medical degree is from Harvard, and I did my medical residence at Mount Sinai, and have hospital privileges there and at New York Presbyterian as an orthopedic surgeon."

Keane knew he was gawking, but he couldn't help it.

"If any of that is true—"

"It's all true."

54 *Shelly Laurenston*

"—then why are you—"

"Here? Because I get fifteen hundred *an hour* treating some bored, rich housewife who gets stress-induced migraines. Now get up on the table and do me a favor for the next five minutes, would ya? Stop being a cat."

Chapter 4

Charles had parked the car around the corner and was standing across the street from Weng-Lee's office. He never parked in front of where he left the Zhao family. He'd learned that the hard way a long time ago.

He'd been working for the family for more than thirty years. Scraped off the pavement in Perth by the Zhao family matriarch when he was thirteen, he'd been a shifter cub about to hit puberty when helped by the Zhaos. That meant losing temporary control of his fangs, claws, and fur as his body taught itself to become a snow leopard. And once he got through all that, the question became, what was he going to do with his life? They gave him options, the Zhaos did, but the best options involved staying around to "help" the family. He wasn't stupid. He was a cat. And he knew "help" was "work," but unlike some other big families that did that sort of thing, the Zhaos didn't mean some brutal, demeaning form of slavery. They paid well and treated everyone who worked for them as employees. With time and training, Charles was moved into security, and that's where he'd stayed. Mostly. The Zhaos put you where they needed you, when they needed you there, and you didn't question, you just did your job.

For instance, being the "protection" of Gong Zhao.

Some of the newer guys handling Zhao family security thought getting the job of protecting Gong Zhao was some kind of insult. The black sheep Zhao daughter was considered a non-entity among most of the staff and some lesser cousins, but that was foolish. Nelle, as she

56   *Shelly Laurenston*

preferred to be called, was a favorite of her father and had a reputation among the elder family members as someone to be avoided. Not only because she'd once tossed her own sister out an open hotel window, thirty floors up, but because they all found her rude and disrespectful. Nelle's mother often blamed her daughter's "Americanized attitude" on "the trash she insists on hanging around," but no. That was too easy an excuse. Nelle was simply who she was and, like the tiger he'd just driven to Chinatown had pointed out, she really didn't need Charles's protection . . . and that wasn't really why he was here.

The truth was, he'd been put here by the matriarch for one reason and one reason only: to keep an eye on what Nelle Zhao was up to at any given time. And each day was a new and exciting adventure in insanity.

The white, paneled van Charles had noticed driving around the block six times in the last hour finally came to an abrupt stop, and three men jumped out. One looked around before heading to the door of Weng-Lee's office. The other two stood outside that door and waited.

Charles finally sent the text he had already typed out, and then, he waited.

Your past is coming to haunt you . . . again.

Nelle let out a sigh at Charles's text just as the jingle from the front door went off and she looked up to see a Beretta pointed at her face.

"Get up," the man ordered her, "and go outside. Now. And, if you try anything . . . I'll blow the little shop girl's head off."

She glanced at Layla and saw the Arctic fox's eyes grow wide before she crouched behind the counter. Like badgers, foxes—another small predator breed—were very good at disappearing when things got out of hand.

Always a good trait to have when hanging around honey badgers.

"How much longer do I have to sit here?" Keane demanded. He was bored and freaked out. Was acupuncture supposed to involve this many needles? It seemed like a lot. Like a crazy lot.

"You'll know when it's done," the doctor told him while he continued to work on papers at a small desk. The first thing the wolf had done was take an X-ray of Keane's shoulder, and while staring at the results, Keane heard the canine mutter, "Wow. That's a mess."

Not exactly reassuring words. But then, while Keane sat on the exam table, the doctor began putting in the acupuncture needles. It didn't sting like he thought it would. Just felt weird. But then the wolf had kept going . . . and going . . . and going.

Keane looked at himself in the stainless-steel paper towel dispenser over the sink.

"How many needles is this?" he finally asked.

"A few hundred."

Keane frowned. He really didn't know much about any of this stuff, but even to him, that sounded weird.

"That seems . . . excessive?"

"Not for you. You are one tight, stressed-out ribbon of muscle and bone. If you were full-human, you'd absolutely have to get a shoulder replacement. But, because you're a big cat, you just need to get your body to do what it already does naturally."

"Which is?"

"Heal itself. But, I think you're so wound up about . . . whatever . . . that your body can't make that happen. These needles will stimulate that process, though."

"Good. Because I can't afford a—"

"Titanium replacement. I know. Do you think you're the first pro player I've ever worked with? You're not. The beauty is, you're a shifter. So you won't have to suffer months and months of rehabilitation or any surgeries. Just a few minutes with some needles and you'll be fine. Just calm down. Stress does not help the process."

Deciding he was done talking to the canine, Keane debated just tearing out the needles himself, but the vast number was daunting. He didn't even know how he'd get started. But before he could come up with a plan of attack, he heard noises from the other side of the door. He looked at the doctor, and the wolf was already standing.

"What is that?" Keane asked.

"I think Nelle may have brought some drama to my little office."
Weng-Lee shrugged those massive wolf shoulders. "It happens sometimes."

"Of course it does," Keane growled, automatically feeling angry.
"Because my life is never *easy*!" He spit out the last word between
clenched teeth, and his shoulders automatically began to tense from
his annoyance.

"Maybe you should calm—"

"If you tell me to calm down," Keane warned, "I will wait until
you shift and then tear your goddamn tail off."

The wolf wisely took a step back. "All right then."

Keane heard bodies slam against the office door. He sniffed the air
and caught fox, honey badger, and full-human male, but he didn't
scent Nelle's useless security guard. Where was he? Why wasn't he
in the other room, helping the woman he was being *paid* to protect?

Knowing he'd have to get involved—and not really wanting to—
Keane slid off the exam table. Glaring at the door, he took in a deep
breath, but when he released it, the deep breath turned into a roar that
shook the small, darkened windows, and his body must have tensed at
the same time, because all the needles in his arm shot out and embedded
into the wall on the other side of the room. He barely glanced at
the weird design he'd just accidentally created and stalked over to the
door. He yanked it off its hinges and stepped into the storefront.

The first thing he saw was the full-human male. He was still standing
but bloody. And wrapped around his neck were the long legs of
Nelle; the muzzle of a gun pressed to the top of the man's head while
she used her other hand to control him by his hair.

Keane took three big steps across the room and, once he reached
Nelle's side, immediately grabbed her hand, lifting it so she couldn't
destroy the man's brain with one shot.

"What are you doing?" he demanded, working very hard to keep
calm in the moment.

Blinking those dark eyes at him, Nelle glanced around a bit, like
she was searching for something, before announcing, "Uh . . . killing
this guy?"

TO KILL A BADGER 59

"You can't do that."

He watched her fight a smile, which just pissed him off, because usually his glower terrified people into submission. He found her smirk just . . . rude.

"I can't?" she asked. "Why can't I?" The smirk grew a bit. "Is this a moral issue?"

"That's part of it. Also, bullets are loud."

"It's New York. Who will notice?"

"There will be blood to clean up."

"That's what cleaning companies are for."

"The body."

"I'll call a hyena I know. His clan loves a good meal."

"Hard prison time."

"Zhaos never go to prison."

"You in an unflattering orange prison outfit."

"I look *fabulous* in orange. And he started it. It's self-defense."

"No one's going to believe that."

"He did start it," a squeaky voice said from behind the counter. Keane assumed it was the She-fox.

"I don't care," he informed all of them. "You can't just go around shooting people in the head."

"I've seen you tear people's heads off."

"Yes, but it was tiger me. Tiger me does what tigers do. We kill our enemies. But when I'm human—"

"Aren't Malones known as leg breakers?"

"Some of us. But not the Malone brothers."

"You're *all* the Malone brothers."

"Just let him go."

She took a moment to seem as if she were actually debating about it, before unwinding her long legs from around the man's neck. Before she could jump to the floor herself, Keane let go of her hand to grab her body and bring her safely to the ground. That's when the man turned and reached for the gun that Keane now realized must have been his in the first place.

Just seeing the movement out of the corner of his eye, Keane re-

60 *Shelly Laurenston*

acted, slamming his elbow into the man's face and sending him crashing to the floor. The idiot tried to get up, so Keane slammed his foot over the man's head, which was kind of funny because his foot was way bigger than the dude's head. Keane's large foot size used to really embarrass him in junior high, creating some brutal times in the boys' locker room after football practice. But then Shay came along, and everyone stopped talking about it. Not only because Shay's feet were bigger, but because they'd both hit their growth spurts, and then everyone in school was too terrified to tease them about anything.

Pinning the man to the ground with one foot, Keane stared at Nelle Zhao.

"Now . . . don't you feel better about yourself?" he asked.

She shrugged. "No."

Nelle loved the cat's ability to rationalize. Ohhh, he was in his *tiger* form when he tore those guys' heads off, so anything he did as a tiger was apparently A-OK. But when he was human, suddenly all those human rules applied.

She didn't really buy that. At all. But she knew he did. Maybe it helped him sleep at night. Maybe it helped him not become a monster like the head of the de Medici Coalition. The lion males they were battling against because the de Medici lions didn't have any boundaries like that. Whether big cat or big human, they would do whatever they wanted to, because everyone else was simply beneath them and nothing but prey.

It was cute, though. A tiger with boundaries and a moral code. Who knew that kind of cat existed? She certainly didn't. Not until she'd met the Malone brothers, with all their upstanding morals and life rules. How could that not be cute? Like when she saw tiger cubs hiss at each other, trying to be fierce but just looking adorable!

"You are just the cutest thing," Nelle told him.

"Don't do that," he replied.

"Don't do what?"

"Minimize me. It's rude."

Minimize him? Maybe she had, but what really shocked her was

TO KILL A BADGER   61

that he was using the term correctly. She cringed. She was doing it again, wasn't she? Minimizing him? All this time, she'd only seen him as a very gorgeous but rather stupid brute. Very stupid, actually. She'd initially thought that was Shay, too, but he'd turned out to be smarter than most realized. She knew that because Tock didn't have time for stupid people. How did Nelle know that? Because Tock always said, "I don't have time for stupid people." And she meant it. You didn't need to be a rocket scientist or graduate from Harvard, but you did need to have good, sound logic if you wanted to associate with Tock Lepstein. That's how Nelle found out that Shay wasn't stupid. At all. But she had dismissed his eldest brother as "kind of stupid." Yet every second she spent with him, she was beginning to realize he wasn't as stupid as she thought. It didn't prove he was smart, but he was definitely not stupid.

Malone proved that even more when he looked down at the man under his giant foot and asked, "How many more do you have outside?"

"I don't know what you're—*owwwwww!*"

"I could squash your head like a grape, or you could fucking answer me. Your choice."

"Two outside the door. Four in the van."

Satisfied with that answer, the Malone brother turned those green-gold eyes to her and asked, "So what did you do exactly?"

"Pardon?"

"To have some guy tracking you down here."

"Who says I did anything?"

He didn't respond, simply raised his right eyebrow.

"Fine," she admitted. "He's probably from the Vatican, and it may involve some gold bars."

Mouth dropping open in shock, the tiger finally demanded, *"Who pisses off the Pope?"*

"Please," she sighed out. "He could not care less about gold. He's with God or whatever. But there are others who work for him that might care. Some priests or Vatican security."

"Don't we currently have *enough* problems with the Italians?"

"I did this ages ago. I thought they'd forgotten about it."

62   *Shelly Laurenston*

"Who forgets about gold bars?"

"It's not like they don't have more."

"That's not the point!"

"No need to yell."

She glanced over at the counter. The fox was again standing and next to her boss, the pair thoroughly enjoying this.

Nelle shouldn't be surprised, though. This would not be the first time she'd brought trouble to the doctor's business, but it was the first time she'd brought a big, angry cat along with her.

With a rather dramatic, put-upon sigh, the cat said, "We need to figure out how to get out of this without—"

"Murdering everyone?"

Malone stopped speaking again and simply stared at her for almost a minute before he asked, "What if we gave it back?"

"Gave back what?"

"The gold."

"That's probably been melted down by now."

"You melted it down?"

"I didn't do anything. I just put it in the system."

"What system?"

"The system."

"I don't know what that means."

"Well, if you don't know, then you don't know."

"And what does *that* mean?"

"Didn't your uncles teach you anything?"

"The whole point of my revenge-filled life is that my uncles didn't do anything for me, my brothers, or my mother after my father died, and that's why I shoved them out of our lives."

"Then why didn't we start a war with your uncles instead of the de Medicis?"

"That's because . . ." Malone's words faded away, and he glanced off before asking, "What do you mean, 'start a war'?"

"What did you think we were doing in Italy? Shopping?"

"I didn't think you were starting a war. I thought you were just . . ."

He briefly struggled to find the words. "I don't know. I don't know! I *do* know I didn't think you were starting a war!"

Nelle shrugged. "They shouldn't have made Charlie mad."

Keane looked as if he were about to say something, but instead, he turned his angry glare to the man under his foot.

"Stop squirming!" he viciously barked.

Yelling at someone else seemed to calm Malone a bit, which Nelle found fascinating.

"Okay," he said. "What's the rest of the plan?"

Shocked by the question, Nelle glanced over at Dr. Weng-Lee and Layla. They were now right beside each other, elbows resting on the counter, chins resting in their open palms. Typical canines watching the drama unfold but offering no assistance whatsoever.

"Rest of the plan?" she repeated back to Malone.

"You all do have a plan . . . right? To deal with this war?"

Nelle answered him honestly. "Probably not."

"How do you not have a plan?" Keane exploded.

"It's surprisingly easy," the badger replied. Despite the man on the floor who'd attempted to kidnap her and in the face of Keane's anger, Nelle Zhao appeared completely unfazed. She wasn't angry. She wasn't amused. She wasn't anything but calm. And maybe a little curious. Which Keane found completely disconcerting!

At the very least, she should be reacting to his rage. He would have eleven-hundred-pound polars quaking in the middle of games when they blew a play because they knew it would bring his wrath, so he didn't understand how this tiny badger didn't seem to even notice his wrath.

How could she not notice his wrath?

Quickly realizing yelling wasn't going to get him much from this weirdly unemotional badger, Keane attempted to calm down and instead asked a simple question.

"What exactly did you do in Italy?"

"I'm not sure I should tell you."

64   Shelly Laurenston

"Why?" he asked.

She stepped onto the man's hip, ignoring his grunt of discomfort, to give herself some much-needed height. She raised her arm and stroked Malone's forehead.

"I'm concerned about this triple line in the middle of your head. It suggests stress. Have you thought about Botox?"

"I also do that here," the wolf suddenly piped in. "I'll give you a discount."

"Shut up!" Keane snapped at the wolf.

"You're going to give yourself hypertension," Nelle went on. "Is that what you want? To be a cat with hypertension?"

Keane carefully took hold of the female's wrist—he'd seen what a startled badger could do to an innocent face with their claws—and pushed her hand away.

"Just tell me what you did," he ordered, expecting her to immediately comply like everyone else when he added his signature glower.

Again, she did that casual shrug of hers. "We gave them back their father."

That sounded strange to Keane. What did she mean, "gave them back their father"? The last he'd heard, the head of the de Medici Coalition had been—

"You gave them back the *corpse*?"

"Yes."

"Why did you have the corpse?"

"Oh, that I don't know. That was between Charlie and Max. Zhaos usually bury our . . . inconveniences."

"Is that what you call those you murder?" he couldn't help but ask.

"Yes," she replied, simply. Calmly. He did not understand this woman.

"Let me see if I understand what you're telling me—"

"This should be good," the wolf said to the She-fox.

"—at this moment, we are in the middle of a brutal fight with a gang of vicious Italian lions, and instead of calming that down, you guys up the ante by taking the *corpse* of their patriarch and, I don't know . . . throwing it at them?"

"Putting it at their dinner table for them all to see before having their family home violently breached by Italian law enforcement," Nelle clarified.

Keane gawked at Nelle Zhao for what felt like hours. Because he didn't know what to say or do until the wolf suddenly said, "Wow." Because even the canine thought what had just been said was insane.

Because it *was*.

"Okay, ya know what?" Keane took in and let out another breath. "We need to have a meeting."

"A meeting?" she repeated back. "What kind of meeting? You mean a meeting-meeting?"

"Okay."

"We don't really do that unless it pertains to basketball. We mostly do more informal get-togethers."

When he simply continued to gawk at her, she said, "Okay. I guess I can text everyone to meet us here in about four hours."

"No. Tell them to meet at Charlie's as soon as possible."

"Everyone is still at practice. And Tock has a date with your brother."

"They're already fucking. Why do they need to date? And I don't care."

"Okay, but you should be aware Mads isn't going to like it. You breaking into practice time."

"Just do it."

She walked over to the waiting area and picked up her phone. As she tapped away on the screen, she glanced over. Keane didn't know what she was thinking until she walked back, still typing. When she'd sent the text, she took a step back and, with her gaze still locked on her phone—waiting for a response, he assumed—she picked up the gun she'd been using earlier off the floor and aimed it at the man under his feet.

"What are you doing?"

"Well, we can't go until we eliminate our problem."

"That's not eliminating our problem. That's making more problems." He held his hand out. "Give me the gun."

66 Shelly Laurenston

"Once I kill him, this will be *my* gun and I like it."

"Give it to me."

She turned over the weapon, and Keane was about to tuck it into the waistband of his jeans but . . .

"Is the safety on?"

She frowned. "You don't know how to use a gun?"

"Why would I need to know how to use a gun? I'm a giant man who can become a nearly thousand-pound Amur tiger with giant fangs and claws. I don't *need* a gun."

She did something to the weapon that he assumed meant the safety was now on. With that, he tucked the gun away from the crazed female ready to use it in any situation, and proceeded to deal with the man struggling beneath him.

Malone stepped back from the man he'd managed not to crush under his enormous foot, which impressed Nelle. He seemed like the kind of cat that would walk around crushing things under his big paws simply for the pleasure of it.

Crouching, he grabbed the now fist-swinging man by his shirt. Despite many of those punches making direct contact, the cat showed no reaction. He simply lifted the man up a few inches, then slammed him back down a few times until the man stopped struggling.

"Hey," he quietly ordered his prey. "Look at me."

Blinking, trying to focus his gaze after all that head trauma, the man gazed up at Malone, and immediately his confused eyes grew wide. Because he could see fangs now.

"The two outside," Malone said, "call 'em in." He looked at Nelle. "Open the door a bit so they can hear him."

She wasn't used to anyone giving her orders except during a firefight, but sure. She'd play along. She wanted to see how the cat would handle this, since he wasn't a fan of straight-up "murder" as he insisted on calling what she'd planned to do, which seemed a little unfair. Nelle preferred the terms "self-preservation" or "self-defense." Although, at the end of the day, it was all semantics, wasn't it?

TO KILL A BADGER   67

Of course, now that Nelle had time to think about all this, she was guessing that she'd been wrong about this latest issue. No way the Vatican had anything to do with any of this. They would have never sent someone so inept.

Then who had sent this man, Nelle didn't know. She'd have to find out so she could put a stop to it.

Nelle quickly walked to the door, stood behind it, and pulled it open just enough.

Malone leaned in close to his prey. "Call them," he ordered in a growl that could barely be heard, but it could definitely be felt.

Eyes now wide in panic, the man called out, "Get in here!"

The two men keeping watch outside the clinic immediately came in. They had their weapons drawn—a handgun for one, a submachine gun for another, which seemed excessive—but that didn't stop Malone. As soon as the first man had entered the clinic, Malone dropped the old prey and went after the new, moving across the room in seconds. He grabbed the first man by the back of the neck and yanked him close, holding him so the gun was caught between the two. The other followed close behind, so Malone used his free hand to grab that man's throat. He yanked both inside—Nelle quickly closing the door—and rammed both males into the wall so hard that it left indents in the plaster and knocked both of them out completely.

"Well, that'll need repair," Dr. Weng-Lee blandly noted.

By then, the man that Malone had held captive beneath his foot earlier was scrambling to get up, but before he could make it to the door—not that Nelle was going to let him out—he was hit with the two bodies of his compatriots. They weren't thrown. Instead, Malone had slammed them on top of Nelle's would-be abductor, knocking him out, as well.

"Open the door," Malone ordered Nelle.

She did and he walked outside, holding all three grown, very large men—in full-human terms—in his two hands with incredible ease.

As he stepped off the curb with his prey, the van door slid open, and two men leaned out with automatic weapons. Malone threw one of the prey he held at them, knocking them back inside. Before the two others could replace them, Malone was at the van. Grabbing hold of the sliding door with his now-free hand, Malone yanked it off the vehicle. Pulling it back, he shoved it forward and inside the van. He slammed it from one side of the vehicle to the other, battering the men now trapped inside. When he was done, he tossed the last of his prey in with their comrades before throwing the door in after them.

Once all the prey was inside and unmoving, the tiger stepped back, and the van abruptly pulled off, forcing its way into traffic, proving Malone had left the driver alive and well.

Despite all the locals and tourists staring at him, Malone continued to gaze across the street until he yelled out, *"I thought you were security!"*

"Well—"

"Get the fucking car!"

Nelle realized that Malone was yelling at Charles, and she had to bite back a laugh. She called Charles her "security," but they both knew why he was there. To report back to her mother.

Returning to the clinic, Malone marched inside and up to the counter. "How much do I owe you?" he asked Dr. Weng-Lee.

"You can't put a price on entertainment."

"I don't need handouts," Malone sneered back.

"So you want to pay fifteen-hundred after all—"

"You said *discount*."

The doctor grinned. "Oh, look. A haggling kitty."

Nelle saw the cat's eyes glow gold-green again. Quickly, she put her hands on Malone's arm and pushed him toward the door.

"Put it and the wall damage on my tab, Layla," Nelle said.

"I don't need *your* handouts, either," the cat complained.

"Stop bitching." She reached around Malone and opened the clinic door, but he stopped and faced Weng-Lee again.

"Wait," the cat said. "I need to know . . . what's in that tiger dong tea?"

"Mystical elements from deep in the tropical rainforests of Xishuangbanna—"

"Cut the shit."

Weng-Lee unleashed that dazzling smile. "It's basically chai tea with some cinnamon."

"That's what I thought."

Keane didn't appreciate being shoved into a fancy car by a small badger, but he decided to let it go.

Once Nelle got in beside him, the useless idiot driver asked, "Where to?"

"Charlie's house."

"I've gotta go to Queens?" he whined, which almost had Keane's hands around the snow cat's neck, but Nelle pulled him back in time. But if that worthless alley cat couldn't be useful as security, the least he could do was drive where she told him to go.

"Just fucking drive," Keane snarled, his fangs out.

"I don't work for you," the house cat snapped back.

This time Keane had his hands around the alley cat's throat and was strangling the impertinent bastard when Nelle patted his arm and motioned to the car door.

"Look," she said, pointing, "the water bottles. Why don't you play with them for a while? You seemed to enjoy that earlier."

Keane unhanded the house cat, ignoring his dramatic coughing, and looked at the plastic bottles in the side pocket. He took one, and immediately flung it at the snow cat's head.

"You mother—"

"That's enough!" Nelle yelled, arms spread out to keep them apart. "From both of you!" She cleared her throat and took a more measured tone. "Charles, just drive. And you," she said, turning to Keane, "just calm down."

Folding his arms over his chest, Keane sat there, pissed. Luckily the windows were dark, because he might frighten any small children that could look into the car.

"He has one fucking job," he finally told her.

"Let it go. You always get so upset over everything. You're going to give yourself an untimely heart attack."

"Can't come soon enough."

"Quiet, Charles," she said before relaxing into the leather seat. "Everyone just be quiet and relax. You males. Always so ridiculously angry over *nothing*."

That's when Nelle's phone suddenly started repeating, "Fuck off, fuck off, fuck off," over and over again until she answered.

"What do you want now?" she asked without even a *hello*. "You want me to what? Fuck no!" She sat up straight. "I don't care what they promised you."

Keane could hear hysterical screaming coming from the other end. But it sounded like an Asian language, and he didn't really know any. He just knew someone was screaming.

And always casual Nelle was screaming back.

"I don't give a fuck about your dress! Burn the fucking thing with you inside it and then, maybe I'll come to your fucking wedding!" A little more yelling from the other side and then, even louder than before, *"Go to hell!"*

Nelle disconnected the call and slammed the phone down on the space between them. Arms now folded over her chest, her entire body rigid with rage, she angrily stared out the car window.

After a few seconds of silence, Charles asked from the front seat, "So how's your sister?"

"You can go to hell, too!" Nelle lashed back.

After that, there wasn't another word until they arrived at Charlie's house.

Chapter 5

"**M**om!**"

Tracey Rutowski immediately rolled off the couch, landed on her ass with her back against the furniture, and aimed the Glock she gripped in her hand at whatever was in front of her . . . which turned out to be her four daughters.

"Must you wake me up like that?" she asked her eldest, Nixie. The only one who looked so angry and so much like her father. The two middle ones, Angelika and Annika—fraternal twins whom she called "double trouble" since the day she'd discovered them plotting in their crib at three months old—were laughing, and the youngest, Leni, simply appeared annoyed at everyone's existence but her own.

Trace was surprised how much work her children turned out to be. Tracey and her brother had been such easy kids. Obedient. Reliable. *Excellent* liars. Self-sufficient. All of which was important, because her parents had rarely been around. If she'd waited for Marv and Lisa Rutowski to make her dinner or bring her to school every day or rescue her from an East German prison, she'd have starved to death without being able to read or do basic math, but with a perfect grasp of the German language.

But her own children's generation were so damn needy. When she was growing up, there had been no cell phones to call or text her parents whenever she had a small demand. But now, all she got were whiny, demanding texts.

Mom, what's for dinner?

Mom, are you in the country?
Mom, how do you get out of the trunk of a car?
Mom, your dogs attacked my boyfriend. Again!
On and on! It was endless.

Personally, she blamed their father. Wolf pups were notoriously needy and demanding and couldn't do anything on their own until they were in their late teens. Although nothing about her kids *seemed* wolf-like except their shoulders and feet; she worried their pack-like need for companionship would be used against them one day.

"Must you bring your weaponry into this house?" Nixie demanded.

"I can't leave it in my car, Nix. That would be dangerous."

Deciding not to reply to that, her daughter held up her phone and asked, "Was this you?"

Tracey wasn't wearing her glasses, so she leaned forward and squinted, attempting to read the screen. When that was ineffective, she looked around for her glasses until Angelika walked over and moved them from Tracey's forehead and onto her face.

"Oh. Thanks, baby."

"No problem."

Again, Tracey looked at the small screen of her eldest's phone.

"Wow. Boston has become dangerous."

"Boston has always been dangerous." She pointed. "You did this, didn't you? For that girl."

"She's your first cousin, and why do you always ask questions you really don't want the answers to?"

"You are making things *impossible* for Great-Uncle Edgar."

Tracey dropped her head back, let go a sound of disgust. She was so *tired* of this conversation about how hard she was making it on poor Uncle Edgar! The crankiest canine she'd ever met or been forced to have Thanksgiving dinner with!

"You know he's grooming you, right?" she asked Nixie.

That's when all four of her daughters exploded.

"Mother!"

"Ma!"

"What the hell?"

"Ewwwwww!"

"I don't mean *that*, you pervs! Jesus." Trace got to her feet. "I mean he's *grooming* you to be just another government drone; just workin' for The Man."

"What man?"

"Is there *a* man? Or do you mean any man?"

"Because Uncle Edgar's retired from *being the* man."

"Oh, my God!" Tracey put the safety back on her weapon and placed it on the coffee table. "How are any of *you* my children? I'm starting to think I need proof."

"Just look at our noses," Angelika suggested. "We were all cursed with your nose."

Trace touched her face. "What's wrong with my nose?"

"Everything," all of her daughters replied.

CeCe Álvarez stood back from her most recent painting and studied it as if she were looking at the worst shit on the planet. She wanted to be her harshest critic so that when actual critics said horrible things, she didn't care. At least that had always been her explanation for being so critical of her own work because, for a honey badger, she could be quite sensitive. Something her tough-as-nails family members did not understand.

"Your father and I survived communist dictators," her mother would remind her, "and you can't handle some Anglo calling your work subversive. Pathetic."

Maybe it was, but it was hard putting your ass out to the world and saying, "Tell me what you think," only to have them come back and say, "I hate it, and everyone else should hate it, too."

Over the years it had made CeCe a little . . . reactionary.

In fact, she'd physically assaulted more critics than she cared to count. She slapped one. Headbutted another. And made a terrifying female art critic cry simply by staring at her until she peed herself. And those were the only ones she could remember, because she'd been so-

74 *Shelly Laurenston*

ber at the time. In any other industry, especially as a woman of color, it should have destroyed her career, but in the nineties art world, it had made her a star.

A *feared* star, but definitely a star. Any time she would become an artist-in-residence at some fancy Ivy League school, students would flock to her seminars. And eventually her work would sell for hundreds of thousands.

A few years back, though, she and her work had been considered old and boring and "out of touch." But after being "rediscovered" online, she had sold one of her pieces for several million. Since she had never stopped working, even during the "lean years," CeCe now had more than enough material for several shows. Something Tracey loved because she had always managed CeCe's art career and received fifteen percent from any sale.

"I'm gettin' a boat!" her best friend had giddily announced after that last deal.

Not that Trace couldn't have gotten a boat before then. Hell, she could have gotten a massive yacht. She had other clients whose careers she managed, and her galleries always mounted some of the hottest artists while still giving some up-and-comer a shot if she saw in them what she'd always seen in CeCe.

Still . . . despite the new appreciation in her work, CeCe didn't feel confident enough to say that this piece was worthy of seeing the light of day outside her home studio. Which meant only one thing . . .

"Time to get naked."

CeCe usually only worked naked in her Manhattan studio. For some reason, it made her feel closer to her work when there were no clothes in the way. Unfortunately, her offspring didn't feel the same way. When they "caught" her naked, they complained to their father and anyone else who would listen that she was "embarrassing" them. How she produced such uptight children, she didn't know, but she tried to meet them halfway. And, at least when she was in the studio behind the family home, she tried her best to keep her clothes on.

But her kids were currently in the main house, making breakfast for themselves like they were creating the Mona Lisa—sometimes they were so like their father's restaurant chain–owning family with the cooking—and she just needed a few minutes to see if this piece was working at all.

She stripped off her paint-stained overalls and stood in front of the piece. She was waiting to see if she had the reaction she needed. The one that told her it was working or not working or should be burned in a fire.

It was while she was waiting that the cat, which had been curled up on the tall stool next to her work table, suddenly sat up and hissed.

This wasn't CeCe's cat. It lived here, but she had nothing to do with it. It had just shown up one day in her studio, eating a small bird, and daring her to start a fight. She figured it would find its own way out when it was done. What she hadn't known was that her children had begun feeding it, giving it water, even providing a spot to relieve itself and then cleaning it out every day so CeCe didn't have a chance to complain about the smell. It was like she and the cat had come to an understanding: the cat didn't annoy CeCe, and CeCe didn't tear it apart one night when she was in her badger form.

Besides, every once in a while, it could be quite, dare she say, helpful?

Like now . . . hissing toward the door in that way. Something was outside her studio that this cat didn't think should be there, and it wasn't CeCe's kids or husband.

Steph Yoon stood in her garden and sipped her herbal tea. When she worked, she drank coffee. The caffeine helped her focus. But when she just wanted to enjoy nature, she drank tea.

Her husband had built this garden for her in the backyard of their personal home. He'd tried to do the same at the Van Holtz Pack house, but his family members killed all the flowers by dog-peeing on them every night when they went out hunting. Or when they'd drunk too much tequila and ended up drunkenly pissing in random spots around the territory.

Moving out of the Pack house had been a good decision all those years ago. Apparently, Steph made the Pack "nervous." She didn't know why. She rarely shifted to her badger form while at the house. And she didn't talk much unless she had something to say. She mostly kept to herself when her girlfriends weren't around. She just put on one of her black hoodie sweatshirts—it was always extra cold in the house, summer or winter—silently worked on her laptop, and occasionally took up residence in a kitchen cabinet when she didn't want to be bothered. It wasn't her fault that the wolves yelped in startled surprise any time they found her in there.

It also wasn't her fault everyone thought she was "weird." An accusation tossed at her since grade school by full-humans. She wasn't weird. She just didn't know how to fit in. Or want to fit in. Her neurodivergence helped her create amazing things that people used every day in this now-digital world. If that made her weird . . . well . . . whatever. She had bigger things to worry about.

Like the scent of male lions coming up behind her at this very moment.

Huh, Steph thought, as she had another sip of her tea.

He kicked the back door open and walked into the surprisingly small house owned by a woman with more money in her many bank accounts scattered around the globe than God himself.

His cousins followed him in, and he again wondered why they were bothering with these old hags. Giuseppe agreed, not wanting to waste the manpower on such nonsense, but their uncle—who still ran the coalition, despite what Giuseppe may think—strongly felt they needed to go.

Personally, he thought the younger badgers were more important. Although it had been the nine of them—the hags *and* the sluts—who'd released the family's cargo and taken down their ship the night before. But it had been the younger five that had killed Giuseppe's father and dumped the body in the middle of his family home. So, he couldn't wait to kill every last one of those disgusting rodents. Which was why, he felt, the four old hags could wait.

It wasn't his decision, though. He was head of his own team, but he did not run the family. The coalition. He didn't make enough money for that. Not yet. So he shut his mouth and did his job.

Walking into the house, he passed a high-end washer and dryer and entered the kitchen.

"Vile," one of his cousins noted, pointing at a glass case on the kitchen table filled with scrambling scorpions.

"They eat those," he informed his cousins.

"Filthy rats. All of them."

Once they entered the living room, two of his cousins took the stairs up to the second floor. Two others went to the basement. He patiently waited until they returned a few minutes later.

"Nothing," one said when he walked back into the living room.

"Same for basement."

He looked around the room. "She's here somewhere. I can smell her."

Something moved under the floorboards. It was said honey badgers could slip in almost anywhere.

"Get the axe from outside," he ordered, pulling out his gun. "We'll tear out these floorboards."

His eldest cousin moved quickly to get to the axe they'd passed on their way inside the house, returning in two minutes. After they all moved the fifty-thousand-dollar rug, his cousin eagerly chopped at the wood floor.

"I hear something," a younger cousin said, dropping to his knees and sticking his head inside the hole that had been created.

"What do you see?"

"Nothing yet, but—" His cousin's sudden screams startled them, and they all jumped back in horror as his cousin jerked away from the hole, revealing several vipers hanging from the cat's face.

Arms swinging wildly, his younger cousin stumbled back into the elder, dropping them both to the ground. Now that there was a hole in the middle of the floor, vipers quickly slithered out. They poured from that damn hole and immediately went on the attack, spreading out and going after all of them.

78 *Shelly Laurenston*

He spun around, shifting to his animal form to make his escape, but the snakes were on him in seconds. Fangs digging into his leg and ass, his underbelly, his neck and paws, and injecting him with their venom. Over and over. Immediately he felt the effect, splaying out on the floor before he could get a foot off the ground and jump onto the dining room table in the hopes of getting away.

He looked up and saw the old hag walking toward him. He didn't know where she'd been that he hadn't seen her, but she seemed calm and rational as all those nasty snakes slithered around her. She stopped in front of him, and one of the snakes attacked her ankle. She bent her knee and lifted her leg up enough so that she could yank the viper off her body. Then she brought it, still alive and hissing wildly, toward her face. She opened her mouth, revealing multiple small but bright white badger fangs, before biting down on the viper's head.

Chewing her treat, she crouched in front of him in seven-thousand-dollar shoes that some of her blood had splattered onto and gazed into his face.

"When you come for badger, little kitten," she said around a mouthful of snake, "do not miss."

She stood and began to walk away, his vision and vital signs rapidly fading. But he still heard her when she tossed over shoulder, "Because badgers. . . ? We never miss."

Steph took another sip of her tea and glanced up when the drone flew over her head. She watched it, turning until she faced the five big cats standing behind her.

They all watched the drone get closer until one of the cats swung his arm high and slapped the device out of the air with his hand. It hit the ground hard and broke into several pieces.

"Hey!" she snapped. "That cost more than anything you could possibly own."

"You think your little drone can stop *us*?" one asked in accented English.

"Of course not," Steph replied. "It just automatically responds to intruders." She took another sip of her tea before motioning her head

TO KILL A BADGER 79

to a spot behind her. "This one, though . . . my twins made this one."
She smiled with absolute pride. "And it comes when called."

She watched the cat's gazes move up the metal body of the eight-foot drone that had driven to a spot behind her. Unlike the smaller one that was now destroyed—which she had built—this one couldn't fly, but she didn't doubt her twins would fix that defect in due time. They may grill a steak like their Van Holtz father, but they created robotic devices like their mom.

The twins' toy raised its two arms, each with Gatling guns mounted on the ends.

The cats didn't wait. They simply ran.

The twins came around their toy and stood on either side of Steph.

"This thing still doesn't fire?" she asked.

"We made it for Comic Con, Ma," Dae replied.

"Not for Auntie Ox to annihilate her enemies with," Tae finished.

"Then what's the point?"

Trace, her arms resting on the kitchen island while facing the sliding glass doors, was rolling her eyes again, while her daughter chastised her like a child about "how much trouble you cause this family!" when she realized she was hungry.

She reached for the loaf of plain, grocery-store-bought white bread her husband absolutely hated and banned from his home when Trace wasn't "in attendance," as he liked to say. That's when her cell phone started ringing and, at the same moment, two of her dogs ran by and out the back doggy door.

The Van Holtz Pack and her husband hated her dogs almost as much as they hated plain, store-bought white bread. But she'd always had dogs in her life since she was a kid. She'd taught herself to train them properly and even bred them now. Not for money, though. Just her own use. She'd started with German shepherds after dealing with them in East Germany, but over the years, she'd learned to love Belgian Malinois.

She currently had five, but when only two went by—meaning this wasn't a bathroom break!—she immediately grabbed her still-

80 *Shelly Laurenston*

rambling eldest and dropped them both to the floor. The twins followed suit, but her youngest just stood there until Angelika caught the child's T-shirt and yanked her down. Less than a second later, those glass doors were blown apart by a shower of gunfire. But as soon as it started, it stopped; male screams let her know that her dogs had made their move.

Trace immediately stood and saw two full-human men, trying to shake off the five dogs that had come at them from five different directions, grabbing hold of whatever they could. Arms, legs, groin. Just as she'd taught them.

She was going to let her dogs tear the big bastards apart when she saw two more armed men running toward them.

Softly, she ordered, "Angelika. Annika. Go."

The twins moved, scrambling around the island, and disappearing back into the house.

"Mom?" Nixie asked.

"Stay here." She pushed her youngest at her eldest. "You two keep down."

Trace stood and yelled out, *"Hier!"*

Her dogs instantly released their prey and ran back to the house.

Once her dogs were safe beside her, she called out to the men through what remained of the glass doors, "Looking for me?"

The two full-humans raised their weapons and took aim at her. Meaning they were here to take her out, not capture. Interesting.

"Mom!"

Ignoring her eldest, Trace begged, with no energy whatsoever—she really needed a very large cup of coffee—"No. Don't. I'm a mother."

She heard her youngest snort and decided she'd have to deal with that later when, outside, the twins attacked before triggers could be pulled.

Angelika just walked up behind one of the men, put a gun to the back of his head, and pulled the trigger on the .45 Trace had given her for her eighteenth birthday.

Annika, however, liked things a little messy. She jumped onto one

TO KILL A BADGER 81

of the men's backs and began stabbing with one of the kitchen knives. Something her father was *not* going to like at all.

The other two men, the ones her dogs had attacked, had finally picked up their weapons, trying to focus on Trace's daughters.

"Pass Auf," she said to her dogs, and they immediately focused on her. Her lip curled a little before she snarled, *"Fass."*

The dogs charged outside once more and, again, attacked the men they'd attacked a few seconds before. This time, however, they took the pair down. Trace's two females gripped the men's throats and bit, blood spurting on their muzzles from torn arteries.

When the men stopped moving, her dogs let go. But Annika . . .

"He's dead," Angelika told her twin. "You can stop stabbing now."

"Nice," Nixie sneered, now standing next to Trace. "You've ruined Dad's kitchen."

"How is that my fault?"

"You've started a fight with people willing to slaughter your entire family."

"I didn't start anything."

"And you've turned the twins into murderous psychopaths."

"Oh, my God, Nixie." Tracey let out a sigh. "Get off the cross, we need the wood."

Her phone started to ring again, and Trace answered, already knowing it was one of her friends.

"Yeah?"

"You alive?"

Ox. Of course. "Yeah. But they fucked up my kitchen."

"The wolf will complain."

"Yep. You hear from Steph and CeCe?"

"Steph, yes. Not CeCe."

"Shit."

Trace disconnected the call and started toward the front of the house.

"Is Aunt CeCe okay?" Leni asked.

"I'll let you know. Nixie, call in a clean-up."

82 *Shelly Laurenston*

"A . . . a what? What are you talking about? Wait. Oh, my God . . . are you talking about cleaning up these bodies?"

"Forget it. Leni, you handle it."

"On it!"

"Wait . . . the fourteen-year-old? *Mom!*"

Amelia was into her second serving of waffles and bacon—her brothers were into their third—when her aunts walked into the family kitchen. The four family homes of these honey badgers were all on the same suburban street. So them showing up at any time of the day or night was not exactly shocking.

But when she saw that all three were armed—her Aunt Tracey covered in glass and a little blood from nicks, her Aunt Ox covered in viper bites that hadn't killed her but had managed to make her a little woozy from all the toxin flooding her system—she knew there was trouble.

"What did you do?" she asked.

"What makes you think we did anything?" her Aunt Tracey wanted to know.

"Nope," Amelia told her brothers. "There are not enough waffles in the world to deal with their crazy this early in the morning."

"It's the afternoon, sunshine, and you don't have to be rude. I didn't do anything wrong. *I didn't,*" she insisted when they laughed.

Of course, that's when the back door opened and Amelia's mother walked in. She was naked, drenched in blood that was not her own, and carrying a blood-and-gore-covered machete that she kept taped under one of her work tables.

Silently, they all watched her walk past them toward the hallway.

Once she'd exited the room, Amelia and her siblings refocused on her aunts by marriage and friendship.

"It's not my fault," Trace insisted. "It's not!"

Disgusted, Amelia went back to her food. But her youngest brother had one big concern as he reached for more bacon . . .

"Someone needs to check on the cat."

Chapter 6

Keane watched, in horror, his younger brother beaten into the ground by two hundred pounds of pure fury. Paws hit his face. Claws tore across his chest. Drool poured into his mouth. And all his brother could do was scream like a panicked child. "Get it off me! *Get it off me!*"

Disgusted, appalled, Keane folded his arms over his chest and allowed the devastation to continue raining down on his brother, completely ignoring the cat's pleas for help.

"What is wrong with you?" his even younger brother wanted to know, shoving Keane aside with a big shoulder. "Why won't you help him?"

That's when Keane realized his brother Finn was talking to *him*.

"Why won't *I* help him?" Keane watched Finn pull their massively sized brother to his feet. "I don't help weakness."

"Give him a break," Finn ordered. "He just got run over by a tank."

"A tank?" Keane barked, incredulous. "What tank? There is no tank." He pointed. "That's a dog!"

"Two-hundred-pounds-of-pure-muscle dog."

Shay, panting like he'd run a marathon, held up a small capsule. "I was just trying to give him this pill, and he went insane."

Finn took the pill from Shay's hand and held it out. "Here. You give it to the dog."

Keane looked around the yard they were all standing in. "I know you are not talking to me."

84 *Shelly Laurenston*

"Why can't you ever help?"

"I help by not beating you both to death from base disappointment."

"He has to take it!" Shay argued, sounding pathetic. "He has an infection. It's an antibiotic."

"I am not getting anywhere near that thing."

He turned away from his brothers, only to face his ten-year-old niece, Dani. She looked so angry down there, trying to appear as if they were eye-to-eye. It was adorable.

"What are you looking at?" he asked.

"You are so *mean!*"

"It's not my dog. And—" Keane blinked. "What the hell is that on your wrist?"

She held her arm up in reply but, for some reason, she thought he couldn't see it well enough, because she abruptly demanded, *"Daddy!"*

Shay immediately came over and lifted his daughter so that she could put the new watch directly in Keane's face.

"Really?" he asked his brother as the further proof of weakness was displayed for the world to see.

"It's either this or she starts the squealing again. She can hit notes that break eardrums."

"This exquisite watch," his niece began to intone, "is from Switzerland, and these are pink Swarovski crystals. It keeps exact, *precise* time and is water resistant up to three hundred meters and will never leave my wrist for the rest of my entire existence on this planet."

"What is wrong with this family?" Keane asked, as he always asked, even though he never got a satisfactory answer.

"Isn't it beautiful?" his niece went on.

"It looks expensive."

"Probably!" she eagerly agreed. "The crystals alone most likely cost millions of dollars!"

"I doubt they cost that—"

"Millions!" she insisted.

"Fine."

"Down, Daddy," she ordered, and her father did as she said, because Keane came from a very weak line of Mongolian-Irish cats, apparently.

"Now let's get this done," Shay said, holding out the capsule again for Keane to take.

"I am *not* dealing with this dog."

"You're not going to help at all?" Finn asked, appearing stunned, which just confused Keane.

"You wanted those dogs—"

"No, I didn't!"

"—you can deal with those dogs! Because if I had my way," he continued, walking toward the MacKilligan sisters' house, "I'd have tossed all of them, including their puppies, into the damn dumpster!"

"You are a bad uncle!" Dani accused, pointing an accusatory finger. "A very bad uncle!"

The back door opened, and Charlie MacKilligan walked out. She wore a black apron over her jeans and green T-shirt, but he could easily see all the flour and sugar on her that told him she'd been making delicious baked goods for the last few hours. It was all over her. Why even bother with the apron? Shouldn't it be more effective than that?

"What's all the yelling?" Charlie asked. She was very calm because she'd been doing so much baking. It was something that calmed her. Like football calmed Keane.

"They're having trouble giving that idiot dog a damn pill, and they want me to help. I don't help with dogs."

"That's beneath you?"

"They're *dogs*," Keane insisted, positive he was making his point.

Charlie grinned, and as pretty as it was, it was surprising. The woman didn't smile much. Not that she had that much to smile about when she had so much on her plate. A psychotic, unstable younger sister and, also, Max. Dealing with a psychotic female who could snap at any time and cause great damage like Stevie had to be much easier than being responsible for Max MacKilligan.

Walking past him and over to his brothers, Charlie took the capsule Shay still held and motioned to the dog he'd been struggling with.

86 *Shelly Laurenston*

It came instantly and sat without being asked. She then held out the capsule, and he took it without prompting. He gulped it down and then sat staring at the wolf-badger hybrid no one really understood. After digging into her front apron pocket, Charlie produced a couple of meaty treats and gave them to the dog. She then motioned it away with a swipe of her hand, and the dog took off to play with its brother while its sister was probably somewhere else in the house taking care of the pups that also none of them had wanted.

"See?" Charlie asked, facing them. "So easy."

"How did you do that?" Shay asked, in awe. "When I tried, he went for my face."

"He was playing."

"Didn't feel like he was playing."

"If he wanted to tear your face off, Shay, he would have torn your face off. Trust me. He was playing." She winked and gave Keane's niece a high-five as she walked back to Keane.

"So I assume you guys are here for a reason," she prompted.

"What exactly did you do in Italy?"

"Nothing you want to know about."

"So you go to Italy and you start a war."

"We didn't start anything. They did."

"Yeah, well, they've come here, I think. Nelle got attacked in Chinatown."

Charlie waved that away. "That wasn't them."

"How do you know that?"

"Nelle and I talked about it. It wasn't the de Medicis. It was probably the Simons."

"Who are the Simons?"

"Why do you ask so many questions?"

"Why do none of you ever give a straight answer?"

"For *so* many reasons."

The back screen door opened again, and Max leaned out. "You better get in here, Charlie. The bears are out front, and they're getting restless. They want treats."

"You shouldn't feed the bears," Keane told them.

TO KILL A BADGER 87

Charlie chuckled, but it eventually faded away. "Oh. You're not joking."

"I don't joke. You feed the bears, they become a nuisance. They lose their natural fear of humans and become aggressive."

Frowning, Charlie asked, "Wait . . . are we talking about full-blood bears or shifter bears?"

"There's no difference between the two. A bear's a bear's a bear."

"Okay, I'm . . . I'm . . . um . . . going inside . . . now."

Shay and Finn came to stand beside Keane.

"What did you say to Charlie?" Finn asked.

"I told her not to feed the bears."

"Oh, my God. Not your 'a bear's a bear's a bear' speech again."

"It's not a speech. It's a simple fact of life."

"You just don't like bears."

"I really don't. But that doesn't mean I'm wrong."

Keane heard annoying and constant crunching noises and turned toward a large tree. Hanging from one of the low branches by his knees swung Shen Li, chewing his bamboo and being annoying just by existing.

"See?" Keane pointed out to his brothers. "Annoying."

"Suck in that jealousy, kitty cats!" Li happily shot back between bites of bamboo. "Because we all know, *everybody* loves pandas!"

"For fuck's sake," Keane sighed before heading back inside the house.

Nelle sat on the love seat across the living room from the big couch that could fit at least two Alaskan grizzlies in their bear form. That's where Keane Malone sat and, with the angriest, most confused scowl she'd seen on anything not in a superhero comic book, he watched Charlie walk back and forth from the kitchen to the front door to hand out different treats to all the bears.

They were lined up down the block, hoping she'd have enough for all of them. She didn't always, and that's when—according to Max—they found their neighbors, in their bear forms, digging through their garbage at night, searching for any mistakes Charlie might have tossed out. Bears didn't mind if something was burned around the edges or a little uncooked in the center. Charlie didn't allow her "failures" to be handed out to anyone, so the garbage diggers usually found something to eat.

Cats were not exactly known for their patience. And the longer Charlie took to finish her current, self-imposed task, the more pissed Malone became. He wanted answers, and he wanted them now, but he'd already learned a very valuable lesson when it came to Charlie MacKilligan. She wouldn't be rushed. Ever.

Over the years, though, less-intelligent people had tried. They would try to rush or push Charlie. Especially in high school, when the government kept wanting to force their way into Stevie's education and move her into a more contained job. Something that they had complete control over. They thought they could push her along and into college and out from under Charlie's watchful gaze, but all those government bigwigs managed to do, instead, was make her mad.

Every once in a while, she'd just show up at her grandfather's Pack house with blood on her hands, an angry snarl in the back of her throat, and a vehicle none of them had ever seen before that would need new plates and VIN. She'd never tell them what had happened, and they'd all known better than to ask, but Nelle always knew it had something to do with the government, because if it was anyone else, Charlie would come home raging about her "bastard father" and how he'd "dragged them all into his bullshit!"

Still, it was fascinating to watch the poor kitty fight his urge to start yelling for attention. Especially when he realized that some of the bears liked to chat while getting their treats. They didn't just take their treats and scurry home so the process could go faster. Some leaned against the doorjamb and chatted about whatever with Charlie. And she was smart to let them. Charlie and her sisters were only lasting on this block because of the good graces of the bears that lived here. Not easy to do when one's sister insisted on raiding their beehives and the other sister hid in trees because they'd been scared up there by squirrels. So Charlie kept the locals fed and happy and protective of their food source.

Finally, after nearly an hour, the last of the bears left. Nelle could see the front door from where she was sitting in the living room and watched Charlie close it. She went back to the kitchen, and eyes that were now gold with annoyance watched her. When she returned with a tray of big blueberry muffins, Nelle thought the cat was going to spin himself into a rage. She even saw fangs peek out from under his lips. He didn't realize that the muffins were probably for the rest of them. Nelle loved Charlie's blueberry muffins. They weren't too sweet, and the blueberries were always bursting with flavor.

Charlie stopped in the middle of the living room, ready to offer them, when the front door slammed open and Mads's aunt and her lady friends burst into the house.

The explosion of noise alone had Max, Mads, Streep, and Tock suddenly appearing from the kitchen, Malone's two brothers behind them.

Mads's aunt pointed at Charlie and ordered, "We gotta go kill some people. Let's go."

Not needing to hear anything else, they all moved.

Keane was close to tearing down the house he was currently sitting in, so that it would force Charlie to move out of this house, and he would no longer have to deal with a line of annoying bears waiting for treats like they were animals in a Russian circus.

How long had he been sitting here? Hours? Days? *A lifetime?* He didn't know anymore. One day had faded into another as he'd waited and waited and waited for her to stop handing out food! It was like she was a nun feeding the hungry lurking around her church.

Then, when she'd come back with that big platter of blueberry muffins, he'd realized he'd have to kill all the adult bears so he could get five minutes of Charlie's precious time. No wonder the woman was always late for practice. She was an astounding defensive tackle. The other teams were going to be shaking in fear when she finally took the field during an actual game. But she needed to be pushy in her daily life, too. Because this was ridiculous! This was New York! There were bakeries on every other block! These bears could find food *anywhere*!

90 *Shelly Laurenston*

But before Keane could start killing all the neighborhood bears, those four older She-badgers had stormed into the house and announced, "We gotta go kill some people. Let's go."

He expected at least one of the younger badgers to question that order. Max usually questioned everyone just so she could annoy them. And he tolerated Charlie so well, because she was logical. She didn't just do things. She asked questions. Got more information. Did follow-up. But that's not what happened.

Nelle moved first, reaching over the back of the love seat she'd been sitting in and pulling out a pump-action shotgun. She tore off the duct tape that had held the weapon to the back of the furniture and, with one hand, pumped it while using her free hand to reach for a blueberry muffin.

He didn't know what appalled him more. That there was a shotgun within easy access to his precious niece? That after Nelle tossed the weapon to a waiting Max, she reached behind the love seat again and pulled out another, then pumped a live round into that one, too? That all the guns in this house were already loaded? Or that while Nelle did all this, she was also eating a muffin nearly as big as her head?

More weapons were retrieved from under tables and behind bookshelves, and not one badger asked a goddamn question. He looked at his brothers, but they seemed equally stunned. Like they didn't know what they were supposed to do in this absolutely insane situation.

"Ready?" Tracey Rutowski asked the younger badgers once they were all armed. They nodded, and she said, "Okay. Let's go."

That's when Keane snapped, and he unleashed a roar that was so loud, shifters from different blocks responded in warning and claiming their territory.

Nelle wasn't about to throw away the rest of her delicious muffin, so she pushed it into her mouth before aiming the Mossberg shotgun at the other side of the room. They all aimed. All the badgers. Violence was their reaction to any strange sounds, and a loud, pissed-off tiger roar was definitely something that was strange. Maybe that was because it just wasn't as common to hear as lion roars or wolf howls.

TO KILL A BADGER   91

But by the gods, when tigers did unleash that thing, a person felt it ripping through their very soul. It was terrifying.

Nelle also wondered if Keane knew that he was so pissed at the moment that he'd shifted to his tiger form. He was on that big couch, his clothes tossed around the room during the shift, with that insane coloring the Malone brothers had in their fur. No orange. Just black with white stripes. It was an extremely rare anomaly among tigers, and she'd never actually seen it before she'd met the Malone brothers. It made them damn near impossible to see in the darkness.

Then there was their size. From nose to tail, a standard Amur tiger could be about ten feet. Without his tail, Keane was about ten feet. With his tail, about . . . thirteen feet? Maybe fourteen. And he swung that tail around like a weapon. It was typical for most shifters to be bigger than the full-bloods anyway, which was definitely the way of badgers. But the Malone brothers were massive. Maybe that came from the Mongolian ancestors that were rumored to be fifteen feet from nose to tail. Nelle didn't know, but she was damn curious to find out more. And what did he weigh in his tiger form? Eight hundred pounds, at least. Maybe nine. Even over a thousand? Wow.

Fascinating! No wonder he walked around like he ruled the world. Because he probably could if he wanted!

Even better? The big cat hadn't realized that he was no longer human. Because he was roaring and snarling and roaring and growling and roaring. In other words, he thought he was talking, but he wasn't. Tock had gone through that, but she'd been in the hospital and recovering from being drugged. What was Malone's excuse?

The big cat continued on, yelling at them, when there was banging at the front door.

"Charlie? Honey? Are you okay?" a She-bear asked from the front porch. Then there were more bears at the windows.

"Hey! Who's that cat?" a male bear demanded, banging on the windows. "I think we need to kill it!"

He may have been in his cat form, but Malone could still understand English. He leaped off the couch and, in one fluid move, was across the living room toward the window and that bear. But with an

92 Shelly Laurenston

ease that had always amazed Nelle, Charlie tossed the tray of muffins to Max—which she caught without dropping a muffin—before grabbing the giant cat by its front legs, spinning him around, and slamming him to the floor with such force, she took out the heavy wood coffee table they all loved.

"No, thanks, Mr. Angelopoulos!" Charlie yelled back, her voice calm. Even relaxed. "We're fine."

"Yes, yes," the bear said with a laugh, pointing at a snarling Keane, whom Charlie was holding down with nothing more than her two arms and a knee. "I see that you truly are. Call us if you need us, though!"

"Will do!" She looked down at Malone. "Stop snarling."

And to Nelle's eternal shock . . . he did!

Keane had no idea when he'd shifted to cat. He usually had ultimate control of that. It was one thing if he was feeling physically threatened. Then a shifter did what it had to do. But shifting because he was majorly pissed off? You couldn't do that. No one could do that. That's how things turned bad for their kind, when a man couldn't control his rage. But he'd snapped, hadn't he? What else could he do, though? With all these irrational badgers, doing irrational badger things right in front of him.

Thankfully, Charlie had been here. She'd gotten his attention and calmed him down in one brilliant move. Because a shifter who didn't know how to control his ability to shift didn't live long. Their kind made sure of it.

"Everyone in the kitchen," she said, looking around the room. "I'll be right in. We'll all talk."

"Yeah, but—"

"Now!" she barked when one of the older badgers began to argue the point.

When everyone was gone, Charlie released his fur and sat down so that her back rested against his chest.

"Just so we're clear," she explained, "I was not going to let them go off and start killing things because Mads's aunt told them to. I was

TO KILL A BADGER   93

letting them get geared up in case they needed to be, but we weren't walking out that door until I knew what the fuck was going on."

Keane let out a breath he hadn't realized he'd been holding since he'd sat down in the living room and shifted back to human, Charlie's back still pressed against his bare chest.

Which was how Charlie's grizzly, Berg Dunn, found them when he walked into the house.

He stopped short as soon as he spotted them on the floor and immediately wanted to know, "Should I ask?"

"Probably not," Charlie replied.

"Not even about the coffee table?"

"Nope."

"Should I order a new one?"

"Yeah. The same one would be nice. We all really like it."

"Okay. Anyway, I got your text. I assume you didn't tell me to come over to see . . . this."

"No, just need you to do me a favor and take Dani and her dogs over to your house so your sister can watch them."

"We are not keeping those dogs, Charlie."

"I already told you I wasn't."

"Good. Because I think one of them ate one of the street cats last night."

"Probably," Keane muttered.

"Is that what I heard last night?" Charlie asked. She scratched her forehead with her thumbnail. "Okay, let's not mention that around Stevie. She's under enough stress right now."

"Why would she care?" Keane had to ask. She was terrified of easily startled squirrels; why would she want anything to do with street cats?

"Because she rescued a kitten, and she'll worry."

Keane sat up a bit. "You have a kitten here?"

"I haven't seen it around," Dunn noted, his head turning from side to side as he desperately searched the room.

"It's fine," Charlie said, finally getting to her feet.

"How do you know?"

94 *Shelly Laurenston*

She pointed her forefinger at the ceiling, and that's where that poor kitten was hanging.

"How is it . . ."

"Yeah, I don't know. She seems kind of young to be able to cling like that." Charlie picked up Keane's clothes and tossed them over so he could put them on under the watchful, accusing eyes of a grizzly. "But Stevie started hanging from the ceiling when she was, like, three, her mother said . . . when she dropped her daughter off and never came back." She shrugged. "Yeah, if Stevie wasn't hanging from the ceiling, she was hiding under the couch."

"So you're saying your baby sister is basically a feral house cat?"

"On a good day."

Chapter 7

Stevie woke up in the basement again. This was supposed to be Kyle's rented room, but he'd moved into the garage with his artwork since Stevie started doing some of her science work from here rather than the lab that had been set up for her about an hour away. Some days it was just easier to roll out of bed and get to work, eventually forced upstairs to shower and brush her teeth before being yelled at that, *"You have to eat something!"*

Her sisters should be used to this by now. How she gets when she becomes obsessed. And finding out what someone was using to poison her kind was paramount to anything else at the moment. Because honey badgers shouldn't be poisonable. Their love of poisonous snakes and arachnids made poisoning them nearly impossible. Good badger mothers usually started poisoning their offspring when only a few months old with small, non-lethal emperor scorpions so that they built up a tolerance.

Stevie's mother didn't know she had to do that for her, but that was because her mother was tiger. Then again, her mother didn't know what to do with Stevie in general. When she'd left her with her half-sisters and Charlie's mom and she just never came back . . . it had been painful, but for the best. A prodigy with music and science skills as well as deep clinical depression and anxiety and obsessive tendencies did not a great family tableau make.

And even though she'd only known her a short time before she was killed, Charlie's mom had been the best. She'd just accepted Stevie as she was and taught Charlie to do the same. When she showed her that garter snake, just to see how she felt about snakes, and Stevie had ended up hanging from the ceiling, hissing at it like a panicked tabby, Charlie's mom didn't get mad or disappointed. She simply nodded and said to Charlie, "Okay, no snakes for Stevie. She does not like snakes." Then, before she could toss the snake back outside, Max had bitten the small snake's head off and, while grinning, blood on her lips, her sister had hissed up at her like some kind of mythical demonic being. That was one of their first fights. Stevie had just retracted her claws from the ceiling and dropped on Max and began wildly punching.

That had been the general tone of their relationship ever since.

Stevie stood in front of her work desk. She was about to dive in, but she had nothing. Nothing! No new ideas of any kind that would lead her to a possible antidote, because she still didn't know the kind of poison that had been developed.

She wanted to do that thing where she slapped her head several times, but Charlie got really upset when she did that. It also didn't help that she bruised so easily, meaning her sister always knew when she'd done it.

No. It was better to see what her sister was baking—smelled like blueberry muffins, at the very least—and get a fresh cup of coffee. The caffeine kick may be just what she needed.

Since Stevie had fallen asleep in her shorts and tank top, she didn't bother to change into anything else yet. She didn't even want to shower. She just wanted her coffee.

When she reached the top of the basement stairs that led to either another set of stairs or out the back door to the yard, she glanced through the closed screen to see Shen happily hanging from a tree and munching on his bamboo. She loved that bear. Not only because he was flipping gorgeous and generally kind, but because he actually got her. He understood when he needed to be right next to her, protecting her from whatever was making her panic—yes, even when it was squirrels—and when she needed space to think and be. Even her sisters didn't often get that right. Although Charlie always tried, and Max didn't try at all.

He spotted her and waved, and she waved back, giggling a little when he began to swing a little. How he could eat upside down like that, she had no idea, but he'd mastered the skill.

Turning to the second set of stairs, Stevie headed into the kitchen. But she froze at the doorway when she saw all those people sitting in her kitchen. At least they weren't a bunch of bears this time. She liked when the bears stayed outside. Away from her. Especially the grizzlies. Loving a panda was one thing, but the easily startled, easy-to-rampage grizzlies completely made her panic. The only ones she could tolerate were the Dunn triplets. They seemed naturally calm, and that kept *her* calm.

But most of these were badgers and—shit!—tigers. *Man-eating* tigers! Yes. She knew she was half-Amur tiger, too. Yes. She knew they were the brothers of her half-sister Nat. And yes, she knew they probably would never hurt her, but still. . . .

Man. Eating. Tigers! In her kitchen! Such a small space with all the new, extremely expensive equipment they kept returning home to find had been put in to replace the old oven and refrigerator, and now a massive new freezer that had been set up behind the house and next to the garage. It turned out their landlord had been putting all this stuff into the property because he adored Charlie's upside-down pineapple honey cake, and if he could make it so that Charlie wanted to bake more, apparently he'd do it. Personally, Stevie found that cake much too sweet, but the bears flipped over it. One wanted it for her daughter's wedding. A five-tier one! Whether Charlie would have the time, though. . . .

Stevie looked around the room. All she wanted was her coffee and a muffin. This was too much for her. So she handled it as kindly as she could.

"Get the fuck out of my kitchen!"

Startled at her raised voice, the badgers and tigers all gawked at her while she stood in the doorway, probably not smelling great, because she hadn't showered. And her hair was probably a gross mess, because she hadn't been sleeping long or well lately. But she didn't care.

"Was I not clear?" she asked. *"Get the fuck out of my kitchen!"*

One of the older badgers attempted to be soothing. "Sweetie, Charlie told us to—"

"*Out of my kitchen!*" she hysterically screamed, shaking her head and her hands for emphasis. "*Now! Now! NOWWWWWW!*"

Stevie stepped aside and kept shaking her head and hands until the last of the outsiders had escaped out of the kitchen and into the backyard. That left only Max, who walked by her slowly, eyeing her closely; sneering at her with a turned-up lip and flash of fang before going down the stairs and outside with everyone else.

A few moments later, Charlie walked into the kitchen with Stevie's kitten on her shoulder.

"Look who came down from the ceiling as soon as she heard your soft, dulcet tones."

The pair laughed as Stevie made herself a cup of coffee and Charlie put more blueberry muffins in the oven.

The front door opened, and he had to look down to see the woman who'd opened it.

Big blue eyes gazed up at him. Stevie MacKilligan. The brilliant little nightmare he'd had to intervene with to stop the government from trying to use her for what she could create. He honestly didn't know who was worse to deal with. The hysterical genius? The protective big sister who had made many men "go missing" when they attempted to even speak to her younger sisters? Or the psychotic, Max MacKilligan? Each one was her own, separate challenge.

"Edgar?" Stevie asked. "I thought you—"

"Were dead?"

"Retired. I was definitely going to say retired."

"I am retired. But sometimes it's important to handle things yourself when they get out of hand." He gave a small shrug. "May I come in?"

Stevie's little face scrunched up, and she glanced behind her. That's when he noticed the kitten that was glaring out at him from her hair. It even hissed.

"I don't know if that's—"

"Stevie. Please. I need to see your sister."

"Fine. Fine. But let's try not to make her angry."

"Of course."

With a heavy sigh that seemed a lot coming from a—what? Twenty-three or maybe twenty-four-year-old?—Stevie stepped back to allow him in.

"Are those your dogs?" she asked.

He glanced at the five Belgian Malinois patiently sitting inside the white picket fence in front of the house. He knew those fucking dogs, and he was not happy about seeing them here.

"Sadly, those are not my dogs. I don't have dogs. No wolf should *have* dogs."

"Wouldn't say that to Charlie," she muttered before closing the door.

The word *genius* didn't do enough to describe the power of Stevie MacKilligan's brain. Countries had been trying to snatch her since she'd solved her first physics problem at the age of six. When interest in the child's music career was still going strong, Stevie was getting overwhelmed with performing piano sonatas in front of world royalty. So, she did what any logical seven-year-old would do . . . she switched her interest to math and science and went on to create a theorem that could possibly cause a massive ripple effect that would destroy all land masses around the world. Scientists whom Edgar knew and trusted had been completely freaked out by Stevie MacKilligan's work and had begged him to step in and "stop her. Stop her before she kills us all!" That seemed a little melodramatic until he met the child that first time. She'd been living with her sisters by then, her birth mother having abandoned her a few years before. At the time, he'd thought that a strange reaction coming from a cat. Big cats loved the glamour that a music prodigy child could get them. All that paid-for-by-others world travel and expensive lodgings that allowed her to meet actual royalty and heads of state. What parent wouldn't enjoy that on some level? But even as a young child, Stevie had been different from even the most unique prodigy. Her tiger mom had known it. Known she couldn't handle the child and handed her off to someone who could. Not great mothering, but probably the best the big cat could do at that time.

Stevie's sisters thought that Edgar had first met all of them on the same day. When he'd brought them back from a government facility they'd nearly decimated, and returned them to their grandfather's pack house. But he'd actually met Stevie a short time before any of that. The grandfather had unofficially adopted Stevie and Max, even though only Charlie was his blood. Admirable, but it didn't seem that the rest of the pack wanted the three girls there at all. Because when he'd shown up after the grandfather took the two girls out somewhere, the other packmates had let Edgar in so he could meet Stevie. Probably hoping he could at least convince her to leave their territory.

He hadn't found little Stevie experimenting with the kinds of things smart kids her age liked to try out. Something involving baking soda or the flight pattern of butterflies. No. He'd walked into the kid's dark room—a single, weak desk light that barely helped at all because she had the blackout curtains pulled tight—and found her studying up on Chernobyl and Fukushima and the repercussions to Hiroshima. Apparently, she'd been spending hours studying the pictures from all those events. Especially the damage done to the humans and animals. She'd read and reread about the deaths of those who'd been near the Chernobyl reactor and Hiroshima. Not only the American versions of such things, but documents she'd found that hadn't been translated into English. Apparently she could read Japanese. Or, as she eventually told him, she'd taught it to herself in a few days when she'd started looking at those Japanese-language documents.

Horrified at what such a young child was studying, Edgar had crouched beside her, expecting the little blonde girl with the white streak through her hair to start crying and asking why people were so mean. He had a ready answer, something to soothe her and allow him to remove her from this dark room. It had only been ten in the morning; she should be outside! Enjoying life!

But she didn't cry. And when she turned to him, her face was expressionless and her eyes were dead. That's when she'd intoned with no emotion in her voice, "We, as a society, are doomed, so I should do what I can to end our mutual suffering."

That was bad enough. But then she added, "Like a rabid dog you shoot in the back of the head."

She'd reached out for one of the hundreds of lab notebooks she'd had stacked in her room—apparently, all the spiral binders that held her sheet music had been stuffed in her closet, her clear case of depression making her unwilling to "provide the world with music they no longer deserve," as she later put it—and began writing with a tiny pink pencil that had a little panda topper on the eraser.

Edgar didn't even want to think about what she may be writing down. Where her brilliant but clearly broken mind was taking her. The world couldn't afford for her to finish writing what she had started, so he'd swooped her up in his arms and had taken her outside. Into the sunlight. Into life. He knew some guys, in his line of work, who would have just "vanished" the entire family at that point, but he couldn't do that. He would never do that. In retrospect, he was glad he hadn't. Although she was still what one of his co-workers called "nutso city," Stevie MacKilligan was turning out to be quite the asset. Not for his work. She was way too emotional and sensitive to ever do what he did for a living. But for their kind. The shifters of the world had no idea what a benefit the tiniest MacKilligan had turned out to be.

Still . . . one had to be careful around her. Her exploding into a rage was like setting off a thermonuclear device in the middle of a shopping mall. A nightmare from which one would never wake.

"She's in the kitchen," Stevie said.

"Of course." Charlie MacKilligan was always in the kitchen. He'd offered the eldest MacKilligan sister a chance to own her own bakery or even a bakery chain, thinking if he provided her with stability, she might trust him more; but she wanted nothing to do with a long-term business that would take away the pleasure she got from baking with her own hands. He understood that. He'd gone out of his way to avoid working in his family's fine-dining empire. Not because he didn't love to create a brilliant meal, but because working with a bunch of wolves—many related by blood—in a high-pressure kitchen was a special kind of hell. He'd rather deal with spies, murderers, and government secrets instead.

"You don't age normally," Stevie noted, forcing Edgar to stop and face her.

"Pardon?"

"You still look very good, but I know you're quite old."

"Thank you?"

She stared hard at him for several long seconds, both her brows pulled low.

"Did you get work done?" she finally asked.

"No."

"Then it's genetic. Can I have some of your blood?"

"No."

She kept staring at him, saying nothing. It went on for a while until he finally repeated, "*No.* We've had this discussion before, Stevie. And the answer will always be no."

Stevie led him toward the kitchen without another word. He could smell the scent of Charlie's baking as soon as he'd stepped out of his limo. Christ, he could make a fortune off this girl's baking talent, if only she would let him.

"Charlie," Stevie said as she stepped into the kitchen, "you have another visitor."

"Edgar?" Charlie asked when she looked away from the phone she was staring at like his children and grandchildren all did whenever he met them out in the wild. "Hi. I thought—"

"He retired," Stevie said, sitting down at the kitchen table. "He's not dead."

"Oh. Okay."

The prodigy smiled before going back to her coffee and half-eaten blueberry muffin.

"Can we talk?" he asked Charlie.

"I'm about to get more muffins out of the oven and bring them outside with coffee. Why don't you go wait out there, and we can all talk together."

TO KILL A BADGER 103

"I was hoping to talk to you alone first. In fact, I'd rather not . . ." He took a breath. "I saw the dogs."

Charlie frowned. "My dogs are at Berg's house. You were talking to Berg?"

"No. Not your dogs. The Belgian Malinois outside the house. Those are Tracey Rutowski's dogs, yes?"

"Oh. Right. I forgot that she's married to a Van Holtz. So I guess that would make you her—"

"Please don't say it."

She didn't, but then the kitchen window was shoved open from the outside, and a happy "Uncle!" was yelled at him by four She-badgers he absolutely loathed for the simple reason they always made his job so much harder.

"*You!*" he snarled, unable to help himself from adding nothing but rage and accusation to that one word.

"And it's so good to see you, too!" Tracey Rutowski cheered back. "Come. Join us!" That's when she grinned, showing all her badger fangs, and added in a singsong voice, "We've missed you!"

Chapter 8

Agostino "Ago" Medici watched his eldest brother pace back and forth in the family room while the rest of them patiently watched him. It was always good to be patient when dealing with their brother. He was emotional and spent most of his time in his lion form, because he seemed to not like being human at all.

Something had happened to get him this agitated; they were just waiting to find out the details.

Giovanni Medici looked down at his big paws, lifting one to study it, then the other. After a moment of deep, painful meditation on those paws, he shifted back to human.

"Sorry," Gio said, pulling on some dark blue sweatpants his twin sister, Giuseppina, had laid out for him. "I needed to gather my thoughts."

"So what happened now?" Ago asked.

"The de Medicis attacked wives of the Van Holtz wolf pack this morning."

Pina frowned. "Why would they attack the Van Holtzes? And why do the Van Holtzes have wives? What normal shifter gets married?"

"I love how the whole thing has a very European vibe," Ago joked. "Like the War of the Roses, but with dogs and cats."

When his brother didn't tell him to stop joking around, Ago knew something was truly wrong.

"What is it?" he pushed when his brother continued to remain silent.

"The wives they went after were She-badgers."

"A Van Holtz married a badger?" Pina asked. "Really?"

"Is that important?" Ago asked.

"It's weird."

"Three Van Holtz wolves married three badgers. Friends," Gio explained for his sister. "There's a fourth badger, but she has not married anyone. But all four are a problem."

"More of a problem than the MacKilligan sisters and *their* friends? Because you said everyone was freaking out about them, too."

"The MacKilligan sisters are young and antisocial. Other than the bears near their house that they continually feed to keep them docile, they have no allies. No friends. But these four She-badgers are the opposite of them. They have connections, allies, dating back more than forty years. Allies that can help them wipe us from the planet."

The six siblings were silent for a long moment until baby Bria—now twenty years old, but still a baby as far as they were all concerned— noted, "Ever notice, Gio, you get really dramatic when there may be even the tiniest chance you might have to leave the house?"

"That's not what this is about."

"Isn't it? You and Antonella hate leaving the house. You work from home, you stay at home, you have food delivered because you won't even go to a restaurant. But this. . . ? This situation might force you out into the sunlight."

Their brother looked away because, as usual, Bria was right.

Not surprising, though, when Ago thought about it even a little bit. Gio *lived* as cat, roaming their big house on four legs, as much as he could without getting caught by the neighbors. Yet all his siblings knew that Gio—and their eldest sister, Antonella—would happily roam the Serengeti instead, if he could. All day. Every day. But, sadly for their big brother, he was born on Hewlett, Long Island, along with the rest of them, and fabulous trips to Africa were not in the cards for them anytime soon. Their startup company was doing well, which was great. Each sibling managing to find a department to run that highlighted their skills and education. But they hadn't hit billionaire money status yet, and Ago didn't think they would for quite some time. They cared too much that their products were actually useful and working correctly when unleashed on the public. It made for an extremely strong fan base, but they hadn't hit that sweet spot of loyal fan base combined with average consumer yet. So if Gio thought he'd be able to move to any part of Africa soon and wander around like king of the African plains . . . he was wrong.

So, when their Italian half-siblings—the *de* Medicis—caused a problem for them, it meant Gio had to deal with the world. And the man *loathed* dealing with the world. Too many full-humans running around. Too many canines and bears. He basically hated them all.

"So the de Medicis have gone to war and are dragging us with them," Nicky said, pushing his glasses back up the bridge of his nose.

"But we're Medicis. Not the *de* Medicis," Bria reminded them. "Everyone knows that."

"We'll just alert Katzenhaus," Renny suggested, talking about the global cat organization that kept peace between the many breeds and prides and families of big cat shifters. "Let them know we're not any part of some war our half-siblings are in the middle of."

"It may not be that simple anymore," Gio replied.

"Why?"

"The MacKilligan sisters killed our father and dumped his body in front of Giuseppe and the rest of them."

"They *hunted* our father down?" Pina asked, a little surprised.

Honey badgers were known to be "crazy," but they didn't usually *seek out* trouble. The way it had been explained to him by an aunt, trouble seemed to find them. Constantly.

"No. He went to them. He threatened them. And Charlie MacKilligan killed him."

They should all be angry. He was their father . . . biologically. But he could tell from the calm silence that none of them could muster more than mild indifference.

Besides, he couldn't blame the MacKilligans for defending themselves. Although, dropping their father's corpse at their psychotic half-brother's big feet seemed . . . a tad reckless? No, no. He didn't mean

TO KILL A BADGER   107

that. He meant it was insane. What they'd done was insane, and he was starting to understand why Gio was so worried.

"But . . . come on," Renny argued, looking around at the rest of them. "They're *badgers*. Right? Aren't they like rats or something?"

"You didn't even know there were badgers, did you?" Ago asked his younger brother.

"Because I refuse to believe anyone would *choose* to be a badger. Who would do that?"

"This," Pina snarled, "*this* is why we've asked you to read a book. Just once. So you can gain knowledge."

"I watch TV."

"Honey badgers are their own, unique, *horrifying* thing," Ago explained. "Shifters, yes. But *soooo* different."

"Rasputin was a honey badger," Nicky pointed out. His brother loved studying Russian history.

"The Borgias were badgers," Bria chimed in.

"Walsingham, who helped Queen Elizabeth I in the first part of her reign . . . badger," Gio added.

"Thomas Cromwell, who took down Thomas More *and* Anne Boleyn," Pina tossed in.

"Trotsky, of course," Gio remembered.

"I heard Judas was a badger."

"No, no, Ago," Pina corrected. "That was just hyena propaganda back in the day. But Pontius Pilate . . . *definitely* a badger."

"Wait." Ago turned to his younger brother and asked, "Do you have any idea what we're talking about?"

"Aren't you just making up words to confuse me?"

"Dear God!" Pina exploded. *"Read a fucking book!"*

"Why are you four here?" Edgar demanded, glaring at the four females that had ensnared his nephews. Tracey Rutowski. CeCe Álvarez. Stephanie Yoon. There was also Oksana "Ox" Lenkov, who hadn't married any of his relatives but hung around the other three so much, she might as well be family. He knew she was always at Easter dinner!

"Why are we here?" Rutowski said, smiling. "To bring you joy and laughter, of course."

Letting his fangs slip out of his gums, Edgar snarled a little. He couldn't help it. These women drove him to it.

Since they were young teens, these four honey badgers had been making Edgar's life a living hell. And despite his retirement, it seemed the nightmare part of his old life would never be over. Not when they constantly, continually, never-endingly started shit!

"This isn't about Konstantin Chernenko again, is it?" Tracey Rutowski asked about the long-dead and onetime leader of the Communist Party of the Soviet Union. She tossed her hands into the air and let out a loud, annoyed sigh. "I was just a kid! You need to let that go!"

He would *never* let that go, but he didn't want to get into any of those past issues in the here and now. Not when they had bigger issues staring them right in the face.

Ignoring that badger's mention of her and her friend's old war crimes, Edgar said, "None of you should be involving yourselves into anything that's going on right now."

"Too late," Rutowski sighed out.

"What does that mean?"

"What do you think it means?" Yoon questioned.

Glaring, Edgar demanded, "What did you four do now?"

"What makes you think *we're* the problem?"

"Because you're *always the problem!*" he suddenly exploded halfway through his sentence.

A tray, held by Charlie MacKilligan, suddenly appeared in front of Edgar's face.

"Muffin?" she kindly asked.

"I don't want a muffin."

"It's blueberry."

"I don't care."

"Blueberry can be very soothing," Stevie informed him, as she sat down across from him at the long table in the MacKilligans' backyard. "It's the antioxidants."

TO KILL A BADGER 109

Not wanting to hear about blueberries and antioxidants, Edgar asked Charlie, "Why are *they* here? Why are you working with *them*? Why is this happening?"

Unlike his nephews' wives and their friend, Charlie and her sisters didn't usually cause problems. They simply reacted to problems coming at them. In other words, they were manageable.

Glancing back and forth between Edgar and the others, Charlie finally said, "Look, I'm guessing you guys have a history that I'm not privy to, and that's okay. Because I really don't want to know, and I especially don't care. I've got enough on my mind and, apparently, I'm going to start playing football soon."

"Are you talking about *American* football?" Rutowski clarified.

"Yes."

"No offense, but aren't you a little . . . small for that?"

Ox pointed at an unsmiling male tiger that Edgar knew—for many reasons—was a Malone. Not a normal Malone. He and his brothers didn't live in a caravan, traveling around when the mood hit them and, unlike most of their blood relations, they were only half-Irish. The other half was part of a powerful Mongolian tribe that had once ruled the Steppes. But these three were Malones nonetheless.

"This tiny badger—" Ox began.

"I'm hardly tiny," Charlie noted.

"—took big idiot cat—"

"I have been nothing but polite to you," the cat pointed out.

"—down without much pain and suffering," Ox said, nodding approvingly. "I think she will be fine in the American football."

"Except you already missed practice today," the cat complained to Charlie.

"There's practice?"

"We discussed this, Charlie. There's practice, and you need to be there. Am I going to have a problem with you?"

She held the tray up. "Muffin, Keane?"

"I do want a muffin."

Before allowing the cat to feed, she said to Edgar, "Sure you don't want one? Once I put it in front of the big idiot cats—"

110   *Shelly Laurenston*

"Hey."

"—the muffins will be gone. They are not fans of sharing."

Edgar already knew that, but he shook his head anyway.

Charlie took the tray to the far end of the table and put it in front of the three brothers. By the time she'd walked to a free chair, the three cats had taken what they'd wanted and had left nothing on the tray but crumbs.

"Okay," Charlie said with a surprisingly sweet smile. "So what are we all talking about today?"

"How much our Uncle Edgar still hates us after all these years," Rutowski announced.

"No, no," Stevie said with deep sincerity. "I'm sure Edgar doesn't—"

"Yes," he cut in, adamant. "Yes, I do hate you. All four of you. Always have. Always will. And fucking stop *calling me uncle*!"

Stunned silence from the entire table followed his explosion until Stevie softly said, "Could someone pass me the uh . . . half-and-half? I need a little for my coffee." She cleared her throat before accepting the jug handed to her. "It's a little more . . . *bitter* than I expected."

"We shouldn't suffer because of *that* side of the family," Pina said, pacing around the room like the angry and tense cat she was.

"I'm not sure we can avoid it," Ago reminded her. "They are our half-siblings."

"Not that they acknowledge that . . . at all."

"Pina's right," Nicky agreed, while pushing his glasses back up his nose again. It drove Pina nuts that her brother never seemed to have glasses that actually fit properly. He'd been wearing them since he was six, much to the disgust of their father. By now he should be able to buy frames that fit his face. "We're not considered de Medicis."

"Our brothers don't consider us de Medicis, but the Van Holtz definitely will," Gio said, sliding onto the desk Pina worked on when she dealt with family finances. "Like those fucking tigers, they'll want revenge for what happened to their own."

"All the Van Holtz wives are dead?" Renny asked, horrified.

TO KILL A BADGER   111

"Surprisingly, no," Gio replied. "Considering what they hit them with."

"If we're all that worried what's going to happen in the next few days or weeks"—Bria shrugged—"I can take the kids to safety in Colorado."

Pina questioningly glanced at her twin, but Gio only shrugged.

"What makes Colorado safe?" she asked her sister.

"Our prepper ranch."

"We have a prepper ranch?"

"Of course we have a prepper ranch."

"Except we're not preppers."

"No. We're not. But we still have a prepper ranch."

"Every day I discover exactly how weird this family is."

"Wait," Ago cut in, "I don't understand. Why would we have a prepper ranch when none of us are preppers?"

"What's a prepper again?" Renny asked. "The people who believe the end of the world is coming? Right?"

"Yeah. Due to God." Ago shrugged at Bria. "But you're an atheist."

"Agnostic, actually."

"Before we decide on anything," Pina cut in, "someone needs to tell . . . Antonella."

The room immediately went silent, and there was a sudden lack of eye contact.

"No one is going to do that," Ago finally admitted.

"Someone has to," Pina replied, before quickly adding, "but it won't be me."

"But you two are so close," Bria lied.

"I still have scars from the last time I was the one who had to tell her something she didn't want to hear." Pina pointed at her lower jaw, which her twin had to fit back into place so it could heal properly. "I am *not* going through that again."

"Well, me, Renny, and Nicky have to start packing if we're going to take the kids to the prepper ranch."

"Stop calling it that," Nicky complained. He once again pushed his glasses back up the bridge of his nose. That's when Pina snatched the pair off his face, adjusting the pads. She'd started doing that for him when he was eight and he'd already lost two pairs of glasses that school year. Their mother had been livid, and had ordered Pina to "fix the problem." It just never occurred to Pina that this would become a lifelong job. The things She-lions were forced to do for the males in their prides.

"Here," she snarled, handing the designer glasses back to her brother.

"Oh. Thanks." He put them on, looked around the room, and smiled at her.

"Gio," Pina said, looking at her twin. "You tell, Antonella."

Her brother stared at her with that wounded expression he always had when she asked him to go grocery shopping with her, and said, "It's like you don't love me at all."

"I need you to hold it together."

Keane gazed down at the She-badger who'd pulled him away from the extra-long picnic table and next to the tree where the panda was still hanging . . . and eating.

Why did he eat so much bamboo? Was it due to ill health? Was he just mimicking pandas in the wild, or was he clinically unstable? Keane really wanted to know if he should be worried about this bear, since his sister was going to spend so much time with her sist—

"Are you even listening to me?"

Keane shrugged. "No."

He expected Nelle to get angry at his blunt response like everyone else did, but he saw the corners of her mouth turn up. "I see. Can you give me three minutes before I lose you?"

"You've got two. After that, my attention will wane."

"Got it. So listen to what I'm telling you . . . I need you *not* to react to whatever happens at that table in the next few minutes. Just know I will handle it."

"Handle what?"

"All of it."

TO KILL A BADGER   113

"All of what?"

Nelle glanced over her shoulder. The old wolf was still on the phone. His receiving a call had allowed for Keane and Nelle to get a few seconds together. But why she was worried about Keane's reactions and not the cranky wolf's, Keane had no idea.

"Just trust me and keep control."

"Okay, but why?"

"Why what?"

"Why do I need to keep control?"

"Because when you react, you freak out Stevie. When Stevie freaks out, she worries Charlie. When Charlie is worried, Max instinctually makes it worse. And when Max makes it worse, Charlie destroys the world. I'm trying to avoid that."

"Okay. . . ?"

"What?"

"I guess I'm not sure why that's *your* problem?"

"I've made it my problem."

"Yes, but I'm not sure why. Personally, I don't make other people's problems my own. My brothers, my niece, my sister . . . their problems, I make mine. Their concerns are my concerns. My buddy Jake—"

"You have friends?"

"—I don't make his problems my problem. Because I really don't care about his problems."

"So you're not friends."

"We have a beer now and then. And when he complains about his girlfriend, I just sip my beer and listen and eat pretzels. What I don't do, is start plotting how to manage his emotional issues."

"Well, these are not just friends. They're like family to me."

"Really? Because any time Streep suggests—"

"She's an annoying pest, so we torment her for our amusement, but that doesn't mean that I don't consider all of them my family and, like most Chinese people, family is absolutely the most important thing in my lif— *Would you stop calling me!*" she suddenly yelled at the phone currently telling her to "fuck off, fuck off, fuck off."

114 *Shelly Laurenston*

"What kind of ringtone is that? I don't want my niece hearing that. She's just a kid."

"Just do as I ask. Please?"

He shrugged again. "Okay."

"Thank you."

With a sweet smile in his direction, Nelle returned to the table and whatever drama was about to happen there.

Keane was about to follow, but then the panda said, "Nelle is nice."

He stopped, looked at the bear, but didn't speak.

"Stevie really likes her. She goes out of her way to keep Charlie calm, and Stevie appreciates that."

Keane continued to stare and waited.

"So I feel kind of protective of her. And I wouldn't like it if some . . . *dude* was just trying to get into her pants."

The panda said this while still hanging upside down, a stalk of bamboo gripped in his fist, which just irritated Keane.

He took a step closer so only the bear could hear him.

"You know, I could bite your head off, chew it, swallow, shit it out, and it would mean absolutely *nothing* to me. So, in future . . . don't fucking talk to me. Understand?"

"Uh . . . yeah. That was, uh, pretty clear."

"Good."

Gio stared out the clear sliding glass doors that led into their large backyard. A huge tent stood over it. Not to block out the sun, but to block out any nosy neighbors or drones that might notice the four-hundred-pound lioness relaxing on a grass-covered dirt mound.

Like Gio, Antonella preferred staying in her animal form. Unlike Gio, however, he wasn't even sure the last time he'd seen her as human. She rarely, if ever, changed into human. Even Gio would shift to go to bookstores or museums. He didn't like being around all those full-humans, but he did enjoy visiting very specific places if he was of a mind. And he couldn't do that in his six-hundred-pound form with a giant mane. His sister, however, didn't seem to want to go anywhere outside the house. Hell, she barely even went into the house. She slept outside, mostly during the day, and roamed the neighborhood at night, searching out small game like rabbits. She sometimes went inside to shower, but mostly she just stood in the rain or turned on the hose with her paw, and had one of the kids spray her down.

Even he had to admit that was a little weird.

Letting out a deep breath, Gio pushed open the big screen glass door and stepped outside. He motioned to the eldest niece, and she rounded up all the younger kids, ushering them back into the house.

Gio moved across the lawn until he reached his sister. She loved sitting there, all day, watching. As a fellow introvert, Gio understand her not wanting to go outside their territory, but even he took hours out of his day to read books. Fiction, nonfiction, history, old, new, even ancient. He couldn't imagine his life without books. But how someone just sat around, watching cubs play in front of her . . .

"Hey, big sis," he greeted the She-lion. That big gold head turned toward him, and cold, predatory gold eyes locked on his face.

What was his sister thinking? he always wondered. Was she just curious about what he wanted to talk about, or was she plotting to rip his face completely off? He honestly had no idea which it might be. His sister could react in a myriad of ways, depending on her mood.

"It's about the"—he cleared his throat—"the de Medicis. I thought I should bring you up to speed on the latest, and some suggestions we have for how to move forward."

Those gold eyes, so beautiful but so flat and uncaring . . . how do gazelles get through a day on the Serengeti when they would find something like his sister watching them all the time? It must be terrifying.

When she didn't move, but simply continued to stare at him and blink, Gio started talking. He told her what he'd already learned. All of it. And told her about how ugly he was worried it might get. He didn't hold anything back from her. The worst thing one could do was hold something back from Antonella and she found out later on her own. That's how he'd ended up reattaching Pina's lower jaw back to the rest of her skull.

"Anyway," he finished off, "we all think we should move the kids

116   *Shelly Laurenston*

to Colorado. You know we've got that ranch there. We figure they'll be safer."

When Antonella only continued to stare at him without making a sound, Gio assumed they were done talking.

"Okay. Let me know if you need anything," he told her before turning around and walking toward the glass doors. That's when he saw his twin's eyes grow huge, and he spun around to find his eldest sister standing in front of him in her human form. Since she never willingly shifted to human, he knew this was bad.

Very, very bad.

"Ohhhh!" Pina and all her siblings cried out when Antonella shifted to human and stood in front of poor Gio. In her She-lion form, she was much smaller than him. But in her human form, their big sister was nearly six-three and could look Gio right in the eyes.

Unwilling to let her twin face Antonella on his own, Pina ran outside and stepped between the pair; Bria right beside her. The baby of the family sticking by Pina's side like always.

Abruptly, Antonella took a step forward, and the three siblings, in the face of their eldest sister's rage, took a step back. Then more steps forward came, and the trio backed up until they stepped inside the house . . . wait.

Pina's back wasn't still heading into the house. Instead, it was flush against thick glass, and she realized that her other brothers had closed the glass sliding door behind them, trapping Pina, her twin, and poor Bria outside with an angry Antonella. To protect themselves!

Cowards!

Trapped between the sliding door and their terrifying eldest sister, the three siblings waited. And, as usual, Antonella took her time.

She let her always-gold gaze silently sweep past each one of them, three times before settling on Pina.

"Your idea is to be weak?" Antonella growled out in that deep, scratchy voice of hers that she'd had since she was a cub. Golden-blond locks reached down to her waist and partially covered her naturally beautiful face. It was like the words were being ripped from deep in-

TO KILL A BADGER   117

side her. It seemed that's how much she hated speaking human words rather than just roaring her unhappiness.

"Well—" Gio began, before one look from his sister shut him down entirely.

"If we run," Antonella continued, "they will only chase us down. If we hide, they will only find us. We will *not* run. We will *not* hide. We will show our strength and stand our ground. Do you understand me?"

"Antonella—" Bria tried.

"Do you understand *me*?"

"We don't know if that's the best idea," Pina said, pretending she was as strong as Antonella. She wasn't, but she'd taken theater classes in high school and had once had the lead role in *Our Town*. So . . . ya know. . . .

Antonella's eyes locked on Pina's face, and the pair stared at each other.

"We?" Antonella asked.

"The family."

"You mean the males. You got *their* opinion on this situation? Why would you do that?"

"They're . . . family?"

"You should have stopped caring about them as soon as their balls dropped. The fact that they still live with us rather than joining another pride irritates me. Then you send one out to talk to *me* about plans for *our* pride?"

"He's my twin."

"No matter what *National Geographic* says, males do *not* run our pride. And we do not live in fear."

"But should we?" Bria asked. "Live in fear, I mean."

Antonella's head slowly turned until she could pin Bria to the spot with those gold eyes that never changed color.

The pair silently stared at each other until Bria added, "I'm asking philosophically."

"Philosophically?" Antonella repeated. "We're discussing actual war here, and you're talking philosophy to me?"

118   *Shelly Laurenston*

"Just trying to find other options."

"There are no other options. There is only one." She held up her right forefinger. "We don't run. We don't hide. And if they come for us, we fight." Her forefinger lowered until she was pointing at them. "If anyone comes for us, we will fight. We will destroy. We will not stop until all of our enemies are dead." She abruptly turned toward Pina's brothers behind the glass sliding door. "And if any of you," she said slowly as she walked toward them, "try to run or hide or don't protect the cubs with your very last breath . . ."

She stood in front of the sliding door, her words hanging in the air as she stared at the others and they gawked back.

She still had her forefinger out, but she curled it into her hand before slamming the glass with her fist. She didn't use much effort, but it was enough to crack the ridiculously thick material. As Antonella turned to walk away, shifting back into her clearly more natural She-lion form, the crack began to spread from its initial spot and snake out across the entire door.

By the time Antonella was again sitting on her grass-covered mound of dirt, watching over her tiny empire, Pina could no longer see the rest of her siblings behind all those cracks.

Bria, unable to help herself, reached out and skimmed one of the cracks with the tip of her finger. That's when it shattered and fell into pieces across the ground.

They all gazed down at the shards until Renny muttered, "That went well."

Chapter 9

Nelle sat down and tapped Streep's hip. "Move, please."

"Huh?"

"Move. I want Keane to sit here."

Her teammate smiled. "Really?" She scrunched up her nose in a very adorable but completely annoying way. "Are you two . . ." She giggled. The giggle was too much.

"Move your fucking ass, Streep. I need to keep an eye on him."

The smile dropped. "Fine. Bitch."

Nelle motioned to Keane, but he merely frowned and reached for a chair closer to his brothers.

"Max," she prompted her other teammate.

"Keane! Get your ass down here!"

With a snarl, the cat slammed down the chair he'd been holding and made his way to the chair Streep had just been forced out of.

Once he was sitting next to her, she smiled at him to soothe his annoyance. But, unlike other males, he didn't immediately fall in lust, which he believed was love—thereby never leaving her alone again—he just seemed annoyed.

"Yes, yes," Edgar Van Holtz said as he made his way back to the table. "Yes. I understand." He disconnected the call and dropped into his chair. He glared across the table at Rutowski and her friends. "My nieces and nephews—"

"*Grand* nieces and nephews."

The wolf's eyes narrowed dangerously. "I was just informed that

120   Shelly Laurenston

they've all gone into a safe house, since you were *all* attacked today at your homes?"

"Hearing from my kid?" Rutowski shot back, turning to her friends. "I told you he's trying to recruit my baby into his little shifter army of government drones. Right, Uncle?"

"Your daughter is an adult. If she wants to work for a proper agency rather than causing problems—"

"We *fixed* things."

"The four of you single-handedly delayed the end of the Cold War!"

"That's ridiculous," Yoon replied. "We were in high school."

"You were in East Germany!" Van Holtz yelled. "Years of work. *Years!* Undone for"—he gestured toward the Russian—*"her!"*

"Fuck you, old wolf! No borscht for you at next Thanksgiving!"

"Oh, no! What will I do without your cold, *boring* beet soup?"

"Okay!" Nelle stood, spreading her arms wide apart, even though no one had gone toward anyone else . . . yet. "Let's all calm down, shall we? What we should be discussing is what's happening *now*."

"Yeah!" Max chimed in. "And not what happened thirty years ago, when you were all . . . what? About forty?"

The wolf, Rutowski, and her friends all turned their glares away from one another and over to Max.

"The end of the Cold War actually took place in 1991," Stevie said. "And if you guys were in high school in the eighties, that would make you—"

"I think we're also forgetting," Rutowski quickly cut in, "that as per school and federal records, Ox was a resident of Manhasset, New York, since she was eight years old. Rescued!" She dramatically added, "By *democracy*."

The wolf glared at the She-badger and yelled, *"Are you kidding me with that bullshit?"*

"I'm sure," Nelle interjected in her best calming voice, "that these wonderful ladies regret everything they did way back then. Right, ladies?"

"Not really."

"I'd do it again."

"We've actually done much worse things. This was nothing."

"You whine like little puppy with wounded foot, Van Holtz. You sicken me."

Edgar turned his frustrated gaze to Nelle, and she sat down again.

"Yeah," she admitted, "as soon as the words came out of my mouth, I realized that was a mistake."

"Why are you here, Edgar?" Charlie asked, and Keane loved how "over it" she sounded.

Honestly, Keane didn't see what Nelle was so worried about. While one MacKilligan sister was starting shit, and the other was appearing to get some kind of anxiety rash based on the way she was scratching her neck and hands any time someone raised their voice, Charlie seemed the only one being calm and rational.

"You know why I'm here. Because *you* decided to drag a corpse to Italy. That was a . . . less than wise move."

"They wanted to know what happened to their father. I thought I was being helpful."

"Then you burned their family home down."

"That wasn't us; that was them."

"Before raiding one of their ships, killing everyone onboard—"

"No," Max corrected. "Not the hostages. We freed them."

"—and sinking the fucking thing to the bottom of the Boston Harbor."

"You *wanted* them to find the foreign bears on meth?" Steph Yoon asked.

"And I wasn't there for that last part," Charlie explained. "I was baking."

"She was," Max agreed. "She was baking. And the Boston Harbor thing wasn't our thing. It was the crones."

"Call us crones again, and I will *gut* you where you sit," Rutowski warned.

Chuckling under his breath, Keane looked down and noticed an ant walking across the table. Without thinking about it, he balled his

122 Shelly Laurenston

hand into a fist and slammed it down. All conversation stopped, and everyone looked at him.

"Ant," he told them, before using a napkin to clean bug juice off his skin. "Probably a scout. It would only bring more. Best to take out now."

"Was that directed at me?" the wolf asked Keane.

"I do not care about you so . . . no."

The canine stared at him for a long moment before refocusing on Charlie.

"Anyway," the wolf continued, "The Group is not happy."

The innocuously named "The Group" was the organization that kept a tight rein on shifters in the United States. Keane had heard about them but didn't really care about their existence, because when his father was killed by the de Medicis, they hadn't helped either. Although he had heard from Shay that Charlie, her sisters, and Max's teammates all worked on a little-known division of The Group. At least they'd done one job for them, but based on the way the wolf was looking at them now, it seemed that recent partnership was probably over now.

"The Board isn't happy," the canine went on.

"What's The Board again?" Mads asked.

"A bunch of snobby, extremely wealthy shifters that think they secretly run the world," Rutowski explained. "Not surprisingly, the Van Holtz Pack has several seats on this so-called Board."

"BPC isn't happy," the wolf announced.

The younger badgers looked to the older ones for explanation.

"That's the Bear Preservation Council," Yoon announced, a black hoodie pulled onto her head. Wasn't she hot in that? It was a short-sleeved tee with a hood, but still. Seemed uncomfortable in the summer heat. "It's a worldwide organization of very annoying bears that pretend they're conservationists, but we all know better."

"And," Edgar went on, "Katzenhaus isn't happy."

"Katzenhaus can fucking blow me," Charlie snapped. When Edgar raised a brow at the sudden anger in her voice, she said, "They could have shut down the de Medicis coalition decades ago, but they did nothing. Now they're going to complain when someone fights back? *Fuck them.*"

"She's not wrong," Rutowski smugly said between sips of coffee.

"No one asked you."

"Watch tone, old man," the Russian warned. "I have no loyalty to you through blood or love."

"And you remember, Oksana Lenkov, I can send your ass back to Russia any time I want." He gave a brutal smile. "I'm sure you still have friends there."

While the Russian badger and the old wolf glared at each other, Rutowski slapped her hand on the table and hissed in anger. That's when Stevie suddenly jumped up from her chair and yelled, *"No, no, no, no, no! No hissing at the dinner table. No hissing at the dinner table!"*

She began panting and shaking her hands.

"All right, all right," Nelle said. She stood and went to Stevie's side, putting her arm around the badger's tiny shoulders. "Everyone just calm down."

"Calm down?" Max gestured to her younger sister. "She's already hysterical over some hissing."

"Shut up, Max!" Stevie yelled, before abruptly bursting into a nightmare amount of tears.

Max rolled her eyes, but her teammates went to calm down the hybrid She-badger. Keane wasn't surprised about Nelle and Streep doing such a thing, but he was surprised that Mads and Tock had joined them.

"Just breathe," Nelle told Stevie. "Slowly. Calmly. Everything is going to be just fine."

Keane glanced at his brothers, but all they could do was shrug. What exactly were they worried about when it came to Stevie? She was so sweet. Crazy emotional, but sweet.

"Is that child . . . crying?" Rutowski asked.

"Is she dying?" Yoon wanted to know.

"Should we get her a doctor?" Álvarez suggested.

"Her weakness sickens me," the Russian announced.

Keane watched as Max's gaze moved to the four older She-badgers.

124   *Shelly Laurenston*

She locked onto them like they were delicious snakes that had just slithered into her den. Apparently, it was one thing for Max to mock her baby sister, but it was another for someone else to do it.

With a small smile, she said, "Just ignore my sister. She's just emotional because she probably got her period. You guys remember what that's like, right? You know . . . before the menopause hit."

When Stevie's eyes had shifted color from blue to green to gold to golden green to blood red, Nelle knew she had to step in. They'd all known. They couldn't afford for her to shift into her true form in front of Edgar Van Holtz. He'd have Stevie put down, and Charlie would kill . . . well . . . everyone. Everyone on the planet. You did not mess with the woman's baby sister. You just didn't. Only Max could get away with that.

So Nelle, Mads, Tock, and Streep had rushed in to calm the hybrid and situation down. And it had been going great . . . until Max had made that direct hit on the older She-badgers.

Rutowski, despite her age, was nearly over the picnic table with her hands around Max's throat when her three friends caught her and dragged her back. Her attack was so aggressive and unexpected that even Stevie was quickly distracted from her panic attack. Now she was watching the three She-badgers trying to get control of their friend with the rest of them.

There was only one who didn't seem to care about any of that drama, though.

"You never answered Charlie's question," Keane said to Van Holtz.

It was said low, quiet. Yet they all heard him over the snarling of Rutowski. Because it was so dangerous, that low voice. That low, angry voice.

The gazes of many predators turned to the tiger, and Rutowski calmed down, but her friends still kept their tight grip on her arms and waist. They were all waiting to see what the male tiger would say next. What he would do next.

"What?" Van Holtz asked the cat, clearly not used to anyone speaking to him the way a Malone was speaking to him.

"Answer her question, old man. Why are you here? What do you want?"

Van Holtz's eyes narrowed and went from dark brown to a bright yellow. Wolf eyes. But a smart wolf always knew when he was outnumbered, and with three Amur tigers in attendance, the canine was definitely outnumbered.

"You want to know what I'm doing here? Fine." Van Holtz turned his gaze back to a waiting Charlie. "I'm here to tell you that you're on your own. All of you are on your own."

"What?" That flabbergasted question didn't come from Charlie. She was completely unmoved by this announcement. Instead, it came from Rutowski. "What do you mean, they're on their own? How can they be on their own? They're kids."

"They're hardly kids. And it's been discussed and agreed upon that since badgers all started this—"

"Actually, we didn't."

"—you can finish it. On your own."

"It's been 'discussed and agreed upon' by whom?" Yoon demanded to know.

"The Group. BPC. Katzenhaus. And The Board."

"That is bullshit," Álvarez said with a harsh, bitter laugh. "Not only are de Medicis *selling* human beings, something none of us are supposed to be doing as per *your* rules. But they've already attacked Van Holtz territories. *Our* territories."

"You're telling us that the Pack is going to let them get away with that?" Yoon asked.

"They attacked *your* personal homes. Badger territory; not our territory. Each of these houses are personally owned by each of you, *not* my nephews."

"My daughters were in the kitchen with me when they started shooting," Rutowski growled out through clenched teeth, "and you're not going to do *anything*?"

"You are more than welcome to get assistance from other badgers, of course. Oh, that's right. None of you work together unless it involves a heist of some kind or the destruction of an entire country."

126 *Shelly Laurenston*

"Oh, my God, Van Holtz," Álvarez snapped. "You are such a baby."

"Look, I'm sure more than one of my brothers will be happy to help. But when it comes to the organizations that protect us as a whole . . . all of you, as I said, are on your own."

It was clear none of the older She-badgers could believe what they were hearing from this wolf. But Charlie, Max, and Stevie had no reaction, which seemed to confuse the wolf.

Van Holtz asked Charlie, "Do you understand what I'm telling you?"

Charlie nodded and stood. "Yep."

His confusion grew worse, brow pulling low as he watched Charlie pick up her empty plate and coffee mug.

"And you grasp that there will be no help coming from any of our organizations going forward? You and your sisters and"—he dismissively gestured at Rutowski and her friends—"will be completely on your own in this fight? You understand *that*, right?"

"Okay."

Charlie stepped back from the table and walked toward the house. Watching her go, Van Holtz turned in his chair.

"Okay?" he repeated. "Is that all you have to say?"

Charlie stopped; faced him.

"What else is there to say, Edgar? I never expect anything from any of you anyway. When my mother was killed, none of you did anything. You, personally, attempted to take Stevie for your organization, but only to use her. And my father should have been put down a long time ago like a rabid circus monkey, and yet . . . you let him live. Much to my great annoyance. So excuse me if I don't fall over in shock that the four organizations that let three little girls make their own way for the last twenty years aren't coming through now."

With that, Charlie walked away. Max followed her sister, her silent but threatening gaze locked on Van Holtz.

Wiping the wetness off her cheeks with the back of her hand, Stevie also followed her sisters. But she did say to the wolf, "We do appreciate you coming here yourself to tell us this, Edgar. Thank you."

She took a few more steps, but abruptly stopped when she found Max standing in front of her, glaring.

TO KILL A BADGER 127

"What?" Stevie demanded.

" 'We do appreciate you coming here yourself, Edgar,' " Max mimicked back in a high-pitched, baby voice. "Really? Can you suck up to these people any more?"

"I will always *hate you!*" the tiny badger hybrid bellowed at her sister before pushing past her and storming back into the house.

"Are you going to cry again?" Max mockingly asked.

"I am not crying!" Stevie sobbingly replied.

"Great plan, Edgar," Rutowski taunted, with a thumbs-up. "Excellent."

"Don't you have a nuclear reactor to sabotage?" the wolf asked dryly.

"I'll say it one more time, *Chernobyl was not our fault!*"

Chapter 10

Keane sat on the top porch stoop in the front of the MacKilligan sisters' rental house. He'd walked away from the backyard when the older honey badgers couldn't calm down Mads's aunt. There was a lot of screaming. He didn't like a lot of screaming.

So, he sat on the stoop stairs and watched Edgar Van Holtz make his strong, steady way out of the backyard, through the picket fence gate, and over to his stretch limo.

Who still used a stretch limo in this day and age? The wolf couldn't just hire a car service like a normal shifter?

Although, Keane did have to admit to himself that he hoped he was as strong and steady when he was that age. Then again, he had been battered so many times over the years, hit by guys two to three times bigger than him who just wanted to get past Keane in order to sack the quarterback, that maybe he should simply be grateful he could still walk and talk and form complete sentences when he was that age.

While Van Holtz briefly stopped outside his limo to answer a call on his cell, Charlie sat on the stoop banister.

"The balls," she said to Keane, also watching the old wolf, "to tell us they wouldn't be helping."

"Dogs always have balls. You know that because they spend so much time licking them."

Still talking on the phone, the wolf got into his limo. The door held open by the driver. Another, much younger wolf, who briefly glared at Keane and Charlie with Arctic blue eyes that reminded Keane of his neighbor's husky, closed the door and returned to the driver's seat.

"So what do we do now?" Keane asked her.

"You need to get Dani and Nat to safety."

This, *this* was why he trusted Charlie so much. It surprised both his brothers, because Keane didn't trust anyone outside of his immediate family. Yet Charlie's first thought, always, was the safety of those who needed it.

"My mother and her sisters are coming back," he told her. "They'll go to a Malone family house out in Jersey . . . or Mineola. And, most likely, they'll probably bring those goddamn dogs. The family won't like that."

"You and your brothers should go with them." When Keane frowned, Charlie added, "I don't want to be the reason Dani loses her Uncle Mean."

"You won't be. Besides, the kid already knows what it means to be a tiger."

"What does it mean?"

"Vengeance."

"Good to know."

"Besides, the kid won't be safe until we deal with the de Medicis."

The limo finally drove off.

"You know this is going to get bad, right?" Charlie asked him.

"How could I *not* know that? It's already bad."

"Yeah, but I don't think *they*"—she nodded toward the limo turning at the corner—"know how bad it's going to get. Paolo de Medici is not only meaner than his father, he's actually crazy. These organizations Van Holtz is so loyal to may think they're protecting all their fancy big-breed, non-hybrid predators, but someone like de Medici won't stop at us. He wants more than just to fuck with some badgers who tossed his father's rotting corpse into their dining room. He wants what every male lion wants. Territory. As much as he can get."

The older badgers finally reached the picket fence, three of them desperately holding onto Tracey Rutowski. It appeared as though

130   *Shelly Laurenston*

she was ready to run after that now-gone limo, but when her friends wouldn't let her go, she instead leaned over the fence and screamed. Just . . . screamed. No words. Just a guttural scream that had bears stepping out on their stoops to see what was going on. The entire thing almost made Keane laugh, because the She-badger screamed like any middle-aged Long Island housewife when the gardeners cut back too much on her shrubs.

"Good God," Charlie finally said, watching the four She-badgers.

"Yeah, I know. They're . . . a *lot*."

Nelle finished sending a text to a smuggler contact in Sri Lanka when she came around the corner of the house and saw Malone and Charlie talking on the porch steps. She stopped, assuming they were making next-step plans and not wanting to interrupt, but also keeping close by in case she had to step in and soothe things.

"What do you think is going on there?"

After glancing over, Nelle replied to Max's question, "Two normal people having a discussion? But I'm assuming you're going to somehow twist it into—"

"Think he likes her?"

"I don't think that cat likes anyone."

"I can tell you Berg won't be happy about any of this. Those two getting all close and friendly during a dramatic time like war."

Nelle lowered her phone to stare at her teammate. "Are you trying to start something between your sister and those two very large predators?"

"No."

"I thought you liked Berg. I definitely thought you liked him for Charlie."

"He's perfect for Charlie."

"Then why are you trying to break them up?"

"I'm not."

"Then what are you doing?"

"Noticing."

Nelle let out a breath. "Max, I come from an ancient, powerful family of shit-starters. I know when anyone is about to start shit. You're about to start shit."

"I'm bored."

"I see."

"And what's a little shit-starting between—"

"Stevie!" Nelle called out. "Max is trying to break up Charlie and Berg because she's bored!"

Max's face dropped. "That was unnecessarily mean."

"I still owe you for that wed—oh."

Stevie slammed into Max with such force and outright rage that she immediately took her sister to the ground, screaming in her face, and attempting to punch her with wildly flailing arms. The panda came running, doing his best to pull his girlfriend away. Even the older badgers stopped screaming at the long-gone Van Holtz and joined in the fray of attempting to separate the sisters from each other. Nelle's teammates, however, simply stood back and watched, doing absolutely nothing.

Of course, they'd been watching Max and Stevie fight since junior high. This was nothing new.

"Nelle?" Charlie called out.

Nelle made her way over to Charlie and Keane, ignoring the continued screaming coming from behind her.

"What's that about?" Charlie asked, once Nelle stood in front of them, so they didn't have to yell over Stevie and Max.

"Your sister being a bitch."

"She asked about Stevie's meds again?"

"No."

"Threw a rabid squirrel at her?"

"Not this time."

"Set her hair on fire?"

"No, but we do have a good conditioner for that now should it happen again."

"Then what?"

"Max was bored."

132   *Shelly Laurenston*

"Ohhhh."

Malone glanced between the two females before asking, "Does her boredom explain something?"

"When Max is bored, she starts shit," Charlie explained. "What this time?" she asked Nelle.

"You and Malone are sitting a little too close together."

Charlie's eyes crossed in minor exasperation, but Malone was instantly confused.

"What does that have to do with anything?"

"She says something to Berg," Charlie explained. "He goes into a grizzly rage out of jealousy, which he shouldn't because he knows better. And you, being a cat, take the bait—"

"Unfair."

"—and Max is briefly entertained by a brutal apex predator fight in the middle of bear town."

"Is she mentally ill?" Malone asked.

"Actually, no. According to Stevie and several specialists, she has a personality disorder. There, apparently, is a difference."

"What difference?"

"One is treatable with medication and psychiatric care and one is, probably, not. Guess which one Max is."

"The one that's going to piss me off the most?"

"Yep!"

Keane didn't understand what badgers called "logic," but he really didn't have time to either. War was no longer coming; it was here. The de Medicis had attacked the older badgers in their homes, trying to kill them. Might have succeeded, too, if these suburban ladies were anything but badgers.

Homes with offspring inside were usually off-limits in most shifter battles. This was not the Serengeti, where one hunted down a yummy cub that was standing alone in the tall grass, waiting for its mother to return from a hunt. Fights between adult shifters was one thing, but the offspring. . . ? Never. So Keane had to start making plans and getting shit done so he could protect his niece and sister. Meaning that, for once, football would have to come in second in his life, or even third for the time being.

Speaking of which, he'd forgotten all about his youngest brother Dale. . . .

Eh. The kid was probably fine. He was currently surrounded by Malones.

When all this had gotten serious, the Malone family had suddenly appeared in Keane's neighborhood to "help out," as one of his uncles put it. Keane still didn't trust any of them, even his aunts and female cousins. They were, however, convenient. If they wanted to help now, fine. But he'd never forgive that they'd done nothing for his family when his father had been murdered, leaving his mother to deal with it all on her own. True, she had her own family more than ready to help, but a majority of his mother's family still lived on the Steppes. That was a bit of distance to travel to help with cooking and getting her boys off to school while she was grieving the loss of her mate.

Yet despite his inability to "let it go," as Finn put it, his main concern right now was protecting his immediate family—yes, including Dale. And to do that, he would have to work *with* the badgers. Maybe not the crazy older ones. They seemed incredibly unstable.

He also didn't want to work directly with Max. That female had no boundaries whatsoever. Life and death were nothing but party favors in her daily existence.

Charlie MacKilligan, however . . . they understood each other. He didn't have to explain anything. Didn't have to make excuses. They both just got it.

While Nelle continued tapping into her phone like it was the only thing regulating her heartbeat and ability to breathe, he looked at Charlie and asked, "What's our first move?"

She didn't even hesitate. "If the de Medicis are willing to send kill squads into homes with kids, I think my sisters and I should leave. Find a new safe place."

"Berg isn't going to like that," Nelle said. Keane was shocked to realize she was actually listening. Because her tapping away on her phone had not stopped.

"Everyone here has been so kind to us. I can't put them or their kids at risk."

"These bears are not going to let you go, Charlie."

"Why do you say that?"

Nelle finally focused on Charlie. "You provide them food. You can't stop now."

"Sweetie, that's ridiculous—"

"Excuse me. Sir?" Nelle said to the older grizzly walking by the house at that moment. When he stopped and looked at her, she added a sweet smile that, Keane knew, melted the grizzly's heart right on the spot.

"Sorry to bother you, but just a quick question."

"Of course."

"If Charlie had to move out for some—"

"Move?" The grizzly's smile abruptly dropped, and he turned all his focus onto a startled Charlie. "Where? When? Why would you move, sweetheart? Has someone bothered you? Did someone say something to you? Was it him?" the old bear demanded, brown eyes narrowing on Keane. "I know the Malones. I don't like the Malones. Is he giving you trouble? You just tell me who said something to you, and I'll fight 'em myself. I'll fight 'em all. I was a bare-knuckles brawler back in the day. You just say the word, sweet Charlie, and we'll all have your back."

Nelle smirked at a shocked and gawking Charlie.

"Thank you, sir," she said to the old grizzly. "That was very helpful."

"You sure you don't need anything?"

"We're sure."

The grizzly took a step closer and asked, "Sweet, Charlie, you wouldn't happen to have any burned bits from your earlier baking, now would ya? Something you might have tossed away?"

"You want my trash?"

"One badger's trash is one bear's—"

"The cans are over there. Help yourself, Mr. O'Conner."

"Thank ya, sweetie," he said, stepping past the gate and into the yard. The five dogs that the older badger had brought with her barked at the bear invasion, but O'Conner roared back and kept moving toward the trash cans.

"Now do you understand, '*Sweet* Charlie'?" Nelle asked with air quotes.

"Shut up."

Nelle didn't know why Charlie was so shocked. The easiest way to attract and keep a bear was to feed it. Of course, then you couldn't get rid of it, and they got real mean when you didn't have food for them. Which meant if Charlie moved now, the bears on the street would tear the house apart, looking to see if she'd left anything behind they could eat. Then, since most of these bears could actually drive, they would simply track Charlie down to her next home, and demand more baked goods anyway.

No. It was best they all stayed right where they were and let the bears know exactly what was going on.

Nelle did briefly wonder if Charlie had planned to live on this street forever. Because she'd have to now.

"If we stay—"

"You'll stay," Nelle told her.

"—how do we ensure their safety?" Charlie asked Malone. "I'd hate for anything to happen to them."

"They're bears," Keane pointed out.

"Yeah. And lots of bears are stuffed and in the homes of rich men."

"If the de Medicis start attacking bears, maybe that'll pull BPC in," Malone suggested.

"No, no," Nelle quickly said. "That won't happen."

"I thought BPC was about protecting their people."

"On a global, mass scale, yes. But the de Medicis only hire bears. So it will be bears fighting bears, and BPC doesn't involve itself in that. Plus, it will only be grizzlies and polars. The other bears will not get in the middle of that."

"And Katzenhaus—"

"We all talk about 'big' cats, but there are really only two. Maybe

136   *Shelly Laurenston*

three. Lions, your kind, and some jaguars. And we all know it's much easier to take down a cheetah than it is to take down a drug dealer's pit bull."

Malone's eyes narrowed. "How do we *all* know that? It seems pretty specific."

Ignoring his question, Nelle explained to Charlie, "As far as Katzenhaus is concerned, this fight is between one lion coalition and one family. They'll never get involved."

"You're right," Charlie agreed.

"Of course I'm right. I'm always right when it comes to this sort of thing."

"What sort of thing?" the cat asked.

"Information. Information is, and always will be, power. And power means money. And my family loves money."

Looking back at her phone and replying to another text, Nelle added, "All that to say, I can get any information you need. Just let me know."

"Okay. Good. That makes me feel a little better." Charlie looked around the street. "I just want to keep everyone as safe as I can."

"What is this obsession you have with the safety of apex predators?" Malone demanded. "Is this some *human* thing you're doing?"

Charlie glanced at Nelle before replying, "Yes, Keane. It's a human thing I'm doing."

"Well, stop it. It's off-putting and offensive."

"Okay."

"I do understand how you feel and everything. . . ."

"Uh-huh."

"But get over it."

"I . . . I'll work on getting over this *human* thing. Thank you for your guidance."

"My pleasure," he replied, with an arrogance only a cat could have.

"If you want," Nelle suggested, "I can make some discreet inquiries. Maybe meet with some people."

TO KILL A BADGER 137

Charlie frowned. "For what purpose?"

"Find out where the de Medicis are. Find out who their connections are. Find out how many people they have working for them."

"Make a move before they do," Charlie guessed.

"Exactly."

"Yeah." Charlie smiled, nodded. "That would be great."

"I'm on it."

"Keane, you go with her."

Keane was only half-listening to the conversation once he realized it had nothing to do with him, but now Charlie was trying to involve him, and he didn't want to be involved. At all.

"I don't wanna."

Without even looking away from her phone, Nelle snorted a laugh and grinned. But Charlie just stared at him.

"What?" he asked when she didn't say anything.

"You're going."

"Going where?"

"Wherever Nelle goes, you're going. You are now officially her protection."

"Don't you already have a bodyguard?" he demanded of Nelle.

"Awww, Charles," Charlie said. "How is he?"

"Doing well last time I talked to him."

"I'm not following her around," Keane insisted, since both women didn't seem to understand what he was telling them.

Charlie slipped off the banister and walked down the stoop steps until she was in front of him.

"Now listen to me, Malone . . ." She paused. "Hold on a moment." Turning her head, she yelled out, *"Max! Leave Stevie alone right nowwww!"*

Keane crossed his eyes; the way the badger's voice went up several octaves there at the end nearly broke his eardrums.

"Me? I didn't do anything!"

"Do not argue with me! Just do it!" She focused again on Keane. "Where was I?"

"You were pissing me off."

"Yes. Right." She jabbed her forefinger at him. "You're going to do what I tell you to do."

"You are not a female who gave birth to me, so I don't have to do anything you tell me to."

"He'll do it."

Keane glared at Nelle. "No, I won't."

"Yes. You will. Charlie," she said with a smile, "let me handle this. I'm sure you have other things you need to do right now."

"I need to bake."

"You do," Nelle agreed. "You need to bake."

"I may have more ideas after I bake." She glanced off, then asked, "Pie, cakes, or brownies?"

"Whatever you want," Nelle replied. "Whatever gives you ease."

"Okay. Thanks. And thanks, Keane."

He opened his mouth to say he wasn't doing anything, so she didn't need to thank him, but Nelle's hand slapped across his mouth, and she didn't move it until Charlie had gone back inside.

"I am not following you around," he said, once Nelle removed her hand from his face.

"If Charlie tells you to follow me around, you follow me around."

"Why would I do that?"

"Because you do whatever Charlie tells you to do."

"Because. . . ?"

"Because you don't want to set her off. Have you seen her when she's set off? I have. I don't need to see it again. And when she starts baking like this. Just batch after batch after batch of food . . . you do whatever she says and keep out of her way."

"Well, unlike you, I'm not afraid of her."

She lowered her phone, looking him right in the eyes. "Yes. But you *should* be."

Chapter 11

Silvio de Medici entered the massive marble bathroom. A room meant to recreate the Roman baths of his ancestors. The fact that it was in the New Jersey penthouse of a tall building his father had built many years ago didn't mean they had to leave their culture completely behind. Even now, the females of their coalition were making them a big dinner that they would enjoy on the roof so they could look over at the city they planned to invade while dining on fish, meat, and handmade pastas along with the best cheeses and wine.

Like all big cats, his brother Paolo loved to eat. Unlike the lower-class cats, he insisted on only the best. "I wasn't born in an alley; why would I eat from the garbage cans there?" he'd ask, while watching pumas and leopards dining in outdoor restaurants back home.

Silvio had no plans to live in this dirty, newborn country longer than necessary, but wherever Paolo went, he followed. It had always been that way, and he didn't question it. His father had made it clear that brothers stuck together until death. Infighting might be necessary to keep things organized and running smoothly, but you never sided with anyone over a brother. Not a sister, not a mate, not your own child. It was what kept their coalition going strong since the late Middle Ages. Why would Silvio fuck with any of that now?

Stopping by a bench, Silvio slipped off his pool shoes and robe before sitting naked on the edge of the bath, his feet dangling in the extremely warm water.

"Well?" Paolo asked, without even opening his eyes as he floated by.

"It didn't go well," Silvio told his brother. "We lost some of our cousins to dogs and snakes."

Paolo's head slowly turned in the water to stare at Silvio. "What?"

"Poisonous snakes. They were in the walls and floors of the entire house. The Russian crone. It was her house."

"Disgusting. It's disgusting we have to bother with that species at all. What about the younger ones? That murdering whore and her sisters."

"They've ensconced themselves with bears."

"So?"

"My contacts tell me those bears will die to protect them."

"Bears will die to protect little vermin? Why?"

"Something about muffins."

Paolo gawked at him, then shook his head and swam over to the edge of the bath, pulling himself out. He sat on the edge next to Silvio. One of the younger nephews brought over a towel, and Paolo placed it around his shoulders.

"Has there been any retaliation from the others?"

"The others?"

"The cats? The bears? The dogs?"

"No."

"Good. Then we try again."

"We just lost blood. I'm not sure going after them again right now—"

"I am not letting some *whore* get in my way, Silvio! I want that cunt dead at my feet! *I want her cunt sisters dead at my feet! I want* anyone *helping them dead at my feet! Do you understand me?*"

Silvio kept his gaze down, focused on his own feet still under the clear water rather than on his brother.

"I understand."

"Then make it happen." He leaned in so his nose nearly touched Silvio's cheek. "Before I get angry. . . ."

"Have you heard from Mom?"

Hearing his brother's question, Keane walked out of Mads's newly

TO KILL A BADGER 141

purchased house, where he'd gone to escape all the bears swarming Charlie's house. Once all those baking smells started to permeate the air, they'd come out of the woodwork. Like bear-sized locusts descending on a crop of corn. But Mads's place was just across the street from Charlie's and down a few doors from the Dunns' house, where his baby sister and niece were staying at the moment until they were picked up and taken somewhere safe by his mother and her visiting sisters.

At least that had been the original plan, which he'd been completely involved in. Now, however, Keane didn't know what was going on.

Standing in front of Mads's house next to Finn, Keane watched as another RV drove down the bear-only street. Past Charlie's house, past Mads's, until it reached the corner, two blocks away. Moments later, another RV turned onto the street. Then another . . . and another. The RVs that couldn't find parking moved to surrounding streets.

And behind all those RVs came cars. Lots of cars. Some were old beaters, often abandoned as necessary. Other cars were high-end vehicles made tacky with bad paint jobs, off-market car parts, and ridiculous rims that would look awful in a low-budget, nineties rap video.

And in every one of those vehicles filling up the streets . . . were Malones.

So many Malones.

"What the fuck is going on?" Keane demanded. The last time he'd seen his relatives, they'd all been hanging out on *his* street, next to *his* house. Much to the consternation of his neighbors. Now they were all here. Why were they here?

Keane started to walk over to those cars, so he could pick each one up and toss them off the street, with his relatives still inside.

But Finn yanked him back and held him in place.

"Calm down."

"I don't wanna calm down."

"Shay!" Finn called toward the house.

A minute or two later, his middle brother lumbered outside and stood behind Keane and Finn. Unlike at Charlie's house, Mads's place

142   *Shelly Laurenston*

didn't have a full porch or a sunroom. So they had to crowd onto that tiny stoop and those two small steps that led to the tiny front yard.

"Did you call Mom?" Finn asked Shay. "Or heard from her?"

"No. I thought you were handling that."

"I thought I had. Last I heard, they were going to pick up Nat and Dani and take them back to the house. But now . . ." Finn watched all those vehicles park on the street. "But now this."

"Maybe they're just accompanying Mom as she picks up Nat and Dani," Shay tried to reason.

"All ten thousand of them?"

"Don't snap at me, Keane."

"This is quickly turning into a disaster, and I've decided to blame you two."

"What did we do?" Shay asked.

"I don't care what you did or didn't know. I just want you to fix it. Before I get angry. Because once I get angry—"

"*Yes,*" Finn barked. "We know."

An enormous, tricked-out RV that must have cost hundreds of thousands of dollars parked in the middle of the street. The side door opened, and Keane's mother stepped down the stairs.

Shay and Finn rushed over to her, giving her warm hugs. But Keane held back and waited until she'd walked over to him.

"Get that angry look off your face," she told him. "Everything's fine."

"How can everything be fine when *they're* here?"

Keane's Uncle Cally leaned out of the RV and called, "There are my boys!"

Disgusted the old cat would even attempt that level of closeness after going *years* without doing anything for Keane's family, Keane appropriately roared his rage and bared his fangs; his brothers ran back to his side to grab his arms and keep him from physically attacking their uncle. Keane's roar was so loud and angry that every other Malone in the vicinity responded in kind, while the bears surrounding Charlie's house finally came off the sidewalk and onto the street to get a closer look at the sudden cat invasion on their territory; while the shifters

TO KILL A BADGER 143

on other streets that made up this insane Queens neighborhood added their own roars and howls to the mix.

It went on for several seconds until Keane's mother yelled, *"All of you, stop that!"*

They did, because his mother had a way of controlling a situation that had made her the head of every parent-run bake sale and high school dance committee she had ever joined.

His mother took a few steps and, in an effortless move he envied, she launched herself up, landing on top of a cousin's purple Camaro. She looked at the predators surrounding her.

"Now, I'm going to say this only once," she explained, raising her voice so everyone on the street could hear her, "to all of *you*," she added, looking directly at Keane. "We're not here to cause problems. This is just temporary. But we are here to protect the *family*. That means everyone will be polite, kind, and on their best behavior. If anyone has a problem with that, feel free to discuss it with *me*. Until then . . ."

With that, she dismissed them all with a hand wave. The bears refocused on the MacKilligan house and Charlie's baking. The Malones began the process of temporarily settling into this space until, one day, they would simply be gone. Keane hoped that would happen sooner rather than later, but he wouldn't say that to his mother. It would just make her angry.

His mother was walking past him now and into Mads's house. Without saying a word, she made it clear she expected her sons to follow. So they did.

Texting on her phone, reaching out to her contacts, Nelle followed her teammates into the living room she had set up for Mads for just this kind of scenario. How Mads could be pissed that Nelle had done nothing but help her was beyond rational understanding.

Why were Vikings so damn moody? If she'd left it to Mads, they'd all be sitting on the floor or cardboard boxes right now!

"What is happening? Why are *they* here?"

Nelle looked away from her phone to see Keane pacing. He was a

144 *Shelly Laurenston*

very poised cat. He usually just stayed still until forced to move. So seeing him pace alerted her that he was unhappy. Although it seemed he was never really happy, he never seemed unhappy either. Unhappy, she was guessing, was probably not good.

An older She-tiger stood in the middle of the living room, arms crossed over her chest, gold eyes locked on a pacing Keane. Nelle knew in an instant that this was his mother. Not only because she looked a lot like Finn, but because she gave off the same energy as Keane. Innate physical and mental strength with a *soupçon* of barely controlled homicidal rage.

The way she spoke to him was a huge clue, too.

"I know you're not barking at me like some stray cat you want out from under your house . . . are you?"

Nelle lifted her gaze long enough to watch as Keane practically twisted himself into literal knots trying to calm himself down before he replied between clenched teeth, "No, ma'am."

"Good. Because we wouldn't want me angry . . . now, would we?"

"No, ma'am," all three Malone boys said together.

Nelle bit back a laugh, but she still got a little glare from Keane, which she adored. He was just so cute when he was full of disappointment and unbridled fury!

Clearing her throat, his mother began, "When I went to retrieve Dale—"

"Who?"

The tigress blinked before replying to Keane's question with, "Your *brother*. . . ?"

"Oh. Right. Him."

Max was standing behind Nelle, and she felt her teammate press her head against the back of Nelle's neck, trying so hard not to laugh. Even Nelle had to cover her mouth and stare at the floor.

"Anyway," Keane's mother went on, "Cally and I—"

"Cally and *you*?" Keane growled out. "You two are friends now?"

Nelle saw the look of horror on Finn's and Shay's faces as the mother and son squared off. Realizing that neither of those weak males would intervene, she quickly moved over to Keane's side and took hold of his forearm.

"Could you come with me a minute?" she sweetly asked.

"I'm busy explaining to my *mother*—"

"I don't need you to explain anything to me, *son*."

Nelle gave a healthy pull, and the obstinate male allowed her to drag him deeper inside the house until they reached the kitchen.

Once they stopped by the big wood table, she released him, answered one more text, then faced the cat.

"Why are you making this hard?" Nelle asked.

The cat stared at his arm. "How are you so strong?"

"I'm an elite athlete who has to hold my own against She-bears three times my size that are well aware I smell like honey. So, moving you from one room to another is not exactly a challenge for me."

"Whatever. What do you mean *I* am making things hard?"

"Starting fights with your mother? Are you insane?"

"I don't like her hanging around Cally. And I don't see why I shouldn't point that out. I mean, did you see the way he looked at her?"

"I can tell you with all sincerity that if there is one thing your mother knows how to do, it is handle your lusty uncles."

"You don't even know my mother, and don't call those old bastards 'lusty.'"

"Keane, I know when a woman is manipulating men she has no interest in."

"What?"

"Your mother wants her daughter and grandchild safe. If she has to use your uncles to make that happen, I'm guessing she will. Let her do it. Having this street filled with bears *and* cats will make Charlie as happy as she ever can be, and the rest of us can get to work hunting down and annihilating the de Medicis. Isn't that what you want? Or would you rather stand around instead, arguing about the uncles that *didn't* kill your father?"

Keane glanced off, baring a bit of fang. Although she didn't think it was directed at her.

146   *Shelly Laurenston*

"I won't be polite to them," he announced.

"You're not polite to anyone, so your mother will probably never notice." She took a step closer to him and pressed her hand against his chest, bringing his attention to her face. "Just don't turn this into a war between Malones. At least not one that your mother will notice. Your enemy right now are the de Medicis. Let's deal with them first, *then* you can slap your uncles around all you want. Okay?"

He growled a little. "Okay. But understand . . . I'm not happy."

"Awwww, Keane. We all know you're *never* happy."

Nelle took over that room like a champ. He'd never seen anything like it.

Once they'd walked back into the living room, she didn't even let him and his mother get into it. Instead, she simply had everyone sit down. Got Tock to make some "strong Israeli coffee," because apparently she'd made sure that was stocked in Mads's cabinets, along with rows and rows of honey from every country in the world. Then she'd texted Charlie and, within five minutes, Stevie's panda boyfriend arrived with several packages of freshly made Danish and a couple of pies.

By the time his mother started talking, between bites of delicious pie, even Keane was in a better mood. It was strange. Nothing ever put him in a better mood. Why should it? The world sucked.

"I know this isn't exactly what you wanted, Keane," his mother said, before taking another sip of her coffee. "I know the family disappointed you. But if they're willing to step up now and do something, anything, I say we let them."

"What if they bail on us? Again? When we need them most?"

"We'll do what we've always done. We'll make their lives a living hell. And besides, I'm not talking about involving them in any of this. Let's use them for protection. It is what the mob uses them for. Let's not stretch their talents too much. Okay? Let's just put up with them for Nat and Dani and Dale."

"Who?"

TO KILL A BADGER **147**

"Your *brother*."

"Oh. Right."

"The Malones are here for one reason as far as I'm concerned. So you and your brothers can search and destroy." She smiled, but it wasn't a friendly smile. "If the de Medicis had anything to do with your father's death, I want them wiped from the planet. Understand me?"

"Yes, ma'am," Keane and his brothers automatically replied.

"Do you need to stay here for now?" Nelle asked. "I'm sure Mads would be more than happy to make up a room for you. Right, Mads?"

When her friend didn't reply, Nelle rammed her elbow into Mads's side.

"*Owww!* What was that for?"

"You'd be happy to make up a room for Mrs. Malone, *right?*"

"What? She has to stay here, too?"

"What is wrong with you?"

"There aren't a lot of rooms! It's not like all of us were born in a palace!"

"It was *not* a palace! It was a small family castle!"

Keane locked eyes with his mother, and they both had to quickly look away, or they would start laughing.

"All I'm suggesting is that you maybe want to do a little extra for the angry She-cat that might be *your mother-in-law one day*!"

"Do you really think she wants to stay here with the coyote?" Tock asked.

"The coyote shouldn't be here!"

"He was here *first!*" Mads argued.

Nelle threw her hands up. "I can't have this conversation again!"

"It's fine," his mother cut in, staring down at the third piece of pie Streep had placed in front of her. "I'll be staying in one of the RVs with my sisters. Right outside that bear house where my niece and granddaughter are staying."

"You're going to let them stay at the Dunns'?" Keane asked.

"If they stay there, then I don't have to listen to the whining of puppies all night long, now, will I? Plus, the triplets are professional

148   *Shelly Laurenston*

and *proper* protection people and don't do it for gangsters. They will be a nice yin to the yang of the Malones."

"Okay," Keane said, nodding. "That makes sense."

"See?" Finn said. "Solved." His brother, always trying to calm things down. Not an easy job when it came to this family. "What do you think of the pie, Mom?"

She pointed at her half-eaten slice with her fork. "This is the *best* pie I have ever had."

"Amazing, right?" Streep said. "Charlie has such talent. For food, I mean. Not for calm reason."

"Okay!" Nelle quickly cut in, eyes briefly widening at Streep. Based on the way Streep quickly reared away from Nelle, Keane was guessing that expression was some sort of warning.

"You know what, Mrs. Malone," Nelle said, putting on that ridiculously fake smile she used with everyone but him. "Now that you'll be staying here for a while, I'll ask that when Charlie bakes if she'll put some treats aside for you and your sisters. Before the bears can get to them."

"Oh. That . . . that would be very lovely . . . thank you."

"Welcome."

His mother stood. "Let me get back outside. Check in with everyone. Let your Uncle Cally know about more recent things. All that. And please, Keane, try to be nice. To everyone."

"No."

His mother let out a sigh. "Just like your father."

She walked toward the door, but stopped and came back. She took the remainder of the pie that Keane had every intention of finishing himself, and left.

"I was going to eat that," Shay muttered.

Staring at Mads, but gesturing to Shay with a sweep of her hand, Nelle waited for her teammate to realize what she was telling her. It seemed she would be waiting until the end of time.

"What?" Mads finally asked.

"He wants pie."

TO KILL A BADGER 149

"So he should get pie. I think there's another two or three in the kitchen."

"I am trying to teach you the simplest of lessons. And you refuse to learn!"

"Learn what? How to be a little kowtowing bitch?"

"Okay!" Finn got to his feet. "Hey, babe?"

"Babe?" Mads turned her glare to Finn. "Did you just call me *babe*? Like I'm some *whore*?"

"Yes," Nelle calmly told her. "That's exactly what he meant. He was calling you a whore."

"Shut up."

Finn pushed on. "Why don't we go out back with your teammates, and play a little ball?"

"At Charlie's house? While she's baking? Are you insane?"

"No. In your backyard."

"I don't have a hoop in my—"

"Yes," Nelle told her, focused on her phone and a text she'd just received from one of her father's contacts. "You do have a half-court in your backyard."

When Nelle didn't hear anything else, she lifted her gaze to find Mads now scowling at her from the other side of the L-shaped couch.

"Did you have a half-court built into my backyard without talking to me first?" Mads asked.

"Yes."

"And that didn't seem weird to you? Or, I don't know, out of line?"

"You *weren't* going to have a half-court put into your backyard?"

"I just moved in!"

"I knew you'd want one. So I took care of that for you. Just be grateful and let's move on."

"Stop. Doing. That."

"Doing what? Exactly? Putting a half-court in your backyard that you're going to make us all train on? Or taking care of things you never think about because you have such a sad, limited view?"

Finn caught Mads in his arms before she could make it across the room to Nelle.

150 *Shelly Laurenston*

Nelle didn't react to her friend's sudden bout of anger. After all these years, she was quite used to it. Although the hyena laugh Mads let out was disturbing. She didn't usually release one of those unless she was *blindingly* pissed off. Berserker rage from her Viking blood, perhaps. And no one wanted to be on the wrong side of that.

"Let's go look at your new court!" Finn kindly suggested, while lifting the She-badger up and carrying her out of the room.

"I have a date tonight," Tock reminded them.

"Forget it," Nelle replied. "You'll have to wait to date the guy you are already fucking."

Tock sighed. "Because she'll make us practice now?"

"Yes."

"We better get changed," Max agreed. "Come on, Streep."

"I have no energy to practice. I am a fragile flower and—"

"Cut the shit and come on."

Nelle typed into her phone, answering important texts. She didn't know how long she was at it, because of the annoying text she'd just received from her mother. A text that was *ordering* her to go to her sister's dress-fitting tomorrow, as if Nelle had nothing else to do with her life. But she did have other things to do. Important things.

Nelle closed her eyes and took in a few deep breaths to calm her simmering anger and disgust. All that was going on, and the only thing her mother and sister could think about was that ridiculous, multimillion-dollar wedding!

When Nelle had calmed herself down, she opened her eyes. That's when she quickly discovered she was alone in the room with Keane.

"What?" she asked when she realized he was watching her. She assumed he was wondering why she was taking deep breaths and soothing herself. Her assumption was wrong.

"You actually built a half-court in her yard without asking her first?" he asked.

"Do you really think she's *not* going to use a half-court in her yard?"

"That's not the point. It's *her* yard. Her house. She decides if she wants to add or take away from it."

TO KILL A BADGER   151

Fascinated, Nelle lowered her phone. "Do you really want me to feel bad about this?"

"Based on what I know from my honey badger sister, I'm sure that's asking too much of you. Instead, I'd suggest you think a little more about your actions before taking them."

"I love that philosophy is coming from *you*, of all cats, but I do think about my actions—very carefully—before I take them. For instance, I thought, do I get her a half-court or just a basket for her to practice her free throws? Do I get her a fresh set of workout clothes or let her continue to use those nasty, smelly things she's been using since junior high? Do I add a shed in her backyard to hold extra balls and gear? By the way, that one was easy. I went with the shed."

The cat did what cats do when they didn't really have anything to say. He just continued to stare.

That's when Nelle added, "I also put a wine cellar in her basement and filled it with the best wines. Some that I actually purchased rather than pilfered. She still hasn't noticed, even though she's actually been to her basement several times since she got the house. So, you do see what I'm dealing with."

Keane shook his head and looked away.

"What?" she wanted to know.

After a few seconds, he returned to staring at her face, but this time, his gaze roved over it for some reason.

"Why are you looking at me like that?"

"I'm memorizing your face. So when Mads claws it off your skull, I can remember what you once looked like and not focus on the horror you will have become."

"I have to say," she told him as she returned her focus to her phone, "I am shocked and awed by your correct usage of the future perfect tense."

Keane grabbed the remote from off the coffee table, turned on the TV, threw his big feet up on the expensive mahogany Nelle had paid extra for so the furniture would last the oncoming abuse, and leaned back into the bear-sized couch without any discomfort. It should really be called a bear-and-big-cat-sized couch.

With a shrug, he explained, "I simply calls 'em like I sees 'em."

"Annnnnd, you have returned to being a typical American, butchering the English language. Welcome back, my friend."

The cat grinned. "Always glad to be here."

"*Nelle!*" Mads bellowed from outside. "*Put on your gear and get your ass out here! We're training!*"

Nelle's head dropped forward in defeat, and she heard the cat chuckle.

"Hung by your own petard, my lady," he muttered.

She stood. "Finding out every day that someone like *you* reads actual books fascinates me."

"Don't be bitter. It doesn't become you."

"Shut up."

Chapter 12

Charlie stood in the doorway that separated the kitchen from the dining room. She'd removed the swinging door that was there, because it got on her nerves going through it constantly and having it open when she least expected it. She'd tried to properly take it off with a screwdriver, but someone had painted over the hinges, and not being in the mood to scrape that off, she'd just torn the fucking thing off with her bare hands.

Berg had been walking toward her when she'd done it, and all he said was, "Awww, babe, I could have done that for you." And she knew he'd meant tearing it off with his bare hands, not removing it properly. She'd quickly discovered bears didn't really do "proper removal." Not when they could just, ya know . . . tear it apart with their brute strength. Something she really loved about bears.

Now she stood in that empty space and stared at the four older badgers, whom she barely knew and wasn't sure she even liked, sitting at her dining table, not speaking. That discussion with Van Holtz had really upset them. Well, it upset the three married to Van Holtzes. The Russian badger didn't seem too bothered about anything as she scrolled through her phone like a fifteen-year-old in science class.

The fact that the four badgers were just sitting there, in her house, for no obvious reason, and not speaking, was making her uncomfortable. Honey badgers were cranky monsters. They did not sit in stillness like meditation masters. Besides, she'd assumed they would leave like everyone else. Go home or to the safe house where they'd sent

154   *Shelly Laurenston*

their adult kids. But nope. They didn't do any of that. They simply sat there. Not speaking.

It was weird!

"What's going on?" Max asked from behind her. Charlie had heard her sister coming in the back door and stopping behind her. Sadly, she couldn't smell her. Her allergies were acting up again. That's why she enjoyed baking, though. She could always smell her food once it started baking in the oven.

"I don't know," she told her sister. "They're just sitting there. Have been for a while." She glanced at her sister. "You stink, which is saying something, because my allergies are bad today."

"Mads had us practicing all damn day. Like Louisiana prisoners on a work farm in August."

"I didn't see you outside."

"Nelle put a half-court in Mads's backyard. So we practiced there."

"Nelle put a—"

"Don't. They have been arguing about that half-court all afternoon long, and I can't talk about it anymore. Anyway, they'll be ordering dinner soon, but I wanted to get a shower in before I eat." She motioned to the other She-badgers with a tilt of her head. "Want me to handle this?"

"You think you can handle this?"

Max raised a forefinger before walking into the dining room, over to the dining table, leaning in, hands clasped in front of her and bending at the knees so she was at eye level with the She-badgers. Then, once in position, Max yelled, *"Would you ladies like to leave now? Would you like me to call a nephew? Or an older grandchild to come and get you and return you to the home?"*

And she said it like the four had wandered away from some senior center.

Charlie had to twist her lips to stop herself from laughing, because she understood how annoyed the She-badgers must be with Max. The other day, a nine-year-old bear cub had called Charlie *ma'am*, and she nearly decked the kid in her pretty pink tutu and ballet shoes.

Slowly—oh, so slowly—the four She-badgers looked over at Max.

TO KILL A BADGER 155

All four glaring. All four insulted. All four ready to kill Charlie's younger sister.

"Whatever you need, ladies!" Max brutally went on. *"We're here for you! Just let us know!"*

"We'll be back tomorrow," Rutowski announced before she stood up, the other three following suit. "We'll talk more then."

Angry gazes locked on Max; the four females headed out. But just as Rutowski reached the front of the house, she whistled, and five Belgian Malinois ran in from the backyard, into the kitchen, and toward the badgers. It wasn't that Charlie hadn't known the extra dogs were on her property. She'd simply assumed they were extra strays that had wandered into her yard. She had already given them treats. Tested them with the other dogs to see if they were aggressive. Fuck! She'd actually fed them!

"See?" Max said when the She-badgers and the dogs were gone. "Told you I could take care of it."

"You're lucky you still have your skin."

"Yeah," she said with a happy laugh. "I know!"

"Who just puts a wine cellar in someone else's house?" Mads demanded when they were nearly done eating.

"Are you going to keep bringing this up?"

"Yes."

Nelle rolled her eyes and focused back on her food.

They'd found a nearby bear-run diner that delivered and, about ninety minutes later, an enormous amount of food was dropped off by two cranky grizzlies and a very cheery black She-bear. It wasn't exactly the best dining experience Nelle had ever had, but it was good enough. And to make it better, she'd finally had the chance to inform Mads and the others of the wine cellar she'd had built into Mads's basement and then stocked with good wine. Because who didn't want access to good wine when they were eating?

"Did you enjoy the wine you just drank?" Nelle asked, pushing the remains of her platter-sized chicken pot pie in front of Keane Malone. Her meal had been pretty good, but it was made for a grizzly appetite, and she simply didn't have a big enough digestive system to take it all in. Yet the cats had devoured their massive amounts of food like they hadn't eaten in years rather than a few hours.

"I didn't drink any wine," Mads sneered back. "I hate wine. I like beer."

"I know. That's why there's beer downstairs, too."

"That's not the point, Nel—*really?*" Mads demanded, when Finn and Shay jumped up and ran toward the basement to get some of that beer.

"Look how happy they are to have options," Nelle said, knowing perfectly well how annoying she was being to Mads. Sometimes she couldn't help it. And Mads insisted on making it easy for her. "Again . . . that's called being a good hostess."

"I hate you."

The two cats returned quickly with several bottles of beer. Finn tossed one across the room to Keane before he sat down and offered other beers to everyone else.

"You found Mongolian beer?" Keane asked Nelle, staring at the label.

"Yes. A Mongolian lager, I believe. Didn't know anything about it, but thought I had to include that. As well as your typical European lagers and, of course, a few American brews for the unrefined palate."

"You better not mean me," Mads warned.

"Hey!" Tock held up a bottle of beer with Hebrew writing on the label. "I haven't had this since I was at the kibbutz."

"The kibbutz you got thrown out of?" Streep asked with a smile.

"It was the best decision," Tock said. "For everyone involved."

"I don't want this," Keane said.

"Why not?" Nelle asked. "This is the drink of your people."

"My people are from Long Island."

Finn reached over and snatched the beer from his brother's hand, and Shay quickly replaced it with a bottle of Guinness.

"This'll work."

"How could I forget the Guinness of Long Island?"

Keane ignored her, taking several gulps before letting out a satisfied sigh. Almost smiling. She was just grateful he didn't burp. She had an older brother who did that, and it drove Nelle insane.

The front door opened, and Max walked in. Her still-drying hair smelling like honey shampoo and wearing cutoff shorts and an oversized football jersey from her boyfriend, Zé. Nelle, however, had been too busy arguing with Mads the last few hours to get a chance to shower.

"How's Charlie?" Tock asked.

"Baking, baking, and more baking." Max said, standing in front of them. "But it's calming her down, and the demanding bears are keeping her busy. They're lined up down the block like she's giving out cocaine. And there will be chocolate cake for dessert."

"With her ganache?" Streep asked, hopefully.

"*Yes.*"

The squeal had the tigers side-eyeing her, but they didn't snarl. That was nice.

"There's food for you in the kitchen," Nelle pointed out. "I ordered you beef stew with white rice."

"Oooh! My favorite."

"Beef stew is your favorite?" Keane asked, frowning.

"Yes. Why?"

"It just seems kinda normal for . . . ya know . . . *you.*"

"I'm normal." When he only continued to stare at her, Max changed it to, "I can be normal. With some effort. Oh, and Mads . . . your aunt and her snobby friends were hanging out at Charlie's house when I got there."

"They were? Why? Why are they still here? Were they bothering Charlie? Tell me they weren't bothering Charlie. What's going on? What's happening?"

Max simply shrugged at Mads's growing panic and paranoia. "I don't know. They were just sitting there, quietly. Doing absolutely nothing."

"And that's a problem for you?" Keane asked.

"Yes. Because it's weird. Honey badgers don't sit around contemplating life."

158 Shelly Laurenston

"When my grandmother's quiet," Tock noted, "someone's going to feel pain."

"We actually weren't bothering anyone," Nelle's aunt announced from the archway leading to the hallway and the set of stairs that led to the second floor. "Which is new for us."

Nelle pulled the .40 she'd felt between the cushions and aimed it at the four older She-badgers. Her teammates pulled the weapons taped to the back of the couch or on the back of chairs. The tigers, however, didn't react at all, continuing to drink their beer.

"I approve of your reaction time," Tracey Rutowski noted. "But I am not digging the fact that none of you noticed we were here until we walked into the room. The cats knew."

"You use a lot of perfume," Keane muttered between sips of his beer.

"I wanna know: Why do you guys always have weapons just lying around?" Shay questioned. "It's like you don't want my daughter to visit."

"How could you five not know we were here?" Rutowski abruptly focused on Nelle, Max, Tock, and Streep. "I am trusting you four with my niece's safety."

Max frowned. "You are?"

"Why?" Nelle wanted to know.

"Since when?" Tock asked.

"Mads, do you feel weak? Are you dying?" Streep began to cry. "You know we'll all take care of you on your deathbed."

"I'll probably just put a pillow over your face to end it quicker," Max admitted.

"Which is what I would demand," Mads snarled.

"How comforting for me," Rutowski said with great sarcasm.

"We have been here for, like, an hour," Álvarez said with a laugh, before dropping into one of the empty club chairs. She swung her feet up onto the ottoman and threw her hands out so they rested on the armrests. "We had dinner while we were in your kitchen. How could you not know?"

"Dinner?" Max repeated. "What dinner?"

TO KILL A BADGER 159

"Beef stew."

"That was *my* beef stew," Max complained.

"It *was*," Steph Yoon said. "And it was delicious."

"Who knew a grizzly portion of beef stew was enough for four badgers with healthy appetites?" Álvarez happily taunted.

"Did you have to put your dentures back in to eat it?" Max snarked back.

Álvarez laughed, but Yoon and Rutowski had to grab the Russian She-badger's arms to hold her back. Fangs out, the crazed female snarled at Max.

"One day," the Russian threatened, "I will cut off your head and wear it like hat on head!"

"That's enough!" Mads yelled, standing between the warring factions. "Do any of you understand what's going on right now? What's happening right in front of us? *Do you?*"

Nelle leaned in close to Keane and whispered, "Wait for it."

"*Championship!*" Mads bellowed.

Rutowski looked at her friends. "I have to admit . . . I *really* thought she was going to talk about the whole killer lions thing."

"We have a championship coming up," Mads elaborated, "and you four are doing nothing but distracting us!"

"Championship?" Rutowski softly repeated. "Is that seriously what you're worried about right now?"

"Yes! *Because that's all that matters!*"

"Okay," Rutowski said, immediately changing her tone to calm her niece down while raising her hands up to her waist, palms out. "I understand your concern. But you do need to remember that we're *all* in danger right now. Not just you guys. Not just us. But our families. They just sent killers to our homes and—"

"And you killed them all!" Mads reminded them. "So sitting around, worrying about *more* killers that you can probably handle, seems like a waste of everyone's time."

"Okay. I understand. You want to focus on this." Rutowski glanced at her friends. "We can work directly with Charlie."

"*No!*" Nelle and her teammates immediately screamed. The older

160   *Shelly Laurenston*

badgers jumped but, again, the tigers didn't react at all. They seemed to be getting used to life with honey badgers. Something that was not easy for anyone.

Eyes wide, Rutowski raised her hands until they were in front of her chest, palms still out.

"How about we all calm down?" she asked.

"How about you not talk to my sister?" Max shot back.

"Why?" Yoon asked. "Why can't we talk to her? Unlike *you,* she seems completely reasonable."

"The fact that you don't know why you shouldn't," Streep sweetly replied, "is why you shouldn't."

"That makes *no* sense."

Nelle stood and stepped over Keane's long legs, moving toward the four She-badgers.

"Look," she began gently, "we understand you want to be helpful."

Rutowski's eyes narrowed. "Uh-huh."

"And I'm sure you can be. Maybe with . . ." Nelle paused, trying to think of something that could keep these four females busy for the next few days, and out of everyone's hair. "Um . . . your husbands!" she said, suddenly remembering three of the women were married.

"Our husbands?"

"Yes. You can speak to them and see if *they* can get their uncles and . . . the, uh . . . pack or whatever . . . to help. That would be so awesome! Right, Mads?"

Mads looked up from the playbook she was scanning. "What?"

Rutowski's eyes were so narrow now, they were practically slits. "So you're saying we can't actually *help* you guys?"

"No, no. That's not what we're saying."

"It isn't?"

"*Max!*" Nelle snapped.

Keane finished his bottle of Guinness and placed it on the big coffee table next to his brothers' finished bottles of beer. He heard the others bickering about dogs or wolves or husbands or whatever, but didn't want to get involved. So he stared at the empty beer bottles that were unconsciously being lined up as each person finished their own particular brand of beer.

After about five minutes, when everyone was done with their beers, Keane leaned in and, using his forefinger, inched each bottle to the very edge of the table, ensuring they were all perfectly aligned, before knocking each one off. After they'd all hit the floor but didn't shatter against the rug Keane had just noticed, he heard Finn let out an annoyed sigh . . . then his brother placed each bottle back on the table in a perfectly straight line.

Keane again aimed his forefinger at the first bottle when Mads suddenly growled, "You're setting those bottles up for him *again*?"

Startled, Keane looked up to find all the badgers staring at him and his brothers, watching him knock the bottles off the table while Finn would set them up again. A little ritual the three brothers could do for hours, much to his mother's annoyance and something they'd been doing since they were toddlers. And Shay? Well, after stretching his arms up above his head, he had been using the tips of his claws to tear at a small spot where the paint had split a bit, and by now, he had removed a several-inches-wide section off Mads's wall. Keane noted that the previous interior color had been a very light blue. Nice, but not really Mads's taste, he was guessing.

"I'm out of here," Rutowski snarled, reaching into her back pocket and pulling out a set of keys.

"Look, look," Mads said, getting to her feet. "We're sorry, Aunt Tracey."

"We are?"

"*Max!*" the four of them snarled at their teammate.

"There's just so much going on," Mads tried again, stepping closer to her glowering aunt. "And we're really not trying to be difficult. I mean, if you need anything from us, please. Let us know. I want you guys to be safe, too."

"That's great." Álvarez finally slid off the chair and put her hands on Rutowski's shoulders. "And since you offered to help out, why don't you take care of Trace's dogs tonight?"

"Dogs?"

162 *Shelly Laurenston*

"Yeah. She needs a break, and you so kindly offered."

Mads lowered her gaze, and Keane watched her expression change from helpful niece to grudging acquaintance at the sight of the five panting beasts surrounding their owner.

"You want me to take care of those things?"

"They're Belgian Malinois and have already eaten," Álvarez went on, as she gently pushed her friend toward the front door. "A few treats and some friendly petting should keep them happy."

"I'm not really a dog person."

"Really? Then why do you have a big food bowl filled with kibble in your kitchen?"

"That's for the coyote."

Yoon took the car keys from Rutowski, then froze. "You have a coyote?"

"I thought I smelled coyote," Álvarez muttered. "But I thought maybe it was just the first signs of a brain aneurysm."

"I don't *have* a coyote," Mads nonsensically explained. "He just lives here." The four older females stared at her. "Under the house. Squatter's rights."

"On that note . . ." Álvarez pushed Rutowski toward the front door.

"We'll pick the dogs up tomorrow," Yoon said to Mads, even as she gazed at her like a mutant.

The Russian followed after the other three, her gaze for Max and Max alone.

When she reached the door, she abruptly stopped.

"One day," the Russian threatened Max, elegantly drawing one claw across her throat. "One day."

When the front door closed behind the She-badgers, Max joked, "I love them! They're fun!"

"Max!" Streep snapped. "Why are you being so mean to those poor old ladies? Tracey Rutowski is the only member of Mads's family willing to acknowledge her existence! Not one blood relative loves Mads or even likes her besides *that* woman! We *have* to be nice to her and her friends."

"Thanks, Streep," Mads replied with great sarcasm.

Keane was starting to like Streep. She was brutal, but always in the nicest way possible.

"Should we be concerned about what those four may be up to that they can't bring the dogs?" Tock asked. "When my grandmother has that expression walking out the door, someone's nation is taking a hit."

"I say we don't ask questions," Streep suggested. "At times like this, with Charlie baking, all these organizations pissed off, lion males willing to kill cubs and pups, old badgers starting shit out in the wild, and dogs we now have to"—she twisted her lips in disgust—"*pet* . . . plausible deniability is our friend."

"Hi, Daddy!" Nelle greeted her father, waving at him on her phone.

"Is that Mr. Z? Hi, Mr. Z!" Max said from behind Nelle, resting her chin on Nelle's shoulder. "It's been ages, huh?"

"It has. How are you, Maximilian?"

"It's just Max. And I'm great!"

"Haven't you all been attacked by big cats and are currently in constant danger?"

"Yeah!" Max said with a smile before walking away.

"Your friend has not changed."

"I know, Daddy."

"So . . . you're calling. Why?"

"Well, I'm trying to find contacts we can—"

"No."

"No?" She stared at her father's video image. "What do you mean, 'no'?"

"You and your friends will have to work this out on your own."

She immediately started speaking Cantonese. "But . . . I'm your little bird."

"No. I said you were my little crested serpent eagle."

"I like bird."

He smiled. "I have faith in you, Nelle. You don't need me."

Nelle slipped off the raised bar chair she'd been sitting on and walked out of the kitchen.

164 *Shelly Laurenston*

"You're right. I can do this on my own. But one of the family jets would be helpful, if we need them."

"Nelle, you have your own jet."

"I know. But yours are faster and have more weapons onboard. And your cheese plates are always exemplary."

"We already allowed you access to the jets for your friends, and someone picked at the leather seats with their claws, and the whole thing smells like those cats you've been hanging around. Your mother is *not* happy. You know how she feels about cats."

Nelle leaned closer so that her entire face would fill the screen of her father's phone. "Pleeeeeeease, Daddy!"

He laughed. "You're ridiculous. Always have been."

"Well, I was Ma's 'unhappy surprise.' Or . . . what was it? 'Proof of a curse from our dead ancestors.' "

"You know your grandmother loves you."

Nelle reached the couch and sat down. She sighed and leaned back.

"This could be bad, Dad. The Group, the BPC, the cats . . . they're all out. Refusing to get involved and help us. And if my friends aren't safe, I'm not—"

"I understand. You're not safe either."

"No. That's not what I meant."

"Oh."

"In fact, I feel I'm perfectly safe."

"Well, actually—"

"The Zhao name has tons of clout. What I was instead going to say, is if my friends aren't safe, then I'm not *happy*. No one wants me to be unhappy, Daddy. Not even Mother."

"I'm aware. In that one way, you are like her."

"No need to get nasty."

"Listen, my little crested serpent eagle—"

"*Really*, Daddy?"

"—I am wondering what that is behind you. That big angry face?"

Nelle looked over her shoulder at a scowling Keane.

"This is Keane Malone, Daddy," she said in English, reaching back with her free hand to tap his chest. "He's the reason *I* am currently safe. Wherever I go, he will go."

"What about Charles?" the cat demanded. "Isn't he your *actual* bodyguard?"

"He has other things to do."

"You mean besides his *job*?" Keane snarled. "And why are you treating me like a chair?"

"This is my daddy," she said to Keane, attempting to redirect him like she would an angry toddler.

"Hello, sir. Nice to meet you," Keane said, surprising Nelle with the tiger's sudden burst of strict politeness. She had to admit, she didn't expect it, but she appreciated his tone toward her much-loved father. "But you should know . . . your daughter is clinically insane," he added.

Now *that* she had expected from Keane Malone.

When she'd sat down on the couch next to him, despite everyone else being off somewhere in the house doing other things, he hadn't been surprised. He doubted she'd even noticed him sitting there, drinking another Guinness and watching TV. But then she'd leaned back against his arm while she talked on the phone and relaxed against him like it was completely normal and she didn't know he was a man-eating tiger that held grudges.

"Are you saying that Van Holtz came to *tell* you these organizations weren't going to help?" Mr. Zhao asked his very comfortable daughter still leaning against Keane like he was part of the couch.

"Yes, which I thought was strange. And a little rude. Appreciated . . . but strange."

"It is strange. All they had to do was not help. One doesn't really need to discuss that. Maybe they're trying to tell you something with that bit of non-information."

"Like what?"

"Let's think about this logically, shall we?"

"Oh, Daddy, no," she whined, tossing her head back, all that black

166   *Shelly Laurenston*

hair falling onto Keane's arm and shoulder. Some of the solid white strands hit him in the eyes, which he did not like. "Just tell me. No logic problems."

"But you're so good at them."

"I know, but that's not the point."

"Maybe what they're saying is you should find someone *else* to help you," Keane cut in before the whining could continue.

Father and daughter gazed at him a moment before Mr. Zhao said, "So he's smarter than he looks."

"Sometimes. When he's not slamming his head into walls."

"I thought only bears did that sort of thing."

"The bears *are* the walls, Daddy."

"Ahh. He plays *American* football. I understand."

"But this one reads books."

"Oooh. That's not common."

"I know."

"Okay, now this is just getting a little mean," Keane noted.

The badger laughed. "Apologies, young man. And it was nice meeting you."

"You, too, sir."

"And good luck to you, my little crested serpent eagle. Don't do anything too bloody."

"I won't. And, Daddy. . . ?"

"Yes?"

"One of the family jets? One of the fast ones? And an assistant, perhaps? Because you love me so much?"

"*One* of the family jets?" Keane had to ask.

"Quiet, kitty."

"Of course," her father said.

"Yay!" she cheered.

"Under one condition."

Nelle immediately stopped cheering. "You want me to be nice to Ma?"

"I *always* want you to be nice to your mother, but no. I want you to go to your sister's dress fitting tomorrow."

"I'd rather set myself on fire."

"Nelle—"

"I don't want to go! I don't want to go to this wedding. I don't want to be involved. I want nothing to do with this ridiculous endeavor."

"I know. But I'm asking you as your father and the one who is going to allow you to use our fastest jet—"

"*Fine.*"

"Thank you, my little crested—"

"*Daddy.*"

The badger laughed, then ended the call.

Nelle lowered her phone and let out a sigh. "I can't believe I have to go to that stupid dress fitting tomorrow. This is all Max's fault. If I didn't like her so much, I would have killed her for this."

"That seems an extreme reaction over a wedding."

"It's not." She closed her eyes, took in a deep breath, then let it out. When she spoke again, she sounded much calmer. "But at least we have access to the family jets now. Because mine just won't do. Your shoulders alone in that tiny thing."

"*You* have a jet?"

"Why wouldn't I have a jet?"

"And your family has a *fleet* of jets?"

"There are a lot of us."

"And why would *we* need a jet?"

"Do you want us to fly commercial?"

"Like paupers, you mean?"

"I didn't say that."

"But we both know you were thinking it."

"Look, I don't know if we'll need the jet. But just in case . . . I like to be ready for anything."

"I guess that makes sense. Still don't know why I need to be involved, though."

"You don't need to worry about that right now. Just continue to look pretty."

He wanted to be insulted. And maybe if someone else was saying it, he would be. Instead, Keane simply replied, "I always do."

Then, out of nowhere, Nelle asked, "You want to find a room and have sex?"

Where the hell had that come from? Why was she asking him that? What was wrong with everyone in this house? It's like they'd all collectively lost their one mind! *"Pardon?"*

"That's not a no."

"You are so insane."

"All I'm saying is that it's been a long, stressful day. I'm being forced to attend this ridiculous wedding by my own father who *says* he loves me. Now I'm not so sure. And I need to come up with some way to get even with Max."

"How does any of that involve you having sex with me?"

"It's just a lot to deal with. Sex helps me clear my mind so I can plan things. And since you're here anyway . . ."

Since he was here *anyway*?

"Gee, thanks," Keane snapped. "That makes me feel so special."

"Did you want me to bring you flowers? Perhaps a box of imported chocolates?"

Deciding he was done with this conversation, Keane refocused on the TV and completely ignored the badger that was badgering him.

"Wow," he heard her say as she exited the room. "If I didn't know you were cat before, the level of disdain coming off you right now would have definitely clued me in."

Well . . . cat disdain was a genetic feline ability.

Chapter 13

After a couple of quick stops in the city, CeCe and her friends arrived at the New Jersey safe house. She thought her kids would be here, but they weren't. No one was here. Most mothers would be worried, but she wasn't. She knew her kids could handle themselves. Besides, they had a lot of safe houses all over the world. A few of them, the four had had for decades.

She followed Trace into the big, sunken living room right off the hallway from the front door. CeCe watched her best friend drop face-first onto the couch before letting out a long, dramatic sigh into the cushions.

"It's really not that bad," she told her fellow She-badger.

"It is! It is that bad!"

It amazed CeCe that Trace could still go from grown adult woman who handled her life and businesses with the iron paw of a dictator right back to the fifteen-year-old girl whose bedroom walls she used to paint murals on.

Ox dropped onto a second couch and kicked her heels off. She'd been wearing heels with jeans since she'd moved to the States in the eighties and, like then, she still managed to make it work. All CeCe ever wore were Doc Martens. Even now—once broken in, of course—they were just so damn comfortable!

"You should let me kill that MacKilligan badger," Ox said, rubbing her toes. "She is the one upsetting my friend."

"Not only does Mads not have a lot of friends, these friends actu-

170   *Shelly Laurenston*

ally like her *and* are willing to play basketball. *The* most boring sport. We can't kill Max MacKilligan. Besides, we really need her sisters to be focused on something other than seeing you walking around with that girl's head as a hat. And stop smiling, Ox!"

Steph came into the room and sang, "Let's get this party started!"

"I don't want to party." Trace sat up and brushed her hair off her face. "Don't you see? They're right. We're old and useless. We might as well just get in our coffins now."

"Don't forget, I want to be cremated," CeCe reminded her friends. "And don't let anyone piss on my ashes."

"Why would anyone . . ." Steph shook her head. "Forget it. I can't."

"We are just old ladies," Trace continued to whine. "That no one loves. We are loveless."

"Oh, my God." Steph dropped to the floor next to a big, wooden coffee table, crossing her legs under it. "You need to get over this."

"She doesn't even want my help! My own niece. I'm an embarrassment to her!"

CeCe shrugged. "We've been an embarrassment to the United States government for the last forty years, and that never bothered you."

"Because they *deserved* to be embarrassed!"

"Look, my friend, you can sit here feeling sorry for yourself—"

"Which is so much fun for us," Steph tossed in.

"—or you can go change into your grubbies, pull your hair out of your face, and get ready to enjoy yourself at any age."

Grinning, CeCe held up the bags of weed they'd purchased in the city before heading here. "Remember how we used to have to get this?"

"You mean our brothers buying it for us?"

"Yes. That's exactly what I mean."

"Since there are no children to judge, I will get vodka from car," Ox said, jumping off the couch.

"I'll get snacks!"

"Aren't we too old for this?" Trace asked, really wallowing in the moment.

"Trace Rutowski . . . one is *never* too old to get high on primo weed."

"You do have a point."

Keane could hear his relatives on the usually quiet street. There was music and laughing and barbeque smells. Worried they were going to do nothing but piss off the grizzlies, which would lead to a tiger-bear fight—something that should only happen in the wilds of Siberia, not in the middle of Queens—Keane went outside to order them to turn the noise off. But the bears were part of it. It was like a street party. Although, seeing the sides of cow that were being barbequed, he could kind of guess why the bears weren't putting up much of a fight.

Keane grabbed the back of a lawn chair, dumped one of his cousins out of it—much to the cat's annoyance—and set it up on Mads's lawn.

He would keep watch.

Because everything was great now, but it could easily turn. He wanted to prevent that. So he sat and he waited. Ignoring the cousins that kept trying to wave him over or the one who roared at him for five minutes for taking his seat.

About an hour in, he realized that someone had pulled up a chair and was sitting next to him. Nelle had her arms resting on her knees and her scowling gaze scanning the crowd. It took him a moment to figure out she was simply imitating him. Rude!

"Very funny."

Her scowl cleared, and she laughed. "You should see your face."

He didn't need to. When he was fifteen, his mother had taken a picture of him at some random moment and later showed it to him. "See this?" she'd asked. "This is what you look like. This is why the entire school is terrified of you and you have a meeting with the school therapist next week. Fix that face!"

On that demand, Keane had been unable to help her. But the therapist had said he was "fine" pretty quickly, just to get the glowering teen out of his office and life.

"Do you know why you're so stressed?" Nelle asked.

"I'm not—"

172   *Shelly Laurenston*

"It's because you're not having sex."

"Stop talking to me."

"What are you doing tomorrow?"

"I'm not having sex with you then, either."

"No, no. I mean what's your plan for the day?"

"I'm going to practice. Why?"

"What if something else comes up?"

"Nothing else will come up."

"Perhaps."

Fed up with the vagueness of this discussion, Keane asked, "What are you talking about?"

"I've made a few inquiries, and I'm hoping to hear back tomorrow with information we can use to track down the de Medicis."

"Really? And then what?"

She shrugged. "Kill them all."

"See, that's what worries me. Because that's not a plan. That's simply murder in the first degree."

"What do you *think* we're going to do when we come face-to-face with these guys? Have a chat over coffee? Maybe enjoy a strudel together?"

"A strudel?"

"You don't like strudel?"

"I've never had strudel."

"You've never had strudel?"

"Nelle." He paused. "What I am looking for is retribution. I want to look Paolo de Medici in the eyes and, as one cat to another, rip him apart with my claws. What I don't want is whatever crazy thing you might be coming up with that will have me waking up in the middle of the night, for the next forty years, sweating and screaming. I'm trying to get *away* from that sort of thing. Not make it worse."

"And if I get their location anyway?"

"Give it to Charlie."

"You trust Charlie over me?"

"Yes."

"You didn't even hesitate."

"No."

"Why do you trust her more than me?"

"Because she's calm."

"I'm always calm."

"Rational."

"I'm extremely rational."

"And has a family."

"I have family!"

"That she cares about."

"I care about my family."

"You won't even go to your sister's wedding."

Nelle's mouth fell open, and she reared back like he'd just slapped her.

"How *dare* you say such a thing to me?"

"You said it yourself. You called the wedding ridiculous and said you didn't want to go."

"Of course I don't want to go! *No one in their right mind would want to go to that motherfucking wedding!*"

Nelle's sudden—and uncharacteristic—explosion of rage had every tiger and bear on the street focusing on her until she screamed, *"What are you all looking at?"*

When they quickly turned away from the badger that was ten times smaller than most of them, Keane had never been more delighted!

Nixie Van Holtz Rutkowski loved, loved, *loved* her father. He taught her how to cook food for a pack of people, gave Nixie her first knife set that she still used to this day, and handled all the parent stuff when it came to school for his kids. He also made sure his daughters knew he loved and respected them as individuals and made sure they did the same for themselves. He was, in a word, amazing.

What her father *never* did, however, was put a .45 Glock in her sixteen-year-old hand and say, "If something comes through that door that's not your father or me, you shoot until the threat stops moving.

Understand?" Then disappear for three months without any of them knowing if she was alive or dead. Nope. He managed *not* to do that to any of his children.

It wasn't that Nixie didn't love her mother. Of *course,* she loved her mother. Who didn't love their mother? What kind of monster would it make her if she didn't love her own mother?

It was just . . . her mother was a lot. Actually, her mother and her friends were a lot.

When it was just her mother, one-on-one, Nixie mostly enjoyed her company. It was almost normal. So "mom and daughter." And, even when just one or two of her friends was added, it was lovely. A fun lunch. Or a lovely dinner where normal things were discussed and handled.

Not just full-human normal, but normal by honey badger standards. A small jewelry heist. Or the smuggling in of fine art for a very rich buyer. Normal, normal, *normal.*

But, when all four She-badgers united in the same space . . .

These four women "meddled"—that was the word her Great-Uncle Edgar kindly used—in world issues like they were Kissinger. But they weren't Kissinger. Nixie knew that, because the actual Kissinger hated the four honey badgers and had told them so at a White House dinner to celebrate the arts that they'd attended with Nixie's father and uncles. That's how she'd heard about it. Her father had told her during one of their long conversations. The pair of them loved to talk about everything. Books, movies, cooking, hockey. They both loved hockey.

The only reason Nix was here at all was because her father had sweetly asked her to "check on your mom." He and her uncles weren't in the country and, after making sure his "girls" were okay, he wanted to know about his wife and his brothers' wives. As well as Aunt Ox, of course, but no one really worried about her, because it was rarely necessary. The She-badger was a force of nature, full of rage and unpredictability that ensured that, like the wind, few could catch her unaware.

Knowing the four She-badgers were together during a time of cri-

TO KILL A BADGER 175

sis had made Nixie hesitate in searching her mother out, but she'd promised her dad. But still . . . she hadn't expected *this*.

"*Mom!*" she practically screamed. Disgusted! She was so disgusted! Her mother looked up from the bong she'd had her mouth wrapped around and smiled.

"Baby!"

"What are you doing?" Nixie demanded, stepping deeper into the safe house living room, her gaze moving over the four women she adored but resented in equal measure. All of them were ridiculously high. Music from the eighties and nineties blasting through the sound system, *The Breakfast Club* silently playing on the big-screen TV, snack foods of all sorts half-eaten and spread out over the coffee table, and these She-badgers draped over the couch and on the floor like sixteen-year-old idiots that don't know any better!

"What are we doing?" her mother asked back. "Uh . . . getting high." She held up the bong that Aunt Steph had made out of one of her Renaissance Faire–purchased dragon statues and asked, "Want a hit?"

Aghast, Nixie had only one response to that . . .

"*MOM!*"

"We need to shut this down," Keane told Nelle, gesturing at the street party with a toss of his hand.

"Because you hate fun?" she asked.

"No. Because it's very late, and I don't like *that*." He pointed at ten-year-old Dani hanging out with her cousins and an aunt. "Kids shouldn't be up this late."

"Her father is right over there. He doesn't seem bothered she is spending time with her cousins. And I doubt they can give her all the ins and outs of leg-breaking while dancing and eating boar ribs."

Keane's eyes narrowed a bit. It amazed him how easily Nelle saw what really bothered him. "I love Shay, but he can be an idiot."

"Do you even know how to be nice?"

"No."

"At least you said you loved one of your brothers."

"If you tell anyone, no one will believe you."

"Especially Shay."

"But, I will say," he added, just to piss her off, "if nothing else, I would definitely go to Shay's wedding."

"Oh, my God!" she yelled, throwing up her hands. "Are any of you going to let that go? Speaking of which . . . could you hand me that?"

Keane looked at his hands, which were empty, and then around his body.

"The football?" he asked, when that was the only thing nearest his chair that wasn't an empty beer can.

"Yes. That."

Confused but interested, he handed her the ball. She took it and held it between her hands, a little confused because it wasn't a basketball.

"Here." He reached over and fitted the fingers of her right hand around it, pulled her arm back a bit to indicate how to throw it. When he was done, she stood, narrowed her eyes on a distant spot, and let the ball go.

It slammed into the back of Max MacKilligan's head, knocking her forward and down.

Keane exploded into laughter. Shocked and amazed! He hadn't thrown that well until he was on the junior high team, and this little princess had nailed a hard-headed badger on her first throw. Fucking impressive!

"What was that for?" Max demanded, when she'd been helped to her feet and she'd stopped stumbling around, rubbing the back of her head.

"You know what it's for!"

At first, Max frowned, confused. But then the frown faded and a huge grin broke across her face.

"You gotta do something for the wedding?" she asked with obvious glee.

"I hate you."

The badger laughed, and Nelle pulled her fist back, ready to start swinging, but then Zé was there, the jaguar taking Max by the hand

TO KILL A BADGER   177

and dragging her away. As a running back, the guy always had amazing timing. Almost always caught the ball, and he always knew when to get his girlfriend out of the line of fire.

"Feel better?" Keane asked, getting to his feet.

"I don't feel worse."

That made Keane laugh more, and that was when he finally noticed that his entire family was gawking at him. He didn't know why. He'd been known to laugh on occasion. He couldn't remember a time, but he was positive it had happened before now.

"Did you really just offer your own daughter drugs?" Nixie demanded.

"You're an adult now, and I just assumed—"

"That I got high?"

"Well—"

"I don't."

"Oh." Trace shrugged. "Okay. Good. I am proud of you. Being drug-free. All kids should be."

She watched her daughter come to a realization. Eyes narrowing, then widening, her hands briefly covering her mouth, before she accused, *"You've gotten high with the twins, haven't you?"*

"Of course . . . that's . . . I would never . . . *they offered!"*

"Mom!"

"Smooooooth," Steph laughed, while wearing sunglasses and hanging upside down on the couch so that her legs dangled over the back.

Her friends began to laugh, Steph sliding off the couch onto the floor, Ox curling into a ball, and CeCe warning them to "Stop! Stop! I'm gonna piss myself!"

"All of you," her daughter said in her haughtiest tone, "disgust me! Hell is coming. Hell! And you four are doing nothing but getting high!"

"What do we care?" Trace asked, unable to hide the despair. "What does it have to do with us?"

178   Shelly Laurenston

"What?"

"It doesn't affect us, my sweet baby, because apparently we're too old to do anything."

"Uh-oh," CeCe muttered, as she reached for another Reese's Peanut Butter Cup from the coffee table. "Here we go."

"Mom, what are you talking about?"

"Didn't you hear? The women who took down the Berlin Wall—"

"You didn't."

"We helped."

"Mostly because we degraded the reinforcements holding it up after digging under it a few times to get from one side to the other unseen," Steph explained.

"Its eventual removal still involved us, no matter what Kissinger kept saying," Trace insisted. "Well, *we*"—she gestured to herself and her friends—"no longer matter. The younger set is going to take over and handle it, because we're so decrepit . . . apparently."

Nixie pointed a damning finger. "You . . ."

"Bitches?" Ox helpfully offered her niece-by-friendship.

"Women," Nixie went with, "better not have involved my sisters and cousins in any of this insanity!"

"Not them," Trace said. "Your cousin and her friends."

"I have a *lot* of cousins, Mom. You'll have to be way more specific."

"Sweet Mads. Who I thought liked me, but she and her friends just think I'm old and useless."

Her daughter watched her for several moments before asking, "What are you doing?"

"Sobbing?"

"No. You're not. You're just making noises. And there are no tears."

CeCe leaned in, studied her face. "She's right, Tee. Dry as a bone."

"Well, I *feel* like I could cry."

Nixie shrugged. "Maybe they're right. Maybe you are too old for this sort of thing."

Now it was Trace's turn to point a damning finger. "Don't think for a minute that I can't shove you *back* into my womb until you learn to be *respectful*!"

TO KILL A BADGER 179

"Okay, that's *disgusting* and all I'm saying is that one day . . . I plan to get married—"

"Married?" Tracey asked, appalled. "Why the fuck would you want to get married?"

"You're married," her daughter felt the need to remind her.

Trace dropped her head back and said, "Because your father *whined* so much about it. 'No Van Holtz will take you seriously as my mate if we don't get married,'" she said in that high-pitched imitation of his voice he hated. "And let me tell ya somethin' . . . that oh-so-important marriage changed *nothin'* with those dogs."

"I'm half-dog, Mom."

"Not really. My badger genes wiped those dog genes right out. But you did get your father's height and his lovely cheekbones."

"Anyway," Nixie continued, "one day I will get married and have pups, and don't you want to be that kind of grandmother they come to for cookies and love and hugs?"

Trace stared at her daughter a moment before telling her, "Grandma Rutowski taught me how to strip a Tokarev PPSh-41 submachine gun by the time I was seven. And put it back together again. By the time I was sixteen, I could use it to mow down as many men as were in my way. *That's* the kind of grandmother I plan to be." Trace paused.

"Yeah," she said, feeling a flush of energy shoot through her veins. "Yeah. That's the kind of grandmother I am going to be, and that's the kind of mother I am *now.* Wait! Where are you going?"

Her daughter stopped in the entryway, glaring back at her. "I am going to tell my father that his wife is alive and well, and that he should divorce her as soon as possible! Then I'm going to make sure that my sisters and cousins are safe and *not* involving themselves in whatever crazy shit you four are about to do to make things even worse than they already are! That's what I'm going to do!"

Trace cringed when the front door slammed shut. Her daughter was very angry, and she hated when the kid got that way. But she was just so damn sensitive.

Shaking her head, Trace looked at her friends. She began playing with the strings on her thin-cotton hoodie.

180 *Shelly Laurenston*

"Uh-oh," CeCe said. "She's got that look, ladies."

"We are in so much trouble," Steph said, giggling.

"I look forward to our honorable deaths."

"Shut up, Lenkov."

Trace began chewing on the hoodie strings she'd tied together before washing so they didn't come out yet again, but they tasted gross. So, instead, she began tugging them up until they framed her head. It was so ridiculous, and they were all so high, and they began to laugh hysterically.

"What were we talking about?" Trace eventually asked. Because she'd completely forgotten.

"The kids . . . or something," CeCe suggested.

"No, no. The big cats."

"What big cats?" Trace asked Ox.

"The lions. The angry lions . . . I think."

"That's right!" Trace slapped her hands on the coffee table. "I *think* I have an idea."

"An idea that will make things better or worse?" Steph asked.

Trace took a second to think that through before replying, "Both?"

Chapter 14

"**M**orning!"

Keane opened his eyes to see Charlie standing over him with several bakery boxes, a thin piece of string wrapped around each one to keep them closed.

"I brought you guys pastries before they're all gone. The bears are already lining up for what I made last night."

Using his elbows to prop himself up, Keane asked, "Did you get any sleep?"

"Not really. But I don't need to sleep as much as everyone else. Due to my father's fucked-up genes."

Swinging his legs off the couch and dropping his feet to the floor, Keane asked, "Do you mention your father's fucked-up genes to my sister often?"

"You mean *our* sister, don't you? And I don't need to mention it to her. She already knows she has fucked-up genes."

"Why? Because she's deaf?"

"Being deaf is probably the best thing that could have happened to that kid, because she can never hear the level of his stupidity."

"Okay," Keane admitted. "You have a point."

She placed the boxes of pastries on the table in front of him.

That's when Keane warned, "Unless you want me to eat them all—"

Charlie quickly picked up the boxes again and headed toward the kitchen at the back of the house. A few minutes later, she returned.

182 *Shelly Laurenston*

She didn't bother to say anything to him this time, most likely sensing his bad mood. A brief wave, and she was gone again. That was another reason why he liked Charlie so much. She really *got* him.

Keane buried his face in his hands. He hadn't slept great. A lot on his mind about the de Medicis; the Malones being around his niece, teaching her things like pickpocketing or breaking legs; the way his father's brothers kept looking at his mother . . . none of it made him happy!

"Good morning, big brother!"

Hearing Finn's cheery greeting as he entered the room made Keane immediately bare fangs and give off a roar that had Finn spinning around on his heel and heading back the way he'd come. Shay stepped into the hallway, but Finn grabbed their brother's arm before he could open his mouth—and make Keane angrier—and dragged him away.

Probably best for all involved.

"Should I even ask why all of you are in the shower together?"

"For hot girl-on-girl action just to entertain you?"

"Try again."

"Because we're all so hungover, we can't stand up straight without all of us piled in together?"

"There you go."

Wolf Van Holtz reached into the large shower and helped his wife out. His brothers grabbed their own wives while Ox informed them, "I need no help. I am not weak like you Americans."

"You're speaking to the wall, Ox."

She realized he was right and spun around too fast, causing her legs to give out. She dropped to the wet floor.

Wolf put his wife on the closed toilet seat and went back for one of her best friends.

"I am okay, weak American."

"Are you? Because you are just sitting there. Unable to get up."

It didn't matter to him, seeing a naked Ox. He'd known Ox since he'd been forced to help the four teenagers escape East Germany. He'd only been twenty at the time, and to find a bunch of American schoolgirls fighting their way through Stasi officers had been . . . weird. Just weird. Of course, then he hadn't really heard about honey badgers being part of the shifter pantheon. He knew about bears, big cats, and wild dogs of all kind. But honey badgers? Really? He had never heard about them as normal animals in the wild, much less that someone looked at the very small species and thought, "I gotta be that!" Yet there they had been, stabbing, shooting, and hacking Stasi officers to death to get their Russian friend to safety. He'd been forced to help simply to avoid an international incident, lecturing them the entire way. Not that any of them had taken him seriously. But, over the ensuing years, he'd watched these dangerous "girls" grow into adult honey badgers—and he'd become much more frightened for the world.

Which was why he didn't know how he'd finally ended up married, with pups, to one of those She-badgers. To this day, his mother insisted she'd cast some kind of Eastern European spell on him, and some days he agreed with her. Because being married to a honey badger when one wasn't a honey badger was just not easy.

Sliding his hands under her pits, Wolf carried Ox out of the shower she was still sitting in and put her on her feet in the hallway. One of his brothers handed him a towel, and he wrapped it around her.

Then Wolf focused on his mate, who had slipped off the toilet and onto the floor.

"Nixie is pissed, babe," he told his wife while helping her up. It was why he'd come home. Because of Nixie. They'd had the *Can't you just divorce her?* discussion again. Never a good sign.

"She's always pissed at me," Trace slurred. "She started punching me while still in the womb. But all I care about is that all our kids are safe."

"They're all safe," he promised. "But Nixie is terrified, babe. That you are going to do something insane. We thought we should come back and get ahead of it."

"I wouldn't say it was insane . . ."

With a sigh, Wolf's brother Hel lifted his own wife into his arms and carried Steph from the bathroom. The rest followed. While holding Trace in his left arm, Wolf briefly stopped to grab a confused Ox with his right and brought both women to the master bedroom with the others.

He put the Russian in a chair and his wife on the wooden chest at the foot of the bed.

"So what's going on?" he asked. "You haven't gotten this wasted in years."

When the four She-badgers looked at one another, Wolf realized he may not be right on that particular point.

"Is this about Uncle Edgar?"

"That wolf holds grudge like cat," Ox complained, standing and walking-stumbling out of the room.

"He hates me."

Wolf pushed Trace's hair off her face. "Sweetie . . . of *course* he hates you. The man had his paws in some of the most nightmarish shit from the eighties, including the Cold War, the Iran–Contra affair, Chernobyl, and the rise of MTV. And yet, he still calls our wedding the darkest day of his life."

"Well, however he feels, about us—"

"You mostly, though."

"Shut up, C. We're going to prove him wrong."

"How and what is going to be the blowback? Are we going to have to move out of the country again?"

"We never moved out of the country. It was a vacation."

"Two years in Switzerland," Hel barked.

"A very *long* vacation, I'll admit."

Ox returned to the room. She was walking steadier now and had four duffel bags. Two black, one of which she tossed to Hel for Steph. A gray one that she heaved at Wolf for Trace. And a bright purple and dark red one that she handed to Lot for CeCe. The second black one she kept for herself, opening it and pulling out a cookie tin with holes opened at the top.

"What's in there?" Lot asked, with a tone of very necessary paranoia.

"Hair of wolf," Ox said, taking the top off.

Hel reared back, allowing his mate to fall back on the bed. *"Tarantulas?"*

"Tarantulas are not venomous."

TO KILL A BADGER   185

"Yes, they are!"

"Not to us. And these aren't tarantulas at all."

Cringing, Wolf watched Trace, the woman he loved more than life, stick her hand into a tin of crawling spiders.

"What are those, then?" Lot asked.

"Funnel-web!" Trace cheered, pulling one out. "From Australia." She crunched down on it like it was a celery stalk. It started biting her as soon as she'd picked it up, and she never even winced.

Trace closed her eyes, and her head dropped for a brief moment, but when she looked at him again, her eyes were clear and she was smiling.

"Whew!" she shouted. "Now that's what I'm talking about!"

She stood, briefly stopping to kiss his forehead. "Love you so much, Puppy."

"Awww," his brothers said in laughing unison, "puppppeee—"

"Shut up."

Ox dug into Trace's duffel. "What mood are you in now, my friend?"

"It's a PJ Harvey day."

The Russian pulled out an old T-shirt that Tracey had gotten from a PJ Harvey concert back in the nineties. Wolf immediately cringed. When Trace was having a "PJ Harvey day," that meant she was in a *mood*. A mood that never led to anything good. Ever.

It must have been on his face. The worry. Because Tracey immediately leaned in to wrap her arms around his neck and hug him tight.

"I love you," she said, and he knew she did. Even after all these years, she loved him like she loved nothing else. "And I need you to go protect our family and trust me. Trust me to handle this."

"Last time you said that to me, we were all investigated by the FBI for sixteen months."

"And cleared of any wrongdoing!" she replied with a smile.

"Awww, baby. That's really not the point."

Keane had put off his shower to eat. He'd been starving, and the smell of all those fresh treats from Charlie had him and his brothers tearing through all of them while sitting in the living room with a couple of gallons of milk and the Cartoon Network playing on the TV.

"We didn't leave the badgers any," Shay noted, gazing at the empty boxes.

"That sounds like a *you* problem and not a *me* problem," Keane reminded his brothers.

Fed and satisfied, he cracked his neck before announcing, "Okay. I'm getting in the shower, and then we are off to practice."

His brothers knew not to complain about that, so they simply nodded and focused on the TV. He was about to stand and get ready when the front door was thrown open and more badgers walked into the room. Badgers he was in no mood to see.

"Good morning, kitty cat!" Tracey Rutowski loudly cheered once in the living room. He knew that door had been locked. How did they just walk in? Without kicking it open? Without any warning? Without even a knock? Without general politeness!

"Ooooh. Sexy bare-chest wake up," Yoon leered, while staring at him and putting Keane's teeth on edge. "Nice!"

"I see why they keep you around," Rutowski noted. "Because it's not for your brilliance."

"Where is everyone?" Álvarez asked, as Mads's aunt simply walked toward the back of the house like she owned the place.

"How the fuck should I know?" Keane demanded, already feeling a headache pounding inside his skull.

Yoon snorted. "Kitty not a morning person?"

Keane was about to shift to tiger and bite the heads off all these bitches when a dressed and smelling *awesome* Nelle entered the room.

"Good morning to all," she greeted, before sitting down on the couch next to Keane. "How is everyone this beautiful day?"

"Big kitty's cranky."

"Maybe because you're calling him 'big kitty.'"

Álvarez flopped into a club chair across from them, one leg tossed over the arm.

"You guys are all so serious," she complained. "Do any of you

TO KILL A BADGER 187

know how to have a little fun these days? Or are you too busy showing your asses on the Internet?"

"Fair question," Nelle shot back, "but let's table that to find out if you own *any actual underwear*?"

Álvarez looked down at herself. She wore a pair of denim overall shorts with very wide legs. This one bright red and covered in old paint stains. It was clearly made for a much bigger person, so when she splayed her legs apart, Keane had seen much more than he'd wanted to this early morning. She also wore no bra under her bright, white, and too-tight T-shirt.

"I'm an artist," Álvarez said, as if it explained anything.

"So you're too poor to buy underwear?"

"*No*, heifer. And you sound like my mother."

"Because she wishes you'd wear underwear, too?"

"I don't understand why anyone needs underwear. The world is an amazing and beautiful place. With so much to see! Who cares if the person next to you is naked or not?"

"What does that have to do with underwear and you not wearing any? And just to let you know that although you're wearing a T-shirt, your nipples are hard and for all the universe to see."

"Of course they are. Because I love *life*!" she roared, which just seemed to harden her nipples more. "Besides," she added, "my tits are fabulous."

"For your age?" Nelle brutally asked.

"For any age, bitch."

And, much to Keane's annoyance, she was not wrong. Her tits, for any age, were amazing.

"Where are my dogs?" Rutowski asked as she walked back into the room.

"I haven't seen your dogs since last night," Nelle said. "Did see that coyote, though." She looked at Keane. "It was waiting for me outside the bathroom this morning. Personally, I find that odd."

"What about you guys?" Rutowski asked Keane and his brothers. "You see my dogs?"

188 *Shelly Laurenston*

"Yeah," Keane said. "I saw them about three or so. They were staring at the door, so I let them out."

When he didn't say anything else, she barked, *"And then?"*

He shrugged. "And then I closed the door and went back to bed."

Álvarez covered her mouth and turned her head. But they all heard the snort of laughter. Yoon cringed, and the Russian just stood there in extremely high heels. How did any female, full-human or shifter, ever walk around in those things?

"You didn't let them back in?"

Keane reared back a bit, because the She-badger was hysterically yelling at him. It seemed an excessive reaction when discussing five pet dogs. Couldn't she just go to a rescue and get more?

"How is letting your dogs back into the house *my* job?"

"You were the one who let them out!"

"It seemed that was what they wanted, and I didn't care either way." He jerked his thumb toward Nelle. "But I knew this one would be really annoyed if those things shit in the house, so I let them out."

"He's right," Nelle calmly agreed. "I would have been annoyed." She crinkled her nose. "The smell. Ech."

Rutowski stormed toward the front door. "If something has happened to my dogs—"

"Then you should get smarter dogs."

She spun around, glowering at Keane. *"You sent them out alone onto a street with tigers!"*

"My cousins don't want your ball-licking canines. Maybe if they were goats . . ." He glanced at Nelle. "People have pet goats, right?"

Sensing that Keane was not having a good morning, and not wanting the old badgers pissing him off any more than necessary considering the day she'd been planning and needed his assistance with, she asked, "Is there something specific you ladies want? Or are you just here to annoy everyone with all that perfume?"

Álvarez, Yoon, and Lenkov looked at Rutowski, and she, after taking a very long moment to silently glare at Nelle, said, "I'm not dealing with any of these basketball-playing bitches. Let's go."

As one, they all walked out of the house, slamming the door behind them.

"My, they are free-wheeling with that word."

"I'd say that it was because they've been hanging around a lot of wolves for decades," Finn reasoned. "But honestly, I think they just use it about any females they don't like."

"I'm just glad they're gone," Keane muttered.

"Now, see?" Nelle teased him. "The last few minutes could have totally been avoided if you'd just taken me up on my offer last night."

"What are you talking about?"

"If you'd slept with me, you'd be so much more relaxed."

"Oh, my God!" Keane exploded, his brothers' eyes wide in surprise.

"Look how tense you are right now. As if you're about to snap. Cats should never be this brittle unless they're old and about to die."

Rubbing his face with both hands, he growled out, "Nelle—"

"Even if you're not going to sleep with me, you should definitely sleep with *somebody*."

"I don't want anyone else."

Startled, Nelle immediately looked at his brothers, but they were already getting up and leaving the room. Neither wanted to be involved in this. Not that she blamed them.

"Now everyone is going to know you love me," she told him.

"I do not love you, and you completely misunderstood—"

"I didn't misunderstand anything."

"Shut. *Up*," he snarled, his jaw clenching and unclenching.

Finally, he said, "I didn't mean it that way. What I said. I meant . . . I don't want anyone at all. Too much on my mind."

"Okay."

"So stop staring at me."

"I can give you moon eyes, if you'd prefer."

He looked at her. "Moon eyes?"

She tipped her head to the side, opened her eyes wide, and blinked at him several times while hitting him with a small, shy smile she'd learned to do from Japanese anime.

Keane snorted a laugh and quickly looked away.

190   *Shelly Laurenston*

* * *

Charlie was handing out treats to her bear-neighbors when Tracey Rutowski walked up to her and demanded, "Where are my dogs?"

"Well—" was all Charlie got out before the impatient female pushed past her—her big badger shoulder ramming into Charlie's even bigger badger-wolf shoulder—and stormed into Charlie's rental house. A few seconds later, Rutowski's three friends ran after her.

"Sorry, sorry," one of them said. "We've got her. No worries."

Once they all disappeared inside, one of the grizzlies waiting outside her house for treats sweetly offered, "We can kill those women for you, sweetie. Just say the word."

The other bears in front of her house all grumbled in agreement, but it honestly wouldn't help. The more annoying a honey badger was, the harder they were to kill.

"Don't worry about it, Mrs. Brooks. But thank you."

Charlie followed the older She-badgers into her house.

She didn't know why Rutowski was worried. No way could Charlie keep the woman's five, perfectly trained Belgian Malinois that had wandered into her yard early this morning. Not if she wanted to continue living with Berg. He kept telling her, "No more dogs!" But it wasn't really her fault. Dogs just liked her, and she liked them. And all the dogs she'd taken in permanently had all needed homes. They were street dogs that had been scrounging for food and living in filth. She wasn't okay with that. Thankfully, Berg wasn't against dogs as a whole. He and his siblings had one of their own. Some giant Russian breed his mother bred and raised. She would send them a new puppy when the old dog died. The triplets mostly used their dogs for general home protection, since the large dogs were used in Russia to hunt bears and guard prisoners, but they treated them well and even petted them sometimes.

"You're obsessed with strays," Berg would still complain when another dog he didn't recognize wandered by him. But Charlie didn't think that was fair. She simply refused to ignore suffering. How could she?

"Hey, Zé," she said to the jaguar just waking up on top of the china cabinet in the dining room. She didn't know why he ended up there most mornings, still in his shifted cat form, but he'd only recently discovered that he was an actual shifter. Maybe he enjoyed doing a little stalking at night before finding higher ground to get some sleep. Charlie couldn't shift, so she had no idea what his thinking was, but Zé had hooked up with Max and deserved a safe space to wake up every day. Even if it was the cabinet in her rented home.

Walking past the dining room table, she brushed her hand through the hair of Kyle Jean-Louis. A jackal with genius artistic skills and a disturbing level of psychology knowledge for an eighteen-year-old. He'd been crashing at her house for a while now. Apparently it was hard for him to "create" with his other siblings around. He had been close friends to Stevie for more than a decade, so it didn't seem like a problem for him to stay at the house for a little while, too.

"Got any plans today, Kyle?" she asked.

"Just more disappointment," he said around a mouthful of chocolate muffin.

The kid had been struggling with his art or whatever, and Charlie knew how frustrating that could be, because she'd seen it with Stevie. Which was another reason she didn't mind him staying at the house. She knew how bad that kind of doubt and strain could be on a young mind. Even one as arrogant as Kyle's. He was still a kid, but prodigies took their work so seriously that to dismiss his stress was just a recipe for trouble.

"As long as you're remaining positive, kid," she teased.

"Was that CeCe Álvarez that just walked through here?" he asked.

"Yes. Want to meet her?" Apparently the She-badger was some well-known artist, and her work sold for six to seven figures apiece.

"Meet her? Why?"

"She's a fellow artist, right? Maybe she has some ideas for getting you through your current slump? Oh. Or are you a fan? Are you shy about meeting her?"

"I'm not a fan."

"I see."

Chewing another bite of his muffin, he glanced up at the ceiling,

192   *Shelly Laurenston*

then said, "I've always found her work a little derivative. Honestly, Basquiat did it better, and her particular brand of politics is *so* obvious. I find it irritating. Honestly, if I wanted to see some random artist's political stance, I'd check out Picasso again. Some people think he actually had something to say."

"Okay," Charlie said, keeping her tone light. "Don't ever say any of that in front of Álvarez, you know . . . ever. In your lifetime."

"But—"

"No, no. It's rude. We both know it's rude and, unlike your big sister, I am not going to have hours-long discussions with you, debating if saying something like that to a fellow artist is actually rude or not. Instead, I will happily beat you. Without shame or guilt. Just like I do with Max when she gets mouthy. Understand?"

"Yes."

"Good."

Charlie moved away from the kid and to her kitchen. But she stopped in the doorway and stared. At the kitchen table sat her half-sister, Nat; Shay's young daughter, Dani; Stevie's panda, Shen; and Max's best buddy, Dutch, a wolverine that Max, Stevie, and Charlie had known since high school. They were all eating breakfast and chatting; Nat was speaking sign language to Dani, who easily responded back in ASL.

Besides the fact that Charlie loved how the ten-year-old had already been taught another language with the help of her uncles so she could always be close to her aunt, Charlie also realized something possibly much more important . . .

She did collect strays.

Dear God! It was just like Berg had said. Her house was literally filled with strays that she'd blindly welcomed into her home. Was she an animal hoarder? Would the neighbors soon complain about the smell until the house was condemned by the city? And she was forced to live under a bridge like the strays she'd attempted to save?

Moments from going into a full-blown panic about her future under a bridge—where was her valium? Her doctor had given her valium just for these moments—Stevie walked into the kitchen from her basement lair, where she'd been attempting to produce a counteragent to the poison the de Medicis had been using in an attempt to kill as many honey badgers as possible.

Throwing her arms wide, Stevie announced, "I'm a failure, and we're all going to die! *And it will be all my fault!*"

Instead of staying quiet, Dutch joked, "I see those new drugs your doc has you on are working great, Stevie-weevie!"

Dutch laughed at his own joke until he caught sight of Charlie in the doorway. He pushed away from the table and announced, "If you'll excuse me. I'm going to now go outside and run into a tree."

"I better hear the thump," Charlie warned before the back screen door closed behind him.

Pausing from eating from his bowl of raw bamboo with milk, Shen asked, "He's running into a tree?"

"When I still lived with the Pack," Charlie explained, grabbing Dutch's bowl and putting it into the sink, "I used to throw him into trees any time he pissed me off. He has a surprisingly hard head, so it never really affected him, but it usually did the job of curbing his tongue. Now what's going on, Stevie?"

"Well—" Stevie began, but Charlie raised a finger, stopping her words. She listened carefully until she heard a loud *thump* from the yard. With a nod of approval, Charlie said, "Sorry, sweetie." She motioned to the others in the room. "Could you guys give me and Stevie a moment?"

Shen grabbed his bowl of bamboo and stood. He leaned down, kissing Stevie on the forehead before whispering against her skin, "I love you." Without another word, he walked out.

Dani started to follow, saw that Nat wasn't because she was too busy on her phone, and went back to grab her aunt's arm and pull her toward the back door.

"I can't even hear them!" Nat complained, but she could read lips better than she let on. So the kid was being wise beyond her years.

"Okay," Charlie said, when they were alone. "What's going on?"

"What if I can never figure it out?" Stevie asked Charlie. Although she could hear the panic in her sister's voice, she could also sense the panic. It came off the badger-tiger hybrid in giant waves. Like a tsunami. "What if all the honey badgers die, and it's all my fault? What then?"

Giving herself a few seconds to think, Charlie walked over to the counter and slapped at the grizzly paw reaching through the narrow window to grab whatever Charlie had cooling on it.

"Wait until I bring treats out, please," she reminded the interloper.

She then walked over to the window that looked out over the side yard.

Relieved to see Dani and the weirdly sensitive Rutowski chatting—with actual smiles—while the kid petted the five Malinois at Rutowski's feet, Charlie felt she could now relax. Rutowski's friends and Nat were silently using the lounge chairs around the pool, so she didn't have to worry about that dynamic either. Good.

She glanced at Stevie. "Want a cinnamon muffin?"

"I'm not hungry."

"It has a strudel topping," she said in a singsong voice.

Stevie glanced off. "Still warm?"

"Of course."

Her sister angrily stomped over to the kitchen table and sat down, arms folded over her chest. "Fine, then."

Charlie put a plate of four regular-sized muffins in front of Stevie and then gave her a steaming hot mug of coffee. While allowing her sister a few seconds to enjoy the first muffin, Charlie poured herself a cup of coffee and sat down on the other side of the table.

"Okay. Talk to me." Charlie ordered, after taking a sip of the French brew.

"I can't figure out this poison that they've been using against honey badgers. I've looked at everything, and I've just run out of ideas. How can I create an antivenom if I don't know how they made the venom in the first place?"

"You're getting frustrated."

"*Very.* I thought about burning the house down to hide my failure, but I knew you wouldn't like that."

"I really wouldn't."

"But I feel like such a loser."

"What did I tell you about using that word to describe yourself and not just our father?"

She sighed. "That you'd make me kiss Max on the cheek and tell her how much I love and respect her."

"Is that what you want?"

"You know I don't."

"Then stop it. You haven't failed. You probably just need more information."

"Where can I get that? It's not like I can find a de Medici and ask them where they got this shit from."

When Charlie saw her sister's gaze move to a spot behind her, she quickly told her, "Stevie MacKilligan, you are *not* going to track down the de Medicis and ask them anything."

"What? No. I would never—"

"Don't lie to me, Stevie-anna."

"That is *not* my name."

Chapter 15

Keane pulled on a black T-shirt and dark blue sweatpants. He grabbed his equipment bag and walked out of the room his brother shared with Mads. He'd showered and gotten dressed as quickly as possible, wanting to get back into the city and to practice early, the way he liked. That hadn't been happening as it should of late. Too much going on. But if he got there early, he could get some additional stuff done. What he really wanted was to at least get into the playoffs this year. The last few seasons hadn't exactly been about winning. More like about not dying of embarrassment.

He quickly walked down the stairs, passing that full-blood coyote heading up to the bedroom Keane had just left. The animal smelled like strawberries, and he realized that Mads had washed that canine with the same shampoo that was in the bathroom he'd used.

It annoyed him more that he smelled just like a coyote than it did that Mads was washing wild animals! Although both were ridiculous!

Keane had just entered the hallway when, heading to the front door, Nelle stepped in front of him. She had on denim shorts and bright, white sneakers that appeared fresh out of the box. The cropped white T-shirt showed off her toned abs, including what looked like a knife scar on her left side.

It was a perfect late-summer outfit, and it was driving him crazy! Especially the scar. He really liked the scar.

Dammit!

TO KILL A BADGER 197

"Oh, good," she said, lifting her foot so she could scratch her ankle. "You're ready."

"Ready? To do what?"

"I have to deal with some things today, and you're coming with me."

"No, I'm not. I'm going to practice."

"We should stick together."

"Why?"

"Charlie said."

Apparently if Charlie said anything, it was law?

"I don't care what Charlie said."

"You should."

"Because. . . ?"

"She's been *baking*."

"I don't know what that's supposed to mean."

"Still? *Really?*"

She glanced at the diamond-encrusted watch she wore on her wrist. "We better go, so we can stop at Charlie's first. Maybe get you a muffin."

"I've already eaten, and I need to get to practice."

"You need to practice pouncing on people when their backs are turned? Because that seems like something already built into your DNA."

"Coach will get pissed if I'm not there today."

"*I'm* not going to practice today. Do you think I won't have to hear about that later from Mads? But I'm willing to put up with that to save the lives of our people."

He had to say it. "You are so full of shit."

The grin spread across her beautiful face. "I am!"

She came around to his side and slid her arm through his. He tried to pull away, but she yanked him forward with that surprising amount of strength he'd noticed yesterday.

"While you were getting dressed, I went outside and offered to get your mother some coffee," Nelle told him as they walked through the living room toward the front door. "Her response was rather unpleasant."

"Of course she was unpleasant. She's a *cat*."

"I come from an unpleasant people, as well." They stepped out of the house. "But we still have basic manners."

"Only when you're getting ready to manipulate and steal from your next target."

Nelle looked up at him, like she was ready to correct such a disparaging remark about her "people." But she only shrugged instead.

"You know, I can walk without you clinging to me like a spider monkey."

"Rude like your mother, I see." She unhooked her arm from his.

He silently let out a relieved breath until she took his hand in hers, intertwining their fingers. An action which only made things absolutely worse!

"Better?" she asked with that damn smile.

"No."

"Great. Let's go."

She tried to walk away, but he pulled her back. "Where? Where are we going that I have to miss practice? Are you going to try to shoot people again? And where's Charles? Isn't he your protection? And do you even need protection? I mean, *what is happening?*"

Nelle released his hand, so she could take the tiny purse with its tiny chain strap off her shoulder and pull out the phone from inside. Did she have anything else in that ridiculously small bag? He was thinking that other than maybe a credit card, she probably didn't. She couldn't fit anything else in there!

She held the phone in front of his face and waited.

"What am I supposed to be looking at?"

"You can't read it?"

"No. I can't read Chinese."

She gasped. "It's Nihongo! You don't know Nihongo?"

"I don't know what that word is."

Nelle let out a long, labored sigh. He hated when she made him feel stupid. He wasn't stupid! Sometimes he had memory loss after colliding into a seven-four grizzly with a grudge, but that didn't mean he was stupid!

"It's Japanese. This is in Japanese. How do you not know that?"

"Because I know one language. English." He thought a moment and added, "American English." Thought a moment longer, then, "New York English." Blinked. "Long Island English." He nodded. "Yeah, I know *Long Island* English."

Clearly disgusted, she stuffed her phone back into her tiny purse, put the tiny strap over her shoulder so the bag hung right under her armpit, and—again!—intertwined her fingers with his.

"Just trust me," she said.

"I don't. I don't trust you."

"That's okay. Let's just go."

He refused to move, but that didn't stop Nelle from yanking him forward again.

Not wanting a fistfight with a badger, Keane went along. But he quickly noticed their little discussion in front of the house had attracted the attention of the entire Malone clan. Well . . . they had attracted the attention of the females. But it was Nelle on her own that had attracted the attention of the males. The lusting, worthless males! His kin. How he hated them.

Deciding it wasn't the right time to slap his cousins around, he kept walking but picked up speed so that they could get out of this particular area a little faster. But they'd barely gotten ten feet from the door of Mads's house when his mother stepped out of one of the RVs, her eyes going wide at the sight of another son's hand clasped with yet another honey badger.

That poor woman. What she must be going through.

The expression on her face gave Keane flashbacks to the time his mother had terrified his first girlfriend when he was fifteen. Laura De Cicio had run from his house, never to return. Or talk to him again in the hallways of their high school. Or even look at him in trig class. Not that he blamed her. In the end, she'd finally just changed schools.

"And what's going on here?" his mother asked, gaze moving from his face to the hand gripping his and back to his face. "Hhhmmh?"

Keane didn't know how to answer that question, but he didn't have to, because Nelle volunteered, "Your son is madly in love with me, and I haven't quite figured out how to shake him from my life yet. But you know what? Maybe I shouldn't shake him. Maybe we were meant to be together. Forever. True soul mates."

His mother stared at Nelle a moment before returning her gaze to his. "Keane?"

Again, Keane didn't know what to say. So he just stood there, silently panicking, gawking at his mother. He'd been hit by four polar bears at the same time, and that had done less damage than Nelle Zhao and her words.

When his mother continued to wait for him to say something—anything!—he let out a confused, "Uhhhh . . ."

"You know, Lisa—"

"Lisa?" his mother repeated, shocked "some whore"—the word she would probably use later to her sisters when she told this story—had the nerve to use her first name like they were girlfriends.

"—we're actually running quite late," Nelle said. "But we'll definitely check in with you sometime tonight. We can discuss the plans of our upcoming wedding. You are going to *love* working with my mother on the color scheme and bridesmaid dress designs!"

Keane didn't think he could move, but that didn't stop Nelle from yanking him away from his stunned mother.

"What did you do?" he asked when they were crossing the RV-filled street.

"I lied to your mother so we could distract her from our business. I do the same thing with my own mother. Although I usually involve Max if I really need to un-focus her." She glanced at him. "She hates Max."

"Everyone hates Max."

"Not true. I find her delightful."

"I think that's because you're clinically insane."

"Doubtful," she insisted, before leaning in and whispering, "I haven't heard the voice of Satan coming from the family cat in *years*."

★ ★ ★

TO KILL A BADGER 201

Lisa Zaya-Sarnai Malone watched the smart-ass little honey badger walk across the street with her son. That's when her sisters "attacked."

"Are you okay, hon?" her older sister, on her right, asked with fake concern.

"That was just so awful for us to watch," her younger sister on her left lied.

"So awful."

"I thought for sure you would have ripped her tiny little badger head off. Especially when she talked about wedding plans." Her baby sister dramatically cringed, briefly showing her fangs. "You poor thing!"

"And now you've lost a total of *three* sons to badgers," her older sister said with a sad, fake sigh of sorrow. "You must be *devastated*."

"I would be devastated, I guess . . ." Lisa began.

"But?"

"But that one is rich."

Her older sister blinked. "How rich?"

"Gold-toilet-in-her-Fifth-Avenue-apartment-type rich. Her-family-has-a-fleet-of-jets rich. They-have-a-giant-yacht-with-a-fleet-of-smaller-boats-attached-until-the-orcas-destroyed-it rich."

Her baby sister swallowed. "Oh."

"Yeahhh." She grinned at her stunned sisters. "My son with a girl so rich he'll never have to work a day again in his life, and all my grandchildren will be running the world by the time they're in their early twenties." Lisa stepped back and asked, "And how *are* my wonderful nieces and nephews? Happy? Satisfied with life and in their marriages? Gosh, I hope so. They're all so deserving and, of course, you two will have less to worry about as you gently age."

Smiling, Lisa returned to the RV, a morning news show, and a cup of hot coffee that she'd made without that little bitch-badger's help waiting just for her.

"Do I attract strays?" Charlie asked.

Stevie looked up from her second muffin—it was *so* good—and frowned. Usually, when Stevie had a meltdown, all Charlie did was focus totally and exclusively on her. The fact that her big sister had something else on her mind for once, something personal, and was willing to change the topic of conversation made Stevie feel downright normal! It was *awesome!*

"Of course you collect strays," Stevie told her, glancing down at the mixed-breed canine standing by Stevie's chair, hoping to get some of her muffin. It was a good guess on the dog's part. She could be a messy eater. "Look at this thing," she added, gesturing at the dog.

"No, no. I mean . . . do I attract people-strays?"

"You have a house *filled* with people-strays."

Her sister winced. "But isn't that weird?"

"Charlie, everything about us is weird. But, honestly, no. I don't think it's weird at all. You make people feel safe and comfortable, so they *want* to be around you. That's a rare gift." Stevie thought a moment and realized, "I just make people feel anxious, and Max never lets anyone feel comfortable for too long. We're disasters," she sighed out. "But you. . . ? You're just like your mom."

"I am?"

"Oh, my God! Yes! Before my mother dropped me off at your apartment, I never felt comfortable anywhere. *Especially* with my mother and her parents. But as soon as I met your mom . . ." She shrugged. "I knew I'd finally found a home. And when it was just the three of us, nothing changed. I still felt I was home. And that was because of you. It was definitely not because of Max. Why are you asking, anyway?"

"Just worried. I don't think Berg is used to being around this many people."

"Are you kidding?" Stevie shook her head. "The man lived in his mother's womb for nearly nine months with two other people. Then, when he came of age, instead of moving to some woods in the middle of Minnesota somewhere, he got them a house they could all share, on a bear-friendly street. People aren't his problem. Your dogs, however . . ."

"But the dogs actually need me."

"That's why I have cats. I can't be responsible for the multiple and varied needs of dogs. I honestly don't know how you do it without snapping from the constant pressure. Speaking of which . . ." She looked around the room. "Where is that kitten I took in?"

"In the walls."

"Is she starving to death?"

"No. She comes out at night, and Nat feeds her."

Stevie lifted her hands and dropped them. "See how wonderfully easy cats are to deal with? Start rescuing cats instead of dogs. I'm sure Berg would be fine with that."

"Yeah . . . I'm not sure that's accurate either."

They walked into the kitchen of Charlie's house and stopped right in the doorway.

"Morning," Nelle happily greeted. Keane merely gave a noncommittal nod.

The two sisters sat at a table with coffee and muffins between them. One of Charlie's stray dogs was trying to beg food off of Stevie.

Eyeing Nelle and Keane, Charlie relaxed into her chair, slinging one arm over the back before asking, "Why are you two holding hands?"

Keane had been trying to shake Nelle's hand off since he knew they were no longer seen by his mother. She'd simply refused to let go. She was sure he was wondering why that was.

And as always, her answer to that question would be, *why not?*

Besides, he reminded her of a toddler cousin she'd once been forced to babysit for a day back in high school. He'd tended to go off and steal things from stores, but he wasn't subtle about it, and the whole thing quickly became embarrassing. So she'd held on to the little brat's hand, because she'd be the one to get in trouble if the child got caught stealing again. And, like Keane, he also tried to shake her off.

"He's madly in love with me," Nelle happily lied.

"She won't let me go! Why are all of you badgers so strong?"

"Hush now. You're fine." She looked at Charlie. "Everything okay?"

"Stevie's just frustrated."

"Max again? Or the squirrel?"

"Neither." Stevie took a bite of her muffin, and muttered words around the food in her mouth.

Nelle looked at Charlie again. "What?"

"She can't figure out the formula for that poison that took down Tock for a while. She wants to get some more but—"

"More? More than what we picked up when we took down that ship a couple of days ago?"

Stevie's head snapped up, and she said something, but she'd already taken another bite of her muffin, so all she managed to do was spray crumbs at Nelle and Keane.

Now just disgusted, Nelle again focused on Charlie.

"What ship?" Charlie asked for Stevie.

"The one we hit with the crones—"

"Please stop calling them that."

"They said they found more of that stuff, and they were going to give it to Stevie. They didn't?"

Growling, Stevie jumped up from her chair and ran out the back door. The screen door slammed behind the She-badger, and Nelle could hear angry bickering that quickly turned into one of Stevie's weird, window-shaking, hiss-roars. A moment after that, she heard the small feet of what she was guessing was Max MacKilligan running across the floor above, a window being thrown open, and a screamed, *"I've got her!"* before Max landed hard outside the kitchen window in the side yard. Once again, she'd managed to miss her sister completely and hit the unforgiving ground instead.

Shaking her head, Nelle refocused on Charlie. "So we're going out to get some information. Might help us track down where the de Medicis are hiding. What I've learned so far is that they're definitely now in the States."

"Makes sense."

"If we can track them down, though, and deal with the oldest sons . . ." She shrugged. "Maybe we can end this before it even starts."

"It's already started because of you," Keane complained.

"Hush."

"Stop saying that."

"Let's hope that ends it." Charlie didn't seem that convinced, but that was okay. Nelle dealt with this kind of shit so Charlie didn't have to. "Do you two need any extra backup?"

"No. Keane is good enough for this."

"Gee. Thanks," he muttered, finally giving up on shaking loose of her hand.

"But it would be great if you could let the football coaches know he's doing something important and won't be in for practice. I don't want him to get in trouble because of me."

"Yeah, I'll tell them."

"You don't need to do that," Keane quickly said to Charlie.

"Yes, she does," Nelle informed him.

"My brothers can do it."

"Not well," she insisted. "Charlie can handle this for us. Yes?"

"Of course," Charlie replied. "It won't be a problem."

Charlie had a way of imparting information that had others not wanting to fight with her. When she handled school business for Max and Stevie, there were teachers and even a principal that hated when she came through their door. From what Nelle could tell, Charlie was never rude or even raised her voice. But she had a way of looking at a person that could be, in a word, concerning. They often wanted to get rid of her so badly, they would agree to damn-near anything.

Nelle smiled up at the cat, which seemed to annoy him even more, and said, "See? Handled."

"I didn't ask you to handle."

"But I did anyway."

"While you're out, watch your backs and stay very alert," Charlie warned. "We don't know who works for the de Medicis."

"Yes. Of course."

"Anything else you need me to handle?"

"No. I don't need you to do anything else. At all. I've got this in hand."

Nelle heard the screen door open again, and Stevie happily bounced up the small set of stairs, her arms wrapped around the metal briefcase the older badgers had been carrying when they'd left that ship. With a

206   *Shelly Laurenston*

huge grin on her pretty face, Stevie did a full spin in the middle of the kitchen, her bright pink summer dress billowing out and showing the white shorts she wore under it—unlike Álvarez, who wore nothing under her clothes—then headed back downstairs.

A minute later, Max came into the room. Blood poured from her nose, and a lump was already developing on the right side of her forehead.

Charlie poured out a cup of coffee from the pot on the table and pushed it toward Max.

"You really need to stop flinging yourself out windows every time you hear Stevie hiss-roar."

"I am trying to save the *world*." Max paused to glare at Nelle after she'd snort-laughed. "Because if she snaps . . ."

"Once she has the baby," Charlie explained, "I'm sure she'll be—"

"How can you be okay with her having a baby right now?" Max exploded, making the big cat standing next to Nelle jump a little. *"How? It's insane!"*

From what Nelle had heard privately, Stevie wasn't planning on having kids of her own any time soon, but she'd been torturing her sister with the idea for days.

As someone who'd grown up with siblings, Nelle knew better than to intervene between sisters. But no one else told Max she had nothing to worry about either, because it was nice to see Stevie messing with her head for once. It was usually the other way around since the time Nelle had met Max all those years ago. It was Stevie's due to torment the master of torment.

"Max—" Charlie began.

"Seriously! *Who knows what kind of freak she'll have!*"

"Hey!" Charlie barked, pointing a finger at Max. "Do not disparage Stevie's panda-honey badger-tiger baby! You'll be the aunt to that thing one day, and you better love it! No matter what unholy beast Stevie births!"

Nelle turned her head to hide her smile, brushing her face against Keane's bulging bicep. He smelled nice, and he didn't seem to mind, so she sort of stayed that way for a bit.

"When that thing turns nasty," Max ominously warned, "don't come crying to me!"

Nelle had her head buried against Keane's arm, and he had no idea why. Then Max was standing in front of him, pointing her finger up near his face—she'd have to go on her tiptoes and stretch her arm completely out to reach his face—and demanding to know, "Are you okay with Stevie having a demon baby?"

He knew that saying "of course not" would be what would soothe her in this moment. Instead, he said, "Yes, I'm completely fine with it. I think it would be great."

Keane didn't make that statement with any sort of real conviction—because, again, he hadn't been listening and had no idea why Stevie would be having a demon baby—but it was enough to send Max stomping off while swearing. So much swearing.

He could have asked after she'd left what was going on, but that seemed like too much trouble. Also, he didn't care. Besides, his niece ran in and stopped long enough to hug him around the leg before heading into the dining room for some breakfast.

Behind Dani came Rutowski.

"I love that kid," she announced to the room. "She is so great with my dogs!"

Keane rolled his eyes. He wasn't okay with his niece's sudden love of dogs. She was a cat. She should hate dogs on principle.

"You Malones did a great job with that kid." Rutowski smiled at Keane. "You should be proud."

"I'm not."

"I've had dogs since I was a little girl," Rutowski continued, ignoring him. "They make you more empathetic, more loving. Teach you about the cycle of life, love, and death in the best way possible."

"My niece is an apex predator. When she's an adult, she *will be* death. And dogs should be nothing more than whimpering toothpicks she uses to get the bits of bison out of her teeth."

"Wow," Rutowski said, eyes wide. "You don't say much but, like your dad, when you do speak . . . it's mighty powerful. And weird."

208   *Shelly Laurenston*

Keane froze at the She-badger's words. Nelle squeezed his hand as if she sensed the sudden tension.

"You knew my father?" he softly asked.

In that moment, with that simple phrase, "like your father," everything about Keane changed. She was worried she'd have to hold him up. That She-badger had no idea how impactful it would be that she had known Keane's father. But Nelle understood. Not simply because of the love she had for her own father and understanding the devastation it would have caused if she'd lost him. Especially at such a young age.

But also because she knew Max and her sisters. The three had lost Charlie's mom when they were so very young and it had affected absolutely everything they had done since then. How could it not?

Making it even worse for Keane, though, was that—from what she'd overheard from his brothers—no one wanted to talk about his dad. Either because they couldn't for reasons involving their father's work at the time, or because talking about it hurt too much. Like for their mother.

So, to meet someone willing to talk about his dad with such ease . . .

Nelle, desperately wanting to help, leaned in and held on to Keane's hand. Then she, in that moment, did nothing more than hope. She *hoped* this crazy female didn't say anything that would make this entire situation awful. "Of course I knew your father," the She-badger replied with a warm smile. "He threw me off a building once."

Oh, for fuck's sake!

When Nelle glared hard at her, Rutowski quickly added, "It was to save my life, but it was traumatic in the moment." She picked up a half-eaten muffin from off a plate on the kitchen table and said, "You look so much like him. It kind of weirded me out when I first saw you. I thought I was having one of my flashbacks."

"Flashbacks?" Keane asked.

"Since I mixed Gaboon viper venom with this amazing Pakistani weed . . . I occasionally get flashbacks. Or maybe they're hallucinations. Or waking nightmares. I'm not really sure. It was the nineties, so it was a wild time."

"Are you CIA like Keane's dad?" Charlie asked.

Rutowski laughed until she realized no one was laughing with her. "Oh. You're serious."

"Yeah."

"Well . . . I think one or two may have suggested me and my girls for a job with the CIA, but apparently they were told that was an"—she made air quotes with her forefingers—"'insane suggestion,' and they should rethink their 'life choices' if they really think that's a good idea. And 'how could you even suggest such a thing?' It got pretty rude. So we just stayed independent—"

"Pains in the ass?" Charlie suggested.

"I was going to say contractors, but it really depends on who you talk to."

"Anyway," Rutowski continued.

Anyway? Did this female just dismiss his father with an *anyway*? The cat Keane could never forget? Did not want to forget. But sometimes whose face he could barely remember without the help of the few pictures they had around the house. Everyone said Keane looked just like him, but he didn't know. He did know he looked more Mongolian than Irish, and his father was nothing *but* Irish. But honestly, he didn't want to think about it too much. Because he couldn't help but wonder how hard it must be for his mom to see her husband's face every day when she looked at her eldest son.

Someone squeezed his bicep, and he realized it was Nelle. She didn't say anything. Didn't even look at him, since she was now talking directly to Rutowski. But somehow, she knew. She knew he was about to spiral into a quagmire of depression from which he might have a little trouble digging himself out of. He tried not to get into that quagmire too often. Tried to hide it from the rest of the family. They all had enough to worry about. It wasn't easy, though. To not sit around, being depressed. Football, though, helped with that. All the

210 *Shelly Laurenston*

work he had to do to keep the team going. That's why he loved the game so much. It never let him wallow in his own misery for long. Not when three grizzlies were trying to take out his quarterback and he had to stop them with nothing but his body and his rage.

"I have a contact," Nelle was telling Rutowski. "She might have some information. About where to find the de Medicis. We're sure they're in America now that they can't go home."

"Oh, they're definitely here."

Rutowski made that statement confidently as she ate a half-devoured muffin that Keane assumed Stevie had left behind. Who ate people's half-eaten food? Not when there was fresh, uneaten muffins all over the damn kitchen.

And also, hold on a second. This woman knew something about the de Medicis, but she hadn't told them immediately? Why? Was she playing with them? Withholding information for her own benefit? A move, he'd recently learned, was kind of typical of the manipulative honey badger.

Or was she just kind of a dingbat because she used to smoke weed combined with snake venom?

"You know where they are?" Nelle asked.

"No. But I know they're here. I meant to tell you guys that earlier, but I got distracted." She wagged a finger at Keane. "That was his fault."

"How was that *my* fault?"

"You were the one who let my dogs out in the middle of the night and didn't track them to ensure their safety. I was distracted by that! My poor babies! Where were they?"

Keane looked down at the five dogs sitting behind her. Five powerful, well-trained protection dogs that could easily kill a man, and he was supposed to worry about *them*?

"So, yeah," she pushed. "Your fault."

The badger grabbed another muffin—uneaten—took a big bite, and then said around a mouthful of food, "The de Medicis are here, but we don't know where yet. But more importantly, I have an idea."

"What idea?" Charlie asked.

"How we can get real information. Real help. That will allow us to shut down the de Medicis for good."

"And how do we do that?"

"Let's discuss over coffee and more of these muffins!"

Rutowski motioned to the coffee pot and pulled Stevie's chair out, about to sit.

"Come on, Charlie, let's sit down and—*ack*!"

Nelle moved so quickly that Keane didn't realize what was happening until she'd grabbed the older woman by the throat and thrown her out of the room, those five dogs chasing after their owner.

Standing in front of Charlie, Nelle smiled in a way that was meant to be soothing but Keane only found disturbing. What the hell was going on?

"You know what, Charlie," Nelle said in a gratingly chipper voice, "you have a ton of bears out there. Hungry bears. You know how they get when they're hungry. Why don't you finish passing out all these lovely treats, and I'll go talk to Ms. Rutowski. Handle whatever idea she has. A stupid idea, I'm sure, but don't want to insult her."

Since when?

"Would you mind, Nelle?" Charlie asked, appearing deeply relieved. "She seems like a *lot*."

"She is a lot, and I don't mind at all. Anything for you, you know that."

"Thanks, Nelle. Just let me know if you need me involved in anything."

"I absolutely will!"

Grabbing a cake box, Charlie exited out the back door. When Nelle faced him, again, the smile she'd had for Charlie was already gone, replaced by what Keane had now learned was her pissed-off expression.

"Fucking crones!" she snarled, storming out of the kitchen.

"I don't think Charlie wants us calling them that."

Chapter 16

"What do you think you're doing?" Nelle quietly demanded once she'd stepped onto the sidewalk in front of Charlie's rental house and faced the She-badger she was beginning to truly dislike.

"What am I doing? I'm trying to have a discussion with Charlie."

"That's what I thought, and that's unacceptable."

"Unacceptable? Who are you? My mother?"

"I can already tell that you are a problem-causer, and I'm not going to let that happen."

"Ugggghh! What did I do now?" Rutowski asked, sounding like a disgruntled teen. And, yet, there was something about the woman that was so elegant; so solid and comfortable in who and what she was. From her expensive haircut that perfectly framed her face because she'd allowed her hair to naturally go gray and silver, to the designer jeans covering her ass. Nelle had a pair of the same ones from the designer herself, and one could only purchase them in Milan.

Still . . . there was a part of this elegant, married mother of four, who ran a mega-successful global art business, that was still a sixteen-year-old girl.

A whiny, *annoying* sixteen-year-old girl.

"Do you know what my job is?" Nelle asked Rutowski, glancing over as Keane came to stand by her side. She was a little surprised he'd followed her.

"I don't know," Rutowski replied, as if she had just been caught behind the high school locker rooms smoking cigarettes. "Something with a ball and your friends?"

"No. My job is to keep the world in balance. Not just my world, but the entire world. And do you know how I do that?"

"With obvious delusion? Because I don't think you have anything to do with keeping—"

"By managing Charlie, Max, and Stevie."

"How did *that* become your job?"

"From my family's earliest ancestors, we have been maintaining balance in the world."

"Are you talking about that emperor's concubine? Because I don't think she really had anything to do with—"

"And because that's also my job—"

"Being a concubine?"

"—I take this very seriously."

"I . . . I'm sorry. What's your point exactly?"

"My point, Ms. Rutowski, is that you don't come to Charlie with whatever crazy bullshit plan you've come up with while high off your ass."

"Who says I'm high?"

"I can smell the weed leaking from your pores."

"Grade-A weed, thank you very much."

Nelle leaned in a bit, took a sniff. "With vodka infused with. . . ?" She sniffed again. "Barba amarilla venom?"

"We didn't start drinking that until *after* I got my brilliant idea."

"See?" Nelle straightened; circled her forefinger at Rutowski. "This is what I'm talking about. *This* insanity is unacceptable. You can't go to Charlie with half-baked—"

"Baked," she laughed.

"—ideas and think that you won't cause problems. You will cause problems, and I can't have that."

"So . . . what does that mean to *me*? Because it's a great idea! I promise!"

Nelle didn't want to do this. She didn't want to have this con-

214   *Shelly Laurenston*

versation. This . . . person was irritating. More irritating than Nelle's mother, and that was saying something, because her mother drove her insane. But her mother, at least, was an adult! A full-fledged, smart adult. Not a teen in an old She-badger's body!

But she knew if she didn't step in now . . .

"Fine. Tell me your idea."

"Are you suggesting that you are going to *vet* my idea?"

"I'm not suggesting anything. That's *exactly* what I'm doing."

"I don't think—"

"It's either me now or Max later. And I can assure you that you do *not* want to deal with Max."

"I wouldn't, no." She smiled. "But Ox would. She hates that kid."

"Do you want my help or not?"

Another dramatic eye roll. "Fine," she said on a long sigh. "So what I'm thinking—"

"Is my uncle . . . *hitting* on my mom?"

Both startled out of their conversation, Nelle and Rutowski looked over at Keane. He was turned away from them, his gaze leveled to the other side of the street, where one of his uncles and his mother were quietly talking.

"Yes," Rutowski said, now on her tiptoes to see over Nelle's head. "I believe he is hitting on your mom. I recognize those old-school moves," she said to Nelle.

"It's his brother's widow!" Keane snarled. "And he's married! My aunt just took off to pick up her grandkids from day camp an hour ago!"

"Based on the body language alone, kid, I don't think your uncle cares where his wife is at the moment."

Keane growled, taking a dangerous step forward, before Nelle grabbed his arm and held him in place.

"We don't have time for any of that," she said to the cat, hoping he didn't get excessively angry. She could never hold him back if he released the true resentment he had toward his father's family.

"I wouldn't worry, kitty," Rutowski told Keane with a pat on his shoulder. "From what your father told me about your mother, I'm sure

TO KILL A BADGER   215

that She-cat knows exactly how to handle her in-laws." She smiled at Nelle, but it slowly faded. "Wait . . . what were we talking about?"

"Dear God."

The female really didn't remember. It had been five seconds, and she'd already forgotten! Was this caused by old age or Russian vodka infused with goddamn snake venom?

"Oh!" Rutowski snapped her fingers, her smile returning. "I remember now. My great idea."

"Fine," Nelle sighed. "Tell me your 'great idea.'"

"I don't think the air quotes were necessary, but this is too important to debate that point at the moment." Raising her hands, she announced, "We combine forces against the de Medicis."

Nelle gazed at the woman and waited for more. But when she kept smiling and saying nothing else . . .

"That's it? That's your great idea?"

"It's a wonderful idea."

"Lady, we've already combined forces with each other. The drugged-out old crones and the young, gorgeous She-badgers working together! It's like a romantic comedy."

"I'm not talking about *us*," she said with a tone that suggested Nelle was the stupid one.

"Then what are you talking about?"

"*Them.*"

"Do you understand that at this point, I simply want to beat you to death? Because you're being quite vague."

"I am?"

"*Yes.*"

She pressed her fingertips to her temples. "I should have had more coffee. You know, rather than the funnel-web spiders."

"That is *not* the hair of the dog that bit you, if that's what you were going for," she told Rutowski. "You should have had orange juice infused with cottonmouth instead. Wakes you up, but doesn't . . . you know . . ."

"Kill you?"

"Yes."

216 *Shelly Laurenston*

"I think I remember that." She moved her hands from her temples and rubbed her eyes. "Anyway, what I'm talking about is uniting *all* honey badger families to fight the de Medicis."

Nelle stared at Rutowski a brief second before she couldn't help herself—she burst out laughing.

"Are you fucking insane?"

Keane was about to shake Nelle off and go beat his uncle until he was nothing but a stain on the sidewalk when her loud, nearly hysterical laughter caught his attention.

"What?" Rutowski demanded. "What's so funny? That is a great idea."

"What that *is* is an idea that will *never* happen. There is no uniting all the badger families. That's not humanly possible."

"Yes, it is."

"Why can't you unite them?" Keane asked, actually curious. He figured he should know at least a little more about this species since his baby sister was half-badger, though he often pretended she wasn't.

"We're just not set up that way," Nelle explained to him. "We usually work with full-humans or one or two other badger families. For instance, my parents often help Streep's parents with their Vatican acquisitions."

"You mean the Catholic stuff they steal?"

"You say tomato. I say to—"

"I really think this could work," Rutowski cut in.

"It hasn't worked for millennia," Nelle replied. "Why would it magically work now?"

"Because now we have a badger-specific threat. The de Medicis are trying to decimate our entire population."

"So did Alexander the Great. They didn't join forces then."

"We also didn't have planes. Or the Internet. Times are different. Circumstances are different. And without the other organizations helping us—"

"You need to let that go."

"How do I let that go? I mean, I understand Katzenhaus not helping. Or BPC. But The Group? They were created to help *all* shifters. Are we not shifters? If you cut us, do we not bleed? If you punch us, do we not cry out? If you shoot us in the head—"

"Do we not get up and walk away with little to no brain damage?"

"True. But we're not immortal. My great-great-grandmother eventually died. She was one hundred and sixteen at the time, and one of her aunts is continuing to go strong in Poland, but still . . ." She waved her hands around. "It doesn't matter. We don't *need* The Group. We don't need the cats or BPC . . ."

Rutowski's words faded away, and she suddenly looked off into . . . nothing. She stood like that for nearly a minute, just staring at nothing. Finally, when it seemed Nelle couldn't stand it anymore, she waved her hand in front of the female's face.

"Hello?" she said. "Anyone still in there? Do I need to get you that orange juice infused with cottonmouth? I put some in Mads's wine-cellar fridge."

"I hope that's clearly marked," Keane told her, horrified.

"It is. Calm down." The She-badger was still staring off, so Nelle clapped her hands together. "Rutowski! Hel-*lo*!"

She blinked; came back to the moment. "Yes. Right. I'm here."

"What just happened?"

"Nothing."

Nelle's eyes narrowed. "Really? Because it seems as if—"

"High. Still high. I'm still high. That's all." She shook her head. "Right. Okay. So you'll handle it," Rutowski told Nelle.

"I'll handle what?"

"Getting the agreement of the most important families."

"Oh, I see," Nelle said, folding her arms in front of her chest. Keane knew that smug look on her face. He'd seen it often. The woman could be quite smug when she wanted to be. "You want *me* to corral my family into this ridiculous idea of yours, is that it?"

For a few seconds, Rutowski appeared truly confused. Keane thought maybe the venom and weed were still damaging her brain.

218 *Shelly Laurenston*

But then her expression cleared, and she just gazed at Nelle like she was this pitiful little thing she found on the side of the road. Like a lost kitten.

"Oh, sweetie . . ."

"*What?*" Nelle low-growled.

Rutowski winced a bit before replying, "You think the Zhaos are one of the most powerful badger families in the world?" She slowly shook her head and whispered, "They're not."

"Uh-oh," Keane muttered.

"Excuse me?" Nelle snapped.

"I know you *believe* your family is, and I'm sure in Asia they maybe are . . . a little."

"A little?"

"But they're really not."

"The Ming-Zhaos have built and destroyed ancient dynasties. We helped take down the Mongols." Nelle glanced at Keane. "No offense."

"It had to happen. Otherwise, we'd *all* just be distant cousins of Genghis Khan."

"We *are* a very powerful family," Nelle insisted.

"Your family is very wealthy. You pay for what you get. I'm looking for badgers to just unite. You know . . . for free." She smiled at Keane like they were friends. They weren't. "I do love a tight budget."

"So who do *you* think are the 'most important' families that are *not* related to me and can unite all or most honey badgers?"

"Again, not liking the air quotes, but my first suggestion is the Von Schäfer-Müllers of Hamburg. Although they're based out of France now."

"The Von whos?" Keane asked.

"German royalty," Nelle told him. "Absolute snobs that will help no one but themselves."

"Not always true," Rutowski argued. "They had to leave Germany in the thirties because Hitler was *not* a fan. And they were a big part of the French Resistance and the British spy network."

"Who else?" Nelle pushed.

"The Santiagos. Out of Cuba and Brazil, but with a lineage that dates back to the time of Philip the Second."

"Soooo . . . more European royalty?"

"Well, they're descended from that, but they're considered Latin American now. I mean, they were never *related* to Philip the Second. They just helped start a war with England by ensuring that Mary, Queen of Scots, lost her head. But the family's main point of contact these days lives in Needles, California."

"There's a place called Needles, California?" Keane asked.

"There is!"

"And who else?" Nelle wanted to know.

"The Joneses."

When silence followed, Keane asked, "And?"

"And what?"

"And just the Joneses? You're not going to provide a titillating backstory? There was no running from Hitler? Taking out the Romanovs? Messing with Genghis Khan? Dealing with all of Elizabeth the First's Catholic enemies? Nothing?"

Rutowski shrugged. "Nope. They're just the Joneses."

"In other words, the majority of the most influential families are from Europe and North America?" Nelle noted with some disgust.

"You should know better than I, Nelle Zhao, that Joneses are from absolutely *everywhere*."

"I truly believe none of that will work," Nelle finally told Rutowski.

"Okay. I'll see what Charlie thinks," she said, turning toward the house.

But with one hand on Keane's arm to keep him from wandering away since he wouldn't stop snarling at his uncle and mom, Nelle used her other hand to grab Rutowski by the face and force her to look directly into her eyes.

The badger gawked at the hand holding her before locking that shocked expression directly on Nelle.

"Yes?" she asked through pursed lips as Nelle squeezed her face.

220   *Shelly Laurenston*

"I need you to hear me," Nelle said slowly, so there was no misunderstanding. "You are *not* to speak directly to Charlie. About this or anything. Ever. She's baking."

"But my idea—"

"Is stupid. And a waste of time." She let out a sigh, rolled her eyes, but said, "And I'll handle it."

"You?"

"Yes. *Me.* She of the ineffectual Zhaos."

"I didn't say they were ineffectual. Ow!" Rutowski slapped Nelle's hand off her face. "You're breaking my jaw!"

"Because you're pissing me off. But I will do this, just to prove how wrong you are about your grand plan."

"Okay but, honestly, I can do it myself."

"Negotiating with someone like the Von Schäfer-Müllers requires a delicate hand. You are not delicate, Ms. Rutowski. You're a sledgehammer."

"I am not! I'll have you know, I have successfully worked with some of the most complicated and complex and *difficult* artists in the world. I actually got Mapplethorpe to take a picture of me and CeCe with our clothes on, which was a good thing, because he was unaware that we were underage at the time."

"That is a fascinating and disturbing story, and I don't care. *I'll* handle it."

"If you think it's not going to work, why—"

"Because we need to do *something,* and I can already tell you're going to do nothing but make a big deal out of this. So let me handle the Von Schäfer-Müllers. I'll rule them out, and we can then focus on other, more viable plans."

"Rule them out how?"

"Well—"

"Oh, my God."

"What, Rutowski? What?"

"He's still talking to her," Keane complained.

Nelle tightened her grip on his arm, but kept her focus on Rutowski.

"You're going to email or text, aren't you?" the annoying crone asked.

"That's how we do it in modern times."

"There is a cornucopia of reasons that's a bad idea. You need to go there and *talk* to Johann."

"No one wants to talk to Johann," Nelle complained.

"Of course they don't. He's an idiot. But if you're going to be the one to do this, you really need to—"

"Fine!" Nelle swiped one hand through the air to stop the She-badger from going on and on. She had a feeling she was a rambler. "I'll handle it in person."

"Good. Thank you."

"And what will you do?"

"Live life to the fullest?"

"Stay away from Charlie."

"I know you *think* you can tell me what to do—"

"I'm telling you what you're *not* going to do, and you're *not* going to bother Charlie. Understand?"

Rutowski looked off, let out a long breath, then returned her gaze to Nelle.

"Fine."

"Excellent."

"And when are you going to go?"

"I have to take care of something in the city, and then I'll go."

"Great. Good."

"Yes. Good."

The pair stared at each other for a minute. Nelle, however, wasn't sure that Rutowski understood what Nelle was being extremely clear about. So she decided to say it again. Maybe this time adding a punch to the face or a kick to the groin. But before she could do any of that, Nelle gasped as she was lifted off her feet and carried across the street by a crazed cat who'd managed to miss the last few minutes because he was obsessing over something ridiculous.

Keane didn't grab her and haul her off, though. Instead, he started

222 *Shelly Laurenston*

walking with her already attached to his bicep. He simply lifted his arm a bit so her feet didn't drag. It was kind of fun, to be honest.

Cutting through his many Malone relatives, Keane marched over to his mother and uncle.

"Oh, hey, kid," his uncle said; the older cat barely glanced at Keane, because his predatory gaze was securely locked on Keane's mother. "Whatcha need?"

In reply, Keane simply took his free arm, slid it between his mother and uncle, and then swept the same arm out, knocking his uncle back into an RV and forcing immediate space between the pair.

"What the fuck?" Keane's uncle roared.

"You okay, Ma?" Keane asked her, while *his* gaze stayed locked on his uncle and the cousins that now swarmed the older cat.

She cleared her throat, but didn't react with any anger. "I'm fine, hon."

"Well, if you need anything, or anyone is *bothering* you, just let me or Finn or Shay know. Okay, Ma?"

"Okay. Thank you, baby."

Keane took several steps forward that put him toe-to-toe with his uncle, glaring right into the older cat's gold eyes. "Anytime, Ma," he said. Then, with fangs out, drool dripping from the pointy tips, he added in an inhuman growl, "Any. Fucking. *Time.*"

Trace and her friends watched the younger She-badger walk through the crowd of cats and bears, expertly moving around them without taking her eyes off the screen of her phone. The tiger loped beside her, snarling and snapping at any of his relatives that got too close to him. He really didn't like those other cats, did he? Not that she could blame him. The Malones had dropped the ball when it came to one of their own, and she doubted the kid would ever forgive them.

She smirked. That "kid" was in his thirties, but these days . . . everyone looked like a kid to her.

"Are you sure about this?" CeCe asked, standing next to her.

"This is perfect. We need her out of the way."

Trace was making urgent plans in her head, so it took a bit to realize her friends were currently staring at her.

"I don't mean we need to kill her," she finally told them.

"Ohhhh."

"I just need her busy. This will keep her busy."

"And while she's busy . . . what are we doing?" Steph asked.

Trace shrugged. "Doing what we do best."

"You mean start shit that makes everybody hate us?" CeCe asked.

"Well . . . that, too." Trace nodded. "*Definitely* that, too."

"Who hits on their dead brother's wife?" Keane wanted to know, following behind Nelle as they left the street filled with his obnoxious family. "Who?"

"Your uncles, apparently," Nelle replied, not even looking up from her phone.

"Maybe I shouldn't leave her on her own."

"Your mother can handle your uncles." She stopped by a more than three-hundred-thousand-dollar sports car and slid her hands under the wheel well until she located the key fob.

"Want to drive it?" she asked, smiling.

Keane snorted. "You really think I can fit in that thing?"

"An NBA player has one, and he's seven feet tall."

"Yeah, and probably half my weight."

She looked him over and nodded. "Yeah. I forgot about those ridiculous shoulders."

"I *love* my shoulders."

"Fine." She put the fob back and started walking again until she reached a black Mercedes-Benz SUV that he was *sure* cost at least six figures. Nelle found that fob and handed it to him.

"Let's go," she ordered.

"I should be at prac—"

"You're coming. I need you."

His next words briefly caught in his throat until he realized she wasn't talking romantically. Then he was pissed at himself for wanting her to be talking romantically. Dumbass. He was a dumbass!

"Um . . . okay." He got into the SUV and started the engine. "Where are we going?"

"To the city," she said, putting an address into the car's GPS system.

Hands on the wheel, Keane asked, "Should we be worried?"

"About what?"

"Rutowski says the de Medicis are here. Already. Should we be doing something to address that?"

"We are."

"No. We're appeasing Mads's aunt. That seems counterintuitive right now. Guys like Paolo de Medici don't sit around waiting to make the next move. They're going to make a move. We should be ready."

"We will be." She glanced away from her phone long enough to tell him, "But I know a little about those four She-badgers from my father. We need to appease them, because what we *don't* need is them making this worse than it already is."

"Is that possible? Making it worse?"

"Yes. It is. Trust me . . . we disprove Rutowski's little scheme, and we're golden. Then we can just focus on wiping out the de Medicis. Okay?"

Keane nodded, pulling out into the street.

"Are you all right?" he asked when she said nothing else, but also stopped looking at her phone. The device simply sat in her lap, making a soft *tink* sound every time she got a new text—which was every few seconds, some *tink*s overlapping another—while she glared out the passenger side window.

"I'll be fine. I'm just annoyed. Very, very annoyed."

"At Rutowski?"

"That's part of it."

"Don't feel bad," he told her, reaching over with one hand to pat her shoulder. "I am sure that somewhere, in this world of ours . . . your family is *very* important."

"Bastard," she said, chuckling a little in surprise. Allowing him to, at least for a little while, stop worrying about his mother and his disgusting, inappropriate uncles and instead focus on giving one-word answers to the beautiful, annoyingly chatty She-badger beside him.

Chapter 17

Bernice MacKilligan stuck her hand into the hive and tore off a chunk of honeycomb. The African killer bees that she'd had smuggled into the country—they were considered an invasive species—immediately attacked her arm, but she ignored them, taking a big, messy bite of the warm comb. She ate the honey, larva, and adult bees with gusto. It was her way of starting her day before the entire world annoyed her. Her hives were her pride and joy. Much more than her children were, but that wasn't surprising. Her children were one of the things in the world that annoyed her so much.

They all lived together in her fifteen-thousand-foot mansion, despite the many times she'd thrown her adult offspring out. Now, she also had to deal with her half-brothers and their sons from Scotland. They'd arrived not long ago for a funeral, and now she couldn't get rid of them. They'd almost left, but their private jet had been blown up with them on it, and they'd been thrown out of the shifter-run hotel they'd been staying in. They'd even tried to stay at their nieces' house first, but Freddy's three girls had quickly—and wisely—thrown the lot of them out. Now here they were. In Bernie's house and refusing to leave. At least all their wounds and burns had healed so she didn't have to look at that anymore, but they still wouldn't get the fuck out!

Some days she really did believe honey badgers were an invasive species, too.

Keeping a small cube of the honeycomb so she could drop it into her morning coffee, Bernice started back toward the house, free

226 *Shelly Laurenston*

hand slapping at the aggressive bees still attacking her head and neck. She abruptly decided to go around and enter through the front. She wanted to see what was going on with the flowers there, so she could discuss it with her full-human gardener. She liked her gardener. He knew when to keep quiet. Sure, he'd asked her about the small black animals with a white stripe running down their backs that he'd spotted around the property sometimes. Quick to note that he didn't think they were skunks. But when she started paying him a little more, he stopped asking, and it was never discussed again. Besides, it was because of him that she had award-winning roses. One can overlook a lot from a full-human when they help a person win awards.

Bernice was just coming around the corner of her home when the gardener called out to her from the opposite direction. She had just stopped to go back when she saw her half-brother Will get into one of her cars, a favored Mercedes Class S that she didn't want his stupid ass riding around in.

She opened her mouth to tell him to "get the fuck outta my car!" when the engine turned over and the accompanying blast sent Bernice flying back at least one hundred feet. She hit the ground and tore up her precious lawn as her body continued to slide another fifty feet before coming to a stop.

"Ms. MacKilligan! Ms. MacKilligan! Oh, my God!"

Her gardener had an arm around her back and another on her shoulder, helping her to roll over and sit up.

"Are you all right?" the man asked, out of breath and clearly beginning to panic.

"I'm fine. I'm fine," she said, between panting and ignoring the pain in her currently broken neck. It would heal in no time. One of the few benefits of being born a MacKilligan. They even healed faster than most badgers.

"No, no," the gardener begged, openly gawking at the way her head was twisted on her body. "Don't get up. I need to call an ambulance."

She put her hand over his phone to stop him from dialing. "Not yet."

"But—"

She grabbed her skull with both hands and, gritting her teeth, yanked it back into place so it properly aligned with her spine.

The color in her gardener's normally suntanned skin quickly drained away, and he stared at her with his mouth open.

Then the next hit came . . .

"Fer fuck's sake," a voice with a Scottish accent growled out from the remains of the destroyed vehicle. "What the fuck happened?"

Will pulled himself from the rubble and, after shaking his head and body to dust off, he looked around. Other than some second-degree burns on his face and hands, he was as strong and sound as anyone who had *not* just been in the middle of an explosion.

"Why do they keep trying to blow me up?" he yelled, as their offspring came running out of the house to see what had happened.

Letting out a sigh, Bernice looked up at her stunned and horrified gardener. At the same moment, several bones on her neck and spine loudly snapped back into place.

She cleared her throat and said, "Uh . . . let's just say you're getting another raise. Okay?"

The gardener closed his eyes and nodded. "Yes, ma'am. Thank you."

Keane didn't know what was going on. They'd been sitting in the SUV for at least fifteen minutes, but Nelle wouldn't get out. She simply sat there, both hands clenched into tight fists, head bowed, eyes closed tight.

He'd never seen her like this. Uptight. She looked uptight. She never looked uptight. She was one of the most relaxed people he'd ever met. But not right now. Right now, she looked like she might snap at any moment.

"Maybe we should—"

"I'm fine," she snipped back.

"Really? 'Cause you don't look fine. Is this because of that stuff with Rutowski?"

"Who? Oh. No. Nothing to do with her."

228   *Shelly Laurenston*

"Yeah, but—"

"I'm fine!"

"She snarls through gritted teeth," he muttered.

"All right," she said, after taking a deep breath and blowing it out, "are you wearing a watch?"

"Yes."

"Is it a good watch?"

"I got it downtown on the street from this Haitian guy."

"Oh, God."

"His stuff is really good. I mean, I *know* that Rolex isn't spelled with two extra Ls, but—"

"What about your phone?"

"I'm pretty sure it's made in China like the Rolllex I'm wearing."

"Gimme your phone," she snarled.

He unlocked it and handed it over. She found the timer app he used during practice and put fifteen minutes on it.

"When this goes off, you go into *that* store."

"That's a store?"

"It is. You come in, you get me, you drag me out. No matter what is happening, no matter what I may say, no matter what *anyone* may say . . . you *drag* me out. Understand?"

"No."

"What don't you understand?"

"Why I need to drag you out no matter what's happening? What do you think will happen?"

"I don't know. But this is what it means to be my backup?"

"It means following your nonsensical orders blindly?"

"Yes."

"All right."

She started the timer, handed back his phone, and got out of the SUV.

"What are you doing?" he asked himself out loud, watching her disappear into what appeared to be an abandoned space waiting to be sold to whomever put in a bid.

"I know what you're doing," he replied to himself. "You're waiting to get the hot girl out of a store when she's bored. Because you're

TO KILL A BADGER 229

pathetic. She's obviously playing with you, and you're buying into it. Because you're pathetic. And now you're talking to yourself like a serial killer, which is even more pathetic."

He entertained opening a book on his phone—which he hated doing. He liked to actually *hold* a book, not read it on his damn phone—but he knew if the book was any good, he'd get lost in it and forget all about the timer. He was known to even ignore alarms when he was into a great book. That was why he didn't read anything but sports magazines on his lunch breaks during practice. The articles were usually short, and he wasn't completely distracted, because they were all about full-human sports. Although he didn't know why any full-human played sports. They were all so fragile.

Finally, the alarm on the timer went off. An annoying sound that had him gritting his teeth as he desperately tried to turn it off. Once that was done, he got out of the car and walked up the street until he reached the storefront with the windows covered by brown kraft paper so no one could look in.

Worried about exactly what illegal nightmare situation he was about to find behind this closed door, Keane entered . . . and immediately froze in the doorway.

He'd expected all sorts of horrors, but not this. Never this.

Nelle slammed the fellow Asian female into the floor and straddled her chest, knees on either side so that the arms were pinned there. Then Nelle began to pummel the other woman in the face. Punch after punch after punch.

Maybe it wouldn't look so strange if the other Asian wasn't in a white wedding dress and Nelle wasn't in a champagne-colored, full-length gown. At first, he thought the dress was sleeveless, but it had a thick strap over the left shoulder. It was made of silk or satin or something shiny and smooth that was popular at weddings.

There were two sets of non-Asian women attempting to pull the pair apart. There was also lot of screaming and crying and threats to call police ". . . if this doesn't stop right now! You're ruining the dress!"

If Keane wasn't so horrified by the whole thing, he'd be really entertained.

230   *Shelly Laurenston*

It took longer than he would have liked to snap out of his temporary psychosis, but when Nelle grabbed the other female's head between her hands and slammed it against the floor over and over again, he knew he had to step in. The two females fighting might be shifters—probably Nelle's dreaded sister, by the way she was going after her—but everyone else in this place was full-human. He could tell, despite all the expensive perfume these ladies had practically *bathed* in to block their natural human scent.

Fighting the urge to sneeze from everything invading his poor nose, Keane strode across the open showroom. Racks pushed close to the wall were filled with wedding gowns. Designer ones, he was sure. He doubted any Zhao would buy off-the-rack.

He reached the battling females and, leaning past the hysterical full-humans, he grabbed Nelle around the waist and yanked.

Tragically, she still had her hands dug in deep into her sister's hair, using that to keep control of her head while she slammed it into the floor. Which meant that when he pulled one sister up, the other came with her. Keane stopped lifting for a moment and proceeded to shake Nelle until she finally released her fellow She-badger. It wasn't his best move, but it was surprisingly effective. And way better than trying to pry her hands out of her sister's hair.

Once Nelle had released her sister and was seconds from turning on Keane, he lifted her up and began to carry her back to the front of the store. When they reached the door, he released her, placing her bare feet on the ground.

She didn't look at him, but when he opened the door for her, she started to step out.

"You better get that dress repaired and cleaned before the ceremony, you lazy heifer!" her sister screamed after her.

Nelle spun around and started to run back to beat her sister some more, but this time, Keane immediately caught her and put her over his shoulder. Using one arm to keep her pinned there, he walked out and took her back to the SUV.

He unlocked the doors and put her into the passenger side. He started back to the driver's door, but stopped long enough to glare at the guy using his phone to film the She-badger's continuing screams. It took the man less than five seconds to turn off his phone and run away. Keane didn't even have to say anything.

It's why he loved being a cat. He never had to say anything. Body language and facial expression did most of the work for him.

He got into the vehicle and started it, but decided to wait until Nelle composed herself. She was, after all, still a very rich girl from Hong Kong with hyper-elite, British-trained manners. He was sure she'd be fine any second now.

Nelle, beyond any rational emotion, decided the best thing she could do at this moment was crawl into the footwell of the SUV and scream. Just for a few minutes. Just until she felt better. She screamed.

And screamed.

And screamed.

She didn't stop until her vocal cords were nothing but raw tendons. Then, finally, she looked up. She assumed Keane would have been long gone by now, running back to Queens as a tiger. Anything to get away from the crazy badger in the footwell. But he was still sitting in the driver's seat, gazing down at her. He didn't appear as angry as she was sure he must feel after witnessing some female screaming her head off out of frustration and rage. A side of herself she rarely showed anyone.

Calmer, she finally said, "Sorry about that."

"How we doin'?" he asked, sounding more like a Long Islander by the second. "Feelin' better?"

He was teasing her. But the way he was doing it . . . it didn't annoy her as much as she would expect.

"No."

"So that was your sister? The one with the wedding you don't want to go to?"

"Yes. That was her."

"You two seem tight. Call each other every night? Talk about boys? That sort of sisterly bonding thing?"

Nelle closed her eyes and did some deep breathing exercises. Stevie had taught her this skill after signing up for anger management classes, for some reason. Usually, they were given to minors due to illegal activity that revealed anger issues. But apparently, Stevie just wanted to go and taught Nelle all she'd learned one day over cookies and milk. Cookies and milk Stevie always had after returning from one of her college classes. She'd been about eleven at the time.

Keane kindly remained quiet while she worked on getting herself under control, which she really appreciated. Although when she heard a knock on the SUV, her anger immediately frothed back up.

Lowering the window, Keane nodded at the full-human female waiting for him.

"Hi!" the woman squeaked, like a little mouse that Nelle would toy with before spitting out the remains in someone's yard. "I wanted to give Gong back her clothes and purse before she left?"

Was that what she was going to do? Or was that what she wanted to know if she should do? It was hard to tell, since she seemed to be one of those women who said everything like a question.

Keane took what was handed to him and reached over to put it all in the back seat.

"It was good seeing you again, Gong?" the full-human either told her or asked. Although Nelle had no idea who this bitch was or when she'd ever met her before. "Really glad you're coming to the wedding?" Probably good to question, since Nelle would take any excuse *not* to go. "And that dress looks great on you? Okay, bye?"

She waved at Nelle and Keane before returning to the store.

Keane closed the window and, after a long moment of him staring off, he asked, "Is it my imagination, or are all your sister's friends blonde?"

"You're assuming that after meeting just one of her bridesmaids?"

"No." He pointed, and the gesture forced her to get out of the wheel well and sit in the passenger seat like a rational person. Looking straight ahead, she saw all of the bridesmaids standing outside the store, watching the SUV. Maybe they were worried that Nelle would come back and finish off her sister. She'd like to. It would be deserved!

"Yes," Nelle admitted to Keane's questions. "They're all blonde. Even the ones not naturally blonde, are blonde. I think one or two of them dyed their hair that color just so they can keep hanging around my sister and be in her wedding. That way she can be the only brunette in the wedding party and all eyes will be on *her*. Because that's completely normal behavior. Because when one gets married, one really wants to make sure that this lifelong commitment of love and caring is all about *you* and the media blitz you can make of it."

Nelle took a deep breath.

"But, as I've been told," she said to Keane, "her wedding is none of my business. I just need to show up, wearing this"—she glanced down at herself—"gaudy gown and pretend I don't loathe everything about her and this entire fucking event."

"That dress isn't gaudy, and that's what sisters do. At least, that's what my mom says. And she has sisters. They barely tolerate each other, but they are still very close."

His hands on the steering wheel, Keane asked, "So do you want me to take you back to Mads's house? Or—"

"No. We have to get to Jersey."

"What's in Jersey?"

"The jet."

"What jet?"

"The jet taking us to France."

His head jerked around so he could gawk at her. "France? Why the fuck are we going to France?"

"Where did you think we were going?"

"Not to France! I can't go to France!"

"You have to come to France."

"I do?"

"Yes. Charlie said you're to stay with me. So you're staying with me. And I'm going to France."

"I am not going to . . . you can't . . . this is . . ." He roared, the SUV shaking a little. "*This is insane!* Why are we going to France?"

"Because we have to see the Von Schäfer-Müllers of Hamburg!"

"*The who?*"

"Were you not listening at all to Rutowski? We discussed this in depth!"

234   *Shelly Laurenston*

"Of course I wasn't listening! I was too busy watching my uncle hit on my poor defenseless mother!"

"Your mother is anything but defenseless." When he glared at her, she said, "Although I am sure she has absolutely *no* interest in whatever your dirty evil uncle is up to."

"Look, I understand you have something important to do in France. But I can't go. I don't have any clothes; I don't have my passport—"

"We're not *staying* in France. And I already have your passport."

"Why do you have my passport? *How* do you have my passport?"

"I have everyone's passport in case we have to leave the country."

"How is that okay? What if I have to leave the country without you?"

"When have you *ever* left this country?" Nelle demanded.

"I've gone to Mongolia to meet my family."

"When you were. . . ?"

She saw a bit of fang before he replied, "Fourteen."

"Exactly. You and Mads, always bitching instead of being happy that *I take care of everything!*"

"Even when we don't ask you to."

"Yes. Exactly. Be grateful. I don't know how half of you would function without me."

"I've happily managed this long!"

"Oh, my God, just drive!"

They drove in Manhattan traffic for nearly thirty minutes before Keane decided that he was ready to have a conversation with this insane female without pointing out that he was *not* going to France with her. He'd get her to the airport and dump her on whatever person was there that handled all this shit for Nelle's father. He didn't know who that was, and he didn't care. He just knew he couldn't keep going round and round with her over such bullshit.

Because he was *not* going to France! Now or ever!

Letting out a breath, he said, "That wedding dress your sister had on . . ."

"Yes?"

"Is it the one for her actual wedding?"

TO KILL A BADGER   235

"One of them, yes."

"You kind of . . . fucked it up then, didn't you? Won't that ruin her wedding or whatever? That should make you happy."

"She always has a designer make several copies of her dress. Just in case. So, no. I didn't ruin her wedding. Maybe if I'd torn her face off her skull . . . but even that would heal eventually."

"She has copies of the dress? But it looks really expensive."

"Three hundred and fifty thousand dollars, give or take."

Keane quickly realized that Nelle didn't have her seat belt on when he hit the brakes and she was thrown forward into the dashboard.

"*What the fuck?*" she snarled.

He should have apologized for that and made sure she was okay, but all he could think to ask was, "How much is that dress? And she has backups in case the first one gets damaged?"

Nelle pushed herself back into the passenger seat, wiped the blood now dripping from her nose, and calmly replied, "Actually, that's nothing. Our cousin's wedding dress from last year was worth several million because of all the diamonds she had on the bodice." Nelle shook her head. "But you know what? This tells me everything I need to know. The fact that my sister went so *cheap* on this dress means she doesn't care about this dude."

"Are you kidding?"

"No. Not kidding at all." And she wasn't. He could tell by her voice. She was still too angry to be joking or teasing.

"And the exact copy of that dress is another . . ."

"Actually, she has three copies of all her wedding-day dresses. At least she had three for her ceremony dress. Now she has two, unless they can get the blood out."

"So all together, more than a million in wedding dresses?"

"Ohhhh, much more than that."

"How much more?"

Someone came to the driver's side window and banged on the roof, most likely wanting him to move his car, since he was still sitting in the middle of traffic.

"*Move your fucking—*"

236   Shelly Laurenston

Keane roared once at the man outside his window, who squeaked and ran away.

"And why does she need so many dresses?" he asked, finally moving again with traffic.

"Well, there's a dress for the ceremony, a dress for the reception, a dress for the dinner, and a dress for the dancing afterward. Then, of course, there's the dress for when she leaves the wedding for her honeymoon. She'd have backup for each of those and some extras looks from the same designer in case she has a mood change and wants to wear something different from what she'd planned for that day—or, of course, I slit her throat during the dinner, getting blood everywhere, which would force her to grab something that's not covered in an arterial spray . . ."

"And that's . . . how much?"

"Several million."

"Just for dresses?" he softly asked.

"Just for dresses."

"Okay."

They turned a corner and kept going.

"That seems excessive," he told her.

"For most of humanity, of course it does. But for my sister . . ."

"I see."

She was quiet a moment, but he saw her finally give a little smile before she told him, "And just so you know, I plan on my wedding being a much more low-key affair. One dress. Just friends. Probably not a blonde in sight except Mads."

"Okay, but why are you telling me this?"

"In case it comes up at *our* wedding."

Keane hit the brakes again, but this time, Nelle was buckled in.

Ignoring the horns blasting and the cursing from other drivers, he asked, "Feeling better, Nelle?"

Suddenly laughing, she admitted, "I am!"

Chapter 18

"So someone blew up one of Max's Scottish uncles."

"Wait . . . what?" Keane tried to turn to talk directly to Nelle, but the "family assistant" that they'd been "assigned" was too busy blocking his way and shoving a small duffel into his hand.

"Clothes," the She-cat said. "And a few other necessary items if you're staying a night or two."

In his other hand, she shoved a wallet.

"Here's some francs and a credit card you can use."

"I don't need—"

"This is a busy trip. You won't have time to get money exchanged or worry about how much you'll be charged on your American card. Just take it and be grateful."

Keane never thought he'd meet someone who was as short-tempered as he was, but he hadn't met Marti Hinds. A bobcat that had worked for the Zhaos for years, apparently. She may have the title of "assistant," like some young kid who ran to get someone a latte when demanded, but she ruled with an iron paw. Ordering him and Nelle around like they were very stupid people with no sense. It irritated him, and normally he'd bully a smaller cat just by being himself. But his instincts told him not to make her mad. A surprising reaction to a cat with a short tail.

"Here's your passport." Keane tried to take it, but she pulled it back. "Can you keep hold of it, or should I give it to Nelle?"

"I can keep—"

238 Shelly Laurenston

"No. I don't trust you. You take it." She handed it to Nelle. He knew by the way Nelle wouldn't look at him that she was loving all this.

The bobcat studied her very thin tablet.

"A car will meet you at the airport and drive you to Paris. I booked you a suite at the Llewellyn Arms for the next two nights, just in case you need extra time."

"You know the Llewelyn Arms are owned by lions, right?" Keane asked.

Gold cat eyes coldly stared at him. "Of course I know that."

"And you do understand that we're in a fight with lions, right?"

"You're in a fight with the de Medicis. The Llewellyns are *not* associated with the de Medicis, and I can assure you they never will be."

"How do you know that?"

"Because I know."

"Can't we go to the Four Seasons?" Nelle whined, diverting those cold eyes from Keane's face. "With a view of the Eiffel Tower?"

"Not with an alley cat, you can't."

"Hey," Keane weakly complained.

"The Llewellyns' establishment will have the same level of comfort *and* be able to feed this one without you pretending to order for twenty people."

"I'm standing right here," he reminded the bobcat.

"Zeus will be your driver when you get to the hotel."

"Zeus?" Keane asked. "Dude's name is *Zeus*."

The bobcat stared at him. "Do not irritate Zeus."

"How can I, mere mortal, irritate a god named Zeus?"

Marti turned her back to him and addressed Nelle. "The plane will be ready to board in a few minutes. Please don't let this one"—she gestured to Keane with a toss of her hair—"tear up the seats like the other tiger did."

"That was Shay. His brother. But this time I'll be much more diligent."

"Good." Marti gave one last glare to Keane before telling Nelle, "I'll meet you on the plane."

TO KILL A BADGER   239

"She's coming with us?" Keane asked, ignoring the fact the bobcat was still standing there . . . being annoying.

Bobcats weren't even one of the "big" cats. They were too small, too North American, and couldn't even roar! Plus, they were *rude*!

"Of course she's coming with us," Nelle replied. "If we need assistance while we're in Paris—"

"You said we weren't staying. Why are we suddenly staying?"

"I know this is hard for you, but you need to let me deal with everything. When we get back, you can boss your brothers around again, and all will be right in your world."

"I don't boss them around."

Both females laughed at him, and he didn't appreciate it. Especially since Marti didn't even know him.

"I do my research, Mr. Malone," Marti said to his unasked question, "so let us not begin our working relationship off by lying to each other."

"What working—"

She walked away.

"Now I'm just getting pissed," he told Nelle.

"Sit, sit." She took his arm and made him sit in one of the plastic seats. The airport was small and nearly empty, except for a few employees and some passengers waiting to board. It took a moment, but he eventually recognized a few of those passengers from the news. Full-human billionaires who also had their own fleets of jets. He often wondered what that would feel like. Being that rich.

Seeing his mother stressed over bills after his father died had been hard. Knowing she could never scrimp on food for her growing cubs, his mother had been forced to downgrade their five-bedroom home to a small rental house, where Keane had ended up sharing a room with Shay and Finn, while his mother had shared her room with Dale, since he'd still been so young. Originally, he'd hated all of that. Wanted to complain about it endlessly, but knew he couldn't. Not once he looked into his mother's sorrowful eyes. So he'd gritted his teeth and kept moving forward. Although, in the end, he had been grateful to being forced to share space with his brothers, because it meant he was

240   *Shelly Laurenston*

there when they woke up in the middle of the night crying or having a nightmare.

Studying the rich with their entourages and multiple assistants, Keane wondered if they even saw their kids. Did they check on them late at night like his dad used to when he'd been out on assignment or whatever the CIA called that shit? Or did their kids sleep alone with a nanny nearby? Keane couldn't even imagine anyone else but him and his mother taking care of his brothers during those first dark months after Dad's death.

"Did you have a nanny?" he asked Nelle.

She didn't look up from that phone, and he briefly wondered if she had surgically sutured it to her hand to ensure she never lost it.

"A nanny? Yes. But only because my grandmother said I was a curse against the family, and she refused to help raise me like she had for my older brothers and sisters."

"Why did she do that?"

"I think because I stabbed her in the knee once with a bunch of colored pencils I'd just sharpened. She still limps a bit, but I think she does that to make my mother feel bad . . . which, of course, she doesn't."

Keane couldn't help but chuckle. "Why in the world did you stab your grandmother in the knee?"

"She took the book I was reading, and I did not appreciate that at all. So I stabbed her. She did really try to make my mother feel bad about it, until my mother pointed out that a three-year-old shouldn't have had access to pencils in the first place. I should have only been using crayons at that point."

"She's right."

"I know. But my mother didn't see me moving the chair, climbing the chair, grabbing the pencils off my father's workspace, *then* climbing down again, moving the chair back to where it was, and lying in wait . . ."

"At three?"

"At three. But I'm a badger. She's a badger. She raised my mother . . .

she really should have known it was coming as soon as she snatched that book from my hand."

"Wait . . . you were reading at three?"

"Yes. I was quite advanced for my age."

"Were you like Stevie?"

"God, no. I just liked reading on my own. Besides, no one is like Stevie."

Keane let out a sigh. "By the time Nat was three, she was taking computers apart. By five, she was putting them back together again with new components and new features. It was disturbing. Especially because I hate computers. I mean, they're great for porn, but what else do you really need them for?"

"I know I should have asked this earlier but . . . could you please elaborate on the whole 'someone blew up Charlie's uncle' thing?"

Nelle held up her finger to tell Keane to hold while she requested an orange juice and croissant from the flight attendant assigned to their jet.

"And you, sir?" she asked Keane.

He gazed up at the pretty attendant, eyes blinking slowly. "What?" he finally asked.

"Would you like something? Something to drink or some lunch, perhaps?"

He continued to stare at her, and Nelle couldn't take it anymore, so she ordered for him. God, sometimes she did take after her mother. How horrifying.

"Roast boar sub with extra meat. All the . . . uh . . . fixings, I think it's called, on the side, please, Janette. And a pitcher of cold milk with a glass. Must keep those bones strong for football."

"I can order my own food," he told Nelle.

Nelle and the attendant waited for him to give his own order.

After a moment, he said, "Roast boar sub with extra meat. Milk."

"Very good, sir." The fox smirked at Nelle before moving off.

"Shut up," Keane said, still snarling.

"I didn't say anything!"

"But you're thinking. I can hear you thinking and laughing at me."

"That's paranoid, because we both know I would just laugh right in your face."

The captain came on the comm to tell them in Cantonese that they were in for a nice flight to Paris and to just sit back and relax before concluding with their calculated arrival time.

Keane's eyes grew wide and he asked, panicked, "Does he only speak Chinese? I don't speak Chinese. What if we're on fire and we need to jump from the plane, but I don't understand what he says?"

"Okay, first . . . if the plane is on fire, *I'll* make sure to tell you we need to jump. And second . . ." She pointed up, and the captain came on the comm again to repeat his message in English.

"Oh." Keane turned toward the window, gave a little chuff, then shook his head. It was a very big-cat move, and she loved it.

"So you were asking about Charlie's Scottish uncle?" she reminded him.

"What? Oh. Yeah. Yeah, I was." He looked at her. "You said they tried to blow him up?"

"No, I said they *did* blow him up. The aunt's Mercedes is totaled, from what I understand."

Keane frowned; blinked. "Uh . . . and her uncle? You know . . . the one *in* the Mercedes?"

She shrugged. "He's fine. He's a honey badger. Not only that, he's a MacKilligan honey badger. That family seems to have evolved into a superior species of indestructible badger. It's a shame that the males seem to have lost some brain cells in the process. If it wasn't for the sisters and female cousins . . . honestly, though, I'm not sure if even a shot to the back of the head would kill a MacKilligan. I think as long as they keep their head on their shoulders, they'll be fine. Once it's separated from the spinal cord, however . . . I'm pretty sure that's unfixable."

"Really? You're *pretty sure* that's unfixable?"

"What can I say? Honey badgers are a wonder to behold."

★ ★ ★

The sub was served on fine china. A platter, specifically, because the one sub was actually three foot-longs. The pattern on the platter was, if Keane was guessing, the Zhao family's insignia around the edge. Seemed kind of fancy and expensive, but he was hungry and honestly didn't care. He especially felt that way after he took his first bite. The meat was fresh and perfectly seasoned, and the milk was cold and fresh and full of fat. None of that one-percent crap.

"Personally, I think it was the de Medicis," Nelle was blathering on about Charlie's uncle, but he'd stopped caring when he realized a bomb would never get past the Malones or any of those bears surrounding Charlie's house and his sister and niece. Not after the Malones' experience with Westies—New York Irish gangsters—and the IRA. "But I also must admit that the MacKilligans are not a well-loved badger family, and those MacKilligan brothers are quite involved in gangster-type activity in Great Britain."

"The MacKilligan name is well known among my leg-breaking uncles," he said around his first sandwich.

"Exactly. So this could easily just be some criminal enterprise sending a message to the MacKilligan brothers." She took a bite of her croissant, chewed, swallowed. "Everybody hates the MacKilligan brothers."

She sipped her orange juice. "But it should be looked into. Charlie will start to feel responsible for everything if the de Medicis do any real damage to that side of her family."

"Isn't she kind of responsible for all of this?" he asked. "She did plop their dead father in the middle of their house, then burned the shit down."

"The de Medicis started the fire, and we were simply returning their father's remains."

"You're so full of sh—"

"You know, I need to change."

"Why?"

"We're going to Paris! You want me to look presentable, don't you?"

"I don't care what you do."

244   *Shelly Laurenston*

"You're so cute." She reached over and tweaked his nose between her thumb and forefinger. "So very cute!"

And Keane was beyond insulted, because he'd seen full-humans do that kind of shit with their house cats on the Internet!

"What about this?" Nelle asked, turning one way, then the other.

"I don't understand what you want from me," the cat admitted.

"Do you think this outfit is okay? Or should I try something else on?"

"I don't know."

Useless. Why were men so useless? At the very least, she could always get some fashion guidance from Streep. She did have a terrible *personal* fashion sense, but she did all right with everyone else. And Max was always great. She had a good eye, considering she personally lived her life in either jeans and sneakers or kilt-like miniskirts with steel-toe Doc Marten boots.

Deciding the simple black dress with black heels was always perfect for a Paris run, she sat in the leather seat across from Keane. His long legs nearly bridged the distance between them, his knees occasionally brushing against hers. She grabbed a copy of the latest Italian *Vogue* from the seat next to her and began flipping through.

"Are you pissed at me?" he asked.

"No. Just annoyed." She was surprised he'd noticed anything, since his gaze was focused out the window.

"Annoyed about what?"

"I was looking for a little feedback. Would it have killed you to say I look nice?"

"Why do I need to say that?" he asked, and she wanted to slap him. "You always look nice. Do I really need to pump your ego anymore when you never look bad in anything?"

She looked up at him and said, "Awwww."

His head snapped around, and his gold gaze locked on her face. "What was that noise?"

"That was my 'you are such a cute thing' noise. Just adorable."

"I am not adorable. I simply lay out the facts as I see them. Coldly and bluntly."

"So if someone you thought was unattractive had asked . . ."

"Would I tell them they're ugly?" Keane frowned. "No. Why would I do that?"

"Lots of people do that."

"Lots of people are assholes. Doesn't mean you have to be one, too."

The cat had no idea how that response only managed to make him appear even sweeter.

"Stop smiling at me," he growled.

"How can you tell I'm smiling at you? You're back looking out the window."

"I can see you out of the corner of my eye."

"Is that your cat sight?"

"No. That's healthy human eyesight. Most of us have a decent peripheral vision until we move into our late forties."

"That's weirdly . . . specific."

"I have an interest in ophthalmology."

Nelle had to work hard not to laugh in astonishment. "You have an interest in ophthalmology? Seriously?"

"Don't you find eyes interesting?"

"Not when I want to dig them out and study them, no."

"They can do so much. That interests me."

"Am I about to find out you always wanted to be a doctor, but your tragic background stopped you from your one true dream?"

"My one true dream was to be a starting linebacker on the Pittsburgh Steelers in the nineteen-seventies alongside Jack Lambert and Mean Joe Greene, with Terry Bradshaw as our quarterback. Being a doctor was never part of that dream."

"Fair enough."

Nelle went back to her copy of *Vogue*, but she wasn't really comprehending much. She had too much on her mind. Plans on top of plans on top of plans. Plus, she was kind of hungry again.

"So what are we going to do when we get to France?" Keane abruptly asked her.

"Meet with Zeus."

He let out a little sigh. "Yes. I am aware we're meeting Zeus. I mean, what's our main goal there?"

"Marti is setting up a meeting with the Von Schäfer-Müllers of Hamburg as we speak."

"Do we actually have to call them that?"

"It depends who we end up meeting with."

"And do you think this will really"—he shrugged—"help anything?"

"I don't know. But if we don't do it, trust me, one of those crones would have simply made everything worse."

"You really should stop calling them that."

"You're worried about them?"

"Based on what Van Holtz said at that lunch, it seems they single-handedly extended the Cold War. So, personally, I wouldn't mess with them. But you do you."

"No, no. You have a point. And they are trying to be helpful in their own drug-addled, post-menopausal way."

"Yeah, sure, keep saying shit like that."

"I'm just joking."

"Look, I have uncles who grew up in the eighties. That generation are a breed unto themselves. Not to be fucked with lightly. They may have gray hair and complain about back pain, but don't fool yourself. My uncles and those broads are *mean*. We're better with Rutowski and her friends on our side than on anyone else's."

"I'll make sure to keep that in mind."

"You should. I'd hate to see that pretty face torn right off your head."

Nelle held back her laugh and asked, "You think I'm pretty?"

Keane finally looked away from the window. "What is wrong with you? I keep trying to have a nice, logical conversation, and you keep trying to make it about—"

TO KILL A BADGER 247

"Us?"

"There is no us. Why would you think there's an us?"

"Because you like me."

"I do not."

"You do, too. I can tell, because you're still here. When you don't like someone, you're like my great-grandfather. You just walk away."

"So you're saying I'm like a cranky old man?"

"You *are* a cranky old man. But it really works for you." She tilted her head to the side to study him. "We should have dinner tonight."

"Why wouldn't we eat?"

"Not just eat. I mean, we should have *dinner*. At a nice place. Just the two of us."

"So no Zeus at dinner?"

"It'll be lovely. Some place with delicious food and excellent ambiance."

"You mean like a Van Holtz restaurant?" he asked, sounding less than enthused.

"It's Paris. There are all sorts of shifter-owned restaurants there that can cater to us. Besides, if you want to go to an amazing Van Holtz restaurant, you should go to the one in Mülheim. It's huge, and the food is amazing. Their red wine pepper sauce is to die for." She smirked. Just to annoy him. "I'll take you there sometime."

He shook his head, but she saw a hint of a smile. "You're hopeless."

"A hopeless romantic?" she asked, fluttering her eyes.

"No. Just hopeless."

Chuckling, she slipped off her heels and put her feet on top of his outstretched legs.

When he didn't push her off, she leaned back in her seat and returned to reading her magazine.

"This is Zeus."

Keane gazed up at the seven-and-a-half-foot polar bear staring down at him.

"He'll be our protection while we're in Paris."

248   Shelly Laurenston

"*Bonjour,*" Keane thought he heard grumbled from deep inside the bear's chest.

"*Bonjour,* Zeus," Nelle said back, as she walked up the grand stairs leading to the Llewelyn Arms. She said something else in French and gestured at Keane.

The bear nodded at him and grumbled, "*Bonjour.*"

"Hiya," Keane replied back before following Nelle inside.

"Mademoiselle Zhao!" a very loud Frenchman called out before rushing over to her.

Air kisses to cheeks followed and some gibberish in French before Nelle was immediately led to the elevators. She didn't even have to check in at the front desk.

Keane followed behind her, but when he tried to step into the elevator, the Frenchman stepped in front of him.

"May I help you, monsieur?"

"Oh, he's with me, Paul."

"Are you sure, mademoiselle?" he looked back at Zhao. "Cats are very tricky. And American cats are the worst."

Keane gazed at what he now knew was a French wolf. "Who says I'm an American?"

The wolf sneered. "Seriously?"

Keane started to unleash fang, but a push from behind sent him into the elevator, and Zeus followed. By the time he turned around, the doors were already closing.

The elevator went up and up until it reached one of the three highest floors. When the doors opened with the help of a keycard that Zeus had, it opened right into a massive suite.

With three bedrooms, he didn't know how many bathrooms, and a layout of caviar, fresh fruit and salad, crackers, bread, and what Keane was guessing was very expensive champagne on the large coffee table in the middle of the living room, he knew he was seeing what the very wealthy had at their disposal every day. He was usually just happy when the hotels his team used on away games had twenty-four-hour room service and a stocked minibar.

"This is nice," he had to admit.

TO KILL A BADGER 249

"Is it?" Nelle asked. She had an annoyed look on her face. "I still smell past jackal. Zeus . . . be a dear. Call housekeeping."

The bear grumbled something and moved toward the house phone.

"Seriously? You smell jackal?"

"I smell everything, but jackal is prominent. They should have done a better job cleaning for what we're paying."

"You're not paying anything."

"My family is."

He shrugged. "I think it's nice."

"It's good enough."

"Wow."

"Don't worry," she said, smiling at him. "I don't feel that way about people."

"Wow."

After an interminable flight and drive from the private airport, Nelle desperately needed a shower. She did that and changed into a simple summer dress and five-thousand-dollar heels she'd recently purchased in Manhattan. She accented her outfit with a simple gold necklace and gold hoop earrings. She left her hair down and strapped a .32 auto in a black leather holster to the inside of her right thigh.

Grabbing her phone and another small purse she was positive Keane would hate, she walked out of her bedroom and into the living room. She immediately stopped and glared.

Keane stared at her before asking, "Friends of yours?"

"Not really."

"Again," he felt the need to say, "I have to question what your family calls protection."

"They're fellow badgers. Zeus probably didn't even—"

"Do his job?"

Deciding not to start a debate at this moment with Keane, Nelle focused on the head badger. "Hello, Travers."

"My sweet Gong. So good to see you again."

Maurice Travers was her least favorite person next to her sister, but sometimes one had to put up with people they didn't like. Especially

250 Shelly Laurenston

when they were pressing a gun into the side of the tiger she'd been planning a lovely dinner with just two seconds ago. Keane could easily survive a gunshot wound to the side based on the caliber of that Beretta Travers held, but he might also lose a kidney in the process. She didn't want that.

"Why are you here, Maurice?"

"To see you and talk about our unrequited love?"

"That statement makes me want to bite your head off," Keane informed his captor.

"Ahh, don't be mad at me, angry American. I have been nothing but polite to you."

"I'm sorry, but that wasn't an idiom," Keane felt the need to explain. "I mean I *literally* want to bite your head off. It will not be the first time I have done such a thing to small men who threaten me."

"Okay, gentlemen . . ." Nelle said, stepping fully into the room. That's when all the guns were trained on her. Because any true honey badger knew that the real threat in the room was the female badger instead of the male tiger.

She smiled, held her hands up so they could all see. "Everyone calm down. I'm unarmed."

"Liar."

"Yes. I'm lying. But you knew that. And instead of getting angry and making threats—"

"Or promising retribution."

"Not helping, Keane," she told the cat before looking back at Travers. "Let's all discuss this calmly."

"We are not here to talk, *chérie*."

"You want to get nasty with *me*, Maurice?"

"No, no. I am just the transport, yes? Here for you and your friend."

"So you come with guns?"

"Your reputation, as always, proceeds you, Gong Zhao. We were being cautious."

"I see."

"We're not going anywhere with you," Keane told Travers.

"Fine. Then we could kill you here, kitty."

TO KILL A BADGER 251

"Well," Keane said, "you and your friends can definitely get off shots as I move toward you, but the question will be if it stops me or will I keep coming . . . just for *you*?"

Travers quickly calculated the speed of an angry, vengeful cat and that of his weapon, plus the lack of help from the other badgers he had with him, because their kind was known to do that sometimes.

The odds were not in his favor. And they all knew it.

So, he looked at Nelle.

"Let's just go, Keane. Get this over with."

"Are you sure?"

"Actually," Nelle said, reaching for the silk wrap she'd left on the club chair outside her room, "I am."

Chapter 19

The drive was long, and Keane was ready to start killing everyone on principle alone. But he knew that biting off the heads of a bunch of badgers—even those not connected to her in any way— would only piss Nelle off. She was already angry at him for shoulder-checking Zeus into the wall face-first when they'd walked out of the elevator on the first floor and he had just been standing there . . . *not* protecting her. What was his purpose if he couldn't prevent a group of badgers from entering their penthouse suite?

Besides, seeing the rude bastard with a bloody nose and dented forehead while they sat in the back of the limo, glaring at each other, gave Keane a lot of brutal satisfaction.

He definitely wanted to bite off fewer heads now.

Keane glanced down at Nelle. She was sleeping peacefully against his arm. Apparently, the world traveler had quite the bout of jet lag. Luckily, he felt just—

Nelle knew as soon as the cat fell asleep beside her, because he growled-snored. He sounded like an irritated puma on one of those nature documentaries.

She knew he'd try to stay up to protect her, but she'd rather he sleep on their drive to their next location instead of dropping cold in the middle of their meeting. That never looked good. Especially with whom they were going to meet. Manners were quite important to royalty. Even fake royalty.

TO KILL A BADGER 253

Sitting up, she smoothed the skirt of her dress over her legs and looked at Zeus.

"Really?" he asked in French, gesturing to Keane. "I offer you everything, and this is what you choose?"

Zeus was Swiss-born, and his English had a heavy German accent. But the twelve other European languages he spoke were absolutely flawless. He came from a bear-only enclave in the Swiss Alps. Her father had recruited him when the family went on a skiing vacation one year. And no matter what Keane may think at the moment, Zeus had been a great choice, because he knew Paris so damn well. Even better than Nelle.

She knew there was no point in explaining to Keane that Zeus had absolutely been doing his job when he'd allowed Travers and his badger gang to sneak into their suite through the walls. She'd been waiting for them anyway. But she thought they'd at least give her the night before arriving. She'd really wanted that date with Keane.

But, alas, some things were not meant to be. At least not right now. Besides, she could not forget that she was here for business. Important, life-or-death business. The kind that would keep people up with worry.

Not Nelle, of course. She could sleep through damn near anything, but others, like Charlie and *definitely* Stevie . . . they liked to stay up and worry.

Nelle, however, simply liked to get things done.

The drive to their destination lasted more than three hours. Nelle stayed busy working on her phone and a tablet that Zeus kept at the ready in his briefcase. There were cars in front of them and behind them that kept an eye out for trouble . . . even if that trouble came from Nelle.

Hanging out with her teammates for the past decade or so had spread Nelle's reputation across the globe and separated her from the family's more refined one. A situation that had bothered her mother, although Nelle always thought it had less to do with Nelle's growing reputation among shifters and more about how Nelle had gotten that reputation while hanging out with Max MacKilligan. Of course,

254 *Shelly Laurenston*

her mother had been anti-Max since the day the kid had walked into their immaculate Wisconsin home in her big, dirty boots she refused to remove and announced to everyone, "Mind if I see what's in the fridge? No, no! I can do it! Thanks, Mrs. Z!" The look of horror that had been on her mother's face that day still haunted Nelle's dreams.

The entourage turned onto a dirt road and traveled deep into a forest until they reached the forest's edge and the massive château within, bright lights shining down on it and what appeared to be a party going on inside.

Realizing they'd arrived at their destination, Nelle reached over and gently slid her fingers through Keane's hair; his head resting on her shoulder. His eyes immediately opened, and he sat up, looking directly at Nelle. The smile that bloomed across his face at the sight of her nearly took her breath away.

Zeus growled, and Keane seemed to become fully aware of where he was and who else was in the SUV with them.

The cat's head snapped around, his gaze locked on Zeus, and his brutal snarl filled the space like a hard clap of thunder.

"Gentlemen?" Nelle warned when she heard the badgers in the front seat begin to growl. "How about we hold off on this apex predator fight until *after* our meeting?"

The SUV stopped in front of the château, and her door opened.

"Mademoiselle Zhao, please come with me," Travers said, holding his hand out.

Nelle reached for that hand, but a large hand with scars from past football games reached past her, grasped Travers's hand, and yanked the badger over her lap.

She pulled back a bit, hands raised so she didn't touch Travers's stunned body.

"She goes nowhere without me," Keane told Travers through his extremely large fangs, drool dripping down on the badger's face. "And if you try to separate us in any way, I'll *eat* your skin."

She'd heard a lot of insults and threats in her life—many of them from opponents on other teams toward herself and her teammates—but that was definitely a new one. And, to be honest, she didn't doubt

Keane's words at all. Which she found kind of hot. Not the eating skin thing—that was disgusting—but the willingness to do that for her.

Keane shoved the badger out of the vehicle and onto the ground before saying to Nelle, "Let's go."

After they stepped out of the vehicle and over Travers, they followed the other badgers inside, Nelle slipping her arm through the cat's and whispering, "Subtle."

"I am known for my subtlety. It's a cat gift. Like our flexible spines." He looked around at the amazing grounds and asked, "Do we need a plan?"

"A plan for what?"

"In case this gets weird."

"I'm sure it'll get weird," she promised. "But not positive a plan will assist in any way."

"That is *not* comforting."

She used her free hand to rub his arm. "I know."

This wasn't a mansion or a simple country house. This was a castle. An actual castle in the middle of the woods. Who could afford this? Such a ridiculous thing. To live in a place like this. He wasn't against normal-sized homes, but castles . . . really?

They were led to the side of the building to another entrance that had no guests. Keane assumed "servants" used this one, and he was immediately insulted. But he kept his mouth shut and his simmering annoyance under wraps as he and Nelle were escorted into a room filled with a big desk, a leather chair, and floor-to-ceiling cases filled with books.

Once inside, the badgers left, indicating Zeus should follow them. With a nod from Nelle, Zeus did what he was ordered and left.

"Isn't he your bodyguard?" Keane asked. "Shouldn't he be with you during all this?"

"I don't need protection from other badgers. And there is no blood feud between my family and the Von Schäfer-Müllers."

"Is that a thing you have to worry about? Blood feuds between badger families?"

256 Shelly Laurenston

"Sometimes. If we're bored and there's nothing else to do."

"I know from life with Nat that a bored badger is a problem."

"Oh, it is."

Keane walked over to the bookcases and studied the titles. Almost everything was in either German, French, or Italian, except for three books in English that were all about getting "amazing abs."

"See that Monet painting?" Nelle whispered.

He turned in the direction she was pointing. "Yeah."

"My cousin did that. He's really talented. See how he captured the way Monet played with light? Brilliant."

Keane stared down at her. "Does the family you need to ask for help know your cousin painted this?"

"Probably not. They picked this up at Musée d'Orsay right here in Paris during a nighttime heist. Replaced it with the one a cousin of *theirs* did, thinking they were taking an original, and here we are."

"Does that sort of thing happen often?"

"Yes."

She kept gazing at the painting. "Sadly, their cousin isn't nearly as talented as my cousin. Soon, someone is going to figure out the one at the museum is a fake. My cousin's version, though, had been there for over a decade. No one ever spotted it wasn't an original."

She patted his arm. "Best to keep that quiet while we're here, though."

He shrugged. "I'd have to care about stolen paintings between badgers to say anything about it."

"Excellent. They do have a lovely book collection, though." She pointed. "A very early printing of Dante's *Divine Comedy*. A signed copy of Kafka's *The Metamorphosis*. Oooh, and a Hermann Hesse signed first edition. Damn. How did they get that?"

"Wait . . . wasn't Hesse a—"

"That was Rudolf," she quickly cut in. "Wrong Hesse."

"Oh. Okay."

Keane heard metal scraping against metal and looked around the room. When he glanced down, he saw a head stick up from a grate built into the floor.

TO KILL A BADGER 257

"Uhhh . . . Nelle?"

Nelle leaned around him and stared at the space next to the desk. "Johann? Hello!"

"My dearest Gong!"

The badger crawled out of the hole in the floor, briefly stopping to push the metal grate back into place.

"Sorry to keep you waiting. It's never easy to get away from eager guests."

The badger held his hand out for Keane to shake, but he just gawked at it.

"You just crawled out of a sewer," Keane noted. "I'm not touching your hand."

"It's not a sewer. It's just a simple way to get around the house unseen." He swept his arm in a big arc. "Through the walls! Much better than walking out of a room in full view of everyone."

Keane focused his attention back on Nelle. "*This* is who you desperately need to talk to?"

She smiled up at him. "Yes."

"This, Keane, is Johann Frederick Ludwig Emmanuel Von Schäfer-Müller the Fourteenth. Grand Duke of—"

"I can't express to you how much I do *not* care about the man's title."

"Well," Johann said, "you are American."

Keane's eyes narrowed. "And you're wearing an ascot. What's your point?"

"Gentlemen," Nelle quickly cut in—she couldn't afford for Keane to be Keane this early in the game—"can we just get started?"

"Of course," Johann agreed. He moved around his desk and sat down in the big leather chair, pulling out a cigar from a case in his jacket pocket, and motioning to the chairs across from him. "Please. Sit."

Nelle took Keane's arm, tugged him over to the chairs, and pushed at his chest until he reluctantly sat down.

"Excellent," Johann said when everyone was seated. "Now would

258   *Shelly Laurenston*

either of you like something to drink?" He held up a clear container containing live scorpions. "Perhaps a little nibble?"

Keane's hands gripped the arms of his chair, fangs beginning to show again, and Nelle motioned the treats away with a quick wave of her hand.

"No, thank you, Johann."

"So, my dear," Johann began, putting the scorpions back into a desk drawer, "I'm guessing you're here about the Austrian royal jewels, yes? Name me a price!"

Nelle sat up straight in her chair. "No, no, no. That's not why I'm here."

"It's not?"

"No."

"Do you only know thieves?" Keane asked.

"Thieves?" Nelle glanced around the room as if looking for someone. "What is this word *thieves*? I do not know this word. English is not my first language."

"You already bragged to me how you only went to British schools in Hong Kong."

Ignoring Keane, Nelle said to Johann, "Actually, Johann, I'm here to ask for a favor."

"A favor? From me?"

"From your family."

"Ah. I see. So, I'm guessing this has to do with the de Medicis."

"It does."

"Yes. That whole situation is most unfortunate. But I'm sure we can come to some arrangement if you want my family involved with protecting your little friend. We have a delightful chalet in the Swiss Alps she might like."

"I'm sorry?"

"Everyone knows."

"Everyone knows what?"

"That some nasty cats are trying to kill your little MacKilligan friend, yes? The Chinese one? With the colorful hair? Although we can only protect her so long, because a *lot* of people want Max

MacKilligan dead. I think your own mother does. There may be no stopping that train."

"Johann—"

"I know for a fact your mother has a real issue with that tiny girl not taking her shoes off—"

"No, Johann. I'm not talking about Max; I'm talking about all of us. The de Medicis are trying to wipe out honey badgers."

He leaned back a bit in his chair and pressed his free hand against his chest. "But, my dear Gong . . . we are beloved."

"Are you?" Keane asked.

Nelle slapped Keane's shoulder with the back of her hand and continued on, "Of course we're beloved, Johann. We're delightful. But that's why the de Medicis hate us. Not just the MacKilligans—"

"Whom everyone hates."

"—but every honey badger. They see us as a threat and want us all dead, and they're going to great lengths to make it happen."

"I see. And what do you want from us?"

"Your influence. We need to combine the forces of all honey badgers, uniting to fight back against this. And with your help in Europe, talking with the European families, I know you can make that happen."

Johann took his time fixing his cigar before puffing away on it. Throwing his legs up on the desk and leaning back in his chair, staring up at the ceiling in what he probably thought appeared to be "deep thought."

Finally, after a few minutes, he said, "You're absolutely right. I can make that happen. But what would *I* get out of it?"

"You?"

He smiled at her. "Me."

Nelle wanted to leap over Johann's desk and choke him to death, but she was too busy stopping Keane from doing that himself. She grabbed his arm and held on for dear life.

"Johann, I don't think you understand the situation we—and I mean *all* honey badgers—are in," she told him.

"I'm afraid I do understand, my dear Gong. I mean, if you want to hire me to assist in this matter, that's different. But just doing something out of the kindness of the heart I do not have . . . you're asking a lot of me."

Keane stopped trying to pull away from Nelle and instead said, "I need to pace."

She understood and immediately released her grip. Keane stood and walked to the far side of the room, away from Johann and the desk, where he proceeded to pace the length from the door to one of the bookshelves. Back and forth.

"You do understand that if they get past us," Nelle explained to Johann, "they'll eventually come for you and everyone else."

"Of course!" he replied amiably. "But by then, my family will know what to expect, because they've already killed all of you!"

Nelle was about to explain how ridiculous that logic was—giving lions a chance to learn from their mistakes was always the wrong way to go—when something flew over her and at the male badger.

She knew it was Keane, but still . . . it was a shock to see his tiger form soaring over her head and onto Johann's desk.

Keane's forearms lifted up, and giant paws landed on the badger's shoulders, shoving him and his chair back and into the floor-to-ceiling window behind the desk. Except that particular window wasn't close. It was about seven-and-a-half feet from the desk. Keane's back paws were still firmly on the desk, so he had more length to stretch if necessary.

She knew Amur tigers could be that long, but to see it up close like that. . . .

Johann let out a panicked snarl, and the study room door slammed open. The group of badgers that had brought them here walked in, and Keane turned his massive head, unleashing a walls-shaking roar.

Never ones to back off, the badgers pulled their weapons—mostly guns and a few knives—and started forward, but Nelle held up her hand.

"I wouldn't," she told them calmly. "Especially if Johann isn't the one paying you."

They all stopped and waited. Nelle took her time getting to her feet and stepping around the chair, resting her hands on the back of it.

"Before this turns . . . unfortunate," she said, "I think we should take a moment and wait."

"Wait for what?" Travers asked.

The study door opened again, and she walked into the room.

Dressed in a simple gray dress from some common store and high-heeled shoes that were less than one hundred euros, the She-badger let out a sigh when she saw Johann snarling up at a raging Keane.

"I swear, Johann, you can't handle *shit*," she said in Polish.

"How is this my fault?"

"Shut up." She held the door open and motioned with a wave of her hand. "Everyone get out. Now."

Travers and the other males walked out at her order.

"Tell your cat to release him, Gong Zhao," Jules Kopanski-Müller said in perfect Cantonese to Nelle. "So we can talk."

"Keane."

He heard Nelle's voice, but really didn't want to let his dinner go. It had really pissed him off. But then a She-badger in human form appeared beside his tiger form, and she bravely slapped his snout a few times with her claws until Keane backed away.

He debated biting her head off, too, but Nelle slid her hand down his right hip, pausing to grip his fur between her fingers. That's when all he could think about was her.

Keane turned and leapt off the desk. He turned again and came to a stop next to Nelle. She pressed her hand against the back of his neck. Warm. Reassuring. Silently telling him she had this.

"Go," the older She-badger said, and Keane thought she was talking to him and Nelle. But she wasn't.

"He started it!" the male badger complained.

"You turn everything into bullshit. Go."

Shoving his chair back again as he stood, the male badger stomped out of the room, baring fangs at Keane as he did. When the door slammed behind him, the She-badger gestured to Nelle.

"Come, Gong Zhao, let us go talk. And bring your big kitty with you."

Chapter 20

"What about Chinese food for dinner?" Charlie asked her mate. He hadn't told her he was hungry yet. Instead, he'd just walked into the kitchen and stood there. Staring at her. Then his two siblings joined him. The triplets standing there and staring.

That's when she'd asked about Chinese food. She didn't know why they didn't just come out and say they were hungry like everyone else in the world. That's how she did it. Even Max just walked in and said, "I'm hungry. What you up for?" But not Berg and his brother and sister. It was some weird bear thing, Charlie guessed, and she didn't think she'd ever understand it.

"Okay," Berg replied to her suggestion.

Yet he and his siblings continued to stand there until Charlie said, "Yes, make sure to ask everyone else what they want and then order. They're probably hungry by now, too. And let's have it delivered."

"Okay."

The three turned and lumbered out of her kitchen in a single line. It had to be a single line, because the three of them were too big to get through the open space in any other way. Their sister was smaller than her two brothers, but she was still a grizzly. Her shifted form was only a few inches shorter than her brothers. All three of them nothing but massive amounts of muscle, adorable charm, and easily activated rage.

Once they were gone, Charlie focused back on the tablet she'd been studying, reading local news about attacks that had happened in the tri-state area that even remotely suggested something involving the de Medicis. Like what had happened at her aunt's house in the late morning. One of her cousins had called to tell her. They were all assuming it was a move by the de Medicis, although Charlie didn't understand what Paolo thought he'd get out of it. It's not like she or her sisters were close to her father's family. They didn't hate them, of course. Not like they all hated Freddy, but his three daughters were tainted by association.

So making a strike against the other MacKilligans would do nothing but irritate the family. Seemed a poorly planned move. The MacKilligans that called Scotland their home were crazier than most badgers, and harder to kill.

"Pssst!"

Charlie swiped her hand across her face to deal with the bug that she assumed was flying around her. She could hear it.

"Pssssssssssst!"

Realizing that noise wasn't coming from a bug, Charlie glanced over her shoulder and saw her baby sister peeking around the corner of the stairway that led to the back door and basement.

"What are you doing?" Charlie asked her.

"Shhhh!" Stevie motioned to her again.

"Can't you just tell me?"

Her sister flashed fangs, which she rarely did. Instantly realizing she'd briefly lost control, Stevie immediately gasped, her fangs disappearing into her gums, and her hand slapping over her mouth. She gazed at Charlie with panicked, wide eyes.

Seeing that panic, Charlie quickly stood and followed her sister into the basement.

"I'm sorry, I'm sorry, I'm sorry," Stevie kept chanting in a whisper as she went down the stairs. "I'm just . . ."

"It's okay, Stevie. Just breathe and tell me what's going on."

Stevie led Charlie to the table covered in science-looking stuff. Charlie recognized a few things from her high school days, but the rest of it . . . other than the massive desktop and three large screens, on a desk pushed up against the far wall, Charlie didn't know what she was looking at. But she knew her little sister did, and that's all that really mattered.

Stevie took a few seconds to practice the breathing exercise they'd both learned over the years to calm their panic or anxiety.

"There's a slight issue . . ." Stevie finally said.

"Why are you whispering?"

"I don't want anyone else to hear."

"We're in a house with shifters who all have enhanced hearing. They're more likely to ignore you if you're speaking naturally. But they will definitely notice you're talking about something you don't want them to know if you whisper, because you'll sound like prey trying to sneak away."

"Fine," she said in her normal voice. "I may have made a mistake."

"You need more samples?"

"No."

"Did you accidentally kill Max?"

"No."

"Did you shoot yourself up with something again, and now you have only a few hours to live?"

"*No.*" Stevie glared. "And I only did that once, and I was twelve. I am wise enough now not to do that again. So can you stop bringing that up?"

"So then what's the problem?"

"Well . . . I am pretty sure I found a counter-agent to the current poison they are using against us."

"Oh! Stevie!" Truly surprised and happy, Charlie gave her sister a quick hug. "That's awesome!"

"Yeah." She clasped her hands together and pressed them under her chin, her knuckles pressing hard into the skin. It would appear to someone who didn't know any better that she might be praying. But for Charlie, she knew that was *not* a good pose for her sister to take. And not simply because Stevie was a staunch atheist.

"Stevie?" Charlie pushed.

TO KILL A BADGER   265

"I have designed it so this formula can evolve along with whatever they come up with—as long as the base of what they use is the same, which it has been so far—and we won't need to keep reinventing a new antidote."

"That's excellent."

"Yes. But there is a chance that at some point, we may need to fight it to the death if and when it changes into a sentient being determined to rule the universe."

"Huh." Stunned, Charlie blinked. "That . . . that could be a problem."

"Yeah. Not a definite one, though. But something to seriously . . . you know . . . consider. And work to not let happen."

"Okay. So that's why you were whispering before?"

"No."

"Oh. That's unfortunate."

"Yeah, uh . . . you see, there's another issue."

"Another issue besides your antidote becoming sentient?"

"There is."

"Okay."

"Um . . ."

"You still don't want to say it out loud?"

"No. But here . . ."

Stevie went over to a bookshelf filled with black-and-white composition notebooks. Hundreds of them. She grabbed one from the middle of the fourth shelf down. It appeared her choice was random, but it wasn't.

She handed the notebook to Charlie and mouthed, *Page forty-nine.*

Charlie turned to page forty-nine, but it was all in Latin. A language she did not and would never know.

She looked at her baby sister, and Stevie said, "Oh! Right." She grabbed a black light from off a table and then ran to the stairs and turned off the lights from a main switch. She made her way across the room, ramming into several tables and barking "ow" each time before again reaching Charlie. Did she forget that both the animals she was made of had great night vision? Or was that particular ability cancelled out due to her unfortunate birth defect of being Freddy MacKilligan's daughter? Charlie really didn't know.

Turning on the black light, Stevie held it over the open notebook, and Charlie saw that underneath all that tiny Latin were other words. Words that could only be seen with a black light in total darkness.

Her sister had created an ad hoc palimpsest as only Stevie could.

Leaning in, Charlie attempted to read what was written until her sister shoved an extra pair of Charlie's glasses at her. Stevie always kept an extra pair around her lab so that Charlie could actually read things she handed her without squinting.

"Thank you," Charlie muttered, slipping the glasses on and reading her sister's words. Her eyes becoming wider with each new sentence. "Oh, shit."

"Exactly. I'm sorry, Charlie."

Frowning, Charlie asked, "For what?"

"For creating . . . *this*."

"You didn't do it on purpose."

"I know, but—"

"No buts. It's not your fault."

"Okay. It's not my fault. But we've got to do something. Right?"

Charlie looked off, thinking through their options, when Berg's sister called down the stairs with, "Charlie, you better get up here."

Stevie immediately panicked. "They all kno—"

Slapping her hand over her sister's mouth, Charlie yelled back to Britta, "What's going on?"

"Lions."

"Keane," Nelle said, "this is Jules Kopanski-Müller."

Still in his shifted form, the big cat turned his head, studying Jules.

"I know," the She-badger guessed Keane's unasked question, "you wonder how the Von Schäfer-Müllers and the Kopanski-Müllers mix, yes? Well, it is too hard to explain, and it no longer matters. My brother represents us among the royals, but it is *I* who runs this family. Which is what he should have told you right away. I apologize, Gong Zhao."

TO KILL A BADGER 267

"That's fine." She looked around the massive kitchen Jules had led them to in the back of the house. "I thought this room would be bustling with staff for the party," Nelle noted.

"This is the family kitchen. There is another kitchen that we use for events. Sit, sit," she said, gesturing to the stools at the island in the middle of the room.

"Here. Bread and cheese."

She sent a freshly made baguette down the length of the marble top, and Nelle caught it. She ripped off a large chunk and gave it to the tiger standing beside her high stool. Keane had not shifted back, and she got the feeling he wouldn't until he felt safer.

"Wine?"

"Red, please."

Jules studied several bottles sitting on the counter before choosing one. She took down wineglasses, used a wine opener to take out the cork, and filled two glasses halfway.

"I am assuming the cat—"

"The bread will do."

They took a moment to sip their wine, and Nelle ate some cheese and bread. Then, Jules began.

"Why are you here, Gong Zhao?"

"I need you to use your family's influence."

"For what?"

"For the badger families of Europe to join forces against the de Medicis."

"You want *badgers* to join forces?"

"I know. It's an unusual request."

"It might be slightly insane." She looked Nelle over. "It was not your idea."

"No. But I said I'd try."

"I see." She took another sip. "You know, some may feel that you simply need better friends. The MacKilligans are known to attract trouble."

"Don't blame this on them. The de Medicis are out to get us all, and it's not because Charlie MacKilligan killed their father."

268 *Shelly Laurenston*

Jules looked up from her glass, eyes wide. "Charlie MacKilligan killed Giuseppe de Medici?"

"Oh. You didn't know that already?"

"No." Pushing her glass aside, Jules rested her elbow on the table and her chin in the palm of her hand. "What a fascinating life you manage to live, Gong Zhao."

Britta, like her brothers, was not one for big emotions unless she was startled. So the quiet urgency in her voice had Charlie handing the notebook back to Stevie—who immediately returned to the bookshelf to stow it away in plain sight among the many other composition notebooks she had in order to confuse the unwitting—and running up the stairs.

The She-bear was already heading out of the kitchen and to the front door of Charlie's rental house.

"What's going on?" Charlie asked as they neared the exit.

"Berg got a call from the pride on the street over. Said a van was headed this way that they didn't recognize, and it smelled like lions they did not know."

Charlie was in the living room now when Britta made that statement. In response, Charlie held her arm out and, pulling it from behind the couch, Max tossed her sister a sawed-off shotgun that was already loaded and ready to fire.

"How many weapons do you have in this house?" Shay demanded from the love seat.

Ignoring the question of a concerned father, Charlie walked out of the house, across the porch, and down onto the street. But Charlie wasn't alone. Not only were the triplets, Max and her teammates, and Stevie beside her, but now Malones were coming out of their RVs, adult bears out of their houses, and everyone else who had been in her rental house, all coming onto the street to surround her. Protect her. All waiting until a white van came speeding onto their street from a different direction than they'd been expecting—meaning they'd taken a circuitous route for some reason. Maybe to confuse the cats on the other block who'd ratted them out?

TO KILL A BADGER 269

But the van didn't stay long. Charlie heard the back doors open, a thump, and then the doors closed. With that, the van screeched off, leaving nothing but something wrapped in a tarp and duct tape.

"Shit." Charlie tossed her weapon to Streep and took off running, pushing past everyone who wanted her to wait. But she knew what she was looking at. It was a body.

She crouched beside it and sniffed, hoping she could guess the remains without actually looking. Unfortunately, her sinuses were acting up after she'd made the mistake of standing by the blooming bushes next to her fencing, and now she couldn't smell *anything*.

Glancing over her shoulder and seeing Stevie coming up behind her, she gestured to Max to stop her, and unleashed the claw on her forefinger to carefully tear open the top layer of tarp that wrapped what had been dumped on the street. But she quickly realized she had more layers to rip through, tons of plastic, black garbage bags, tearing down and down until she finally reached the face of her . . . father.

Charlie yanked the wrapping harder and exposed the deep wound to her father's neck. His throat had been cut, literally, from ear to ear. Nearly decapitating him.

Eyes narrowing, her mind racing, she motioned to her sister with one finger.

Max took off running, her teammates right behind her.

Nat started to run with them, but Finn caught their sister in his arms and kept her from going anywhere. She was a little young for that sort of thing. Of course, once she hit eighteen, there would be no holding her back, but Charlie would deal with that when they got there.

"Oh . . . Daddy," Stevie sighed, crouching beside Charlie. "Poor Daddy."

"Yeah. Sure. Whatever."

"You could be a *little* upset," Stevie admonished her.

"I am," Charlie said.

"Then why are you smiling?"

"I am *not* smiling! I am very upset at the death of our father."

"Because it's our dad? Or because the de Medicis had the nerve to kill a MacKilligan?"

"Does that matter?"

"Charlie!"

Charlie waved her sister's recriminations off. What she needed at this time was to understand what was happening. Had they hunted down her father to kill him? Or had he been dumb enough to go to them? She'd only killed the de Medici patriarch because he'd come to her without warning and begun the conversation with threats to her family. There had been no other way to deal with it, at least in her mind. But if the de Medicis had hunted the idiot down. . . ?

Berg put a comforting hand on Charlie's shoulder. "You want me to call the cops?" he sweetly asked.

"Are you kidding—" was all Charlie got out, as her father's body jerked and he coughed up blood; his brown eyes opened to look right at his daughter. Proving that, despite the brutal, normally life-ending wound—even for a honey badger—the old bastard wasn't dead.

He. Still. Wasn't. *Dead!*

"Oh, for fuck's sake!" Charlie roared, startling shifters for miles.

Chapter 21

"What you're asking for, Gong Zhao, is unusual. And I do want to help but—"

"But you can't. I understand." She slipped off the stool. "We'll go."

"Unless we can come to some arrangement . . ."

Nelle stopped mid-step and let out a long sigh.

She faced the badger. "You and your brother are more similar than I realized, Jules."

"Nothing is free in this world, Gong Zhao."

"What do you want, Jules?"

"You know, there was a time when the badger families of Europe all joined forces to fight an enemy."

"Let me guess . . . Hitler?" Nelle asked.

"Of course Hitler," Jules huffed. "It is always Hitler. But those were full-humans. Now you are asking us to fight big cats."

"So?"

"That's a much bigger risk."

"It is?"

"And we should get something for taking such a dangerous risk."

"Let me get this out right now," Nelle said. "I'm not killing anyone for you. And if this involves the Pope . . . forget it."

"Ach! Don't bore me with what other people ask of you and your American friends. I have another issue I need your help with."

"Okay, then what do you want?"

"I need a book back."

"A book? You can't buy a new one?"

"It's a special book that someone stole from me. The loss of it has made me look weak among this small group I run."

"What small group?"

"A Satanic cult." Jules held up the wine bottle. "Another glass, Gong Zhao?"

Damon turned the corner and almost lost control of the small truck, but he righted it and kept going. As he sped down a random street, he saw the badger standing there, blocking his way. He could run her down and—most likely—she'd be just fine. But there were a couple of full-humans at the end of the block, chatting. He knew if he ran the badger down in front of them, they'd call the cops and get the license plate and all that other bullshit. They would definitely see it as a crime.

He didn't have time for that.

So he hit the brakes and stopped inches from her. She didn't even budge.

"D," his brother said.

"Keep it calm," he replied. "They're just badgers."

She walked over to the window, climbed up onto the rig, and politely knocked at his window.

He thought about not opening it, but knew a crazy badger would just bust it open with her fists.

"Hello," she said, when the window was down. She draped her arms inside, so he couldn't close it again without trapping her top half inside the truck. "Whatcha doin'?"

He didn't let that innocent-sounding phrase or her cheerful smile fool him.

"Nothing."

"Really?" she said. "Look, I'm short on time. So either you tell me what you guys are up to, or I'll—"

"Batter me with your tiny fists of badger-rage?"

"Or I'll blow your brains out all over this dashboard."

TO KILL A BADGER   273

Damon started to laugh, but stopped when he felt the barrel of the gun pressed against his temple. The passenger door swung open, and another gun was pointed at his brother.

Two more females stood in front of the truck, blocking him from just driving away. One with a sawed-off shotgun in her hands.

The full-humans had stopped talking and were watching, but neither made a move to call the cops. He didn't know if that made him happy or sad.

He'd forgotten that honey badgers had no moral code like cats and even worthless dogs. They would use guns, knives, anything to harm their enemies.

"Start talking," the badger pushed, finishing in a happy, singsongy voice with, "or I'm gonna get angry!"

Nelle glanced at Keane, still in his big cat form. His gold eyes were wide, and she felt she was mirroring back the same stunned expression to him.

"You run a Satanic cult?" Nelle asked. "You're a Satanist?"

"Of course I'm not a Satanist. What makes you think I'm a Satanist?"

"You just told me you run a Satanic cult!"

"For the money. Everything I do is for the money. Money is my god. And a happy god she is."

Now Nelle understood.

"All your cult members are rich."

"Of course they are!" Jules said, laughing. "And if very rich idiots want to give me money because they think a man with hooves, horns, and a pitchfork help them stay rich rather than their evil business ways and privilege, why would I tell them different?"

"Okay. I get that. But how does the book play into this?"

"It was taken from me by Jean-Pierre Lavoie. I want it back."

"The full-human banker? Why would he take your . . . wait. What kind of book are we talking about?"

"A book filled with rituals."

"So a Satanic book?"

"Yes."

"Is it made out of human skin?"

"Possibly."

"I'm done. If you killed someone—"

"It is an old book, Gong Zhao. I did *not* put the skin on there. I bought it that way in Romania many years ago. But it is part of all I do to keep these idiots involved in my little organization."

"Cult."

"Whatever."

"And Lavoie. . . ?"

"He helped me launder my money from these people. When I would not give him a bigger percentage, he stole the book."

"And you don't want to just pay him for it?"

"Of course not. What message does that send?"

"What message do you want me to send?"

"Not you, Gong Zhao." She pointed her finger. "I want *him* to send it."

Nelle looked down at Keane.

"He is *not* killing for you either!"

"I do not need him to kill." She grinned. "I need him to do exactly what his kind does so well. And what he just did to my brother, although he will never admit it."

"And what is that?"

"Scare the shit out of him."

Nat knelt by their father, patting his head with one hand and brushing his chest with the other, while Shay watched with disgust. There were not a lot of people he didn't like on principle alone, but if there was one . . . it was Nat's birth father, Fred MacKilligan.

He should be dead. Anyone else with a wound like that, shifter or full-human, would be dead. But Charlie was right. The guy just wouldn't die.

Shay wanted to pull his sister away from the idiot, but Finn had shaken his head. Best not to jump in yet. And, instead, sent Dani away with one of the aunts after they'd spotted her coming toward all the street drama playing out before them. She didn't need to see any of this. Especially Charlie's anger. Because that shit was formidable.

Yet, he couldn't figure out if Charlie was mad that the de Medicis had tried to kill her dad and thrown his body on their street like trash? Or if she was mad that they couldn't manage to kill the bastard.

Everyone knew how much Charlie hated her dad. And if it wasn't for Stevie, Fred MacKilligan would have been dead a decade ago. Especially after the time he'd sold Max into indentured servitude. "A less than fatherly move," Max had joked while telling the story. The fact the female could find humor in that childhood experience fascinated Shay and both his brothers.

For a few minutes, Shay was worried that Nat was going to be more like Stevie than her other two half-sisters when it came to Fred MacKilligan. Always willing to give him another chance. The way she was petting him like a wounded collie. But then she pulled a piece of paper from the tarp he'd been wrapped in and handed it to Charlie. That's when Shay understood his baby sister had just been looking for a note or something from the attempted murderers. As soon as she found it, she'd walked away from her father and back to Finn's side. Just leaving her birth father to bleed out on the pavement.

Good.

Charlie looked at the note, frowning, and handed it off to Shay. It basically said there would be more killings of MacKilligans if Charlie didn't give the de Medicis what they wanted. Which apparently was the MacKilligan family fortune?

Were they actually supposed to believe that Paolo de Medici would ever stop coming after Charlie and her sisters, no matter how much money they gave them?

Or that a truce would ever stop Keane from getting his revenge for their father?

Confused, Shay handed the note to Finn.

That's when Tock, Max, Mads, and Streep returned from tracking

276 Shelly Laurenston

down the truck that had dumped their father. Tock stopped by his side, glancing up at him. She didn't say anything, and he didn't take that as a very good sign.

Max stood next to Charlie, leaned in, and whispered something into her ear.

Charlie immediately paced away.

Everyone on this street at this very moment were apex predators. The tigers. The bears. The honey badgers weren't considered apex by science, but they really should be, because they were that mean when pissed off, which was why the other apex predators watched Charlie so closely. Over the short amount of time they'd all known her, they had figured out she was the ultimate apex predator. Her rage may be a rare thing, but when it exploded, it moved through the world like lava from an active volcano. Smooth, hauntingly beautiful, and heartless, destroying the poor Icelandic village it was tearing through.

Max crouched on the other side of her father, across from Stevie. He raised a weak hand to her, and she took it in her own, held it tight against her chest, and said, "Daddy . . . we found the truck."

"Did you kill them all?" he gurgled, despite blood still pouring from his open throat wound. "Did you get our revenge before I . . . die?"

"Unfortunately—"

"They were gone. I understand, baby. It's okay."

"Thanks, Daddy. For understanding. But we actually did catch up to them . . . and talk to them, and they wanted you to know that they're out of this deal, and you still owe them the fifty grand from the Super Bowl loss."

Stevie immediately stood, staring down at him. "Oh, my God, Daddy. *You* did this? To yourself? Just to get money from us and the family?"

"Of course not! That's a lie!"

"Daddy," Stevie pushed, her hands curling into fists at her side. "You're the one lying, aren't you?"

The badger blinked; his slow, tragic mind turned as he tried to think of a lie that would get him out of this.

"Uh . . ."

Finn crumpled up the note he'd been holding, and Nat walked away. He didn't even have to tell her what was said in ASL, because she already knew. Whether she read the lips or just understood . . . Shay didn't know. And it didn't matter.

Snarling, Stevie screamed, *"You are the worst person I have ever known! And I'm including the meth dealers you sold me to!"*

Shay couldn't believe anyone would risk cutting their own throat—deeply! Down to the spine!—just to get money out of his family so he could wiggle out of some gambling debt. Who did that?

Oh, yeah. Fred MacKilligan did that. Because he was an idiot!

Finally, a quietly seething Charlie turned around and, looking down at her father, said in a soft voice, "I've asked you this before, Dad . . . and I am going to ask you one more time . . . why won't you *JUST DIEEEEEE?"*

Lions from the street over roared in response to her scream. Three blocks away, wolves howled. On the very street he was standing on, tigers and bears growled. But all of that could be barely heard over Charlie MacKilligan's bellow of absolute rage and hatred at her own worthless father.

Charlie lifted her foot over her father's head, and Shay knew she was about to stomp his skull into nothing but a puddle. She was that angry. But then Berg was there. He grabbed her around the waist and lifted his screaming, fury-filled mate away. He had to work so hard to get control of her like this that his grizzly hump exploded between his shoulder blades. It was the extra strength that helped him hold on to her. But he was still having a problem, and his two siblings had to jump in to help. Dag grabbed her legs, and Britta wrapped her arms around the She-badger's chest.

"Let's go! Let's go!" Berg ordered, and the triplets quickly made their way back to the rental house, Charlie's roars of rage shaking nearby cars and the Malone RVs.

Vehicle windows were blown out.

Max, gazing down at her panicked father—who must have realized that he was trapped not only in this disgusting lie, but in the tarp,

278 Shelly Laurenston

plastic, and duct tape he'd used to *sell* his lie—stretched her arm out. Shay didn't know why until a simple axe flew past him and into her hand. He glanced over his shoulder and realized that axe had come from Nat. She'd gotten it from somewhere and sent it to Max to finish the job Freddy MacKilligan had started.

She was going to cut off her father's head. *Holy shit.*

"Finn . . ."

But before either of them could move to stop her, Stevie leaped over her father's struggling body—his claws working overtime to tear his way out of his self-made prison—and grabbed the axe handle. The sisters fought over it. Nat started to step in, and Finn grabbed her, holding her back. Because they both were certain now that she'd taken after Charlie and Max when it came to their birth father, which meant she'd be more than happy to cut the badger's head off. Something he didn't want his sister doing! Ever!

Taking his life into his hands, Shay stepped up to the battling sisters and wrapped his fingers around the hands holding the axe. He then yanked them forward and away from their father, since neither sister would release the weapon. The panda and the black jaguar—the two sisters' mates—joined in to protect the females from each other and, as one, they all headed back to the house. Each trying to get full control of that stupid axe.

As everyone moved away from the toxic badger, Fred MacKilligan yelled out, "I swear, you guys, I can explain everything!"

Smack dab between France and Spain, Andorra was one of those places that Steph Yoon loved to visit when she needed a break from everything. She used to own a beautiful house in the region, but she'd sold it about a decade-and-a-half back to help her—at the time—struggling business. Now, of course, she could buy that place and a few hundred more if she wanted, but she hadn't had any time recently to think about real estate. Besides, if anything good came on the market that would be perfect for her, Ox would handle it. The woman had been handling global real estate since she'd been old enough to get her Realtor's license. It had started off with her finding studio space for CeCe and gallery space for Nelle in some of the worst places in the five boroughs to handling available gallery space in London for Nelle's massive business. Even the Van Holtzes had been known to use her skills when they wanted to open a new restaurant in territories not known to be welcome to wolf packs.

Which was why Steph didn't understand what would make anyone think they couldn't be found by her and her girls in such a small principality like Andorra. As it was, Ox could find anyone, anywhere, whenever she wanted. But if one was actively hiding from her, Andorra was not the place to go.

Kicking at the door of the baggage area until it opened, CeCe leaned out to take a quick look around before announcing, "All clear."

Grabbing their backpacks, bottled water, and jars of honey, the four females jumped down to the tarmac.

"You know," Steph felt the need to point out, "none of this would be necessary if you weren't so cheap."

"I am *not* cheap," Trace snapped. "I am—"

"Budget-conscious," they all said before she could, which just annoyed her.

"We are getting too old for this," CeCe complained.

"Especially when we have access to jets we can board like normal people rather than hiding like rats in the jet's baggage compartment." Once on the ground, Steph took a few seconds to stretch her legs out and do a few forward bends to loosen up the now-cranky muscles in her back.

"Do you want people knowing what we're up to? Because everyone and their mother is probably watching us."

"You are so ridiculously paranoid, Trace."

"Am I, CeCe?" their friend asked, very dramatically. *"Am I?"*

"Okay," CeCe said, starting to laugh. "Take it down a notch, Lady Drama."

Steph pulled the straps of her backpack onto her shoulders and waited for the rest of her friends. They were all dressed in black, but CeCe's black jeans, black T-shirt, and black Keds were covered in paint; Trace's jeans, T-shirt, and work boots were purchased at the

Target closest to her main home during a Black Friday sale a few years ago; Ox's clothes were all designer, because she didn't mind spending several thousand dollars on black jeans, T-shirts, and combat boots named after some snobby Italian; and Steph's clothes were the same black hoodie, jeans, and Doc Martens she'd been wearing since she was sixteen and had hacked into the Pentagon one day when she'd been bored. She hated clothes shopping, so rarely had new clothes unless her husband or one of her sons picked something up for her.

Staring at her phone, Trace clicked her tongue against her teeth and muttered something.

"What now?" CeCe demanded. "What's wrong?"

"Nothing, nothing." She waved away their friend's concern before typing into her phone. "Just a more *local* update from our young friend."

"Do we need to—"

"Don't worry. Having it handled there."

Steph knew what that meant and decided not to worry about anything happening in the States while they were away. It was how she managed to pass her advanced calculus class in eleventh grade while running around Europe. By not worrying about calculus until she was home and then passing all the tests the teacher gave her with flying colors. And when that teacher asked, "You haven't been to class in more than week," Steph could reply with a straight face, "Of course I was. We talked about taking college-level calculus at Hofstra over the summer. Don't you remember?"

Turning away from the jet they'd hitched a ride on, Steph saw the stunned security guard watching them from a few feet away. This was probably not what he'd expected from his night. Seeing four middle-aged women climbing out of the bottom of a private jet like rats from a ship. Women who didn't seem damaged from a trip that should have frozen them to death, but didn't, because they weren't women at all.

"I thought you said it was clear," Steph pointed out to CeCe.

"It's just Romero. Hi, Romero!"

The guard seemed to snap out of his trance and fumbled with his

TO KILL A BADGER   281

radio to contact the rest of the security team protecting this small airport that catered to millionaires and billionaires of various repute, but CeCe walked a few steps forward. That move allowed the light from the nearby lamppost to hit her eyes at an angle, showing that they were not human eyes. Not at all. Because they flashed in a way one only saw from nocturnal animals.

Stunned, Romero dropped his radio and stumbled back.

Ox was already on the move, walking past poor, terrified Romero—her eyes shining like CeCe's—but pausing long enough to shove a wad of cash into his hand.

"You never saw us, Romero," Trace said to Romero in Spanish, since she didn't know Catalan, the main language of Andorra. "And that way, we won't ever stop by your house late one night. Because you wouldn't want that, would you?"

CeCe patted the man's shoulder as she passed him, telling him in Spanish, "Sorry, Romero. Didn't mean to startle you."

Steph didn't know how CeCe knew the man, but she also didn't care. Instead, she stopped by his side long enough to press her forehead against his and flash her fangs, opening her mouth wide. He'd probably think they were vampires, but whatever. As long as he kept his mouth shut, she didn't care what he thought.

She did feel bad, though, when he pissed himself. But Ox fixed that with another wad of cash she went back to shove into his other hand.

As they walked off into the night, CeCe asked, "Did you get us transport, Trace, or are we going to *walk* where we're going?"

"I have a Land Rover, paid in full, waiting for us in the nearby woods."

"Paid for?" Ox demanded, annoyed. She had no problem paying money for jewelry, designer luxury goods, and to keep people quiet, but she had never paid full price for any vehicle in her life. Even that three-hundred-grand Aston Martin she took a shine to and drove off in when they were briefly in Monaco.

"Why pay when we can just take?" she would always ask.

"Yes. *Paid for*, Oksana. I paid for a vehicle for us, not only because it's the right thing to do, but because Max MacKilligan is such a kind, sweet soul who actually purchased it for us with the money from her private Swiss accounts that not even her sisters know exists."

"Tracey Rutowski, you didn't!" CeCe gasped.

"So loving, our Max, don'tcha think? I've discovered she also loves to donate money to pug dog rescues in Arkansas. One of them is giving her a plaque to honor the two hundred thousand she's sent them out of the goodness of her heart."

Steph, CeCe, and Ox stopped walking, staring after Trace as she kept going, disappearing into the darkness ahead.

"Come on, ladies," Trace called out over their laughter. "This old *crone* has a lot of work to do!"

Chapter 22

Charlie had her head on the kitchen table. Max was slumped down in the kitchen chair, her gaze locked on the ceiling above. And Stevie watched them all with a bit of disgust.

"You can't kill our father," she was forced to say, yet again. "It's morally wrong."

"You said Max has no morals," Charlie explained into the table.

"And I stand by that."

"Then let me do it." Max sat up straight. "I promise not to have one guilty feeling about it."

"No."

"*You're unreasonable!*" Max exploded.

"There is only room enough for one mentally unstable She-badger in this family—*and that's me!*"

Berg lumbered into the room. "Dinner's here," he said, his naturally baritone voice even lower than usual. "We're eating in the living room. We can put on a horror movie and enjoy the Chinese food, and maybe the flying body parts and splattering blood will help you guys relax a little."

Stevie glanced at her sisters before telling Berg, "I don't think we're hungry right now, Berg. Just save us some?"

Frowning, he stared at the top of Charlie's head, then said, "Okay."

She understood the bear's concern. In some ways, it was definitely *less* terrifying to see Charlie MacKilligan so upset she could only sit and do nothing, but it was also sad. Stevie hated seeing her sister this upset about anything, but especially this upset about their father. A badger even Stevie had to admit was completely worthless. And she didn't like to believe that about anyone . . . except him. Because it was true.

Even worse, he wouldn't leave! He was still in their yard now, trying to remove duct tape from the hairy parts of his arms. Max offered to do it herself, but the look in her eyes—and the fact she was holding a butcher knife at the time—made it seem like a bad idea to everyone.

Since this whole family-only nightmare had begun, the bears, tigers, and the lions from the next street over had come to surround the house Stevie and her siblings were living in, forcing their father to keep his distance. No one was asking for baked goods. No one even tried to swim in their pool. Instead, everyone kept quiet and kept Freddy MacKilligan away from the house and his daughters.

Stevie thought about going to her father alone and trying to "reason" with him. Of course, her idea of reasoning with him was giving him money to go away before his head was separated from his shoulders. Giving their father money, though, was one definite way to make Charlie snap. She did not believe in giving their father a cent, even if it was the easiest way to get him to go. Then again, she had a very good point. Give him money once, he would keep coming back for more.

Berg walked back into the kitchen with a confused expression on his face.

"What's wrong?" Stevie asked, since her sister still had her face pressed against the kitchen table.

"Did you guys ask for *wolves* to stop by?"

"Wolves?" Stevie asked. "What wolves?"

"They say Van Holtz. Older guys."

Finally, Charlie lifted her head, and the three siblings exchanged glances. Then Max said, "Husbands of the crones, I bet."

"Oh. Right." Charlie let out a sigh. "Why would they come here, though?"

"Looking for their wives?"

"They're not here. Wait . . . are they?"

Stevie and Max shrugged. Then Charlie shrugged at Berg. "Let them in, I guess. And Max, do me a favor, don't call those women crones in front of their husbands."

"Even if they are?"

"*Max.*"

Hel followed the grizzly into the MacKilligan sisters' rental home. Of course, he wasn't surprised by the presence of a bear inside, because there were already so many bears *outside*. There were bears literally everywhere. On the porch. In the front yard. In the backyard. All down the street. And all different breeds, too. Grizzlies, polars, black, sloth, Asian black, a giant panda, and Hel could be wrong but . . . a cave bear? Didn't they go extinct in the last ice age? No, no. That was not possible. And the fact that there was a giant man hanging out on their porch—bigger than any other bear there—didn't mean it was a cave bear. That was insane.

Anyway, they were everywhere, and none of them liked the presence of any wolves in this miasma of their own bear smells. Especially Van Holtz wolves. Back in Germany, generations ago, the Van Holtz were well known for hunting down and eliminating brown bears for amusement and meat. It was something most bears from long-standing families had not forgiven.

Then there were the damn cats . . .

Jeez. He and his brothers left the country for a few weeks, and everything went to shit. What made Hel happy, though, was that although their mates were involved, they hadn't *started* anything. Such a nice change of pace! Usually, many a nightmare could be dumped right at the feet of their women, but not this.

That's why they were happy to help when needed if it didn't involve talking to their Uncle Edgar who, these days, barely tolerated Hel and his brothers.

Trace had texted Wolf, and the next thing Hel knew, they were headed to Queens. A place they rarely went to, because it was *Queens*.

When they entered the kitchen that late evening, Charlie MacKilligan immediately asked, "Are you also here to tell us you're not going to help? Because we really don't need to hear it twice."

286   *Shelly Laurenston*

"That's not why we're here," Wolf explained.

"Are you here to cook us dinner?" the little blonde with orange and white roots eagerly asked. Stevie, right? Yeah. The little one was Stevie.

"No."

"Oh. Okay." Apparently done with them, Stevie pushed back from the table, grabbed a bottled water from the refrigerator, and walked down some back stairs.

"Then what do you want?" That was from Max, the middle sister. The last time he saw Max, she had green hair. Tonight, it was orange and, if he cared more, Hel would tell her that color did not work on her.

"We saw your father out in the yard and, with that particular situation, we can help."

"*You are not killing our father!*" Stevie yelled from beneath the house.

"*He tried to scam his own daughters!*" Max yelled back.

"*I'm not protecting him! I'm protecting you guys! You'll never recover from the guilt!*"

"*Yes, we will!*" both older sisters yelled at the same time.

"I said, *no!*"

The two older sisters looked at each other, and something unspoken passed between them. Something that was keeping their hated father alive. It was sweet, actually. That they cared enough for their baby sister to not kill the one being who made them absolutely miserable.

Charlie sighed and asked Wolf, "Can you get rid of our father and *not* kill him?"

"We were never going to kill your father."

"Why not?" Max asked.

"That's not really our job."

"How much to make it your job?"

"*Max!*" Stevie bellowed from below, making the windows shake. A little scary, considering the size of that tiger-badger hybrid when human.

"I'm sorry," Charlie said, holding up her hand, "but knowing your wives and the Russian, I really don't believe it's *not* your job to kill people."

Wolf smirked. "Then let me rephrase. We don't kill anyone without direct orders from the President of the United States. But we can deal with your father in other ways. If you ladies would like."

"Are you calling us 'ladies' sarcastically?" Max asked, using air quotes.

Hel's brother smiled. "I've known my wife for at least forty years. I've seen what a honey badger female can and will do when she feels a male of any species is not being nice or is using his sarcasm to insult her. So when I use 'ladies' with you guys . . . I always mean it politely, if not honestly."

"Totally fair," Charlie replied.

Charlie hadn't slept in more than twenty-four hours, and although she wasn't in the mood to eat, her body was about to give her no choice. The smell of that delivered food was starting to get to her. But she had to deal with the Van Holtz wolves in her house. Giant bear faces, with those adorable small eyes, kept appearing at the kitchen windows, glaring at the wolves. Apparently, it was one thing to have big cats hanging around, but wolves were somehow a step too far? Nope. She still didn't understand the shifter world, and that was probably okay.

"Look," one of the handsome Van Holtz wolves said to Charlie and Max, stepping closer, "I get it." Although, when Charlie thought about it a little, *all* of these wolves were handsome. They looked like those young male models who had salt-and-pepper hair to make people *believe* they were in their forties or fifties. But these three actually were. Yowza. Lucky She-badgers, those three. "You two are exhausted. You *sound* exhausted. And I'm guessing that if Fred MacKilligan is around much longer . . . both of you are going to snap and upset your little sister."

He wasn't wrong. Every time Charlie heard her father call out in pain from *still* removing that duct tape or when he kept insisting that, "I can explain everything!" she wanted to cut his head off. Because it

288   *Shelly Laurenston*

was clearly the only way to be done with him. Cut off his head, salt his body, and toss the head into an active volcano. Anything else, and the bastard was liable to return.

Charlie glanced at Max, and she saw the agreement in her sister's eyes. They both knew the handsome wolf was right.

"So," the canine went on, "let us deal with him, and you *ladies* focus on what's happening here. I promise, nothing permanent and, sooner than either of you will probably like, I'm sure he'll be back. But it will give you guys a little breathing room."

Silently checking with Max once more, Charlie eventually nodded. But she had to ask, "This may be rude, but . . . why are you being so nice to us? Because no one is ever nice to us, and your uncle made it clear—"

"Our uncle was just bringing you a message from those he still works with. We, however, are currently retired. Mostly. Besides," he added, "we're doing this because my wife asked us to."

"She knows our father's here? How? It just happened."

"I have no idea, and I learned a long time ago not to ask those questions."

Max got that look on her face. The one that told Charlie her sister was being completely serious for once.

"Where's your wife?" she asked. "Right now?"

There went that smirk again. It wasn't nearly as irritating as most male smirks. Maybe because he was just so goddamn handsome. "That's another question we don't ask our wives. But," he continued, "for whatever they have done or are about to do . . . we heartily apologize. And I'm sure they meant well."

Charlie and Max simply gawked at the three males until one of them clapped his hands together, startling them both.

"Now! Let's deal with your dad."

The wolves walked out, and Max, with a shrug, went to get something to eat. But Charlie headed down to the basement, finding Stevie reaching for her latest phone.

"I'm about to text Tock's grandmother," Stevie said, without even

TO KILL A BADGER **289**

looking at Charlie. "She's become my point person on managing this antidote. She may come here and—"

Stevie looked down at Charlie's hand over her own.

"What?"

"I changed my mind," she told Stevie.

Stevie's eyes grew wide. "You're going to let them kill Dad?"

"*No*, dumbass."

"Oh. Then what?"

"The mistake you made. Let's keep it . . . for now."

"The mistake I made? Oh! You mean the other stuff. I guess . . . wait . . . why would you want to keep that?"

"Why do you think?"

Stevie thought a moment before gasping. "Oh, Charlie. No!"

"It's a non-lethal way to shut him down and keep him out of our lives."

"It's wrong. To permanently change someone's DNA? It's *morally* wrong."

"*Dad* is morally wrong. And I am running out of ideas on how to keep him under control."

"Yeah, but—"

"Look, *if* he comes back, we'll talk about it. But for now, we just keep it. We won't tell anyone else. Not even Max."

"Especially not Max."

"Okay. I'm fine with that. Just the two of us will handle this together. If and when the time comes. Deal?"

Stevie stared at her work table before taking in and letting out a deep breath. "Okay. Deal."

"Great."

"To work off my anxiety, can I tell Max I think I'm going to give myself twins with science and witchcraft?"

"Stevie, this is a very serious situation, and we really don't have time for that . . . so, *of course* you can."

Finally smiling, her baby sister ran upstairs.

Charlie stared down at the tube of "mistake" that her brilliant sister had created—and which might be a permanent fix for all her Dad-related issues—until she heard Max scream, *"Charlie, you cannot be okay with any of this!"*

Grinning, she yelled up, *"Max MacKilligan, we will all love Stevie's demon twins! And that 'all' includes you, missy!"*

Alexei Huranov followed his security team into his Andorra mansion, with four more trailing after them to make sure no one came rushing in behind. He had men on the roof of his mansion. He also had CCTV everywhere. He was better protected than those British royals. He knew that everyone thought he was paranoid. He knew the world called him "the paranoid Russian" because he worked so hard not to be seen. Not to be known, except by those who could afford his services. But he wasn't paranoid. He was wary. And they all thought he was this way because of where he'd come from. Because of his home country and the way it changed in the early nineties. But that wasn't it. That would never be it. He was still beloved by those who now ran that part of the world. Always would be, because he'd always known how to stay invaluable to those who needed what he could offer.

No. His paranoia came from another reason. Another threat. One he'd been dealing with all of his life.

Walking down the marble-floored hallway, Alexei abruptly stopped and looked at the spot over a Louis XIV side table.

The empty picture frame screamed at him. He'd had an original Picasso in that frame. Some people thought the same painting was in the Picasso Museum in Barcelona, but it wasn't. Because it had been right here for the last few years. In his house. Or, at least, it had been. Now it was gone.

"We go," he ordered his men, and they all turned around and started toward the front door.

The first guard was yanked away and dragged down the hall by a thin rope around his neck. The second guard tripped on something and went down so hard, his head hit the marble, instantly knock-

TO KILL A BADGER 291

ing him out. The remaining two guards grabbed Alexei by the arms, quickly dragging him toward the front door. But a wire around one's legs yanked his feet out from under him, and he slammed into the ground. The fourth guard hit the wall beside them, something from the shadows grabbing him and shoving him into that wall again and again, until he stopped moving.

Alexei ran toward the front door on his own, but a small shadow stepped out, and he quickly turned. Now he headed toward the big ballroom.

As soon as he entered, he tripped on something thin that dug into his ankle and tore his pants. He hit the ground face-first, but immediately rolled onto his back. That's when he saw her. Standing over him like a demon from his nightmares. Just like when they were children.

"Hello, little brother," she said in Russian, before grabbing him by the hair and dragging him across the marble floor. "It's been so long. And how I have missed you so!"

He let her pull him a few feet before he remembered that he was now a powerful man whom people feared.

Digging his heels into the floor to slow her down, he moved his hands away from his head where she gripped him, and grabbed her forearms. He pulled and flung, sending his big sister several feet away from him.

He had to remember who he was! He was no longer Grigoriy Lenkov, most disrespected son of Sergei Lenkov. Now he was Alexei Huranov. He controlled banks and men. He ran guns in and out of foreign countries after starting wars he could not be bothered to care about. He had his choice of beautiful women! He was Alexei Huranov! Not some child afraid of his evil big sister!

Alexei had fought his way up to such wealthy heights after the Soviet Union had been dismantled by doing what he did best. Trading in information and helping people hide their money. As a former KGB officer, it was easy for him to simply keep doing what he'd always been doing. Back in those early days, he'd simply had to stay nimble, avoiding his family and any war crime tribunals. But now he was here.

292 *Shelly Laurenston*

With multiple properties around the world; a seven-hundred-foot yacht anchored in the Aegean Sea, where his current twenty-three-year-old wife was enjoying some fun times with her friends; and with so many cars, he could hold his own at *Le Mans*, if he wanted.

In the global papers, he was often called an oligarch, but he saw himself as an underdog that had fought his way to the top. As someone who had struggled and suffered for all the things he now had. So he didn't have to take any more shit from the sister who used to torment him when he was too young and small to defend himself.

Getting to his feet, he saw Oksana already charging him. When she was close, he caught her around the chest and lifted her off the ground. She slammed her elbow into his face, shattering the nose he'd already had fixed to change his look and to make himself feel more handsome. All that work destroyed after one moment with Oksana Lenkov.

The bitch grabbed him by his five-thousand-dollar leather jacket, using it to spin him around, attempting to disorient him. He grabbed her arms and yanked her close. She slammed her booted heel into his instep and, annoyed at the additional bout of pain, he did what he'd been known to do when some full-human woman pushed him too far.

He slapped her across the face.

Alexei knew it was a mistake as soon as he'd done it. Unlike the full-human women, his sister didn't cry out or sob or start swinging at him wildly with flailing arms and fake nails and a slew of curse words. No. Not his sister.

Instead, slowly, her head turned back until she was looking right at him. She had that terrifying blank expression on her face that he remembered far too well. He hadn't seen that look since he'd turned her in to the KGB as a dissident. He'd gotten an award and a job at fourteen. She was sent to East Germany, for some reason. He still didn't know why. She should have been shipped off to Serbia like everyone else he'd tossed at the KGB for treats and rewards. But for whatever reason, she'd been sent to the Stasi for interrogation. A decision the KGB—and eventually, himself—had soon regretted.

Now he saw that blank expression again, and that's when he knew he was in trouble. So he did what he'd always done when they were both still living on his parents' honeybee farm . . .

He ran.

Tracey cringed when that slap rang out across the room, the three of them turning toward the sound.

When they'd decided this was the quickest way to track down where the de Medicis were hiding because Grigoriy Lenkov had been laundering that coalition's money for decades now, they all knew it might get . . . well . . . out of hand. Ox was not the forgiving type. Her brother had betrayed her in a way no one ever had before or since but, more importantly, he was family. Badger kin did not fuck over badger kin like that and expect anything but retribution. And despite always having a general idea of where her brother was at any given time, Ox had allowed him to live for all these years, because she never knew when they might need him for something.

Trace looked down at the full-human protection lying on the floor at their feet. There had been no reason to kill any of them, since knocking them out would do the job. They really only needed a few minutes to get what they came for and then get out. But they hadn't planned on Grigoriy fighting back. He'd always been such a weasel. Not a honey badger weasel, which he was biologically, but an actual human-like weasel. Because who the fuck betrayed their own family? Even Mads never did that to her mother, and God knew, that girl had had every right!

Stupidly, Trace now realized, she'd hoped that Grigoriy would simply give them what they needed without much fuss. She should have known better, but they'd been using information from him for years by simply having specialists invade his computer and phones to get what they needed. Right now, though, they were exceedingly short on time, and their current "specialist" was very busy. So this time, they'd gone for the direct approach, not realizing how cocky being a Russian oligarch had made the little weasel.

Of course, more fool him. Because no male should ever get cocky around Oksana Lenkov.

Grigoriy attempted to run, but Ox had always been faster. Crazier. She charged after her brother and tackled him from behind, slamming him to the ground the way her father had taught her all those years ago.

"We need him alive, Ox!" Steph yelled out.

Their friend stopped, keeping her yelling brother pinned to the ground with her arms, her beautiful face contorting as she attempted to control her badger rage. Finally, snarling through clenched fangs, Oksana Lenkov made her move.

"*Ohhhhhhh!*" all three of them cried out, instinctively cringing at the sight, although their combined sounds could barely be heard over Grigoriy's horrifying roar of pain and humiliation.

"Nothing worse than an atomic wedgie," Steph said with a head shake.

"This is why underwear to me is always optional," CeCe said, before slamming down her bat onto the head of one of the security guys sitting up next to their feet.

"Is it?" Trace wanted to know. "Optional, I mean? It really shouldn't be optional."

"I will not be forced into garments meant to keep women in their place!"

"When those garments were corsets, I get it. But we are at a point in history where there is an array of underwear, my friend. And I am tired of seeing your pussy every time you step out of a limo."

Ox grabbed her brother around the neck—ignoring his continuing screams—lifted him up, flipped him over, and down. Hard.

"She does love the head drop," Steph noted.

It was true. Ox still loved wrestling from when she was learning it from her silver-medaled father and bronze-medaled mom in shot-putting. Sadly, her baby brother had never been able to pick up any of the techniques as well as Ox did. She had skills, though. Could have gone gold if she hadn't been, ya know, arrested by the KGB and ended up in a Stasi prison in East Germany all those years ago.

All because of Grigoriy.

Ox dragged her nearly comatose brother over to them and shoved him into an antique Louis XIV chair like it was something she'd picked up from Ikea. Trace opened her mouth to tell her friend to "be careful!" but CeCe wisely cautioned her with a shake of her head. Telling Ox to take care of historically important furniture would just have her using each piece to beat her brother for the next hour.

"We have questions, little brother," Ox told Grigoriy in Russian, "and you are going to give us answers." She leaned in close so the badger could hear every word. "Or I am going to start taking organs you have forgotten you have—and desperately need."

"Did you ever think, Ox," CeCe suggested to her friend, "that maybe the reason your brother ratted you out to the KGB all those years ago was because you used to torment him so much when he was little?"

"Not my fault he is weak. And we all tormented him because he always cried like little bitch."

"Yeah," Steph said with a nod, "that is definitely why he ratted you out."

Ox laughed. "You always feel bad for him, my friend."

"Not really. He's a scumbag that runs guns and marries girls more than half his age. But is that because he was born an asshole? Or because you beat him into *being* an asshole?"

"Ahhh," Ox said as they made their way to the helicopter waiting for them far out at the edge of her brother's property. "The question again of nature or nurture. My friend CeCe the philosopher has returned."

"She never left."

"At least we got what we need," Trace pointed out. "And for once, we didn't leave an island worth of bodies in our wake. See? We are *not* out of control!"

Slinging her arm around CeCe's shoulders, Ox softly asked, "Is she ever going to let go what the old Van Holtz wolf say to us?"

CeCe leaned her head against her friend's shoulder. "You'll forgive your brother for turning you in to the KGB long before Trace *ever* forgives that old man for saying we're out of control."

Chapter 23

When Keane trotted back to the château's study, shifted to human, and grabbed his clothes, Nelle assumed he'd get dressed. She was wrong.

Naked, with his clothes in his hand, Keane Malone stalked through the crowd of rich people enjoying overpriced wine—most of it fake, based on the poorly made labels slapped onto old bottles—and out into the night.

She followed after him, watching how the full-humans gawked at him as he stomped by. Some lusted, some feared, and some men with too much testosterone wanted to fight. Keane ignored them all.

When he went out the ornate, double front doors, past the hired badger security that started laughing—until Nelle slapped two of the closest in the backs of their heads—Nelle quickly picked up speed so that she now walked beside him.

"You're angry," she guessed.

"You said this would be quick. You said we'd go and come right back. You said nothing about killing Satanists."

So focused on getting back to their SUV, Keane walked straight at a middle-aged couple, forcing the pair to separate. Instead of being annoyed, they stopped to watch him go by; then the woman said to the man in Greek, "It's *that* kind of party. Let's go!" She held out her hand, the man grasped it, and they *ran* to the front door to get inside.

How disappointed they were going to be in a minute or two.

TO KILL A BADGER 297

When Keane reached the SUV, he put on his clothes. Apparently, he wasn't willing to slide his bare ass across the leather seats.

"I can't believe you agreed to any of this," he complained, tugging on his boots.

"It's not like we have a choice."

"You could have said no."

"And then we get no help, and Rutowski jumps in to make it worse. We at least have to try so that She-badger has no room for argument."

"All this bullshit for that female to—"

"Talk to *all* the badger families in Europe and convince them to join us. Do you know how hard that is?"

"You mean sending what basically amounts to an email?"

"*I* could send an email. Or a text. But she's not blocked on their phones, and her email won't disappear into a spam folder because her mother irritated them once!"

Now dressed, Keane stared down at her for a moment before giving a snarl and getting into the SUV.

Holding the door open, Zeus smirked when the tiger passed him, but Nelle quickly told the bear, *"Don't."*

As they headed back to Paris, Keane kept his gaze firmly focused out the window until the SUV finally stopped in front of the Llewellyn Arms du Paris and they both got out. Zeus followed them into the hotel and to the elevator.

As soon as they reached their penthouse, Nelle went to the bar and began doing something behind it, while Keane and Zeus made sure all the rooms were clear from any more "visitors."

Once done, Zeus went back to the elevator, and Keane asked, "Think you can manage to keep people out this time?"

"Leave Zeus alone," Nelle chastised, not even looking at him.

As the doors closed, and with Nelle's back turned, the bear gave Keane double middle fingers.

Keane's tiger form hit the doors just as they closed shut, slamming him back into the room to sprawl out on the floor.

298 *Shelly Laurenston*

When he looked up, Nelle stood over him with two glasses of liquor.

"Feel better after that?"

He shifted back to human and, naked, stood in front of her.

"I hate him," he said, taking the cut-glass from her hand.

"That appears to be mutual, so I'm not too worried about it."

"I can't believe we have to do this," Keane said, staring down at the brown liquid in his glass. Smelled like scotch. "This dog-and-pony show."

"It is the way of my people," she said, sipping her liquor.

Annoyed, trying to understand, he grabbed the glass out of Nelle's hand before she could take another sip and took both to the bar, dumping them into the sink.

"I was going to drink that."

"I need you sober." He placed the glasses on the bar. "Just so we understand each other . . . I'm not killing Satanists."

"You were there. You heard me tell her you weren't killing anyone."

"I don't like the idea of terrorizing this guy either."

"He launders cult money, and you're protective of him?"

"I don't know this guy. I don't know anything about him."

"You think he's doing it for his sick mother, who may or may not be a Satanist, too?"

"I'm definitely not harassing Satanists just to amuse a bunch of European badgers."

"So you're pro-Satanist?"

"Just because they're Satanists doesn't mean they're horrible people."

"Seriously, Keane?"

"Freedom of religion, Nelle. As long as they're not sacrificing babies or virgins—"

"What about goat sacrifice?"

"I'm *not* killing anyone!"

"I would never ask you to do that. I have no plans to kill anyone either. Especially for Jules. And this isn't about freedom of religion.

These are selfish rich assholes that don't care about anyone or anything, and being Satanists has little to do with any of it."

"I just want to make sure you understand what I'm saying!"

"I understand!"

"Good!"

"Good! Now," she demanded, sounding equally pissed, "do you want to have angry sex with me or not?"

Keane stared at her. "I'm not angry at *you*. Just your kind."

"I know."

"Then wouldn't having angry sex right now just be *me* taking my frustrations out on *you*? And I have to tell you that smiling at that question is really disturbing."

He was just *so* adorable, wasn't he? Where did he come from? How was he like this? She didn't know a lot of men who were this earnest. About goddamn *everything*!

"I'm sorry," Nelle told Keane. "I just find you so cute."

"You make me sound like a puppy."

Nelle walked toward him. "You sound exhausted."

"I am exhausted. I have jet lag, I hate Zeus, and badgers have us dealing with rich Satanists. It's been a long day."

She motioned to one of the bedrooms. "Go get some sleep. I'll wake you up in the morning, and we can make plans."

"So that's it?" he demanded, scowling. Although she no longer heard real anger in his voice.

"That's what?"

"I don't deliver angry sex, and you just turn on me?"

"I am *not* doing that," she said on a laugh.

"I see how it is," he continued, in a grumbling tone. "Just here for your amusement."

"Go to sleep, foolish cat," she ordered.

"Fine."

Keane was so clearly tired, she felt bad for teasing him. He really did need sleep after what would be a long day to anyone who was not a honey badger.

Nelle, however, *was* a honey badger, and not ready for bed. So, once Keane disappeared into a bedroom, she made her way over to the bear-sized couch one could only find at shifter-owned hotels. Pricey, fabulous furniture made of only the best materials. Created to be big and sturdy enough for a full-sized polar bear to sleep on.

Grabbing the remote off the coffee table, she kicked off her heels and sat down on the very corner of the couch so that she had the support of the armrest. Without being so deep inside the giant couch, she would look like a three-year-old girl waiting for her parents to get home.

She turned on the wall-covering, high-resolution TV and immediately flipped through the available channels. Thankfully, there were many, and she had lots of options.

What she apparently had no option about was the eight-hundred-pound Amur tiger that settled on the couch right beside her. She was *going* to say something to him—like "move your ass off my couch"—but when his big, heavy head gently landed in her lap, what could she do?

Apparently, she could only stroke her fingers against the fur covering his head, neck, and under his chin. She also scratched his ears and down the part of his chest she could reach.

Keane was asleep in seconds, and Nelle found even his growling snores and twitching limbs adorable.

Goodness! What was wrong with her?

Charlie sat on the stoop of her home and stared out over the neighborhood. A few locals were lumbering back to their houses for the night, nodding at her as they passed.

She glanced at her phone. It was late here, but it would be dawn in Europe. When Max had told her that's where Nelle and Keane had gone, Charlie had been surprised. Not about Nelle taking off, but Keane? That man was *not* a traveler. He may be descended from nomads on both sides of his family tree, but he was a cat that liked one home and one place to live.

TO KILL A BADGER 301

She, however, was thinking about leaving. Just running away.

Her hope was that Paolo would follow her. Come after her. They could meet face-to-face and end all this between them. She felt bad about what she was doing to this whole neighborhood. To these lovely people. To her sisters. To everyone.

"No."

Charlie looked up to find Lisa Malone standing in front of her.

"No?"

"No."

"I don't understand."

"Whatever you're planning . . . no."

"I wasn't planning—"

"Don't lie. I know that expression on your face. My husband used to get it all the time when he was about to disappear on me or do something crazy. It's how he looked just before he was killed. By the de Medicis."

"Mrs. Ma—"

"You can lie to my boys. I don't care. But you promised *me* you'd work with Nat. And I need you to do that. I never thought I'd say this, but . . . she might be a little more than I can handle."

"She does love you," Charlie wanted the woman to know. "She loves her family."

"Oh, I know. I don't doubt that. But she is . . ."

"Honey badger."

"Yes. And I'm used to cat logic. I don't know how to get in her head, in order to protect her when she needs it. But you do. So, whatever you're planning, it better take place here. In New York. In case you need my help. But if you run off like my Keane—"

"Nelle is very persuasive."

"Yes. I've noticed her legs, too."

"They are amazing."

"They really are. My boy didn't stand a chance." She shook her head. "So you stay. We stay. And we figure this out together. Understand?"

302 *Shelly Laurenston*

"No offense, but I really don't—"

The cat was suddenly right there. Face-to-face. Nose-to-nose. Gold cat eyes relentlessly boring into Charlie.

"Understand?" the She-tiger pushed.

"Yes, ma'am."

"Good. Glad we talked."

Then she was gone. Just walked off, went around an RV, and didn't come back.

Charlie didn't realize she had been holding a breath until she felt a strange vibration that kept going off every few seconds, would stop for a moment or two, then start again.

Letting out that breath, Charlie stood and went in search of the vibration. Stopping at the edge of the yard, she squatted down and began to dig. She didn't have to go far to find the box. She used her claws to rip it open and took out the phone. She didn't recognize the brand or why someone had buried it, but it began to vibrate again. A call from . . . someone.

Curious, Charlie tapped the screen to answer and listened.

Chapter 24

They sat on the veranda of the unoccupied home, looking out over a small town and enjoying the breakfast they'd picked up at a local bakery that hadn't even opened its doors yet. They hadn't stolen anything. Ox just knew the owner and her daughter. Steph had made the coffee, because the woman did love her coffee. All those years working hours upon hours on code and product had made her a connoisseur of the "addictive elixir," as she liked to call it. They'd managed to get a few hours of sleep in the house's cabinets once they'd left Ox's brother's house. He'd already left the country, limping his battered body to his private jet, a new security team helping him. He would attempt to go underground again, but Ox would always know where her brother was located, and she would find him when needed. Or just when she wanted to pull his underwear over his head again.

Right now, they were just enjoying life in Andorra and killing some time until they could catch a ride on another billionaire's jet, because Trace was nothing if not budget-conscious.

CeCe's best friend had been using that term since high school, and she really believed it. Because Trace knew when to spend money and when not to. It was why she had such a thriving business. She never wasted cash. She'd seen too many galleries go under because the owners spent money on ridiculous things. Private jets, Rolls-Royce limos, the best champagne, and overspending on art that was shit. Some people, of course, thought that Trace's galleries thrived because

304 *Shelly Laurenston*

her husband's family money backed her up. Little did they know how that family felt about Trace, CeCe . . . all of them. There were family members who wouldn't piss on the four of them if they were on fire . . . and wolves loved to piss on *everything*.

They'd been sitting on this balcony, watching the sun rise, and enjoying their lives, when Trace glanced at her phone and abruptly sat up.

"Oh, shit."

Steph looked up from the hardback copy of Stephen King's *Misery* she'd found on the owner's shelves. A book she'd read so many times, her own signed copy was falling apart.

"Okay," CeCe sighed. "Who did what to whom, and whose ass do we need to kick when we get back?"

CeCe assumed that something was going on with their three sets of kids. Because they'd grown up together, because their parents were so close, and because the wolves weren't crazy about having honey badgers as part of their bloodline—and didn't like the idea of their pups picking up bad honey badger habits, of which there were many—their offspring were incredibly close. More like siblings than cousins. Which meant stupid fights often broke out about stupid things. When they were young, their fathers handled most of the drama. But now that all but one were adults, they were inherently more dangerous. Meaning it had been up to the mothers to step in when necessary. Or they just sent in Ox. The kids adored her like the sun, and Ox managed to break up fights without starting new ones.

"Did any of you guys know that Manse was back?"

Now they all sat up. Even Ox.

"Since when?"

"I don't know." Trace stood. "But we need to move."

"He can't be involved in this de Medici thing," Steph argued.

"I don't think he is." She showed them her phone. They recognized the contact that had reached out to her, sending a warning none of them could ignore. They had a long, brutal history with Manse, and honey badgers never forget, never forgive.

TO KILL A BADGER   305

Without another word spoken between them, they all headed inside the home they'd borrowed for the night and got ready.

While she pulled on her clothes, CeCe realized she'd have to text Lot when she got the chance. He'd made her promise, years ago, that she'd give him a little warning before all hell broke loose. Especially if her and her friends were the reason for said hell.

Zeus glared down at the couple; mid-morning light from the big hotel windows hitting them, but not waking them up.

The couple, he thought with disgust. They were clearly a couple.

How could she ignore *him* but make herself available to a vile cat? Gong Zhao deserved only the best. Everything—*anything*—she may want, she deserved. And he was more than ready to give it to her. Yet, here she was. Cuddled up next to *that*. On the couch built for *Zeus's* kind, not some worthless *American* cat.

She was turned toward the American, asleep in his big cat form, her arms pulled up tight against her body, her knees tucked in, and her head buried against his fur-covered chest. His forearms wrapped around her like he was holding onto a prized, half-deer carcass he'd found in the woods.

Zeus didn't know how long he stared at the pair, resenting them both. But he knew when the cat was watching him. Could feel those strange gold eyes locking on him.

He glanced up and confirmed what he knew. The cat watched him as Zeus watched the pair. The two males glowered at each other for what felt like ages until he heard Gong say, "I don't know what you two are planning, but stop it."

Her head was still buried in the cat's chest. Her eyes weren't even open. She appeared asleep. And yet . . .

"Zeus," she said, "tell Marti I need a laptop. As soon as possible. Do you have something for me?"

"Yes," he said in French. "One of Jules's people left it for you at the front desk."

"Drop it on the table, and let me know when the laptop arrives."

306 *Shelly Laurenston*

Zeus placed the thick manila envelope on the coffee table. He tried to turn away, but he couldn't stop glaring at the cat, who only glared back.

"Get out, Zeus," Gong pushed.

With a snarl, he returned to the elevator.

If she wanted a worthless cat, she could have it.

"That idiot bear is in love with you," Keane said after shifting back to human.

"Not as much as he's in love with himself. He thinks I'd look perfect on his arm. Nothing more, nothing less. Although, I'm sure my family's money doesn't hurt either."

Keane shouldn't care who was in love with Nelle or not. Then again . . . he shouldn't be cuddling her while in his tiger form either. That was something special one did with their tiger mate. He distantly remembered finding his parents like that, more than once. Two giant cats, limbs and tails wrapped around each other while they'd slept.

Nelle hadn't even been in her honey badger form. She was still wearing her dress from yesterday, now covered in black and white fur. And he . . . well, now he was naked.

Dammit, but he felt comfortable with her like this! In his arms, cuddled close. What was going on with him? Why was he acting like this? Maybe he needed a mate. A nice tigress who was looking to have a cub or two with a virile male. And it was this instinctive desire he probably had—whether he was aware of it or not—that had him grabbing the first female who happened to be lying next to him on the couch, watching TV. This was, tragically, how many shifters ended up with full-humans as mates. Sure. These same shifters often argued later they were "in love," but seriously? In love? With a full-human? Sure. Whatever.

And it was the same with honey badgers. Who could love a honey badger? Thieving, plotting, politically dangerous honey badgers?

Your brothers? They're in love with badgers.

He rolled his eyes at the voice in his head, which always sounded like his dad's and only made an appearance when he was arguing with himself. Why didn't he hear his dad's voice when he had a great game or kept their family safe? Instead, he only heard his dad when that voice was telling him not to be so hard on his brothers or uncles, or asking him not to live his life for revenge.

See? Irritating!

And his brothers' current stupidity regarding women didn't count!

Stupidity? Shay is stupid to choose Tock? She's brilliant and clearly loves my granddaughter. And Mads is psychotic like you with her love of a single sport. So how stupid can your brothers be to find such great females? Just like I did with your mom.

"What the hell are you thinking about?"

"What?" Keane snapped, startled to hear Nelle's voice in the middle of his inner monologue.

"Your face." Nelle was looking up at him. "It's all scrunched up. Are you holding in gas?"

"No."

"Just asking. Because farting is a normal human function."

"I'm just arguing with my dad," he said quickly, not wanting to hear anyone talk about "farting."

Her eyes widened a little, and she leaned back.

"In my head, I mean," he attempted to clarify. "Not . . . *literally* arguing with him."

"Oh." She relaxed in his arms again. "I understand. I mean, I've never lost a parent, but I argue with my mother all the time in my head. I know I can call her and argue with her in person, but that is a dangerous road to go down. She doesn't like offspring that have an opinion outside her own. Even when she's absolutely wrong, she expects us all to agree."

She laid her head on his chest, and they were silent for a little while. Neither of them sleeping, but not in the mood to get up and face the day either, he guessed.

Finally, though, she did pull back a bit and look down his body.

"Yeahhhhh," Keane said, embarrassed. "Just ignore him."

"He seems awake . . . and quite happy."

"Sorry about that. But he has a mind of his own."

308 Shelly Laurenston

"No reason to apologize. And I'll deal with him later."

"Okay. That is *not* helping."

Nelle laughed and pulled out of Keane's arms.

She'd never felt so safe and comfortable before in her life. Even when he started growling at Zeus, she had known that *she* was safe. Although she didn't feel the same about Zeus, who really needed to get over his bear-obsession with her. She wasn't a house that regularly had unlocked trash cans in front of it.

Keane groaned when she pulled away, and she allowed herself to enjoy that moment. However briefly. It was nice that he felt the loss of her body as deeply as she felt the loss of his.

While he got to his big feet, she sat on the couch and ripped open the envelope that Jules had sent her. It was filled with printouts of articles about Lavoie over the last five years or so. Such a waste of paper! She could have just texted Nelle the links to these articles. Did Jules not understand that? It was clear the She-badger had grown up with mimeographs or whatever. All this technology must be confusing. Among all this wasted paper, though, was a handwritten note with an address on it. *That* Nelle could use.

"Switzerland."

"What about it?" Keane asked, after finishing off an entire quart of orange juice he'd just grabbed from the full-sized refrigerator and gulped down while still naked.

"That's where we're going."

"Is that far from here?"

"It's not around the corner, but it's not far, unless we were still coming from New York."

She looked down at the Longines watch on her wrist. It was covered in diamonds, but the time was always precise. Tock had been trying to get Nelle to buy one of those military-type watches that her teammate always wore, but no. She refused to wear one of those things on her wrist unless they were on a very time-specific assignment. They were ugly! And Nelle had lovely wrists to be adorned, not defaced.

TO KILL A BADGER 309

"Get showered," she told the cat, "and dressed. We can have lunch someplace nice before we get started."

"How nice?"

"Jeans and T-shirt will be fine. Sneakers, too. But you will love the food."

"Okay."

"Go that way," she said, without looking away from the papers in front of her; she pointed out the room where a duffel bag of clothes awaited him on the bed he hadn't used.

A few minutes later, the laptop showed up, handed to her by a silent Zeus, who was still glaring. She ignored him like she always did, because . . . who cared?

Nelle sat back on the couch and immediately got online through a protected connection, researching what she could on Lavoie.

"You haven't even showered yet."

Nelle realized she'd lost track of time when she looked up to see Keane standing in front of her. He was dressed in blue jeans, navy blue T-shirt, and black work boots. His black and white hair was wet and combed back from his face, reaching down to his shoulders. She hadn't realized how long his hair was until this moment. And because Keane and his brothers were one of the rare black tigers—a genetic rarity among their kind—there were only a few stray orange hairs in that mane, unlike the rest of the Malone family. Then you add in those sharp cheekbones, chiseled jawline, and green-gold eyes, and Nelle knew she was in very deep trouble.

Especially when she realized she could take him. Right here and right now.

Then again . . . she really should ask him first if that's what he wanted. It was the polite thing to do. Not that badgers were polite.

"Hello?" Keane said, waving at her. "Are you here?"

"What? Oh. Yes. Yes. I was just researching Lavoie." She stood and motioned to the laptop. "You read up on him, and I'll get ready."

"Are you one of those takes-hours-getting-ready people? Because then I'm going to need to order room service."

310 Shelly Laurenston

She glanced at her watch. "I'll be fifteen minutes."

"You will?"

Lot looked at his phone and then to his brothers. "Manse is back."

Wolf's eyes narrowed. "Since when?"

He shrugged. "Don't know."

"Ox won't be happy," Hel said. "She'll want his head on a pike."

Now Lot sighed. "She may get it. They're going after him."

Wolf sat up in his seat. *"What?"*

"Don't even bother," Lot told his emotional brother. "They're already on the move."

"Of course they are," Wolf said, tossing up his hands. "Because they love starting shit!"

"Should we turn around?" Hel asked.

"No." Wolf sighed and—Lot could see—forced himself to relax back in the leather seat of the family jet, attempting to get comfortable for their long flight. "They can handle this."

"That's what I thought we were worried about," Hel said.

"We're retired now, remember? This isn't our problem." He jerked his thumb behind him at the badger. "That is."

Fred MacKilligan couldn't get out of the layers of tape they'd used to secure his body to a seat, but he did manage to keep chewing through the duct tape they'd kept putting over his mouth. They'd finally just given up.

"You'll regret doing this!" MacKilligan continued to yell. "You don't know how powerful I am! The connections I have! I'll destroy you!"

Unable to get the idiot to shut up, the brothers did that thing MacKilligan—and all sensitive-eared badgers, like their kids, actually—hated in any enclosed space. They howled. And howled. And howled . . . until he begged them to stop.

She was fifteen minutes exactly.

He didn't know anyone who got ready that fast. Not even his brothers.

TO KILL A BADGER 311

And, as usual, she looked stunning, despite being in nothing more than worn jeans, a white sleeveless T-shirt with NEW YORK written across it in blue letters, white and gold sneakers, gold rings on her fingers, and big gold hoops from her ears.

She looked like an American tourist, even though she was actually a hardcore traveler who had been more places than he could even dream of going in his lifetime. He wondered if any of the Zhaos would be considered "tourists" in any region, though. The entire family seemed extremely well-versed in most cultures.

Nelle swung a small gold-colored, leather backpack over her shoulder. "Let's go."

They took the elevator down, the idiot bear waiting for them on the ground floor. He followed them to the large exit, but once they stepped outside, Nelle said, "You wait here, Zeus."

"But—"

"We have Charles. Marti will get in touch with you about your next assignment. Thanks."

She walked to the Bentley, with the back door being held open by that idiot Charles. He grinned at Keane, and Keane wanted to slap him, but at least he was better than the bear.

He followed Nelle into the back seat, and Charles closed the door after them.

"I can't believe I'm glad to see him."

"You mean Charles? We love Charles."

"He's as useless as the bear, but at least he won't stand over us . . . staring."

"True."

Charles pulled the Bentley into busy Paris traffic. Nelle slid across the seat until she was pressed against Keane's side.

"What are you doing?"

"Nothing." She held up her phone to take a selfie and told him, "Now glower."

He did, because he was annoyed, and she snapped the photo.

"Why?" he asked as she tapped away on her phone.

312   Shelly Laurenston

"You are perfect to scare away the weak males who won't leave me alone."

"Does that include Zeus?"

"Hopefully."

She started to return to her original spot across the seat, but he wrapped his arm around her waist and pulled her back to his side.

She didn't complain, which was good. Because he was extremely comfortable.

"They didn't give us water."

"You have to ask for water."

"I have to *ask* for water? Are they in a drought?"

Nelle looked over her menu. "This isn't the States. They do things differently here. Or did you not realize that when you went to Mongolia?"

"I was a kid when I went to Mongolia."

Nelle motioned to the waiter, who seemed to have been ignoring them, and said something to him in French. A few seconds later, two glasses of tap water arrived, the glasses placed in front of them.

The waiter went off to ignore them some more, and Keane drank his water.

When he finished—after complaining, "It doesn't have ice. Do they have an ice drought, too?"—he said, "I can't read the menu."

"It's in French."

"I got that."

"Are you always this disagreeable?"

"Yes."

She laughed. "What would you *like* to eat?"

"An entire side of bison?"

"Okay, we're not doing that." She put the menu down, and the waiter returned. She spoke to him in French and, since the waiter was smiling at her, Keane guessed her accent was perfect. As soon as Keane had opened his mouth when he'd walked inside the busy restaurant, he'd gotten nothing but glares from the staff and customers. He couldn't help it! He was an American! And proud of it!

TO KILL A BADGER 313

The waiter left, and Nelle informed him, "In a little while, they will put food in front of you. You will thank them by saying *merci,* and will eat what you are given accordingly. Understand?"

"Yup."

"And try not to say 'yup' to the French."

"Got it!" he said with finger-guns and clicking his tongue against his teeth for emphasis.

"Stop that."

"With ya!" he said with a big American double-thumbs-up and ridiculous grin.

"Keane!"

Chapter 25

Nelle ate her delicious meal while she watched the French full-humans watch Keane Malone devour his food like he'd never had a meal before. He wasn't tacky about it, quite aware of what surrounded him. But, as she'd instructed the waiter, food kept arriving seconds before he shoveled in his last bite from the bowl. And it kept arriving until the tiger finally sat back in his chair and let out a satisfied sigh. The man had eaten a lot, and the French had been fascinated. It wasn't even about their etiquette. It was about the fact any "human" could put away that amount of food and not explode.

Nelle gestured to the waiter, and several staff came over to remove all the empty plates, glasses, and silverware.

"How did you know I was done?" he asked, finally speaking now that he'd had his fill.

"You and your brothers do the same thing every time you feed to your satisfaction."

His small smile was almost shy. "So you've been watching me?"

"I'm observant. About everything."

He chuckled. "I've noticed."

Nelle waved the cheese away with a flick of her fingers, and the waiter returned a while later with a single plate and two forks, placing them in the middle of the table. A dark-chocolate gâteau with curled pieces of chocolate artfully decorating the confection.

"Do we have time for dessert?" he asked.

"Yes."

"So we're flying to Switzerland rather than taking the train or driving?"

"Marti's handling that."

"That doesn't answer my question."

"What are you worried about?"

"Helicopter. Not a fan of helicopters and those tiny planes rich doctors fly on their own."

"*You're* scared of heights?"

"I'm afraid of tiny, aluminum things that can fail in an instant. Or explode."

"As Tock has taught me, anything can explode."

"Yes, but that doesn't mean I need to be trapped inside it."

"If you want," she said, picking up her fork, "I can tell Marti . . ."

Nelle gazed at the empty plate. "You already ate the cake?"

"To quote my dad, 'You snooze, you lose.' "

"Charming."

"I'm all about the charm. It's a Malone thing. When my uncles and cousins break bones while playing hockey or on orders of mobsters . . . they're all about the charm."

Nelle laughed, glancing down at her phone when a new text came in. She read it. It was from Max. It was early morning back at Charlie's house and. . . . *Oh. Dear.*

"What's wrong?" Keane asked as another slice of gâteau appeared between them with fresh forks.

"Uh . . ." She shook her head. Should she tell him? Yeah. Probably. "Max's father showed up at the house last night."

His expression changed instantly into something terrifying. The anger. The rage. Big cats were able to do that without flashing a fang or unleashing a snarl.

"Everyone's okay," she told him. "And I need you to remain calm."

"I don't want to remain calm."

Nelle already knew that. She bet he wanted to *run* back to New York to find out exactly what was going on and handle it all himself. He was

316 *Shelly Laurenston*

probably sizing up the ways he could get back home in a few hours. Like swimming home. Almost logical, really, since tigers loved to swim. But swimming across the Atlantic was probably too much for even a tiger.

"Everyone is fine," Nelle promised Keane and stood up. "Now, give me a moment. Let me see what I can find out. Do *not* contact your brothers. They'll just piss you off more."

Keane watched Nelle walk away from their table. He no longer thought about devouring another piece of that delicious cake. Instead, he pulled out his cell phone and texted Finn.

What the hell is going on?

Finn immediately replied back:

Calm down. Everything is fine.

Why did people keep telling him that? To calm down? What about him suggested he could calm down when ordered? *What?*

Fine? Meaning the fucker is GONE???

Yes. He was taken away by wolves.

What the fuck does that mean?

He would have called by now, so he could get his anger across by yelling his questions, but he didn't have an international plan, and Nelle was halfway down the block of the Parisian street with snooty Charles following about fifty feet behind, which seemed too far away from his subject for Keane's comfort.

Okay. I'm coming home right now.

Why? I said he's gone.

Permanently?

TO KILL A BADGER   317

When there was no immediate answer, Keane completely understood. Charlie and Max wanted to kill the bastard and bury his remains somewhere in Jersey or Staten Island. Wherever mobsters buried their victims. And that way, they could *all* be done with Fred MacKilligan's intrusive presence on this planet. But chances were high that Stevie had put a stop to that because she was protective of that idiot, and no one wanted to upset the little genius, because she could easily destroy the world.

Although, if Keane was in New York right now—where he *should* be!—he could take the hit from Stevie. Her hysterical crying didn't bother him at all, and if she never spoke to him again, he really didn't think he'd care. She was a sweet girl and all, and he was glad she got along with Nat, but Fred MacKilligan needed to *go*. Because the badger suddenly showing up in the middle of all this shit with the de Medicis was not good. Nothing that man ever did was good except for the strange daughters he helped make. Although Keane attributed that more to their mothers and less to that idiot.

He is not here NOW. Stay where U are.

Fine.

JUST STAY CALM!

Yes. Because all-capped communications ordering him to be calm always soothed his rattled nerves!

Deciding not to get into an argument with his brother through text, Keane slipped his phone back into his pocket.

He stared down at the cake in front of him. He really shouldn't waste food . . .

He ate the cake slice in a few bites and pushed the plate away. Still, Nelle had not returned. He understood, though, she was trying to get him more information from back home. He needed her to do that to keep him from doing something stupid that would just upset everyone. Except maybe Charlie and Max.

Keane rested his folded arms on the table, gazed down at the empty water glass in front of him, and worked to keep his rage under control.

318 *Shelly Laurenston*

He focused on the glass and, using his right forefinger, he gently moved the glass across the table until it fell over the edge. A waiter he hadn't noticed was standing beside him, catching the glass in his hand before it could hit the ground and shatter. The man glowered at Keane.

"Monsieur!" the waiter said, managing to chastise with that one word and a look. Must be a French thing.

The waiter kept up eye contact. And it was true, the dude was French. Keane, however, was *cat*. While Keane maintained that eye contact, he used his right forefinger again to slowly move the empty cake plate across the table. Just as it sat precariously on the edge, the waiter's eyes narrowing, Keane used fore- and middle fingers to flick the thing across the outside space, past the surprised faces of the other patrons, until it crashed into the building next door.

The waiter was babbling in French to the other waiters and pointing at him, and Keane realized that Nelle had still not returned. Or even texted him.

That was weird. She knew how dangerous it was to leave him alone around full-humans he could easily irritate or terrorize. Because he would irritate and terrorize them just for his amusement. It was what he did. His sister called his predilection, "Your brand."

He looked over his shoulder again, but still didn't see Nelle or Charles.

Keane decided to look for them. Just in case.

Standing, he didn't immediately notice that all the restaurant's waiters were coming over to him to, most likely, ask him to leave. In the politest, but still rudest French way possible, he was sure. But when he looked down at them while standing at his full height . . . they all stopped. Stared. All—except the one who had been waiting on him—walked away.

Keane knew it was wrong to enjoy the impact his size had on full-humans, but how could he not? It was one of his favorite things when he was ever forced to deal with that species.

Although the waiter didn't move away, he did turn his gaze to a spot behind Keane. That was good enough. He didn't always have to

TO KILL A BADGER 319

make these guys piss themselves or anything. Just deference to his cat-greatness was enough.

Pulling out the wad of euros that Marti had shoved at him, he dropped them on the table. He didn't know if Nelle had paid or not, but just in case she hadn't, he didn't want these people calling the cops on him. And if Nelle had already paid, then the waiter would get a nice, fat tip. The French loved that, right? Who didn't love a tip?

Stepping out from the awning that had kept them protected from the sun, Keane lifted his chin and sniffed the air. He immediately caught Nelle's scent—and that idiot Charles—and set off after her.

Keane had no idea how far he walked. It felt far, but her scent was strong. At least to him. He felt like he could track her anywhere at any time, if he had to.

At least, he felt that way until her scent abruptly disappeared.

Turning in circles, his chin lifted high, his mouth open and tongue out, he tasted the air, trying to track her. When he realized he'd lost her, Keane's rage took over. It enveloped him like an old coat, and he was seconds from shifting. Right there on a Parisian street, in front of all these full-human tourists and locals and CCTV, tearing through them until he found—

"You, you, you! Come! Come!"

Keane stared down at the woman who'd grabbed onto his arm and dragged him into a dress shop.

Once inside, the door closed and locked, she walked around him in a circle, yelling at him in French, and confusing the hell out of him. Not only because he didn't speak French and he had no idea what she was saying, but because he hadn't actually done anything yet. So how did she know to pull him away . . .

Keane sniffed.

The woman wasn't a woman. She was a fox. An Arctic fox.

Keane rolled his eyes. He didn't have time for the antics of foxes! The most irritating and frustrating of shifters! Yes! Even more irritating and frustrating than honey badgers! Foxes were a breed that mostly spent its time following after wolves for food and liquor or aligning themselves with bears . . . for food and liquor. Of course, when his kind met foxes in the wild, they usually just ate them. At least that's what he assumed. He didn't really know. Not a lot of foxes attempted to hang around Malones.

She continued to yell at him until he finally said, "I don't understand you! I'm American!"

She briefly froze. "American?" she repeated, but in that French way that made it sound like he could not have said anything worse. When Keane nodded, she threw her hands up in the air before grabbing his arm again and pulling him toward the back of her store.

She was still speaking, in French, which he still found annoying. And he didn't want to go anywhere with her. He wanted to leave, he wanted to find—

The female shoved him into a backroom. There was another door that led to the alley behind the store, and he was about to walk through that door until he heard a "ding" and, from the left side of the room, what he thought was a closet turned out to be an elevator.

That's when she said the first word he'd understood.

"Allez! Allez! Allez!" she verbally pushed, while gesturing with her hands.

Go. She wanted him to go.

Confused by the elevator, he allowed her to harass him into the small space; Keane forced to lower his head and shoulders so he sort of fit.

She followed behind him and, within seconds, they were traveling beneath Paris.

When the elevator doors opened again, Keane stepped into another world. A world of foxes. All the foxes. Arctics. Reds. Grays. Even a fennec walked by in her fox form, stopping to sniff him, before making a "blah!" dog-sound and sauntering off again. It was rude.

"Allez!" the first fox loudly ordered again, using her hands against him to push. At first, he didn't let her move him, because she needed to understand that despite his casual attitude on her bossiness, he was still able to tear apart every fox in this room—despite their vast number—if he so decided. He just wanted to make that clear. Which he did by standing there and glowering. Once he got his message

TO KILL A BADGER 321

across, however, he let her push him out of the elevator and into the giant underground space. Thankfully, the ceilings were much higher, so Keane could stand at his normal height.

While his escort walked off, yelling for someone named Elise, Keane took a moment to get his bearings and he figured out the deal pretty fast.

While a small portion of the enormous space was being used by seamstresses for the clothes they sold upstairs, the rest was being used by thieves. There was a pile of empty wallets about ten feet from him. Other foxes brought in boxes of assorted high-end electronics from another elevator that was so big, he assumed it was taking that stuff from a loading dock above ground.

Then there was the section he was sure Nelle would love. Designer clothes; shoes and boots; and bags. So. Many. Bags.

Unable to help himself, Keane walked over and picked one up. He opened it, looked inside . . . and smirked. Fake. These were fake bags that he bet cost the foxes a few cents to make and that they sold for thousands to hundreds of thousands of dollars. A lot of Birkins and Chanels and Fendis. Not far from all these bags were more that, when he looked at them, he realized were definitely *not* fake. Those, Keane guessed, were stolen. Like the cases full of diamond-encrusted jewelry that stood across the room like sentries for thievery.

Nelle would probably be surprised he could tell fake from real when it came to bags, but he'd learned that from his mother, because she refused to take anything from a Malone that she wasn't assured was the real thing. She had no desire to go to jail for trading in "hot goods."

"I am much too pretty to go to prison," she'd tell him. "Although I do look fabulous in orange."

"'Allo?"

Keane turned, blinked.

"Down here, genius."

He looked down and saw another tiny fox standing in front of him. Her accent was French, but at least she spoke English.

And yes, Keane knew he was being a typical American right now, but he was stressed out and angry. He didn't have time to worry about being a respectful tourist in a foreign land.

"Is Babette correct?" the Tibetan fox asked.

"About what?"

"Were you about to shift in the middle of Paris? Like some idiot?"

Keane leaned down so the female would understand him perfectly.

"I. Want. My. *Honey badger back!*"

"*Mon Dieu,*" she sighed, her body leaning away from his yelling. "I hate the cats."

Chapter 26

Some of the strongest foxes moved closer to Elise, ready to attack the hysterical big cat if it became necessary. With a simple hand gesture, though, she stopped them from getting too close. She didn't want to pressure such a large beast.

"Calm down, big kitty," she soothed. "And tell Elise what is wrong."

He did. Something about honey badgers and how one had disappeared after a meal. Maybe the She-badger had wanted to get away from him. Elise could understand that. Two minutes and she wanted to escape such an annoying animal.

"Who is your pet badger?" Elise asked when he suddenly stopped talking. She assumed he was done.

"She is not my pet."

"Who is she?"

"Nelle . . . I mean, Gong. Zhao."

Like alert meercats sensing hyenas near, every fox in the room stopped what they were doing and focused on Elise and the big cat.

The Zhaos were well known among their kind.

For some foxes, the Zhaos were enemies, because they continued to disrupt their smuggling businesses throughout Asia and the Indian Ocean. For others, they were business partners that brought in a great amount of money and protection from the bigger predators that would love to get a toehold in this world and push all the foxes out.

Elise, whose family had been working with the Zhaos since long

324 *Shelly Laurenston*

before Elise had ever been born, grabbed the tiger's arm and pulled him toward her private offices.

She knew Nelle Zhao. Had worked with her a few years ago. A very nice badger. Her friends, however . . .

And quite honestly, that's what Elise was worried about. Zhao's friends. An unscrupulous band of young badgers that could cause all sorts of problems for Elise. Something she absolutely couldn't afford. If she lost the Paris territory that her family had been holding for centuries when there was still a king ruling these lands, she would never get it back again.

"*Allez*, kitty. *Allez*," she said to the cat, pulling him inside her office. She motioned for one of her brothers and told him in French to find the She-badger. Immediately.

It was best to help this cat as much as she could before he really panicked and called Zhao's friends. Because once they were involved . . .

"We have much to discuss," she told the cat, after closing the door and pushing him into a chair.

Her poor furniture creaked at the weight of the beast, and she hid her cringing face while sitting across from him. She felt it was best to keep her desk between them. Hopefully she wouldn't need the sawed-off shotgun she had taped underneath it, but it was good to have access in case the cat lost all his fragile cat-control.

When Elise felt she wouldn't show her every emotion on her face, she lifted her head and smiled at the animal across from her.

"What is your name?"

"Keane."

"Keane . . . what?"

He took several deep breaths, closing his eyes, and giving himself several interminable seconds. It was clearly difficult for him right now with Zhao missing.

"Malone," he finally said. "Keane Malone."

Fuck. A Malone.

It was bad enough he was a cat. It was even worse, he was a tiger. But a Malone, too? An *American* Malone, no less? What had she done to cause such hate from the angels above?

Her day was just getting worse and worse!

"So . . . you are protection for, uh, Zhao. Yes?"

"No."

"Ah. Lover, then?"

"No!"

She leaned back at his sudden bark. "No need to yell, kitty. I sit right here."

"Look, it's too complicated to explain."

"I understand. You went on date. She got bored. She abandoned you like alley cat in street."

"That is *not* what happened."

"There is no shame, kitty. I can find you a very nice full-human girl who would not find you repulsive at all."

"She does not find me repulsive!"

"Again, no need to yell." Elise raised her arm and motioned her brother into the room with a twitch of her fingers.

He came over to her desk and plopped down a laptop. A video was ready to go, and he tapped a key, playing it.

"Ahhh, *mon dieu.*"

"What?" the cat demanded.

"Well, Malone, good news is she did not abandon you because of your repulsive personality."

"Thanks," he snarled dryly.

"But, unfortunately, she was arrested."

"What?" He scrambled out of the chair and came around her desk to watch the video, pushing her brother into the wall without even trying.

"You see?" Elise asked him. "Police pick her up and take her away. See? She is fine."

"She is *not* fine! She's in jail!"

"I'm sure not for long."

Her brother, snarling at the cat, tapped on the laptop screen, and Elise was unable to stop the wince that flashed across her face.

"Merde."

"What?" the cat demanded. "What's wrong?"

"This man," she said, pointing at the screen, which showed an older man with short white hair getting into a car and following the police who had picked up Zhao. "This man, Malone, is a problem."

"Why? Who is he?"

"Manse."

"Who's Manse? Who is Manse? *I need to know who Manse is!*"

"He's getting hysterical," her brother noted.

"I know."

"Perhaps we should kill him now. Get it over with."

"We could, but such a mess."

"We can clean that up."

"No, no. I don't mean a physical mess, with blood and everything. I mean, a mess with the Zhaos. I'd like to avoid that. Even if killing him would be easier."

"You know you're saying all that in English, right?" the cat asked.

Elise tilted her head to the side and replied, "Yes. We know."

Keane was trying to stay calm. He really was. In fact, he'd never worked so hard before to remain calm since his mother had informed him that his father was dead and he didn't want to upset her or his brothers by crying.

Of course, right now, it was not about crying. It was about his desire to tear apart the streets of Paris until he found Nelle. Where was Nelle? Where had they taken her? And why had she been arrested? Wait . . . he probably shouldn't ask that last question.

"Can you get her back?" Keane asked, deciding to ignore the fact the foxes were talking about killing him the same way he and his brothers talked about buying morning bagels.

The female fox, Elise, raised a finger and picked up her cell phone; the case was covered in what Keane assumed was yellow crystals, but now he thought maybe they were instead yellow diamonds.

Jesus! He was in a thief den! With thieves! Fox thieves! The thieviest of thieves! You didn't invite foxes over to your house for a party unless you wanted to discover half your electronics and all of your cash gone the next day. They didn't live in your cabinets or bother with high-end artwork like badgers. They just ran around stealing shit, because they could. They were so adorable—full-blood and shifter—that people often let them get away with it, too.

Even Elise, who had to be in her early sixties, was adorable.

Keane felt a hand slip into his back pocket, reaching for his wallet. Turning only his head, as far as it could go, he roared and unleashed his fangs. The red fox—gaze wide—looked at the floor, pulled out his hand, and walked backward out of the room until he could run away.

Elise spoke in French to someone on the phone. If she was upset Keane had threatened one of her people with his fangs, she didn't show it.

The only thing Keane understood from this end was the French word for *yes* and Nelle's name. Otherwise, he was lost, and the fox's expression told him nothing.

Eventually, Elise disconnected the call and, after glancing at the male fox next to her, she looked at Keane.

"What?" he asked, when she said nothing. *"What?"*

Nelle was pissed. Really, truly pissed.

She had been sitting in a mostly empty room in the Paris police headquarters for almost an hour, her left wrist zip-tied to the metal chair she was sitting on.

Of course, she could get herself out of this, but that would just force the police to send out an alert about her to all on-duty staff. She didn't have time to worry about getting out of Paris without getting caught again.

What really irritated her, though, was that she hadn't done anything. Not in France, anyway. Streep and Max had taken on a few things, but by themselves or, as in Streep's case, with family. Nelle had not been involved. There was literally no reason to arrest her, since she was almost positive the statute of limitations had been reached on what she'd done when she was still in high school.

She loved shopping in France so much, she wouldn't have risked not being able to return.

So, then, why was she *here*? Why had she been—

A full-human male walked in. He was older. Probably in his sixties. She could smell that he had diabetes and some damage to his liver, probably from drinking. She expected him to sit down across from her in the empty chair and begin grilling her on something. He didn't do that.

Instead, he said nothing, simply walked around her and dropped the duffel he'd been carrying at her feet. Something heavy and metal *clink*ed inside when it hit the floor. He unzipped the bag and took something out.

He cut off her zip tie and gripped her arms, pulling them back until they were close together. Then he held her like that with one hand while doing something else with his other hand. She didn't know what until she felt cold metal against her bare skin. Then she heard metal against metal, and something ripped into her flesh and embedded itself in the bone. She barely stopped herself from crying out, because this did hurt.

She looked over her shoulder and saw that a long piece of titanium had been placed against her right arm and was now stuck there somehow. Blood oozing from around it. The man took another piece of metal and pressed it against her other arm. That's when Nelle saw the spikes from inside dart out and slam into her flesh.

Nelle snarled, her body instinctively beginning to shift. But she stopped when the man said in French, "Do that and your arms and the bones will be destroyed. Understand?"

She didn't know if that were true. But she knew the damage would take longer to heal than even a shot to the heart.

That wasn't what disturbed her, though.

What disturbed her was that this full-human knew exactly what she was, had something to counteract what she was, and wasn't running around telling every other full-human what she was. No. None of that was good.

Locking her arms together with a big zip tie looped around her arms and the metal attached to her flesh, he grabbed her by the extra skin on her back and lifted her out of the chair. Tossing a black sweatshirt over her shoulders, the hood over her head to obscure her face, he led her out of the room and into the busy hallway.

There was no point in calling out to the full-humans who filled this place. They wouldn't understand what was going on and, if they figured it out, it would only be worse for shifters everywhere. This man understood that, too. He understood it far too well.

Confused, angry, and more worried than she'd ever been, Nelle let the man lead her toward an exit. She glanced back once more to see if there was something she could do. Confusion she could cause. A way to facilitate her escape, but there was nothing.

She did, however, see a cop walking into the room she'd just left before quickly darting out again, his gaze searching the hallway. When gold eyes landed on her, she knew he was a fellow shifter. A small man. She was guessing, a small cat or canine. He silently watched the man take her out before he started speaking into a cell phone.

Nelle didn't know whom he was speaking to, but she could only hope it was someone who could help her. Because this was shaping up to be an enormous problem.

Nope. Keane didn't like the look on this She-fox's face at all when she disconnected the call that had come in a few minutes before. Not at all!

"What's wrong?"

She didn't answer. Instead, she simply said, "We need to go."

"Go? To Nelle?"

"Come, kitty. We do not have much time."

"Why? What's happening?"

As they walked through this thief's paradise, Elise motioned to several different foxes. Without question, they all followed after her. They took the freight elevator to the surface and moved quickly to an underground parking structure more than a mile away.

The security guard—another fox—nodded at Elise as she passed and traveled down to a row of cars that included a brand-new Jaguar and a Volkswagen Golf that had to be at least twenty years old and had definitely seen better days.

330   *Shelly Laurenston*

Elise was heading to the Jag when she stopped and looked Keane up and down. Then she switched keys with another fox and headed to a larger panel van with logos on both sides and the back.

He was grateful. He knew his legs couldn't handle being twisted up so he could fit into that tiny car. Dani's twin bed at home was bigger.

"Where are we going?" he asked once they'd started driving.

"To rescue your lover before it is too late."

"She's not my lover, and what do you mean by too late? What does that mean? *Tell me!*"

The male fox from Elise's office leaned forward from the back of the van and said, "Are you sure you don't want me to kill him? He seems very slow with his mind, and I doubt he will be missed."

Chapter 27

Her flesh had already begun to heal over the spikes embedded in her arms, and she wasn't looking forward to when they would be removed, but Nelle was more concerned with where they were taking her.

The zip tie had been replaced with a titanium chain that held her two arms together and was then attached with a combination lock. That was then attached to a titanium bar bolted to the inside of the black van she was now traveling in and. . . ? Going where? Where was she being taken? She still didn't know.

She hadn't said a word since she'd been taken from the police station, and she hadn't put up a fight. She wasn't trying to reason her way out of this, but she wasn't ready to show her hand either. Not that she had a hand. At the moment, she had nothing. So she focused on her current situation until something came to her.

In this van, there were eleven men total. Six on the opposite bench and, on her side, five surrounding her. They were all full-human but heavily armed. She would guess they were mercenaries who worked for whatever country was willing to pay them.

She thought about all the people who could have arranged this. Who could have hired someone like the man in the passenger seat of the van, giving orders. He was not only able to get her arrested, but also able to take her out of a police station without anyone asking questions. Whoever he was—or had been—he was extremely powerful. Powerful was expensive.

332 *Shelly Laurenston*

It could have been the de Medicis. At least she thought so until he began talking on his cell phone. When this white male spoke halfway decent Cantonese, it was like ice water was poured down her back. She hadn't lived in China long enough to make any enemies. But her father? Her mother? Now she understood her current situation.

She wasn't the target, just the bait.

"Versailles."

Keane knew that word. "The museum? Why would they take Nelle to a museum? Won't there be thousands of tourists there?"

Elise shrugged before taking a turn. "It is closed on Mondays."

"What does that mean?"

"There will only be security for these people to worry about, I guess. I doubt they plan to kill her, kitty. Your lover is worth more alive than dead."

"She's not my—" He shook his head. Forget it. "What do you think they are planning? Putting her up in a palace for a few days? Is that something kidnappers do with their rich victims?"

"My brother is right. You are slow-witted cat and very hysterical."

"I just want my honey badger—"

"I know! I know! We will do what we can. As long as we . . . *merde.* It is too late."

"What do you mean it's too late? How is it too late?"

Keane could still see the trio of black vans that the foxes had tracked down and been following for the last forty minutes or so. He didn't think they were that close to the palace, though, because he couldn't see it. Although he was making the assumption that he could see a palace without straining. They were also on a freeway or highway or whatever the French called an eight-lane road that was split in the middle with traffic going in two different directions.

Whatever you called what they were currently driving on, Keane had no idea what Elise was talking about.

Until that bright red Lamborghini darted past them, heading straight for the black vans.

TO KILL A BADGER 333

"Who is that?"

Elise didn't answer his question, instead hitting the gas, no longer worried about holding back so they weren't spotted. But two seconds later, she was forced to hit the brakes as an F-150 Ford pickup—*in France?*—crashed through the trees lining the road, tearing across the pavement, and slamming into the van's front side and forcing it into the concrete barrier separating the roadway. When the two vehicles came to an abrupt stop, someone from inside the truck began firing a weapon through the windshield.

Was this Nelle's teammates? He knew they could be crazy, but this . . .

The black van that had been leading spun around and came back, while the one behind had already stopped. They were driving straight toward the crashed vans, but the Lambo had turned around, went wide, and came back. The driver made another wild turn and spun out and *into* the first van. Another crash that slid right into the first. The driver and front seat passenger in the first van came through the windshield on impact, but armed men jumped out the back and immediately began firing.

The damaged windshield on the pickup truck was kicked out, and a female in designer jeans and T-shirt, with a gray balaclava over her face, rolled out onto the crumpled hood. She stood tall and, pointing at the armed men, she opened fire with an automatic weapon.

The cars that had been idly driving wherever that morning spun around and drove off in different directions. Some people panicked and abandoned their cars altogether, running for the opposite sides of the road. And some tried to hang around and get all the insanity on video. But two more females came out of the crumpled Lambo and fired at them. They didn't hit any of the bystanders, though, which Keane felt was on purpose. These two females also wore balaclavas: one's, a dark red: the other's, a light blue.

As all the unarmed innocents ran for their lives, another car pulled up, and another balaclava-covered female stepped out. She was armed, but her weapons were holstered. Instead, she moved through the

334 Shelly Laurenston

crowd of fighters. When anyone grabbed at her, probably hoping to use her as a shield, she either punched, kicked, or flipped them out of her way with a simple throw.

Initially, Keane thought these females were Nelle's teammates. But no. He'd seen them in action before. They worked and moved like a military special ops team. These four, however deadly, moved like crazed marauders unleashed from a mental institution. When they weren't trying to scare off onlookers, they were shooting, stabbing, and battering well-trained mercenaries with an obvious glee. Even with their faces covered, Keane knew they were enjoying every second of this attack. And it was an attack. A brutal, unforgiving attack.

Elise still hadn't moved to help or run away, but Keane couldn't wait for that. Not when he saw that man he recognized from the surveillance recording, Manse, yank open the back door of the second van and step in. When he came back out, a snarling Nelle was with him.

He yelled at five of the mercenaries that were still fighting and ordered them to do something in another language. He forced Nelle over the concrete barrier that separated the street and pulled her toward the trees on the opposite side.

Keane opened the door of the van, but Elise grabbed his arm, pulling him back.

"Are you mad?" she demanded. "We will get her back! Do not go out there!"

His rational brain knew she was right, but his tiger DNA had already taken over. All he could see before him was a fox touching him. He snapped at her with a mouthful of fangs, not realizing he'd shifted right inside the van until he'd jumped out and ran across the road on all fours.

Mercenaries were thrown into Nelle when something collided with the right side of the van. The force sent Nelle slamming into the van wall behind her, the spikes pushing deeper into her bones and opening up the wounds that had already healed. She snarled in pain, but stopped when the bullets began tearing through the metal paneling.

TO KILL A BADGER 335

Her legs were free, so she began kicking the full-human men who had fallen onto her off, and forcing them back across the half-crumpled van. These men would have hit her in return if they weren't so freaked out about what was happening.

Nelle turned enough to grab the metal chain attached to the now-crumpled van wall. One yank and she freed the bar secured to the weaker vehicle metal. Crawling her way across the bodies of the few who lay dying from the impact and those still confused and trying to figure out where right-side up might be, Nelle made her way to the still-closed back door. Having to continually stop and twist this way or that to avoid the bullets that kept tearing through the van's walls made it slow-going, but she wanted out.

With time, and all sorts of hell being unleashed outside the remains of this vehicle, Nelle reached the doors. She slapped her hand on the handle, but before she could rip it off, the doors were opened and the man who had arranged her kidnapping stood there, staring down at her. His singular focus meant he would be a problem. He wasn't going to go down easy, and he would make sure to take her out before that happened.

He reached around her and grabbed the skin on her back, lifting her up and out of the van. Pressing a gun to the back of her head, right at the one spot a bullet could actually kill her, he snarled, "Move."

As he dragged her away from the vehicle to—and *over*—an embankment, and then to the other side of the road, he ordered his mercenaries in German, *"Kill them all!"*

Elise jumped out of the van and watched the crazed cat tear his four-legged way across a battlefield with no care for his safety or whether full-humans could see that a fucking *tiger* had now entered the nightmare unfolding on local roadways!

Knowing she would have to now step in, whether she wanted to or not, she motioned to her team in the cars behind her, sending them back home.

"What now?" her brother asked, standing beside her. "And we should have killed that cat."

336 *Shelly Laurenston*

"I know. You were right." She threw up her hand to halt her nephew before he could speed off on his Japanese motorcycle. "You go back," she told her brother and his son. "Do what you can to get this handled with our people." Reaching the bike, she held her hand out. Her nephew removed his helmet and handed it to her. "I'll deal with the rest of it."

"Elise—"

"Go. Now." She straddled the still-running bike and pulled the helmet on. "I'll contact you soon."

Her brother stopped her one last time to say, "If you get a chance, sister . . . *kill that cat!*"

"Manse!"

Now surrounded by ten full-humans, Nelle gritted her teeth when the man holding her abruptly stopped and yanked her around. Again, he pressed the muzzle of his weapon to the back of her head.

Four She-badgers stood there, and despite their covered faces, she knew exactly who they were before she even caught their scent.

"Rutowski," the man called Manse said. "Long time."

"What a surprise to see you again, old friend. Too bad I can't let you go this time. At least not with her."

"I'm not giving her up."

"You better."

"She's coming with me, and you cunts better not get in my way."

American? This man was American? That surprised Nelle since his accent, in any language he'd used, had been so good. That's when she understood this man was probably some ex-agent, probably trained by the best. A man who knew that information was more powerful when used judiciously.

"Come any closer, and she'll get a bullet in the back of the head. What are you going to tell her father then?"

"That she died with honor."

Nelle's eyes widened at that answer. What kind of answer was that? These bitches were crazy! Just like the old Van Holtz had said! Crazy!

The man, unfazed, started to back away, pulling Nelle with him.

TO KILL A BADGER 337

"Kill them," he ordered his mercenaries. "Kill them—*fuck!*"

It was like being in the van again, with something big slamming into her and Manse, both hitting the ground hard. The spikes in her arms tore at her flesh and damaged her bones again. But instead of barely moving in time to avoid a tire sawing off her head, Nelle barely moved in time to avoid gunshots from the mercenaries while big, heavy, rage-filled paws trampled across her body.

Tracey heard the She-badger scream as those metal poles were nearly ripped from the backs of her arms. Dodging the gunfire, she ran over to her and grabbed the metal bar that was caught between the big cat, Manse, and three of his men. They'd all gone down when the cat had struck from out of nowhere.

Keane Malone. He'd traveled with Nelle, but she'd known that he couldn't have been with her when she'd been captured by Manse, because Malones weren't known for their shifter-control. If he'd been grabbed and put in a van, he would have just shifted to cat and killed everyone. Even if they'd been cops instead of mercenaries. And yet here he was, making this thing even messier.

Holding the bar with both hands, Trace kept a tight grip as the squirming pile of human flesh and angry black-and-white cat fur rolled around on the ground. She had to use both hands and keep moving so that the spikes that had been driven into Nelle's arms weren't pulled out yet. She knew from experience the damage it could do to bone and how long that would take to heal.

The men and cats turned one way, and Trace held onto that bar like her life depended on it. They turned another, and she went with them.

While she kept hold of poor Nelle, her friends were fighting mercenaries. But honestly, she wasn't worried about them. They'd been fighting men worse than this group—with all their fancy tech gear and years of training somewhere in the Sudan—for decades.

"*You need to get out!*"

Trace searched for that voice she recognized immediately. Elise!

"*Trace-eee!*" Elise yelled her name with that thick accent Trace loved. "*Go! Now!*"

338 *Shelly Laurenston*

Knowing there was only one way out of this, Trace screamed, *"CeCe!"* CeCe finished cutting the throat of a mercenary and ran over. Together, they dove onto one of their most hated enemies. CeCe stabbed at him, and Tracey kicked Manse in the head and stomped on his hands until he released the chain holding Nelle.

Manse blocked CeCe's knife with his Kevlar-covered arm before shoving her back. He pointed his gun at her, but Ox forced him to run instead of firing as she unleashed a fresh clip of bullets at him and, of course, everyone else.

Trace covered Nelle's body until Ox stopped firing. Then she got to her feet and helped the kid up. The cat was busy taking down the last full-human male, not realizing that Manse had run right past him.

"Go!" she said to Elise. "We've got this!"

Elise nodded and raced off through the trees on a sports bike as Steph came running in from the road.

"Brace for it!" she screamed out as she suddenly dove to the ground, the explosion happening behind her. The power of it shook the ground so hard that CeCe went down on her knees and Ox fell into a tree she stood next to. Trace held on to Nelle, and they managed to keep standing, but it wasn't easy.

When Steph got back up, she gave a triumphant smile.

"What did you do?" CeCe demanded.

"Distracted the cops!"

Steph moved over to a clear spot, dropped to her knees, and began digging. She put something in the hole and pulled out her phone. She pressed the screen, and another explosion opened a hole.

"Let's go!" she said, pulling off her mask and crawling inside.

With an "I am sorry," Trace pushed poor Nelle into the hole after Steph. "It will hurt," she yelled after her. "But you must dig, Nelle!"

She motioned to the others. "Ox! CeCe! *Now!*"

"Manse," Ox snarled through fangs.

"Fuck him! Let's go!"

"What about the cat?" CeCe asked, running to the hole.

"Malone!" Trace yelled.

He faced her in all his fabulous tiger glory.

TO KILL A BADGER 339

"Drop the head!" she yelled at the cat. He was swinging some man's head around like one of her dogs with a new chew rope. *"Drop it!"*

He snarled but finally did what she ordered once Ox ran by, making sure to yank his tail hard. Trace let Ox go before her and waited for the cat. He was over to her side in seconds, but paused when he realized he'd have to go *into* the hole. He was a water cat. A tree cat. He was not a burrow cat. But he was about to learn.

Standing behind Malone, Trace rammed her foot against his ass and shoved as hard as she could. Startled, the cat fell in headfirst, his big cat ass standing straight up out of the hole. She then leapt up and landed on his butt with both feet, jumping up and down on his ass until he was forced to go forward. Once she could only see his back paws, she followed behind him with one warning.

"I swear to God, Malone, if you fart in my face, I will kill you."

Pain tearing through her arms, Nelle kept going. She had to. She could hear the sirens. The one time any honey badger shifter ran was when they heard sirens. Getting caught in the middle of a big pile of bodies and explosions would be a nightmare for all of them.

She kept moving until she saw light and the bottom of someone's Nike sneakers. Hands reached down and lifted her up. Nelle gritted her teeth, not wanting to cry out and appear weak around other She-badgers. They hated that.

Álvarez and Yoon dragged her out of the hole. The pain was so bad that Nelle had no idea where she was. She just closed her eyes and waited until the pain passed. Unfortunately, it was taking a long time doing that.

When, finally, she could open her eyes without doing more than wince, she saw nothing but . . . chest.

A beautiful, chiseled chest.

Nelle lifted her gaze, then leaned back her head, so she could see his face.

His brows were drawn together so tight, she was afraid they would turn into one big brow. Like a Neanderthal.

Then, standing there naked, he spoke.

340   Shelly Laurenston

"Are you okay?"

His voice was soft, his hands barely touching her shoulders. As if he didn't want to hurt her more.

"We need to get this off her," he said to one of the She-badgers.

"No time," the Russian replied, walking around him. But Keane caught her arm; held her in place.

He didn't say anything. Neither of them did. They simply glared at each other.

Honestly, if that particular fight happened, Nelle wasn't sure who would win. It could go either way.

Thankfully, a fight didn't happen. Rutowski pulled herself out of the hole and ordered, "C! Help me get these things off her."

Álvarez came over, and both females pulled out tactical knives. Keane stepped in front of Nelle.

"What are you doing with those?"

"You want them off, don't you?" Álvarez asked.

"Not if you're just going to cut her up."

"We're not. Now move."

Keane looked at her over his shoulder, and she gestured him away with a simple flicker of her eyes.

The two She-badgers went around her, and she waited for the pain to start. She waited. And waited.

Finally, she had to ask, "What's going on?"

"Uh . . . these are different from the ones used on me," Rutowski explained. "Newer. Very fancy."

"You look like you should be on a Milan runway with these."

"Can you get them out or not?"

"Huh."

Nelle gritted her teeth. She didn't have patience for any of this.

"We do not have time for you two to stare and think," the Russian told her friends.

"Yeah, but if we aren't careful—"

The Russian moved in front of Nelle.

"Your sister's wedding comes, yes?"

TO KILL A BADGER 341

Surprised by the question and feeling more paranoid than usual, Nelle asked, "How the fuck did you know that?"

"We are all invited."

"You are?"

"Are you in the wedding?" the Russian asked.

"Unfortunately."

"How sad if arms are too damaged for pretty dress." She raised a blonde eyebrow.

"Do it," Nelle told her.

"Do *not* tear those out of your arms, Nelle, just so you can get out of that fucking wedding," Keane ordered.

"Cops will be here soon," the Russian explained. "We have no choice."

"Nelle," Keane warned. "I'm serious."

"Do it," she told Lenkov.

The Russian grabbed the chains that were still attached to the contraption on Nelle's arms.

Rutowski's eyes grew wide. "Ox, *no!*"

But Ox had already slid her claws under the metal against Nelle's skin and, without even a warning to brace herself, yanked those things out of Nelle's arms. Blood splattered across them all, and Nelle let out a startled roar.

Keane caught Nelle as her body gave out and she dropped. He stopped her from slamming into the marble floor.

The Russian motioned to the horrible thing she held in her hand. "This looks like sick sex toy."

"We need to wrap these," Álvarez said, leaning in to see Nelle's wounds without getting close enough for Nelle to rip her face off with her claws. "I think they may actually need stitches too."

"Stitches?" Keane snarled through fangs. "Don't you mean skin grafts?"

"Why? Her skin is still there. It's just . . ." Álvarez shrugged. "Mangled."

342 *Shelly Laurenston*

"We don't have time for that," Rutowski informed them, even as she paused to also look at the wounds.

He was fascinated by how calm these females were being. All he could hear were helicopters and drones and emergency vehicles bearing down on them. Yet they didn't seem to notice. How could they not notice?

"I don't think we should leave until we get her sewn up."

"Just slap a bandage on these wounds and *let's go!*" Nelle roared.

"First, you need to calm down," Rutowski said in a chastising-mother tone that Keane had often heard from his own mom. "And second, we've got this."

"Do you?" Keane demanded. "Because I'm pretty sure we're in Versailles right now."

The She-badger looked around, smiled. "Very good! We are at Versailles. Beautiful, isn't it? This is one of the bedrooms of—"

"I don't need a tour, woman!"

Nelle pulled out of Keane's arms and spun around, splashing blood on them again.

"Are you crones insane? *We're in Versailles? You dug us* into *Versailles?"*

"We needed a place to regroup." Again, that was said so calmly. So rationally. Even though Keane and, clearly, Nelle were not feeling rational. And it wasn't because *they* were the crazy ones in this current situation.

Nelle had no time for their insane rational tone, either, Keane guessed, because she looked at him and said, "Fuck it, I'm going to shift and—"

"No!" Three of the elder badgers yelled. The Russian just smirked and said nothing.

"You can't shift," Rutowski quickly explained. "You'll get smaller, but those wounds won't. And your bones may shatter when they change. Right now, they're simply broken."

"Who the fuck would invent such a device?" Nelle asked.

Rutowski shrugged. "Manse."

"He's full-human." Nelle stepped into Rutowski, the pair eye-

TO KILL A BADGER   343

ing each other like the predators they both were. "That man is full-human. So mind telling me how he knows what I am?"

Before Rutowski could answer—not that she necessarily would have—Yoon called out, "We gotta go!" She ran back from the big window she'd been looking out of. "Cops. I'll get in first," she added, dropping to her knees in front of the hole they'd just recently left.

"You know where to go?" Rutowski asked.

"Yep."

"Wait, wait." Keane looked at the females. "We're going *back* underground?"

"We don't have a choice." Yoon pointed at the window. "Cops. Everywhere."

Keane understood that. He didn't need to see the cops to believe they were outside and closing in fast. What he did understand, though, was that he did *not* want to go back into that hole.

"Forget it," he finally said. "I'll just turn myself in."

"Do you know how many bodies we left behind? The explosion? They're going to think you're a crazed terrorist. You can't turn yourself in."

"I don't care."

"You're covered in someone else's blood. Trust me when I say, if you turn yourself in, you'll never be outside a prison ever again."

"I don't want to go in that hole," he told them. The last time, he'd felt like he was suffocating. Like it was his grave. He just didn't think he could do that again.

Nelle's hand pressed against his neck, and she gazed up at him. "I won't leave without you."

Behind Nelle's back, the other females rolled their eyes in exasperation. But he didn't care. The way Nelle said it . . .

"Promise you won't leave me in there to die," he begged.

"Never." Nelle smiled. "You ripped a guy's head off for me. That is so romantic."

"Before this gets any weirder," Rutowski cut in, "we're really traveling far. So can we just . . . get moving? Please." She motioned to Keane. "And you'll do better with claws and fur, I think."

344   *Shelly Laurenston*

She was right. He would.

After sparing a moment to gaze at Nelle for another few seconds, he shifted and waited.

Yoon went in. Nelle, after stroking the back of Keane's neck, followed.

Keane leaned in and sniffed around the dirt, debating whether he should really do this, until he felt a foot shove his ass and he fell face-first into the hole.

He really hated when Rutowski did that!

Trace jumped up and down on the cat's big ass until he started to move forward, disappearing into the tunnel that Yoon was creating.

She motioned to a laughing Álvarez and stood back, allowing her friend to head in. Then she turned to Ox.

"You go first, my friend."

Trace's eyes narrowed. "No, Ox."

"I will follow behind."

"You're not going after Manse on your own."

"He is still dangerous. Look what he has done to annoying Zhao. Look what he has caused."

"We'll deal with him later. Right now, we're *all* getting out of here. Now."

Ox took in a deep breath. "When the time comes," she finally said, "you will let me kill him. Not you. Me."

"Absolutely."

"You are good friend, Tracey Rutowski."

"Because friends always let friends take the kill shot."

Ox slapped Trace on the back, nearly shattering her spine. "You are funny, American."

Tracey smiled until Ox entered the hole; then she took a second to crack all the bones back into place where her friend's hand had hit her. When done, she let out a grunt of pain before following everyone else.

Man, it *sucked* getting old.

★   ★   ★

TO KILL A BADGER   345

"You can't do this! This is murder!"

"Stop whining. You big baby!"

Lot rolled his eyes at the chained badger. Since meeting The Crazy Four, as he once called his now-wife and her friends, he had known many honey badgers. They could be polite, crude, funny, tacky, angry, terrifying, sweet, and any other number of things. But he had met very few pathetic crybabies! He'd known newborn cubs less hysterical.

"Why is Uncle Edgar sending us pictures of France?" Hel asked, staring at his phone.

Wolf held up his hand. "I don't want to know."

"We don't know where our wives are," Lot pointed out.

"And we don't need to know."

"What if they're burning down Paris?"

"This looks like Versailles."

Lot and Wolf stared at their brother.

"What? It does."

"We're just surprised you would know."

"I know things," Hel reminded them.

"I say," Lot cut in, "we pretend we didn't get his texts until we get back home. Either our wives will have destroyed France completely by then, or they'll be home and Edgar can yell at them rather than us."

"He'll still yell at us."

"Yes, but it will be less, because the whole thing will have been resolved."

The brothers all silently agreed and waited for their cue.

"You can go."

Lot and his brothers looked at the full-human Nigerian who had spoken to them. He was staring at a laptop, studying coordinates and visuals from below.

They'd parked the jet at a private airstrip to be fueled and readied for their return. Now they were in a supply plane, flying low over an animal park.

"You sure, Henri?"

Henri's half-sister was a wild dog who ran one of their restaurants

346 Shelly Laurenston

with a Van Holtz cousin. Henri was the director of this park that protected the animals full-humans enjoyed hunting. Sometimes for poaching and sometimes because they were bored dentists looking for something to kill.

"Do not insult me, *mon frère*," Henri said with a smile. "I am always sure."

"Apologies," Wolf replied.

"You can't do this!" MacKilligan screamed. *"You—"*

Lot kicked the badger out of the open door, watching him fall as they held on to the sturdy straps that kept them from following.

Wolf looked at his brothers. "I could forget. . . ?"

"Nah." Lot shook his head. "We promised that tiny badger with the big roar. I'm not sure we want to make her mad."

"Good point."

At the right moment, Wolf pressed the button on his phone, and the parachute deployed.

The badger kept screaming anyway until he hit the ground.

As the door closed, Lot's wolf ears picked up Fred MacKilligan yelling out, *"This isn't over!"*

Wolf, staring at his phone, cringed and asked, "Is that some dude's head stuck in a tree?"

"Oh, yeah," Hel said, sitting on the bench next to Henri. "Whatever happened in France—it definitely involved our wives and Ox."

Lot nodded, because his brother was probably right. That absolutely sounded like their wives.

And Ox.

Chapter 28

It didn't feel like they'd been digging for that long.

They came up from the earth to find a dark-red SUV waiting for them, the keys in the ignition. Rutowski drove, and Nelle kept moving her arms so her wounds didn't heal completely. She wanted them cleaned out before that could happen. She also wanted her phone. Or a phone. She needed to contact her father. Let him know to watch his back. She didn't want him blindsided.

Yet, despite all the things crowding her mind, she couldn't ignore what was happening with the cat. He'd been silent since they'd come out of the hole that last time; he'd sat in the vehicle without saying a word. Naked, his clothes left somewhere else, he'd climbed into the back seat inside and immediately opened the window. As they'd traveled the roads leading away from Versailles and Paris—and France's well-trained police force—he'd kept his head outside that window like he couldn't get enough fresh air.

When they arrived at the small, but extremely nice château Nelle didn't recognize, Álvarez cut in front of her while the rest went into the home.

"Just a suggestion," the She-badger said quietly, holding onto a large, red-leather Louis Vuitton bag just out of Nelle's reach, "but you may want to watch out for your cat. I think traveling underground has really freaked him out."

"Really?" Nelle snatched the bag from the female's hand. "I wouldn't have figured that out if you hadn't said anything."

348   *Shelly Laurenston*

Álvarez leaned back. "Are . . . are you okay?"

"I'm fine. Why?"

"You just seem a little . . ."

Nelle stepped closer and snarled, "A little *what?*"

"Nothin'."

Rolling her eyes at this female wasting her time, Nelle went around Álvarez and walked into the house. She dropped the bag on the stairs leading to a second floor, and tracked everyone down in the kitchen. A kitchen that was quite large for such a small-ish house.

At least someone had given Keane a towel, but it was barely covering him, despite his narrow hips. He had to hold it with one hand until he sat down on a kitchen chair and laid it across his lap.

Why couldn't anyone get him a proper towel? Were they *trying* to annoy Nelle? Because it was starting to feel that way.

Then she noticed that Rutowski was on her phone.

"Who are you texting?" Nelle asked.

"My niece. Figured I should—"

Nelle stomped across the kitchen and slapped the phone out of the female's hand. "Are you stupid?"

Gawking at her empty hand, Rutowski asked, "What the fuck?"

"Are you trying to make this situation worse?"

"No, but—"

"Then don't call anyone! Don't text anyone!"

"You seem a little stressed, Nelle."

"Shut up!"

Keane hadn't been listening. Not for the last hour. He'd been too busy imagining himself being buried alive, and what if he couldn't get out? What if he couldn't get out and no one could save him? Every time he had that thought, he would start to quietly hyperventilate. So quietly no one seemed to notice, but he could feel his heart rate increasing and his blood pressure growing.

But then he heard something strange. Nelle Zhao yelling.

Nelle didn't yell. She didn't get truly angry. She could be mean and dangerous, but she didn't go into a rage like Charlie or Mads or, well,

TO KILL A BADGER 349

him. But there she was, standing at one end of the kitchen table, yelling at the stunned She-badgers on the other side of the table who had stepped in and saved them both.

True, according to local news radio—as translated by Álvarez for Keane—the entire country of France was freaking out about the "attack" near Versailles, and every entry into the country was being watched to find the "culprits." But other than that . . . these four lunatics had really been trying to help. In their own Gen-X, kill-or-be-killed, honey badger way.

Nelle grabbed a fresh baguette from the table and brandished it like a long knife. "Did you do this?" she demanded, jabbing the baguette toward them. "Was this you?"

The four badgers looked at one another and back at Nelle.

"Was what us?" Rutowski asked.

"If you're asking if we trashed Versailles. . . ?" Yoon shrugged. "Sorta."

"If you're asking if we saved your ass . . . yes!" Álvarez told her.

"Other than that, we're lost," Rutowski said.

"And do not care," the Russian tossed in.

"We *care*, Oksana," Rutowski quickly insisted. "We *do* . . . sort of."

"They wanted my father," Nelle told them. "Did one of you give me up so they could get to him?"

It was like cold water had been thrown on the four She-badgers. Their expressions changing from mild concern and annoyance to something darker. Of course, Keane recognized their expressions. He'd seen it in his own mirror so often the last two decades. Even the Russian moved away from the counter she'd been leaning against to stand beside her comrades. The four of them glowering at Nelle.

"Let me tell you something, kid," Rutowski growled out, "when we join a team, we are fucking *loyal*. We don't turn tail and run. We don't rat anyone out to cops. And we definitely don't give up snobby bitches to runty full-humans who know who we are. And if that's what you are accusing us of—"

"That's what I'm accusing you of—"

"Okay!" Keane quickly stood, the wood chair scraping against the

350   *Shelly Laurenston*

tiles as it skittered back. He held both his arms out, although the table was between them all. "Ladies, look, I don't know how to do this . . . this . . . right here . . ." He motioned with his hand, trying to find the word.

Yoon guessed first, "Mediate?"

"Yes! I don't know how to do that. That's Finn's job, and he usually is stopping me from . . ."

"Biting someone's head off?"

"Yes! That's what I do, when tiny people annoy me. When it's bears, I just try to take their faces off. But that's not what I want to do right now. Instead, I'd rather . . ."

"Put on some pants?" Rutowski suggested.

"*That* and my loyalty is torn here."

"*Really?*" Nelle snapped.

He moved the hand aimed at Nelle higher. "*Meaning*"—he pointed at the four She-badgers with the other hand—"they saved our lives. And *you*—"

"You want to fuck her?" Álvarez coldly suggested when he pointed at Nelle.

"Please stop talking," Keane begged. "I am just trying to get through this with as much dignity as possible and the limbs I was born with still intact. Is that too much to ask?"

When they all remained silent, Keane continued.

"Nelle, I don't think they ratted us out. And, ladies, I think Nelle has been through a lot in just a few short hours and instead of swarming her like the angry badgers you all are, maybe we should just sit down and discuss what may have happened so we can fix it."

Keane cringed a little, not knowing if suggesting they "fix" things was the right direction. He really needed Finn here for this sort of thing. Especially when he was still naked and had the taste of some dude's hair, scalp, and blood lingering inside his mouth.

He started to think he should have grabbed Nelle and run when the four badgers didn't stop glaring at Nelle and she didn't stop glaring back. But then Rutowski's cell phone pinged, and she reached down to pick it up from the floor. She took one look at the message that had

TO KILL A BADGER **351**

come in and said, very calmly, "Why don't I cook us something to eat? I'm sure everyone's hungry. And while we eat . . . we can talk. Calmly. Rationally. Sound good?"

Yoon nodded. "Sounds good to me." She looked at Nelle. "Your highness?"

"Not helping!" Keane snapped.

Keane had wanted a shower before he ate, but he seemed afraid to leave her alone with the crones while they whipped up some dinner from the fresh supplies someone had left for them. So he'd insisted she come with him to one of the upstairs bedrooms. While he went about showering the blood and dirt off his body in the adjoining bathroom, Nelle had spent time cleaning the wounds on the backs of her arms. Of course, first she had to cut each one open again. Then she cleaned out the dirt and grime the wounds had picked up on their travels through the holes in the dirt. After that, she'd applied rubbing alcohol and wrapped each wound with clean bandages.

Once done, she'd stretched out on the bed, arms and legs akimbo, and stared at the ceiling.

She felt a little more centered now. A little calmer. She didn't want to cut the Russian's throat nor hack off Rutowski's head with an axe . . . so . . . that was good.

"Have you been in touch with your dad?"

She hadn't realized the shower had gone off and that Keane was back in the room with her.

"Not yet." She sat up and froze. He'd pulled on a pair of jeans, but that was it, and *damn.*

She watched him continue to dry off his shoulders and hair. Muscles flexing . . .

What, exactly, was wrong with her?

Oh, honestly! She knew what was wrong with her. She wanted to fuck him! Who wouldn't want to fuck that man? Fresh from the shower, his hair smelling like Olaplex conditioner, and his body just rippling in those jeans. He'd even brushed his teeth. He smelled "minty fresh."

352 *Shelly Laurenston*

"What's wrong?"

She blinked, realizing she was staring at him. Practically drooling. She had to get it together!

"Nothing."

He sat down next to her, the damp towel between his hands. "I'm sure your dad is okay. But if you want to go check—"

"No, no. I know he's fine. Charles immediately contacted Marti, who contacted—"

"Charles! Where the hell was he?"

Damn. She'd meant not to bring Charles up, since she knew Keane would only be angry. But he simply didn't understand.

"Charles did what he was supposed to do."

"Bullshit! He abandoned you!"

She held her hand up. "Keane, I wasn't kidnapped. I was arrested. When one of us is arrested, the family has to be informed by security. That's exactly what Charles did. So the next time you see him—"

"He's not fired?"

"—I expect you to be nice." She pointed a finger at him. "And no head crushing. He may survive, but he'll never look the same again, and we both know it. Understood?"

The tiger looked away.

"Keane."

"Fine." He looked at her again, forcing a terrifying smile that definitely didn't reach his eyes. "I'll be nice."

"Thank you."

That horrible fake smile faded and he said, in earnest, "Whatever you need me to do, just tell me. And if you want to leave right now, we leave."

Warmed by his tone and the way he was looking at her, Nelle suggested, "How about a kiss?"

"Absolutely not."

"The speed of that response was hurtful."

"I didn't mean it that way. I just know what will happen. We'll start kissing and we won't stop and then . . ."

"Fucking?"

TO KILL A BADGER 353

"Yes."

"And you're morally opposed to that?"

"Unequivocally, *no*. Not opposed to it."

"Then what's the problem?"

"Right now, I'm still feeling a little . . ."

"Trapped underground?"

"Oh, my God." His head dropped forward, his face buried in his hands. "I can never do that again."

"I know."

"I thought I was going to be trapped there forever. I felt I was just crawling around my own tomb."

"You weren't, but I get it. I have an aunt that was a great digger. Loved to dig from one house she owned in Yunnan to another house she owned in Chengdu. But then, one day, she had to get an MRI. Thirty minutes in that machine and suddenly she realized she was claustrophobic." Nelle shook her head. "No more digging. She just has her limo take her between houses now."

Keane turned his head away from her, and she got the feeling he was trying not to laugh.

He cleared his throat and said, "I know that if we . . ."

"Fuck?"

"Yessss," he said, looking at her again, "I'll just be using you. Stop smiling."

"I can't help it."

"I know *you* don't care about being used. But that's not what *I* want."

"What do you want?"

"I don't know." He shrugged, looked around. "To hang around outside your house until you start worrying about me, end up feeding me and giving me water, maybe let me in when the weather's bad because I look so sad just sitting in your yard in the rain, until one day you let me in and I never leave again."

"You mean like what happens when someone adopts a stray cat?"

"Yes."

★ ★ ★

354   *Shelly Laurenston*

She gawked at him, obviously confused, but he didn't know why. How else did she think cat couples became cat couples?

"Let's go get something to eat," Keane suggested.

"So you can avoid me and this discussion?"

"Avoid *you*? No. But avoid having this discussion while fighting my desire to put my hands all over you. . . ? Yes."

They both smiled, and Nelle nearly forgot everything but the big cat sitting next to her.

Then . . .

"Are you two fucking in there?" the Russian barked through the door.

Nelle unleashed her claws and nearly had the bedroom door open all the way when Keane caught her around the waist, yanking her back with one arm while slamming the door with the other.

"We'll be a minute!" he calmly called out.

"Do what you want. I do not care."

"Yes, we're well aware of that."

"I hate her," Nelle panted through fangs. "I hate her."

"I know," Keane said, his cheek pressed against the back of her head. "I know. But let's at least try to get through dinner without bloodshed. I'm so hungry."

"I've heard old honey badger is quite tasty."

"It's not."

It was late afternoon when she heard it.

"Hello? You there. Child-sitting . . . person? Hello?"

Charlie looked up from Dani's hair. The kid had asked her to brush her hair and put braids in it. At first, Charlie had suggested Mads do it, but the kid really wanted Charlie. Apparently Mads was being "a little scary right now" about basketball, while Charlie and Dani had bonded over their love of dogs. Not only their love of dogs, but their mutual confusion at the bears and cats innocently asking if, "You want me to throw that thing in the trash for you?" while pointing at some living, breathing dog standing at their feet.

That kind of bonding couldn't be ignored, so Charlie had gotten some hair products from the bathroom—the ones Stevie used, since Charlie's were probably too heavy for the kid's hair—and settled on the top step of the front stoop while the kid settled on the step just below.

Charlie had been barely five minutes into brushing Dani's shiny black hair with white flecks—too young for the full white streaks yet, but black like her father's and uncles'—when she heard a voice she hadn't heard in years.

"Yes, hello," she said when Charlie finally looked at her. "I'm looking for Gong Zhao. Someone said she might be here. Have you seen her?"

Charlie cleared her throat and said, "Hi, Mimi."

The honey badger's eyes narrowed, and she examined Charlie with obvious distaste—the "help" being so forward and all—but Charlie had seen that expression too many times to take it personally anymore.

"Do I know you?" Mimi asked, making it sound like an insult without even trying.

It was strange. How much Mimi looked like her sister Nelle. Despite Mimi's waist-length black hair with one big white streak and Nelle's shoulder-length locks, the sisters could almost be twins, they looked so much alike. Yet their personalities were so vastly different that Charlie felt comfortable telling people they looked *nothing* alike. Nelle was so charming and friendly to everyone, and she stayed that way unless people proved they didn't deserve it; while her sister was . . . less charming.

"We went to the same Wisconsin high school at the same time?" Charlie repeated the facts she'd had to say when they would meet at a 7-Eleven in their hometown during the holidays. "Our sisters are best friends and play basketball together?"

The blank stare told Charlie this girl had completely excised anything to do with the MacKilligans from her mind. Not surprising. In vastly different social circles in high school, the pair had barely tolerated each other then. Now, they might as well be complete strangers. But Charlie knew what would prompt the snobby heifer's memory.

"You called me 'peasant' once, so I set your Gucci bookbag on fire, then drank a chocolate milkshake while it burned."

"Ohhhh . . ." Mimi's top lip curled a little, and Charlie was sure she saw a bit of fang. "Charlie. Of course," she said through now-gritted teeth. "How could I forget?"

"Well—"

"Anyway, where's my sister?"

"France."

"France?" And Charlie smirked at the sudden fury in that voice. "What is she doing in *France*? She's supposed to be part of my wedding!"

"I'm sure she'll be back in time."

"All the festivities are starting *this* week! She can't just blow this off! *She promised me!*"

Both Charlie and Dani leaned away from that abrupt explosion into insanity.

"I'm sure she'll be there the day of. Isn't that what you want?"

"*NO!*"

"Good Lord."

"*It's not what I want! She needs to be here NOW!*"

The yelling. Charlie had forgotten about the yelling. Mimi loved to yell at people back in high school, too. Teachers. The lunch ladies. Other students. The principal. Her own friends. Her sister. But she especially loved to yell at Max. She *hated* Max. Of course, in this one instance, Max hadn't really done anything to prompt such a rampage. At least not from Mimi. Nelle, however, had a whole host of reasons to rage at Max for tying her into this stupid wedding.

"*I shouldn't even be doing this!*" Mimi continued to rant. So loudly, even the uncaring cats and bears had taken notice. "*She's one of my bridesmaids! She's supposed to be by my side at all times! Now she's in France and not doing anything I NEED!*"

While this rant was happening, the front screen door opened, and Stevie walked out, saw what was happening, immediately turned around, and went back inside.

Charlie almost laughed at the insanity that invaded brides like a virus when they were arranging their weddings. But she also knew that laughing would only extend this screaming, and she wasn't in the mood for that. She really just wanted to do the kid's hair. Brushing it was surprisingly soothing.

But she should have known that Stevie would have never completely abandoned her big sister. Not when there was a better victim to toss into the ring. Like tossing a Christian to a Roman lion—quite a few of which were shifters who just liked to eat full-humans for fun and profit! Ahhh, such a different time.

"Hey, Charlie!" Max called out happily, oblivious. "Stevie said—oh, God!"

Max spun back around to return the way she'd come before Mimi could deign to notice her, but despite those superior basketball skills, she wasn't fast enough, crashing into her teammates just as their fellow badger noticed them all.

"You! Demon bitch!" Mimi yelled, now pointing at Max rather than Charlie. "You get my sister back here this minute!"

With a deep breath, Max reluctantly faced the crazed badger.

"Look," she said calmly, "she's doing something very import—"

"You promised she'd be here! *Not in France!*"

"There's been a slight change in plan," Max said, doing really well at sounding reasonable for once. Charlie was super impressed. Look at her sister! Not escalating a problem when they were surrounded by sound-sensitive bears and cats! Charlie was almost proud!

Not that Mimi cared about any of that.

"I don't want to hear about slight change of anything when I am getting *marrieddddddd!*"

Good Lord, the screeching! Charlie had excised that screeching from her memory the way Mimi had excised her. Because, even for a badger, it was a lot. Then again, Mimi's "rich lady screeching" in the front of the jewelry stores was usually distraction enough that allowed her brothers to steal flawless diamonds out the back.

Charlie blinked at that. Distraction. She abruptly looked around, ignoring the hysterical She-badger in front of her. She wondered if someone had a line of sight on her right now. Ready to blow her head off while Mimi Zhao distracted the MacKilligan sisters. But the shot never came, and Mimi continued to be a hysterical bitch.

358 *Shelly Laurenston*

So hysterical, Max was reaching for the tactical knife she kept taped to her back under her practice jersey.

Charlie immediately put her hand over Dani's eyes. She wasn't going to stop her sister, but she knew that Dani was too young to see anyone get stabbed in the neck. But before that could happen, Streep stepped in. It's what she did when Nelle wasn't around to calm an out-of-control situation. She simply did things a little differently from her suave teammate.

For instance, Nelle would never walk up to a screeching badger and . . . burst into hysterical tears.

"You don't understand," Streep sobbed at a stunned Mimi, "she's got to take care of this because so much has happened and everyone is upset and . . ." Streep continued talking, but her words had become so high-pitched that it was impossible to make out the rest of what she was saying. Plus the sobbing. So. Much. Sobbing.

Although it was pretty funny that all the dogs on their street started barking.

Mimi attempted to step away from Streep, but Max's teammate threw herself into Mimi's arms, hugging her tight, and sobbing into her shoulder.

"Please don't be mad at Nelle," Streep begged, as her entire body shook and she hugged Mimi tight. There were tears. Tears! Not just noises, but actual tears and snot pouring down onto Mimi's designer sleeveless blouse. *"Pleasssssssssse!"*

Quickly realizing no one was going to rescue her from this overly emotional honey badger, Mimi pushed at Streep and said, "Okay! Okay! Fine." Wow. The female suddenly sounded so . . . normal. "Just tell her I need her. And to call me when she gets back." When the pushing didn't work, Mimi went with shoving, sending a still-sobbing Streep into Max's open, waiting arms.

Streep's teammates faked concern and patted her back and shoulders until a horrified and disgusted Mimi quickly walked away in her ridiculous six-inch designer heels that probably cost more than Charlie's first legally purchased car.

TO KILL A BADGER 359

A minute or two later, with her shoulders still shaking, Streep asked, "Is she gone?"

"Yep."

Streep straightened up and wiped the tears with the backs of her hands. "I need hydration," she said with a big smile. "I'll get the Gatorade!"

She disappeared around the side of the house, Tock and Mads following.

When Charlie saw that Mimi had crossed to another street and was gone, Charlie halted her sister from going past her and inside the house by raising one finger. When her sister stopped and waited, Charlie picked up her noise-canceling headphones and put them on Dani.

"Hold on, sweetie," she said, before carefully covering the kid's ears. When done, she asked her sister, "I'm assuming we're not telling Mimi that Nelle may be arrested for terrorism in France and won't make her wedding?"

Max's eyes widened, and she looked off before lying. "I don't know what you're talking about, Charlie."

"Really? You're trying that with me?"

"I don't know what you mean."

"Max, I *know* why Nelle is in France with Keane."

Max's gaze flickered over to her. "You do?" Now her eyes narrowed. "How do you know?"

"How do you think I know?"

Max stamped her foot. "Nelle *told* those crones *not* to tell you!"

"Really?" Charlie asked with great sarcasm. "And yet they seem like such cooperative bitches. Don'tcha think?"

Max immediately laughed. "You're right. You're right." She shook her head. "All right. Soooo . . . what do you want me to do? Go over there and get Nelle?"

"So that *you* can get locked up for terrorism, too? Let's avoid that plan."

"Are we just going to leave Nelle there? To go to prison forever? I might actually feel bad if that happens."

"Would you?"

"I might. Especially since I hope to have my own place one day that Nelle will redecorate behind my back so that I have all the comforts but without the costs. Like she did for Mads."

"The unconditional love you have for your friends is quite heartwarming."

"Isn't it?" Max said, grinning. "So what do you want me to do?"

Charlie lifted her gaze to the surrounding houses and, again, wondered about someone being able to take a shot at her. It would have been easy enough, wouldn't it?

"Charlie?"

She returned her gaze to Max. "I've got an idea."

Her sister smiled. "Yeah . . . I see that."

Chapter 29

Nelle and Keane walked into the kitchen, and Álvarez greeted them with a, "There you are! Sit, sit." She gestured to the big wood table as she and Rutowski began placing big bowls of pasta, platters of steak and fried chicken, and fresh bread and bowls of vegetables on the table. Wine had already been uncorked and was now being poured into stemware. An icy bottle of beer, however, was placed in front of him.

Yoon was already sitting at the table and working on a laptop. The Russian was talking on her phone to someone, but Keane couldn't understand what was being said, because it sounded like she was speaking . . . German?

Nelle pulled out a chair and sat down. She crossed her arms over her chest and one leg over the other. She said nothing, but Keane knew that wasn't a good thing.

With the food placed, the four She-badgers sat down. They took what they wanted, like he did, but Nelle simply sat there. Not moving. Not speaking. Just waiting.

"You're not going to eat anything?" Álvarez asked.

"I'm not hungry at the moment." Her gaze moved over to Rutowski. "I have a lot on my mind."

"Like what?" Rutowski asked, managing to smile while asking a question and eating steak.

"I know you four are up to something . . . I just don't know what."

"Sweetie . . . we're *always* up to something."

★　★　★

"Whose house is this?"

Nelle asked because she smelled wolf everywhere, but there was nothing that told her that any of these four badgers actually lived or owned this place.

Between bites, Rutowski replied, "It's Edgar's."

Nelle glanced at Keane, but he was so busy shoving food into his face . . .

"Edgar?" she repeated. "Edgar Van Holtz? The wolf who clearly hates you?"

"He doesn't hate *us*," Álvarez said.

"He hates Trace," Yoon finished.

"And me," the Russian tossed in. "But it is mutual and built on the fires of a very cold war."

"Why would you bring us here? Won't he—"

"Even if Edgar knew we were here, he'd never rat us out to the cops." Álvarez pulled a baguette into two, handing the second piece to Rutowski.

"Plus, when we stay here, we reroute the security system," Yoon explained. "As far as he's concerned, no one is here. If they're searching for us, it's probably in Germany or Lithuania."

"Lithuania?" Álvarez repeated. "Why Lithuania?"

"You know. *Lithuania* . . ."

"Ohhhh. Right. Lithuania. Yeah. She's right. He'd be looking for us in Lithuania."

Nelle held her hands up. "I don't want to know about Lithuania."

"You're right. You don't."

"What I do want to know is why Edgar Van Holtz would be looking for us at all?"

"Well, it may not be him. But it might be others."

"Uh-huh."

"You look concerned."

"Not used to my own kind trying to hunt me down."

"Really?" Yoon asked, clearly shocked.

"When you say 'your own kind,' do you mean badgers or shifters in general?"

TO KILL A BADGER 363

"Either."

"Huh."

"So now I have to worry about The Group? Katzenhaus? BPC?"

"More like the CIA. FBI. Homeland Security."

"The Hague, if this is ever considered a war crime," Álvarez added.

Nelle glanced down at the steak knife next to her plate and debated using it to kill all four She-badgers, but then Keane spoke.

"Am I going to prison?"

Nelle immediately saw that the color had drained from Keane's handsome face as he held an uneaten drumstick in his hand. "I'm going to prison, aren't I, Nelle? I bit a man's head off. I tore out another man's spine. They *definitely* send you to prison for that. I'm going to prison forever. Even worse, they're going to bury me in the ground, aren't they? They have some underground prison, just for shifters, and they're going to bury me in it. Aren't they? Some place no bigger than this room! I'm going to die in an underground prison, aren't I?"

With an annoying amount of *I told you so* in the gesture, Álvarez used both hands to point at Keane.

Nelle's contrary nature wanted to simply leave the room so the four crones would be forced to deal with a panicked tiger on their own, but she cared too much about *him*. Not them . . . *him*!

Reaching over, she grabbed his chicken-free hand and squeezed. "You're not going to prison."

"You promise?" Keane asked, sounding more desperate than she'd ever heard him before.

"I promise."

"We would kill you long before that anyway," the Russian dryly volunteered.

"Shut up!" Nelle snapped.

"Don't worry!" Rutowski quickly stated, pressing her hand to her upper chest. "We protect our own." When Nelle scoffed at that particular lie, the female added, "As I've always said . . . killing together, brings friends together." The She-badger had her hands clasped, as if she were giving a state of address to the United Nations.

"I understand now," Nelle flatly told her. "You're insane."

364 *Shelly Laurenston*

"Not clinically!"

"There is nothing to worry about. This is already being cleaned up," Álvarez told them.

"By whom?"

"By those who know it would be very unfortunate if we were ever captured and interrogated," Rutowski said, with a smile that was so off-putting, Nelle continued to hold Keane's free hand just to keep herself grounded.

"We know things," the female continued, still smiling. "We've done things. If they capture us, all hell would break loose, and they all know I won't care."

"Trace is right," Yoon muttered around her food, the hood of her black sweatshirt pulled over her head, as if she were trying to hide her identity from her own friends. "They can't afford any of that."

"So, I'm *not* going to prison?" Keane asked.

"You're *not* going to prison," Álvarez promised.

"And if you are ever captured, I will put bullet in head before they can ever put you in cage."

Keane nodded at the Russian. "Thank you, Oksana."

"No, no!" Nelle snarled. "No 'thank you, Oksana!' Do not thank her for offering to kill you!"

"But I don't wanna go to prison."

"You're not going to—"

Nelle stopped when she realized she was screaming; clenched her free fist and took a deep breath to calm herself down.

"She's right," Rutowski told Keane. "You're not going to prison. And even if you did—"

"Which is *not* going to happen," Álvarez insisted.

"—we got her"—she pointed at the Russian—"out of East Germany when there was still an East Germany."

"So, we can easily get you out of the American prison system," Yoon said.

"Which we have done several times in the past anyway."

"Hey, hey, hey," Álvarez said to Rutowski. "We are legally obligated *not* to discuss that."

"Right, right. I forgot."

At that point, Nelle released Keane's hand so she could use both her own to rub her eyes and silently wish for death for four old crones.

"Can I tell you something without you coming across the table to kill me?"

"No."

Nelle said that so flatly, Keane had to look away before he started laughing. She was so sick of these four females, she didn't know what to do with herself. It would be hilarious if he wasn't still recovering from the trauma of traveling underground.

"Well, that makes this awkward," Rutowski replied to Nelle's admission.

"I'll grab her before she gets across the table," Keane promised.

"Oh. Okay. Yeah. Because you're really fast. Cat fast." Rutowski nodded. "Cool. Anyway," she said to Nelle, "do you remember when you told me *not* to talk to Charlie?"

"Yes."

"I talked to Charlie."

Keane shoved the drumstick into his mouth, bone and all, so he could catch Nelle when she launched herself over the table.

As he held her with both arms, Nelle desperately struggling to be free, she still managed to ask through gritted fangs, "Why would you do that? Just because I told you not to?"

"Partly. But mostly because I like her. I like her a lot."

"Of course you do," the Russian said, "because she is part dog."

"We did bond over the dogs," Rutowski admitted. She grinned. "There were puppies! I love puppies!"

Nelle allowed Keane to put her back in her chair, but it wasn't until she retracted her fangs and her growls only came low and from the back of her throat, did he completely release her.

When Nelle felt confident she had most of her control back, she ordered, "Just tell me what you did."

"As I said, I talked to her before we left. I told her about my brilliant idea and what you were going to be up to in order for it to happen, and she was totally cool with it. Like, she didn't go on a rage or anything."

"Did she start baking?"

"She was baking when I told her."

"Oh, God."

"First, you need to know that our thing wasn't to crash your thing," Yoon said.

"And what, exactly, was your thing?"

"I had to pull my baby brother's underwear over his head."

Keane watched Nelle mutely stare at the Russian. He was glad he wasn't the only one who didn't understand what the fuck that woman was talking about.

"His underwear needed pulling," she insisted.

"Okay," Nelle said quickly, "what does this have to do with you talking to Charlie when I expressly told you not to?"

Rutowski took a long moment, staring at Nelle the entire time, before replying, "Nothing."

"Then why did you bring it up?"

She cleared her throat. "Clarity."

"Oh, my God," Nelle said, looking at him, but he had no idea what these ladies were on. Weed? Snake venom? Ricin? What?

Nelle blew out a long breath before asking, "Why did you tell Charlie anything?"

"To keep her in the loop."

"You do not keep Charlie MacKilligan in the loop. Not without going through *me*."

"Why not?"

Nelle lifted a finger, her focus on the table. She stayed like that for a few seconds before she asked Rutowski, "What did Charlie *tell you* to do?"

"She wants us to finish our deal with the Kopanski-Müllers."

"With France now accusing us of being *terrorists!*"

Keane flinched at Nelle's yelling.

"They're not accusing *us* of being terrorists. They're just saying

they were attacked by terrorists. Which is wrong, but, ya know . . .
who cares?"

"You idiot."

"What now?" Rutowski sighed out in teenage-like exasperation.

"Do you know what Charlie will do when she finds out we made a
deal with a badger that set me up to be used as bait to trap my father?"

The four She-badgers glanced at one another before Rutowski
asked, "That's what you think Jules did?"

"That's what I *know* Jules did."

"And she did that because. . . ?"

"Because she probably thinks your idea is stupid. Just like I do. And
she knew someone was willing to pay a lot of money to get to my dad,
and she was willing to share that cash with this full-human Manse,
who seems to know what we are."

Now the four She-badgers studied Nelle and, for the first time,
Keane saw it. What had Edgar Van Holtz so worried. It was that look
in their eyes. Especially Rutowski's. Not only were they all hiding
something, not only were they all *plotting* something, but they were
much smarter than anyone was willing to give them credit for, because
they were all just so goddamn annoying. One tended to automatically
dismiss them out of hand, because they were so absolutely annoying.

And the way Rutowski was sizing Nelle up . . .

No. Keane didn't like any of that one bit.

"You know what we should do?" she said to Nelle, those shrewd
eyes still studying the younger female.

"What?"

"We should find out if you're right. Because if you are, we can use
it for leverage."

"Leverage for what?"

"To get Jules to do what we need her to. That's the plan, right?"

"But she was just using me to get to my dad. And you *still* want to
work with her?"

"We still need her on our side."

"Except she's not to be trusted."

368 *Shelly Laurenston*

Rutowski wiped that away with a quick handwave. "Who among us is?"

Charlie scrolled through the news on her phone, cringing at each mention of what was happening in France. How was this *not* going to be an international incident?

"Uh . . . Charlie?"

Lifting her gaze from her phone, Charlie smiled at Streep. "Hey!"

Charlie blinked when Streep abruptly scuttled back out of the room like Charlie had thrown something at her.

"Streep? Sweetie?"

Max's teammate didn't step into the room. Instead, she stood outside the doorframe, looking in.

"Hi," Streep said. "You wanted to see me?"

"Yeah. Do you want to come and sit down?"

"No!" She cleared her throat. "I mean . . . sure."

Slowly, Streep crept into the room, pulled out a chair at the kitchen table, and—still slowly, her gaze never leaving Charlie's—sat down.

"Sweetie, are you okay?" Charlie asked.

"Uh-huh."

"If you say so . . ." Charlie shook her head and continued on. "Anyway, I was thinking—"

"You sure you don't want Max or *anyone* else in here? At this moment."

"I wanted to talk to you first, and then we can fill them in if you agree."

"If *I* agree? Agree to what?"

"Are you sure you're all right?"

Max's teammate was a brown-skinned Filipino-American, but she was so pale at the moment, she could be Stevie.

"I'm fine," Streep said in such a high voice that the dog asleep on Charlie's feet under the table lifted his head and *woof*ed.

Streep cleared her throat and said again, "I'm fine. What's up?"

"I need you to broker a deal for us."

"A deal?"

"Maybe two. The deals Nelle was supposed to do in the States, but now that she's stuck in France . . ."

"I don't really know what you're talking—"

"Tracey Rutowski told me everything before she left."

Streep cringed. "Nelle is not going to like that."

"Why not?"

Streep blinked her big brown eyes at Charlie before replying, "No reason."

Charlie could tell Max's teammate was hiding something from her, but she didn't really care. Not at the moment. She would worry about it another day. "Okay. Anyway, can you do it?"

"Can I haggle? Haggle with honey badgers?" She finally smiled. "My mother would say I've been trained since birth to do just that." She gave a little shrug. "When do you want me to start?"

"Tonight. There's a jet at the ready, because that's a thing now. And I want Max and the others to go with you. It's too dangerous for you to be on your own."

"Oh, but—"

"I know. The playoffs. Look, I thought I should talk to you first, make sure you wanted to do this, and now I can talk to Mads myself—"

"No!"

Charlie leaned back a bit while Streep forced a smile.

"Sorry. This is all so exciting. Um, I mean, *I'll* talk to Mads. She'll take it better from me."

"If you're sure."

"Yes. I can handle everything. You don't have to worry about any of it."

"Great. Thanks."

With a nod, Streep stood and walked out, but a few seconds later, she returned.

"Charlie?"

Charlie, who had already stood up, faced her. "Uh-huh?"

"While we're making deals, and Nelle is in France handling things, what . . . uh . . . exactly will *you* be doing?"

"Well . . ." Charlie reached down and picked up the fifty-pound

370   *Shelly Laurenston*

bag of flour that had been piled on the floor with six others, using the move to give herself a few seconds to come up with a worthy lie. But when she turned around and dropped the flour on the kitchen table, Streep was already gone.

Finn was sitting on the open back door of a cousin's pickup truck, Mads leaning in with her arms around his chest. Dani, her hair in adorable braids, was sitting on Shay's shoulders while she and Tock discussed something about math. And Max was attempting to learn how to throw a football from her cat boyfriend and his team's newest receiver. She wasn't bad at it, either.

It was a lovely evening, and he was glad to just be here, in this moment. Sadly, moments like that never last, did they?

Streep came tearing out of Charlie's house and toward their group. "We have to go! Now!"

"What's wrong?" Tock demanded.

"She's baking!" she yelled as she kept running. "She's baking!"

"Five-pound flour bags? Or ten-pound?" Max yelled at her friend. "Five-pound? Or ten-pound, Streep? *Tell me!*"

Turning but now running backward like she was on the basketball court, Streep told Max, "Fifty-pound! *She's using fifty-pound bags!*"

"Mighty Odin," Mads sighed out before she ran after Streep, Max and Tock right behind them.

The bears, however, ran *toward* Charlie's house. Some started a line that would eventually reach down the block and into other streets. Some sat outside the house, simply waiting.

As for the rest of them, all cats, they quietly watched everyone else until Shay said, "Should we ask what's going—"

"No," Finn said, as firmly as possible. "Absolutely not."

"Yeah . . . I think you're right."

Chapter 30

"Let's take a look at these arms of yours!" Rutowski cheered after they'd all finished eating and talking. Keane was fine with that until she pulled out her tactical knife again.

"No! What's with you broads and knives?"

Rutowski's grin somehow got bigger. "There's that Malone energy I've been looking for!"

"You are *not* touching her with those knives."

"Yeah, but—"

"No."

The Russian suddenly stood. At first, she didn't say anything. Simply stood there, staring at each person in front of her before she announced, "I go to raid neighbor-bear's hives."

She shifted and trotted out the doggy door that was large enough for a Great Dane or a massive wolf. Or a large-sized honey badger.

Álvarez and Yoon followed their friend out the doggy door as well and, after putting her plate in the sink, Rutowski was about to follow.

"We're hiding *here*," Nelle pointed out, "but you guys decide it's a good idea to go harass bears and steal their honey?"

"Well . . . we could stay here," Rutowski said, "get high, and sing down memory lane to Kate Bush songs. She has a really high singing voice that none of us can match. So it's really funny when we try . . . and try . . . and *try* to match it." She flashed a smile that showed practically all her teeth. No fangs this time, but the threat was implied. "Or we can go harass bears and steal their honey. Your choice."

372   Shelly Laurenston

Nelle didn't even have to tell the female to get out. She simply looked away, and Rutowski headed to the door.

And, before shifting and disappearing into the night, she said, "You two should get some sleep. We'll be starting pretty early, and we have a lot to do."

When she was gone, Keane searched the cabinets for a medical kit. He finally found one in the bathroom. When he returned to the kitchen, Nelle had already taken off the bandages and, already cringing, she tentatively asked, "How do my arms look?"

Keane stood behind her and used alcohol wipes to clean the remaining blood off. He took his time, not wanting to damage the area any more than it had been. When he was done, he told Nelle the harsh truth.

"They're fine."

Nelle looked at him over her shoulder. "What?"

Keane shrugged. "They've healed completely. Not even a keloid."

"No, no, no!" She was no longer cringing, but very annoyed. "They should be a mess! Why aren't they a mess?" She bent her right arm at the elbow and raised it so she could examine the skin that had taken the brunt of the damage.

"Is this about your sister's wedding again?"

"That stupid dress is sleeveless. I just wanted to look hideous on her special day! But clearly I can never get a break!"

"And you laughing at me does not endear you to me right now."

"Sorry. I can't help it. I have never met anyone who wants to avoid a wedding as much as you do."

"She won't listen to me. It's a waste of time."

"Maybe she loves him."

Nelle, disgusted by the suggestion, rolled her eyes. "If you're going to say ridiculous things, we can't talk about this anymore."

"You know," he said when she went to grab an apple from a bowl full of them on the counter, "I can come with you. To the wedding. If you want."

Nelle froze, mid-bite, her fangs digging into the apple's flesh and her eyes wide as she faced the cat.

TO KILL A BADGER 373

She bit off a piece, chewed, and swallowed. "Are you joking?"

"I'm not funny."

She shrugged at that. She actually thought he was quite funny.

"You want to come to a wedding of someone you don't know?"

"No. I don't. But neither do you. So if we go together . . . maybe it will be tolerable. I also like the idea of looking down on all those rich people. Maybe scaring some full-humans just by staring at them until they piss themselves." He nodded. "I can find lots of ways to entertain myself. It's a gift."

"And you'll do this . . . because?"

"If I can keep you from getting in another chick fight with your sister in front of all those people so your family doesn't hate you, I think it will be worth it."

"It was not a chick fight."

"You pulled her hair."

"To ruin it for the wedding! It was a cruel and inhuman plan!"

"It was two girls rolling around on the floor in a wedding store while a bunch of other girls tried to stop them. If that's not a chick fight . . ."

Nelle studied the apple in her hand for a moment before asking, "Will you really come with me?"

"I won't wear a tux."

"That's okay."

"Then yeah . . . I'll go."

Nelle charged the cat, slamming into him and wrapping her arms around his waist.

"What's happening?" he asked, confused.

"I'm giving you a hug to thank you."

"Oh. Okay."

"Feel free to hug me back."

"Do I have to?" She looked up at him, and he grinned. "Just kidding."

"Not funny."

"Told ya."

★   ★   ★

He did hug her back. He really wanted to. She was soft and warm in his arms, and it just felt really nice.

The problem was that the nice thing didn't last long. Because the longer he hugged her, the hotter his skin got. The more his muscles tightened. Then, despite his best efforts, his dick got hard. Just like that. With no warning and, as usual, paying his silent commands to "settle down" no heed!

It didn't take her long to figure it out, either. He felt her body stiffen, and she moved back a bit, her gaze lifting to his.

She cleared her throat and pulled out of his arms. He didn't blame her. He was pathetic.

Then, gazing up at him, she said something really stupid.

"Catch me."

Keane was hoping he hadn't heard her right. "What?"

"Catch me." She took off running.

He watched her run out of the room, but refused to follow. She didn't know what she was doing. She couldn't know. She couldn't possibly be that—

She ran back in, sped around the table, punching him in the chest as she passed, then went out the kitchen door again.

When she ran in a third time, he said, "Nelle, you need to stop—"

She slammed into his side with such force, his entire body jerked over several feet. He reached for her, but she ducked under his arms and ran out the door again.

He didn't even realize he was chasing after her until they were in the large dining room, and she moved around him the way she moved around those She-bear players on other basketball teams. She was faster than he thought she would be and was really making him work for this.

At one point, he almost had her. His hand closing on her shoulder, but she spun away from him and went out of the room. The next thing Keane knew, he was chasing her up the stairs, and tackling her onto a bed.

It wasn't until he pinned down her arms over her head and roared with his fangs out that he froze. Horrified at the loss of control.

TO KILL A BADGER 375

She kissed him. With his fangs still out, Nelle Zhao kissed him. And that was the last thing he remembered consciously thinking for a good while.

Nelle was tired of waiting. She was tired of the stoic warrior that appeared anytime they spoke of being together. She appreciated that guy but, at the moment, she didn't *need* that guy. And she knew that under all that stoicism armor was a horny cat just waiting to get let out of its cage. Keane had probably had too many full-human girlfriends. Girls who could never handle his true nature. Or smaller cats that weren't ready for him either.

But she wasn't full-human, and she definitely wasn't a cat. She was a honey badger. And when she saw those fangs and heard that roar . . .

She attacked him like he was a king cobra and she hadn't eaten in months.

She got her arms loose and slammed them against his shoulders, shoving him onto his back. Straddling him, she kissed Keane again. Pressing her mouth against his, easing her tongue against his lips. He opened to her immediately, and their kiss turned passionate so fast, she wasn't really aware what she was doing. Like when she unleashed her claws and tore at his T-shirt until it was nothing but shreds. She could have just pulled it off, but who had time for that? She wanted to touch him *now*. She wanted all of him.

Nelle couldn't deal with any more waiting!

As it was, she didn't even want foreplay. Okay. She did. But not right now. Right now, she had to get *this* out of the way. Then they could do all the other stuff.

She sat up long enough to pull off her shirt, yank off her bra, and nearly rip off her jeans and panties. By the time she was done, Keane was naked, too. His cock was stupendous. And big. She loved big.

She launched herself at him, and he easily caught her, hands on her ass, as he turned around and dropped them both back on the bed.

"Now," she growled against his chest, fingers digging into his skin.

Keane understood, his body pressing against her seconds before he impaled her with his cock. Then he froze.

"Shit."

"What?" she asked, not meaning to sound so desperate, but come on!

"Condom."

"Shit!"

"Hold on." He rolled off her, and she almost told him to forget it. Then she remembered she didn't know when or if she'd ever want kids. So they really needed condoms.

"He must have condoms here."

"Van Holtz is old," she reminded him. "His mate has definitely been through menopause."

"But he has sons—"

"Middle age. Wives possibly menopausal."

"And grandsons . . ."

He stood, lifted his nose, sniffed the air. He smirked. "Incense."

Used by a college kid trying to hide the pot smell coming from his bedroom and who hadn't quite learned all the things an adult wolf could smell even when one was trying to cover it up.

They both followed the scent down the hallway until they reached the last door. A locked door. Keane raised his leg and with one kick sent the door flying across the room.

He went right to the bedside table and opened the top, then bottom drawer. That's where he found the condoms. She heard him whisper, "Thank God."

That was enough for Nelle. She grabbed the already open box from his hand while hooking her foot behind his and lifting. He crashed to the floor, and she was on him in seconds.

"Where do you badgers get your freakish strength from?" he asked as she put the condom on him. Once she'd done that, she straddled him again and pressed herself down on his cock. When he was buried as deep as he could go, Keane wrapped his hands around her waist and rolled her onto her back.

Nelle spread her legs as wide as she could, making sure she was absolutely taking all of him in, then slapped her hands against his hips and dug in her manicured nails. She left her claws sheathed. She didn't want to tear him apart, simply get him moving.

The manicured nails seemed to do the trick, though, Keane slamming his hands on either side of her head and thrusting his hips hard. Which was just what she wanted. Needed. She'd never needed anything more.

It took him a few seconds to get his rhythm; then it seemed like his cock took over. Eyes closed, snarls coming from the back of his throat, he powered into her. And Nelle loved every second of it.

She moved her hands to his shoulders and did nothing more than match him thrust for thrust. She let her mind be wiped of the shitty day that had passed, the worries about her family, the fact she might be the lead suspect in a terrorist attack on French soil. Or that she may never again be able to shop at the Champs-Élysées Louis Vuitton store!

She let this cat and his long, thick cock take every horrible thing away from her but the enjoyment of being fucked by someone she really, really liked.

Wow. That was so weird. She actually liked a male that she was fucking. She couldn't remember if that had ever happened before. She'd tolerated past lovers, but *liked* them? Wanted to spend time with them outside her bed? Wanted to wake up in the morning with them beside her? She couldn't remember that ever happening before, and she had a very good memory.

Realizing she simply liked someone who wasn't a fellow honey badger or on her basketball team or the lead designer at a major Italian fashion house had Nelle arching up against Keane, her legs wrapping around his waist. She squeezed him with her body and her cunt, and the growl that came out of him had her following him right over the edge until they both dropped to the floor next to each other. She knew he hadn't wanted to crush her under his weight, but she wouldn't have minded. He still didn't get that she wasn't some fragile thing, did he? Some full-human that would crumble at the first sign of his cock and those fangs.

Well, there was nothing like seizing the day, as Horace once wrote.

Panting and gazing up at the ceiling, Keane allowed himself these few minutes of absolute blankness. For once, he wasn't worried. He wasn't worried about his family. He wasn't worried about his team. He wasn't worried about anything.

He was, however, a little hungry. But that was to be expected. Actually, getting something to eat while he gave Nelle some time to recov—

"What's happening?" he asked when the badger grabbed his foot and proceeded to drag him from the room.

"We shouldn't fuck in the kid's room. It seems wrong, but I wasn't exactly rational a few minutes ago."

Keane knew he wasn't a light man. Even in his human form. He was more than three hundred pounds. It was the only way he could handle those bears that had cleared the four-hundred-pound human weight range when they were in their teens.

"Where does this crazy strength come from for you people?" he demanded to know.

"There's a rumor we were around when dinosaurs roamed the lands, which means we have adapted, survived, and thrived for at least one cataclysmic event on this earth. Who knows, maybe we were there for the earlier ones, too. So dragging a tiger around a French château really doesn't challenge me."

She pulled to a stop in the bedroom with the adjoining bathroom. Lying on the floor, he watched her take the remaining condoms from the box they'd jacked from the college kid's bedroom and carefully place those on the bedside table. Like she was setting up that cheese plate the She-badgers put out after their meal less than an hour ago. When she seemed satisfied with that, she stood over him, legs on either side, before dead-dropping onto his chest.

With one knee planted against the floor and the other raised so she could rest her elbow on it, she sat there a moment, her gaze focused somewhere else. When he felt that "moment of silence" had gone on long enough, Keane asked, "Is that it?"

"No, no," she said, waving a finger. "I'm still dealing with this."

"I don't know what that means."

"I'm not used to this."

"Sex?"

TO KILL A BADGER 379

"Don't be a smart-ass."

"Okay," he said on a laugh.

"I'm not used to *this*. Where I like the person I'm having sex with."

"Okay."

"I usually just hit it and quit it."

"Good to know."

"But that's not what I want from you."

"Is that why you're squatting on me like a farmer in a field?"

She glanced down at herself and said, "This is how I squat during a game when we're discussing plays with the coach."

"I see."

"Yeah, yeah," she said, motioning between them. "I really like this. Really like you, no matter how much it confuses the fuck out of me."

"If it helps, I like you, too."

"It doesn't help. Not at all."

"Oh."

Nelle closed her eyes, and her face contorted into a mask of pain.

"Are you okay?"

"No. Because I'm realizing I'm heading to a world of family barbeques and Christmases with your unpleasant mother and you and your brothers arguing over who gets to grill the generic, store-brand hot dogs."

"No, no," he quickly cleared up. "We buy Nathan's."

"Oh, my God," she said, dropping her head, her entire body shuddering in horror.

"If we think about it in advance, we can usually snag Hebrew National. They're Kosher."

"That's it, isn't it?" she asked. "This will be my tragic, sad, suburban life if we start a . . . a . . ."

"Relationship?"

She flinched like he'd swung at her. Then she shook her head and said, "Wait. I don't think I'm seeing the big picture."

"What's the big picture?"

"I'm rich. Fabulously, wonderfully rich."

"That is true."

"So at any time, I can jet off to another country or sail the Mediterranean in the family yacht."

"Also true."

"And I will make you come with me."

"Is that supposed to sound like a threat?"

"It is. Because . . . my mother."

"I'm a cat. We can adapt to any horror."

"Good to know."

"A few things, though."

"Sure."

Keane put his hands behind his head. "Can I constantly complain about how much money you spend on stupid things?"

"I'd expect no less."

"Can I roll my eyes dramatically when you whine about the quality of toilet paper I got on sale at the grocery store?"

"As long as you know I will have the softest three-ply delivered each day, whether you want it or not."

"Not a problem. Also, when I have to spend time with your family, can I allow myself to be so bored that I'll start swiping things off the table with my claws until your mother screams at you hysterically for bringing a cat into her perfect home?"

Nelle froze, her gaze locked across the room. Her breathing became shallow. "I'll allow that," she finally said, her voice low, "only if you promise to knock over the Ming Dynasty vase that my mother will lie and tell you is a fake because she actually stole it from the Chinese government."

"Huh. Do you want it to tip over and land on the ground with a smash, or do you want it to fly across the room and hit the wall, bursting into a thousand pieces of ancient and precious art that your mother can never get back or replace?"

"Oh, my God," she gasped out, her entire body heaving. "I am so *wet* right now. I think I just came." She pressed her hand over his heart. "Would it be weird if I asked you to marry me?"

"I'm a cat. Our level of weird is vastly different from everyone else's."

TO KILL A BADGER 381

* * *

Nelle didn't really think much after that. What was there to think about?

Instead, she simply stood, took a step, and dropped down onto his face with a perverse amount of satisfaction. And it didn't help the situation that he proceeded to eat her out like he'd been waiting to do that for decades. He tongued her, fingered her, and nibbled until he had her screaming.

He rolled her over then, a pillow under her hips, pushing her legs apart as he entered her slowly from behind. He'd already gotten off once, so he took his time this go-round. Sliding his hands and lips across her shoulders, down her spine. When she looked at him, he kissed her. A sweet, slow, eternal kiss that made her feel incredibly wanted, which only made her hotter and wetter.

Damn cats and their evil sex ways.

Several hours later, Keane left the room and soon returned with a bottle of wine, a couple of boxes of water crackers, and the cheese plate that had been left on the kitchen table. While they ate and drank right from the bottle, she sat on his lap, facing him, and he had his cock buried deep inside her.

She had never enjoyed brie more.

When they'd finished satiating one hunger, they proceeded to deal with the other until they both eventually fell asleep, holding each other tight.

They'd only been asleep a few minutes when Keane woke up to those cold blue eyes gazing down at him.

"Who kicked door off room?" the Russian asked, uncaring that he was still inside Nelle at this moment.

"Now we must get it fixed," she complained when he didn't answer. She studied them a moment before announcing, "There is food. You are welcome to it. But wash the cum off each other before we are forced to deal with you."

"Yeah," Keane told Nelle when the door slammed behind the Russian. "I completely understand why you hate her."

Chapter 31

"Where's my son?"

Shay gazed down at his mother. She was at least a good foot shorter than he was and yet, he always felt like he was about to be crushed. She always said Keane was just like their father, but the truth was, he was just like her. The two floated on their rage the way butterflies floated on air. So when he didn't want to answer her straightforward questions, he tended to panic.

"What? Huh? Uh . . ."

Finn stepped in front of him. "Hey, Mom! What's up?" He looked at his watch. "You sure are up late. Anything we can do for you? The Malones being too loud? Want me to tell them to shut it down?"

It was when their mother was quiet that she was the most terrifying.

Again, just like Keane.

"My son wouldn't happen to be in *France,* would he? With that badger?"

"France?" Finn said. "Why would Keane be in—"

"Okay." She held her hand up to stop Finn's attempts to tap dance around the question. "I can see that whatever's going on is just going to send me into a spiral of anger the likes no one has ever seen."

"That sounds ominous."

"Doesn't it? But to avoid that, let's just do this . . ."

Their mother pointed across the street to the badgers slipping through the crowd of bears waiting outside Charlie's house for more baked goods.

TO KILL A BADGER 383

"You four!" she called out.

Tock, Mads, and Streep immediately stopped. Max kept going.

"Over here. Now."

Shay hadn't even noticed Tock and the others were leaving. He knew they would be, but he hadn't asked for specifics and hadn't noticed they'd already made their move to leave.

Tock came to his side, her hand slipping into his. Something his mother immediately noticed and, based on the way her eyes narrowed, she did not like. Mads settled next to Finn, and Streep stepped in front of their mother, smiling.

"Hi, Mrs. Malone! What can we do for—"

"Quiet."

"Yes, ma'am." Streep stepped back and kept quiet.

Max ran up a few seconds later when she realized she'd lost her entire team.

"What are we doing?" she asked. "What's going on?"

"I'm not asking that question," his mother informed them all. "Because I don't want to know. I am, however, going to say this . . . you two go with them."

Shay looked at his brother, and he saw the same confusion.

"Mom, are you—"

"Whatever is going on with your brother—and I don't want to know!—this de Medici thing needs to be resolved *now*. I want that coalition wiped from the face of the planet, and I'm sensing whatever idea these rodents—"

"Ratals," Max corrected.

"—have maybe the only way to get it done quickly. But, quite honestly, I don't trust these four to do anything without causing even more problems than we already have. So you two go with them. And that other cat should go with you, too."

"The other cat?" Streep asked.

"You," his mother called out, and Zé sauntered over in his jaguar form, black tail flicking. "This one goes, too."

"But, Mom . . . we should stay," Finn argued. "Nat and Dani—"

"I have come to realize that Nat can take care of herself. And Dani—"

"Has all of us!"

Finn locked eyes on their uncle, who had slung his arm around their mother's shoulders while making that pronouncement.

"If you want to keep that arm," Shay's brother quietly warned, "I'd move it."

"Now, lad, it's just a friendly gesture!"

"You know what else is a friendly gesture?" Streep asked with a big smile, and before Shay or Finn could, in fact, rip the cat's arm off. "Me calling your wife and telling her what you've been doing with your arms while she's gone! Isn't that friendly? I think it's really friendly!"

She pulled out her phone. "Let's give her a ring, shall we?"

His uncle's smile faded, and he pulled his arm off their mother's non-consenting shoulders.

"We won't leave until your mother tells us to go," their uncle informed them before walking away.

"You believe him?" Finn asked their mother.

"I do. Now go. All of you. We'll be here when you get back." She went up on her toes and kissed Shay and then Finn on the cheeks. "And if you have to leave these rats—"

"It's ratals, Mrs. M!" Max happily reminded her.

"—to die, you do it. Your lives are much more important than theirs. Just bury them in shallow graves and keep moving."

"*Ma!*" Shay and Finn said together.

Nat kissed her two big brothers goodbye, checked on her niece to make sure she was sleeping, then snarled a little at the puppies to watch them cower, before returning to the Dunns' finished basement, where she'd made a bedroom for herself.

She was glad she'd gotten to this street when she did; otherwise, she could be trapped like her brother Dale. In an RV with three younger Malone cousins was not what she considered a good time. Besides, unlike Dale, who'd been doing nothing but prepping for college, she had more important things to do.

Important things her brothers didn't know about, but that was okay. They didn't need to know everything. Besides, they'd just get in her way.

When Nat got to the bottom stair and turned into the main basement room, she froze at the doorway. Charlie sat on Nat's twin bed and looked at her over the laptop screen. She'd left it open on the table she'd brought down to have next to the bed, so she could work and watch the TV across the room. Since she'd been staying here, no one had come downstairs. Not even once. Still. This was sloppy on her part. She knew better.

For a minute that felt like an eternity, Nat and her half-sister stared at each other until Charlie motioned her over with a twitch of her forefinger.

God, she didn't want to do this. She didn't want to have this out with Charlie. Especially because Charlie was way tougher than Nat's brothers. All these years, Nat knew just how to handle them. Even Keane, who was tough with her, but never mean like he was to Dale. Charlie, however, wouldn't be fooled by the tricks Nat used to keep her older brothers from giving her too much trouble. She was a badger herself and had basically raised Max and Stevie. She'd found Nat's usual moves almost insulting. And the girl was not afraid to hit when annoyed. Nat's brothers never raised a hand to her, but Charlie and Max didn't have that problem. They'd swing in a heartbeat if they were pissed enough.

Staring at her half-sister, Charlie said, "You've been busy."

Charlie had gotten better about looking directly at Nat when she spoke, keeping her sentences short, and enunciating. Nat was pretty good at reading lips, but it wasn't easy, and she preferred American Sign Language. But Nat didn't hold it against her new half-sisters that only Stevie knew some ASL, since none of them had known they'd had another sister, much less a deaf one, until very recently.

It was funny, though, how they'd just accepted her. Without question. Without resentment. They were angry, but not at her. They blamed their mutual father for all of it, which she appreciated. Especially because Freddy MacKilligan was an asshole.

386   Shelly Laurenston

"Did Tracey Rutowski ask you to do this?" She pointed at the screen. Dumb. Nat should have closed her laptop, which would have forced Charlie to enter a password to get in. A password that combined sixteen letters and numbers, so Charlie getting in would have never happened. Same thing with Max. Stevie, though, could have probably gotten in. She was way smarter than Nat, and Nat didn't say that about a lot of people in the world.

"Yes."

Charlie rubbed her forehead with both hands and blew out a long breath. Then she stood, and Nat steeled herself for a punch or slap, hoping it wasn't too hard. She could handle it, but she didn't want to. Being around her brothers had made her comfortable living *without* random acts of sibling violence.

Standing in front of her, Charlie said, "Don't let your brothers know." She handed her a piece of paper ripped from a spiral notebook. "And I need this information as soon as you can get it. Understand?"

Nat nodded.

"Leave the information in my backpack. It is red and by the door. Okay?"

She nodded again.

Giving a small but sad smile, Charlie pressed her hand against Nat's shoulder, then walked out.

Nat followed after her to make sure Charlie went up the stairs. Once she felt confident her sister was gone, she looked at the paper in her hand.

She didn't think she could be any more surprised than she already had been by Charlie MacKilligan but, for once, Nat had been wrong. She had been delightfully surprised!

Berg opened his eyes when he felt Charlie slip into his bed. He turned over, reaching his arm out to pull her into a hug.

"What's going on?" he asked, happy to have her pressing against his bare chest. He knew she hadn't gotten a lot of sleep the last few days. Actually, most of her "quality" sleep time involved short naps at her kitchen table while things were baking.

"A lot."

"Are you leaving the country, too?" he asked.

"It's not my plan."

"That's not a no, though."

"It's not." She cuddled closer, and he tightened his arms around her. "I hate to ask but—"

"We're not going anywhere, Charlie," Berg told her, speaking not just about himself but his brother and sister. "We can protect Dani and Stevie."

"And Nat."

"Nat doesn't need anyone protecting her."

"I know. That's what worries me." She let out a small sigh. "I'm sorry you're losing so much money right now."

It was true. They were. Berg and his siblings provided security services to very rich and very important people. But the work often took them out of the country for long periods of time. He wasn't going to do that with Charlie and her sisters in such danger.

But, like most bears, the Dunn triplets didn't need much to be happy. A house; comfortable, size-appropriate furniture; and a regular shipment of sustainable frozen salmon; and the three of them were more than content. What money they didn't use, they saved for rainy days like now. And it felt very rainy.

"You do whatever you need to do," Berg told her. "We'll be here until it's done."

She pulled back a bit so she could look into his face. "On your keyring, I put a small safety-deposit-box key. Dutch has the password, and my grandfather has the bank name and location. If anything happens to me and Max, that box has everything Stevie will need. Understand?"

He did understand. Completely. But he didn't like what he was hearing. He knew, though, that telling Charlie he didn't want her or Max in danger, and he could manage all of this himself, was not the way to go—and possibly not true. He had no idea if he could handle this himself. Or even with his brother and sister in tow. Besides, the MacKilligan sisters didn't want anyone rescuing them. They didn't need it.

388 *Shelly Laurenston*

"I'll take care of everything," he promised.

"I love you."

Berg held her even tighter. "I love you, too."

"And if Max ever ends up going to prison, Dutch handles the escape plan to get her out."

He kissed the top of her head. "Always good to know how to help with a felony."

"It's a badger specialty. Felony help."

Analia de Medici was busy doing the washing up when she heard the knock on the back door. When her sister answered it, Milano de Medici walked in. He barely acknowledged her with a nod of his head. Then he dropped into a chair at the kitchen table. His two great-nephews who had accompanied him were dismissed to the nearby living room.

She immediately went to the refrigerator, assuming he'd want something to drink, but when she came over with a glass and glass jug, he waved her away.

Analia returned everything to its proper place and went back to her dishes. She usually had a staff to take care of these small things, but that had been when they lived in Italy and weren't at war. A war her husband had started. Now no one who wasn't a de Medici by blood or marriage was to know where they were. It was said their lives were in danger. But Analia's life had been in danger since she'd been handed off to the de Medicis by her pride. By giving Paolo a girl to marry, her mother and her sisters prevented the murder of their youngest children. Analia's younger sister had been given to Silvio, her mother telling her, "This way, you won't be alone." Her mother had also promised her two daughters they'd be rich and have everything they could ever want. Instead of feeling satisfied with her life, though, Analia often wondered what it was like not to flinch every time her husband moved.

Paolo walked into the kitchen with his shadow and brother, Silvio.

Throwing his big arms wide, Paolo greeted his family. "Uncle Milano! What brings you here?"

"Our money."

Paolo stopped walking and lowered his arms. "Our money? What about our money?"

"We don't have any."

Analia motioned to her sister and the other women helping in the kitchen to leave, and she followed them out the back service entrance. She sent them all up the back stairs to their rooms, but stayed and listened at the door. Analia had learned long ago that to avoid her husband's rage, she always needed to know what was going on. Even if she risked getting caught.

"What are you talking about?" Paolo asked.

"Our money is gone. All the bank accounts cleaned out. Only the cash is left. And there's not a lot of that since you started this fucking war."

"Are you accusing me of taking that money?"

"No, you idiot! We know who took it! The vermin! This is what they do! And why your father told you not to fuck with them!"

"He thought he could control them. And look what happened. They killed him! I'm not making the same mistake!"

"You started this, and now we are all fucked. Do you know why? Because you don't *think*, boy. When your father was alive, we were willing to take the risks, but not anymore."

"Meaning?"

"I've discussed it with my brothers, Paolo. It's time you withdraw from what's happening. I can work with Katzenhaus to handle ending this."

"I'm not ending anything."

"You'll do what I tell you, boy, or—"

Analia knew the second her husband shifted and attacked his uncle. She could hear the two lion males tearing her kitchen apart. Then it all stopped.

Swallowing, she pushed open the door enough to see inside.

Paolo had his uncle pinned to the ground by his neck, while Silvio had Milano by his hind leg. The older lion kept trying to fight them off, battering them with his paws, but they wouldn't let him up.

390   Shelly Laurenston

Paolo readjusted his hold on his uncle's windpipe and bit down harder. For long minutes, they stayed like that until the old lion, finally, stopped moving.

Silently, Analia backed away, carefully closing the door, and went up the stairs. Her sister was waiting for her in her bedroom. They sat next to each other on the bed, but Analia didn't have to tell her sister anything. Over the years, they'd learned to communicate without words.

Now Milano was dead, and the remainder of his brothers would be coming for Paolo and those willing to back him.

But it wouldn't stop there. Not for the de Medicis. If Paolo and his brothers were killed, the uncles would also wipe out any cubs they had. That's how they avoided future retribution when Paolo's sons and daughters were adults.

But they weren't just Paolo's sons and daughters. They were hers, too. Of course, if Paolo went after his uncles first . . .

Whatever her husband and his brothers did, though, after all this, was only going to make everything absolutely worse. And now it sounded like there was no money to hire mercenary cats and bears who could be bought to fight on their side.

Analia looked at her sister, and she knew they were both thinking the same thing.

They had to get the fuck out of here.

After spending some much-needed time with Berg, Charlie slipped out of their bed while he slept. She showered and got dressed, and went back to her house, greeting the bears that were loitering around her property, most of them in their shifted form since it was still dark out.

Once back in her kitchen, Charlie didn't start baking. Instead, she simply sat at the table with a hot cup of coffee that was rapidly going cold, and just gazed across the room. She had so many thoughts, and was busy trying to organize them into something usable. Something that would get her through all this, because time was no longer on her side.

"Are you okay?" Stevie asked as she grabbed a bottled water from the fridge and sat down at the table with Charlie. "You look befuddled."

TO KILL A BADGER 391

"No. Just thinking about things," she admitted.

"What things?"

"Just things."

"Have you heard from Max?"

"No. But I doubt I will until they have something to tell me. I'm sure it will be fine, though."

"I have to admit, I was surprised you sent them out."

"Why?"

"It seems like a crazy badger plan. The kind you usually avoid."

"Maybe. But I'm sure Streep can handle it. She's smart and knows how to cry on cue."

"True." Stevie stood. "If you need anything, just let me know."

"Sure."

She heard Stevie leave, but then her sister was back at the table.

"You're not baking," Stevie noted.

"No. Because I'm sitting here and thinking. Remember? We just had that conversation."

"But everything is okay, right?"

"Yeah."

"Okay. Okay."

Again, Charlie heard her sister walk away, but three seconds later, she was back.

"How is everything okay?" she asked.

Charlie leaned back in her chair. "Huh?"

"What I mean is, *why* are you okay? You should be baking and freaking out. Why are you not baking? You should be baking."

"You sound like the bears. And usually you freak out when I *start* baking."

"That's not true. I love when you bake."

"Okay."

Stevie nodded. "Okay." She smiled. "Okay!"

This time she made it down to the basement before darting back upstairs and sliding to a stop in front of Charlie, who had not moved.

"You know, don't you?" Stevie asked.

"Know what?"

"You *know*."

"You'll have to be more specific."

Stevie stomped her foot. "Charlie!"

"Oh. Do you mean that I know that Nelle had originally told Rutowski not to tell me about her idea? To not involve me at all? That anything that might involve me should only go through her first?"

Stevie cringed and turned to walk away.

That's when Charlie said, "*Or* do I know about the time you ran off to Nepal to join a nunnery?"

Stevie spun around, eyes wide now as she gaped at Charlie.

"A nunnery," Charlie repeated. "Even though you are a very proud atheist, even then. And then Max had to run after you and get back in time for her prom and, of course, before I noticed that you were gone at all. Or do I know about the time Max was arrested in Canada for stealing gold bars from some dude's house, dug herself out of the jail, only to eventually punch a moose for some reason? Thankfully, she was only fourteen, and my grandfather was able to get her back home before I noticed. Although he was told not to tell me . . . and not to let Max return to Canada. Ever."

Charlie leaned forward and said, "Or do I know that you and Max have been working together to track down and kill each bastard that was involved with my mom's death? I believe you've gotten three out of the six, right?"

Stevie groped for the chair before dropping into it, mouth open, eyes still wide.

Finally, her sister tried to speak, "Char—"

Charlie held her hand up. "No, no. No need to apologize, which is what I'm assuming you were about to do. I get it. But let's understand something . . . I always know what you guys are up to. When I don't know what's going on is when you have to worry. That being said, of course, don't tell Max I know what's going on. She's happier when she thinks she's getting something over on me. If she finds out she's not . . . I worry what she'll *really* get up to."

With a full-body cringe, Stevie nodded in agreement.

★　★　★

TO KILL A BADGER 393

Stevie fought the wave of panic that washed over her. When she usually got like this, she would have to go into a dark cabinet and spend *hours* doing her deep-breathing exercises until her heart rate went down.

But thankfully, her new medication was helping control that need—and her heart rate—as was Charlie's calm reaction to all of this.

She knew.

She'd always known.

Max used to wonder if their big sister knew, but then they'd dismissed it. If she knew, wouldn't she step in? That's why they hadn't told her, because they didn't want her to worry or be involved or get mad. There were tons of reasons why, for all these years, they'd kept her on the outside of what was going on. Because Charlie, could be, when provoked, a bit . . . reactionary.

Charlie picked up her phone and read something, texted back a reply, and put her phone back onto the table.

"So," she said, briefly glancing at her phone again before continuing, "why don't you guys ever tell me what's really going on? I mean, I *think* I know, but I'd love to hear your thoughts."

Stevie knew there was no point in lying to her sister at this point. But she wanted to be gentle. She didn't want to hurt Charlie. She loved her!

Satisfied with the direction she was going to take, Stevie began, "Vlad the Impaler—"

"Wow!" Charlie immediately exploded. *"Really?"*

"Okay. Okay." Stevie held her hands up. "Wrong example. Get it. You are *not* Vlad the Impaler." She tried again. "Genghis Khan—"

"Oh, my God."

"—was a master of psychological warfare. He would wipe out entire civilizations so that when he went to the next civilization or city or empire, he could point at the one he just destroyed and say, 'If you don't do what I want, what happened to them will happen to you.' And that plan was quite effective for him."

"Your point being . . . I kill old people and children and take the stronger women as slaves?"

"Not on purpose."

"Oh, my God," Charlie let out in a stunned whisper.

"No, no, no! I mean . . . you don't do *that*. Of course you don't do *that*. But when you're making a point . . . you tend not to see the potential long-term, more wide-ranging damage that could come from your angry reactions. Especially when it comes to protecting me and Max. We try to save you from that so we don't lose you forever if one of the shifter organizations decides you are a danger. Or you're thrown in prison for murdering someone."

Charlie glared at her, but the fact she didn't have an immediate, angry response meant she was listening.

Listening was good. Listening was one of Stevie's favorite things, and she believed the world, in general, didn't listen enough.

"Okay" Charlie finally said. "I get your point. Thank you," she said with a nod. "For being honest."

"I love you, Charlie."

"Love you, too."

With that, Stevie headed back to her basement. She had just opened some files and began to prepare to add a few more things into the notes section when she froze, gazing at the wall behind her desk.

" 'Love you, too?' " she repeated, realizing how foolish she'd been.

Spinning around, Stevie bolted back up the stairs, sliding to a stop in front of her sister and slapping the phone she was typing into from her hand.

"What the—"

Stevie pointed an accusing finger. *"Tell me what you did!"*

When Charlie did nothing in response but smile, Stevie knew everything was fucked.

Chapter 32

"Oooh, bacon."

Keane took the platter of bacon from the Russian's hand and sat down at the table, but Nelle wanted to know what they were doing next. Because she was ready to go home. Now.

"Why are we still here?" she asked Rutowski, who had been using a fresh baguette to "swordfight" with a willing Yoon. Because that was completely normal behavior for two fifty-somethings with children and careers!

At her question, Rutowski did that thing again. The thing that made her look like an irritated sixteen-year-old girl dealing with her uncool dad.

Head dropping back, mouth open, eyes rolling and crossing before huffily announcing, "You ask so many *questions!*"

"Because this seems insane to me. To still be here!"

"Well, we had to allow you time to keep fucking," Álvarez joked, before being distracted by an empty platter presented to her by a hungry tiger.

"You do have more bacon, don't you?"

"This is a wolf house. Of course we have more bacon, but . . . it takes longer to finish an entire platter of bacon when thirty wolves are grabbing at it."

"How does that affect me?" Keane asked.

Álvarez backed away from him and pulled out another platter of bacon from the oven.

396 *Shelly Laurenston*

"Let's not fight," Álvarez admonished, once she'd handed off the platter to Keane and turned back to Nelle. "If we're going to get through this, we'll need each other."

"You're kidding, right?" Nelle asked dryly.

She nodded in agreement. "I was trying something, but even I didn't buy it."

"We're waiting," Yoon said, sitting on one of the kitchen counters.

Waiting for more from that response, Nelle studied the woman who dressed like she was a South Korean teenager living in an online gaming café. Black jeans, black high-top Keds at the moment, rather than the black boots Nelle had seen her in so far, and a long-sleeved T-shirt with a hood. When Nelle had walked in, she'd had the hoodie pulled down to her forehead, but now she'd pushed it back and started eating the baguette she'd been using as a weapon moments before. She had such a pretty face; Nelle didn't understand why she insisted on hiding it.

"Waiting for what . . . exactly?" Nelle asked when the badger didn't add anything to her initial comment.

"We're waiting for Trace to tell us . . ." Yoon looked around the room for her friend. "Where did Tracey go?"

Keane realized his plate was empty of bacon again, so he began roaring until another platter of bacon replaced the empty one.

He began eating again, and Álvarez told him, "You're just lucky we're used to cooking breakfast for entire packs, big kitty."

He didn't know what she expected him to say, and he didn't care. All he knew was that he was hungry. He'd had a night of great sex and was madly in love with a honey badger that sometimes walked outside into a yard in the middle of France, grabbed a middle-aged woman by her hair, and dragged her back into the house they were all hiding in.

"Get off me!" Rutowski raged at Nelle.

"I would let her go, little badger," the Russian warned over the two females screaming. "My friend can be very mean."

Nelle did let the older She-badger go, but she did it by throwing her across the kitchen and into Yoon.

"Why are you throwing her at *me*?"

"What are you up to?" Nelle accused, pointing a finger at Rutowski. "Who were you on the phone with just now?"

While staring at Nelle, Rutowski held her phone out. Nelle reached to take it, but the device hit the floor first, and the She-badger slammed the heel of her boot against the fragile glass.

Nelle, snarling through fangs, went for Rutowski, but Keane was up and over the table before she could get her claws on her; he wrapped his arms around Nelle's waist and pulled her away. Rutowski's friends stood between her and Nelle, using their bodies to hold her back. It was not easy for any of them to keep the two enemies apart. They were ready for a fight, and neither was giving in.

"*I don't owe you anything!*" Rutowski yelled at Nelle.

"Bitch! You owe me *everything! You're lucky you still breathe!*"

Hissing, enraged, Rutowski almost made it through her friends to get Nelle while Keane was busy trying to drag Nelle from the room, but she ripped out of his arms and announced, "*That's it!* I'm done."

She slashed her arms across each other and motioned to the door. "Let's go, Keane. We're going home."

Keane was fine with that. He'd been wanting to go home since he'd gotten on the jet to bring him to France. He followed her out of the kitchen.

As they moved down the hall, Rutowski called out, "I know who gave you up to Manse. It wasn't just Jules."

"I don't care!" she yelled back.

"Really? Because it was done to purposely hurt your family."

He wasn't surprised when Nelle stopped walking.

Nelle Zhao returned to the kitchen.

Trace had known she would. She was too much like her mother not to. Not that Trace was about to say that to Zhao's face. That was just a quick way to get a claw to the head.

Zhao stood on the other side of the kitchen table, while Trace slid onto the countertop. A habit that she'd started in childhood—much to her parents' annoyance—and had not been able to break more than fifty years later.

398 Shelly Laurenston

The big cat stood beside Zhao now, and Trace realized these two hadn't simply fucked. They'd bonded. She knew the signs. The look. The scent that came off them. It was all there. They seemed to realize it, too. Unlike her. In the beginning, she'd refused to believe what she had with Wolf had been anything more than sex. She'd eventually figured it out, though. But she'd made sure to make him suffer for making her fall in love with him. To this day, she was still pretty mad about it, and it didn't help one bit that her friends still called her "Blessed Lady Stockholm Syndrome."

"Is this bullshit?" Zhao asked before Trace could say a word.

"I don't bullshit," she told her. "That's Steph."

"True. I've been trained in the art by my parents, who successfully ran a Ponzi scheme for forty years until they retired and moved to Barbados."

"Still proud about that," CeCe muttered.

"Hey! No one told that dude to involve family and friends and *charities!* Who fucks over charities? Full-humans, that's who! He deserved that prison time."

"So, yeah," Trace cut in before Steph could go on one of her rants, "me and Ox are straight shooters, Yoon bullshits when necessary, and CeCe is an artist, so she can do the abstract thing."

"The abstract thing?"

CeCe nodded. "I have a very direct, unassuming way of discussing things until . . ." She glanced off and sighed out, "Flowers."

The bonded pair waited for more, but there was no more. None.

CeCe shrugged. "See? Perfect."

Closing her eyes, Zhao placed two fingers from each hand against her brow and stroked them across her skin several times. Trace had seen the badger's mother do the same thing. She may have looked more like her handsome father, but Zhao was her mother's child in almost every other way.

"Just . . . tell me who," the kid finally said.

"You'll never believe it coming from me." Trace slid off the counter and picked up the burner phone she'd crushed under her foot. It wasn't her main phone. That she still had tucked into the back pocket of her jeans.

Tossing the burner into the trash, she walked past Zhao and the cat.

"You've got five minutes to get your shit."

"We're going home," the kid insisted.

Trace stopped at the door, looked at Nelle. "If that's what you want. But understand . . . we really don't give a fuck what you do. Think about that a minute and what that might truly mean to you and *all of France*."

"Is it me," Keane asked, when the four She-badgers had walked out of the kitchen, "or does Rutowski *always* sound like a cranky sixteen-year-old?"

Nelle leaned back so she could see his face. "Oh, my God! I thought it was just me who kept hearing that!"

She stepped closer to him. "I strongly suggest we kill all four bitches and then go home. What do you think?"

"Won't Mads be upset we killed her aunt?"

"She'll get over it."

"She hasn't gotten over you decorating her house. I'm pretty sure wiping out her aunt and her aunt's friends will ensure she never will."

He was right, of course. But these females!

"If we let them off to do whatever they want in France . . ."

"Yes, yes, of course," Nelle said to Keane's justified worries. "We'll have to come up with some bullshit excuse as to why they *must* come back with us, and then we'll let someone else deal with their crazy when we're safe at home."

"All right. I think we can—"

Keane slowly turned his head away from Nelle and stared out one of the kitchen windows.

"What's wrong?"

He didn't reply, but he didn't have to when he started sniffing the air—nose twitching, brow furrowing—low, quiet growls coming from the back of his throat.

400 *Shelly Laurenston*

Nelle walked past him and went to the back door. She stepped out and looked around at the beautiful yard and deep into the forest of trees surrounding the back of the property. She still didn't see anything, but the light summer breeze changed direction, and she smelled . . . shifters. Different breeds and species, but they were definitely shifters.

She returned to the kitchen, but Keane was gone. When she heard something right outside, she immediately slid into one of the lower cabinets, pulling her legs in tight, and closing the door. A few seconds later, she didn't hear anything, but she scented a cat. Cheetah. She could hear him sniffing, trying to find her scent. He stopped in front of the cabinets and, when he started to pull the door open, Nelle kicked her legs out, sending the cat flying across the room.

Nelle scrambled out and, unleashing her fangs, came at the cat. He tried to pull a gun, but she was on him, grabbing his hands and biting at his face and neck.

He screamed, trying to get her off, but Nelle unleashed her claws and stabbed them into his sides. She was about to start tearing his organs apart when Álvarez grabbed her from behind and pulled her away.

"What are you doing?" Nelle demanded.

"Trust me, kid. You don't want to kill him."

She didn't? Because she kind of felt like she did.

Álvarez picked up the gun the cheetah had been going for. She aimed it at the cat and pulled the trigger. But a bullet didn't explode out and tear through the male's jugular. Instead, a dart did. He gasped, then passed out.

They weren't trying to kill them, they were trying to sedate them. Like escaped zoo animals. Good to know. But then she remembered Keane.

"Crap!" She ran to the back door.

A brown-haired man with a growing grizzly hump on his back charged toward her, but as she stepped back to move out of his way, black fur with white streaks flashed by, ramming into the bear from the side.

TO KILL A BADGER 401

She knew Keane was fast. She'd seen him attack before. And all cats were naturally fast. But still . . . seeing him move like that in the bright morning light. It was wonderfully terrifying.

"You need to stop him," Álvarez told her.

She wanted to, but she wasn't sure she could. Especially when he wrapped his maw around the fur-covered neck of that grizzly.

Rutowski ran into the room. "We have to get out of here!"

Álvarez faced her friend. "What's wrong?"

"Edgar knows we're here."

She shrugged. "Okay. And?"

"He's sent a Smith to bring us in."

Frowning, Álvarez said, "Edgar doesn't work with . . ."

The two females stared at each other.

"What?" Nelle asked. "Why do you both look like that?"

"We have to leave," Álvarez said, grabbing a black backpack from under the kitchen table. "Right now."

The Russian stalked in, ready to go, the straps of a red backpack already on her shoulders. "Why are we still here?" she demanded, getting a few bottles of water. "She will be here soon."

Nelle had never seen these four She-badgers react to anyone like this. Not Edgar Van Holtz. Not the French government. Not even Charlie! And yet . . .

"Who are you talking about?"

"We just have to go," Rutowski said, moving behind Nelle and shoving her toward the front of the château.

"I'm not leaving Keane!"

"Of course, of course. So in love. It's adorable."

Before she could slap the She-badger simply for her condescending tone, Nelle heard the Russian yell, "Cat! Leave bear toy alone! We must go!"

A few seconds later, there was a loud thud, and Keane ran past her. He was covered in blood and waited at the front door for her, panting hard from his fight. Behind her, the Russian complained, "He has fucked up back door! Now we must pay to fix that, too!"

★　★　★

402 *Shelly Laurenston*

Keane nearly had the grizzly right where he'd wanted him when he heard the Russian yell. He didn't know exactly what she said—he couldn't hear anything over the grizzly's roars—but there was a tension in her voice that he had never heard before, and he let the grizzly's throat go and ran into the house. He had to jump over several other shifters to get to the front door. They littered the hallway, but none were dead. He didn't understand that. He'd seen these older females work. They had no qualms about killing anyone.

Yoon tried to order him to get into the SUV—different from the one last night—but he wasn't leaving until Nelle was with him. He didn't trust these ladies. Not when it came to Nelle.

"Let's go! Let's go! Let's go!" Yoon ordered, while holding the SUV door open so he could get into the back seat.

He ignored her demands until Nelle was by his side. Together, they ran to the SUV and got in. He shifted when one of the women tossed him clothes. Some ill-fitting sweatpants and a too-small black T-shirt that reeked of canine.

"You're covered in blood," Nelle told him as the other females got into the vehicle, Rutowski taking the wheel. She grabbed a towel someone had handed her and tried to wipe his face clean, but he sensed that wasn't effective.

"Anyone have wipes?" she asked, and was immediately forced to rear back when all four She-badgers held out packets of wipes from their bags, Álvarez nearly punching her in the face.

"Moms always have wipes on them," she explained, while gesturing to Rutowski and Yoon.

"And I am often covered in blood," the Russian added to unnecessarily explain her having wipes, as well.

Grabbing one of the packets, Nelle started wiping Keane's face clean. They gazed at each other while doing so. Not so much out of love and lust—although that was there—as confusion. What had these women so panicked? He'd never seen them like this. Not even when the French police were basically on top of them back at Versailles.

"Where are we going?" Nelle asked.

Rutowski shifted the SUV into gear and sped away from the house before suddenly turning into the woods. The vehicle was four-wheel drive, so it maneuvered well enough. Although it was a very bumpy ride—Nelle slamming into Keane, and Keane slamming into the door next to him.

"We are going somewhere safe," Yoon replied, holding on to the sturdy bar above the passenger window she sat next to.

"Where is that exactly?" Nelle snapped. "Since Van Holtz's house was *supposed* to be safe!"

"Someone must have ratted us out," Rutowski said to her friends, ignoring Nelle's concerns. "Edgar has never caught us there before."

"How many times have you used that man's property?" Keane wanted to know.

"Is that really important?"

"Not getting killed is important," he told them.

"They didn't want to kill us," Álvarez said, staring out her window like they were simply sightseeing. "They were just going to dart us so they could transport us to cages and bring us back to the States."

"That's humiliating," Keane admitted, "but at least we'd be going *home*."

"We're not going home like *that*. Besides, we're not done here. Right, Zhao? You want to know what's going on, right?"

"Stop talking to me. I hate you."

"See?" Rutowski mindlessly said. "She agrees with me."

"Edgar must have told The Group where we were, and they came to get us," Álvarez surmised. "Those were all Group people. I recognized a few of them."

"Which means she's *definitely* coming," Rutowski said.

"Who is *she*?" Nelle finally yelled, getting fed up. But again, the females managed to ignore her and her very valid questions.

"You know," Yoon said as she opened her laptop and began typing despite the worsening bumpy ride, "it's bad enough we have to deal with that female every Thanksgiving. But to send *her* to retrieve us is just an act of war."

"I know! Right?" Rutowski agreed.

"Wait a minute." Nelle finished wiping his face and neck, sat down

404 *Shelly Laurenston*

beside him, and pushed the black T-shirt at him to put on. "All this drama over a *Van Holtz*?"

"Not a Van Holtz. A Smith," Yoon replied.

"That's even more pathetic."

"Look, kid, there are Smiths and there are Smiths, and then there are *Smiths*."

"What does that even mean?"

"I get it," Keane admitted. "There are Malones. Then there are Malones. And then there are *Malones*."

"Is this an exclusively American thing?" Nelle asked.

"*Yes,*" they all replied, even the Russian.

Richie was sure he was dying after that fucking badger stuck her claws in his sides like he was a side of beef! So when he woke up to stare into the plain, uncaring face of Dee-Ann Smith, he simply assumed he was in hell.

"How hard is it to round up a bunch of badgers and a cat?" she asked with that *annoying* Southern accent she still hadn't lost, despite living in New York for all these years.

"You said it would be an easy pickup," he reminded her, blood spilling from his mouth and dripping down his chin.

"You said there'd be a cat," his grizzly partner said, as a tech tried to stanch the flow of blood coming from the bear's neck. "Not a goddamn Siberian tiger. I think it nicked an artery!"

"Don't wanna hear your whinin'." Smith stood, motioned to the medical techs to deal with Richie's wounds.

They thought they'd be doing nothing more than transporting the badgers and one "cat" to cages and then back to the States, monitoring their vitals as they were kept under control with something that would actually knock them out. That wasn't easy. Badgers could tolerate extremely high doses of all sorts of toxins. So keeping them down for longer than sixty seconds took skill and lots of backup treatments. Now, however, these techs were forced to treat his entire team for near-fatal wounds.

"Where do you think they're going?" Cella Malone asked as she

TO KILL A BADGER 405

entered the kitchen. For years now, Malone and Smith had been partners, and it seemed to work for them, but no one understood why. It's not like they actually got along.

"Isn't the tiger that tried to kill me one of your many first cousins?" his grizzly partner asked.

"What does that have to do with anything?"

"Couldn't you have just *asked* him to come home with us?"

Malone and Smith shared a look before Malone admitted, "You know, we actually hadn't thought about that as an option."

Bria Medici wasn't really thinking when she opened the front door of her family home. She was too busy fighting with her boyfriend. He was full-human, and everyone in her family hated him, but she didn't care about any of that. She just wanted to know what he thought he was doing with that *whore* Franny Rossi!

"Hold on," she said to her yelling boyfriend—which he ignored and kept yelling at her—and looked at the woman standing in her doorway. "What?"

In answer, the woman held up bakery boxes. Bria figured someone had ordered breakfast, and this was the delivery. She motioned the woman in and led her through the house toward the kitchen.

"Let me tell you something," Bria screamed over her boyfriend, *"if I find out you've been fucking Franny Rossi, I'm going to kick her ass and then I'm going to kick your ass and then I'm going to kick everybody's ass!"*

She disconnected the call and motioned the delivery woman toward the table her older siblings sat at. They were drinking coffee and trying to wake up to start their days. They'd all been tense since all the shit started with their Italian half-siblings. No one really talked to Bria about it, but she heard everything. She knew exactly what was happening, but she simply didn't have time to worry about any of it. She had a boyfriend to destroy.

A boyfriend calling her back. She turned off her phone. She'd turn it back on in exactly eighteen minutes so she could see the barrage of voicemails and texts he'd sent her in that time. And God help him if he *didn't* send those voicemails and texts.

"What's this?" Gio asked, as the woman put the bakery boxes on the table.

"The food you ordered," Bria said, pulling out her second phone from her back pocket to turn it off, too.

Gio looked at their other siblings, and everyone simply shrugged.

"No one ordered food, Bria," he said. "You didn't order it?" he asked her.

"No. Maybe Antonella ordered food."

"That would require her to use a phone. She's not in the mood to use a phone, remember?"

The siblings stared at one another for a moment before slowly looking over at the woman standing by the table.

She wasn't tall, but she wasn't tiny either. African-American with curly black hair in a high ponytail, one white streak shooting through the strands, some of those beautiful curls also in braids. She was muscular with extremely large shoulders—for a female—and a few scars on her neck and bare arms.

"Hi," she said when they all simply gawked at her, trying to figure out who this stranger in their house might be. "Name's Charlie MacKilligan."

Now Bria's siblings all slowly turned to look at her.

"It's not my fault," she immediately told them. "It's not!" She shook a finger at them. "It's my boyfriend's fault." When they didn't immediately agree with her: *"It is!"*

Gio sat on the couch, not-so-patiently waiting for Antonella to be done speaking to the honey badger hybrid that had shown up at their front door.

Of all the things that had been going on, he hadn't been expecting that. Charlie MacKilligan just showing up at their door? Uninvited and without violence. She'd brought Danish! He really hadn't expected the Danish.

He glanced over at his siblings. They'd been enjoying all that food since the hybrid had gone into the backyard with Antonella. None of them seemed too worried about eating food brought randomly by a species of shifter that enjoyed poisons, but whatever.

Pina held a half-eaten blueberry muffin in front of his face. "Are you sure you don't want any? It's *really* good."

He pushed her hand away. "You aren't worried at all?"

"Worried about what?"

"A stranger alone with our sister?"

"If things get out of hand, we'll just bury the hybrid in Mr. Hensworth's backyard. He'll never notice."

Unlike his twin, Gio wasn't as confident about his eldest sister's safety when it came to this particular female. It was true, honey badgers were dangerous. Hybrids were unpredictable. MacKilligans were well-known for being psychotic. But Charlie MacKilligan was all three. They had no idea what she would and *could* do, even to his super-predator sister.

All Gio knew was that the She-badger had come out of nowhere, asked to speak to Antonella, and handed them baked goods before entering their backyard.

He hoped she didn't expect any help from the Medicis to "simmer things down," as his mother liked to say. They were not exactly loved among their Italian brethren, and they were definitely not respected. Besides, they were a pride, not a coalition. Christ, Gio couldn't even imagine how useless his three brothers would be if they'd been forced by their sisters to set off to start their own coalition or join another pride. They could barely manage getting up in the morning, much less fighting to start a new life.

The sliding glass door opened, and the hybrid walked in. She gave a small smile before silently walking past them all and out of the house.

Pina gestured to Bria—because her mouth was full of muffin—but their baby sister just frowned and shrugged.

"What?"

"Go with her!" Pina snapped, spitting bits of blueberry across the room. "Make sure she actually leaves!"

"For fuck's sake," Bria complained before running.

The rest of them stood and went out into the backyard. Pina clapped her hands at the cubs and sent them inside the house with Renny, who had the most tolerance for his nieces and nephews. Once they were gone, Pina approached Antonella. She was where she always was when outside in the backyard—on that grassy mound under the tent-like covering that kept the sun off her.

"She's gone," Bria said, coming outside.

"Did you see anyone with her or anyone following her?" Gio asked.

Their baby sister shrugged. "No."

"Were you *looking* for any of that?" Pina asked.

"You didn't tell me to look for that!" Her phone rang, and she answered it with a screamed, *"Stop calling me!"* But then she stalked off while still screeching at the boyfriend she kept promising she was breaking up with any day now.

Gio and Pina faced Antonella again.

"You're not going to tell us anything . . . are you?" Pina guessed.

When Antonella did nothing but look off across their small yard like she was staring out at the vast plains of the Serengeti, they simply returned to what was left of the baked goods the hybrid had brought.

As they finished the last of the amazing brownies with walnuts, Pina asked, "What are we going to do?"

"Be ready for war," Gio told his twin. "We have no other choice."

Chapter 33

"Why the fuck are we back in Paris?"

It never occurred to Keane that the She-badgers would actually take them back to Paris. The scene of their "crime."

"Where did you think we were going?" Álvarez asked. Keane didn't appreciate how she always sounded like he had to be the stupidest man she'd ever come across. It was her tone. He hated her tone!

"I didn't think we'd be coming back to Paris. The place where we're wanted fugitives!"

"Calm down, cat. It's fine."

Keane reached out for Nelle, and she immediately gripped his hand with her own. That one move was the only thing keeping him from killing and eating the four badgers while they drove past the Champs-Élysées. A sight he would have normally loved to stop and look at, but at the moment couldn't be bothered to do more than simply note it was there.

When they finally parked in the city and got out, he was shocked when the Russian led them through a bunch of backstreets until they reached an entrance that was nothing more than a grate in the ground.

The Russian yanked the grate free and motioned to Keane.

He shook his head. "I am *not* going down there. Nope. Forget it."

When he felt that foot against his ass just before he went flipping in, he reminded himself he would have to kill all these old crones the first chance he got!

★ ★ ★

410 *Shelly Laurenston*

"Stop kicking me!" Keane yelled from the darkness when he landed.

Nelle glared at Rutowski.

"What? I was just helping."

"I hate you."

The female laughed, and Nelle decided to ignore it for now. She knew how Keane felt about underground spaces, and the abandoned mines and catacombs under Paris would do nothing but send her poor cat into a mire of misery.

She landed next to him and immediately put her arms around his waist.

"Are those human *skulls?*" he demanded, pointing.

"Yeah. Let's just go," she said, following after the other four, who had already landed and were walking away.

It was nothing but darkness in these passageways, since the tours didn't come to this particular location. But they were all nocturnal species. They could see most of what they needed.

But as she took Keane's hand and led him deep under the city, she could feel him panicking. He was doing his best to hide it, but his heart rate increased, his breathing became shallow. At any moment, he was going to panic and shift to cat, and then she had no idea what the hell would happen.

Stopping abruptly, she turned to him and went up on her toes. Putting her hand on his shoulder, she pulled him down until she could press her lips against his. She slid her tongue into his mouth and teased his until it reached out for her. He released the grip he had on her hand, so he could wrap his arms around her waist and lift her up.

Nelle completely forgot why she had started kissing him, because she was too busy kissing him. Their hot breath mingling; their hands holding onto each other; her breasts pressed against his chest.

She wanted him to take her right here and now, pressed up against a wall that may very well have some skulls there, too. She didn't care. She just wanted him. Now.

"Are you two *done?*"

Rutowski's teenager voice cut through the darkness and their lust in a way Nelle's own mother couldn't have.

TO KILL A BADGER   411

Pulling away from each other, they both looked at the She-badger and snarled.

"Hey, I get it," she replied. "My husband does the same for me. But we gotta go. *Now.*"

Grudgingly, their bodies heated and ready, Keane lowered Nelle to the ground, and she released him.

"Later," he growled before grabbing her hand again and following after the most annoying females Nelle had ever had the misfortune of meeting.

"It does not open," the Russian said about the door she'd been pushing and then banging on for the last five minutes.

"Is there something behind it?" Keane asked. "Like concrete or boulders?"

"No. It is simply steel and securely lock—"

He slammed his shoulder against the door, sending it crashing into an empty hallway. Taking Nelle's hand, he walked inside, ignoring Rutowski's "Impressive" comment.

It was, however, harder to ignore Álvarez's "He's just horny" response.

But before he could tell all four of the She-badgers to "shut the fuck up," an armed fox came into the hallway Keane was walking down. The male's eyes got big at the sight of Keane, and he ran off in the opposite direction. As they kept going, more armed foxes appeared; this time with more extreme weaponry. Then he saw Elise.

"*Mes amis!*" she gasped. "What are you doing here? Why did you not come through the store like always?"

Wanting to know that, too, Keane faced Rutowski, but she merely walked past him and Nelle and over to Elise.

"I thought you had already fled my beautiful country," the fox said, motioning them closer. "Come, come!"

She led them down the passageway and turned a corner, which led to another door. This one was open and brought them into the big space Keane had been in before beneath the dress shop. Already having been here and knowing what was around and how to get out, he immediately relaxed. He never thought he'd be so happy to be around foxes.

"What has happened?" Elise asked as she led them past all the busy workers.

"The Group came for us."

"So? They are friends, no?"

"Not to us."

"They would drag you home, yes? But you would be home and away from here. You should be home, my friends."

"We're not done here."

Nelle pulled away from Keane so she could stop right in front of Rutowski.

"You keep saying that . . . why?"

"I thought you wanted to know who betrayed you, and you won't believe it coming from me."

"You know what? I don't want to know. Because I'm done. I'm done with you. I'm done with France. I just want to go home."

Nelle faced Elise. "Can you arrange transport for me and Keane?"

"Of course. This way."

"So you're just going to walk away from this?" Rutowski continued, as Keane followed Nelle and the other badgers followed them all.

"Yes, I am."

"That is not going to make your family look good."

"You said my family didn't matter, remember?"

"Yeahhhh. I was kind of shittin' ya about that."

Nelle froze mid-step before spinning around. "What?"

Rutowski shrugged. "I lied. Your family's crazy powerful."

"Then why did you tell me—"

"You were just so insulted when I said they weren't that, ya know . . . I kind of ran with it."

Nelle's hands clenched into fists and, for a moment, there was nothing but silence as the pair eyed each other.

But then, one of the crones snorted, and all four of them burst out laughing, leaning against one another, unable to catch their collective breath. Simply having a grand old time at Nelle's expense.

"I'm sorry," Rutowski said around her laughter. "I shouldn't have . . . it's just . . . you were just *so pissed off*!"

"Still! She's *still* pissed off!" Álvarez said on a burst of more laughter.

Elise quickly stepped between her old friends and her newer ones. The cat was quick, so he grabbed Gong Zhao before she could get her hands around Tracey's throat.

Elise knew she had to calm this situation down quickly. Like her mother, Gong was not a woman who appreciated being laughed at.

"I cannot believe you still play these games, Tracey Rutowski!" Elise admonished.

"It's not my fault she's so sensitive!"

"This is why Edgar Van Holtz sent The Group for you. He hates you, too!"

"He's just an uptight prick."

"You are all so short-sighted," Elise went on, years of annoyance catching up with her. "There is no time for the games you four play!"

"Just get us out of here," Gong said to Elise. "I'm done with them."

She understood the girl's anger and motioned her toward her office.

But then Tracey said, "It was Zeus."

The cat stopped before Gong, but both seemed confused.

"What was Zeus?"

"How do you think Manse knew you were here?" she asked Gong. "Jules knew. She knew you were in Paris, but not where you were at that moment."

"You're lying."

"I'm not. Tell her, Elise. She'll believe it from you."

Elise met Gong's gaze straight on. "It is true. It was Zeus."

"What did you expect?" Trace asked. "He's in love with you, and you hooked up with this one." She pointed at the cat. "You know how bears are. Very sensitive. They either crumble from the rejection, heading off to find a body of water to either feast on salmon or seal, depending on the species. Or they get vengeful and rip up the inside of your car."

The cat very quietly asked, "Where is he?"

414 *Shelly Laurenston*

"That can wait," Elise tried to reason. "You should go back to America."

"No," the cat said. "Where is he?"

Finally, Elise admitted what she didn't think she'd have to and knew, even before saying the words, how badly it would be received, "At the moment, we are sure he is at Schäfer-Müller château with Jules and Johann."

Now Gong and the cat focused back on Rutowski, and Gong said, "Your plan of joining badger families together has been *so* successful."

"This has to be Johann," the crone insisted. "But we can still talk to Jules."

"Are you insane?" Nelle asked with all seriousness. "She betrayed us. She betrayed *you*."

"No way. I've known Jules for years; she would never—"

"She did not want it to work, my friend."

Nelle was so happy to hear the fox's voice cutting through the crazy.

"What?"

"This is your idea of combining badger families to fight together, yes?" Elise shrugged. "Jules was never going to let that happen."

"Since when?"

"Since forever! She likes the control she has when there is anarchy." She motioned to the other foxes near her office. "*We* have people to answer to. Badgers do not. *She* does not. She would not give that up for you, my friend."

"Warned you," Nelle reminded Rutowski.

"Shut up."

Deciding they were done, Nelle announced, "We're going home."

"Not until I kill Zeus."

Nelle turned to Keane. "I'm sorry . . . what?"

"He dies."

"That's a little overdramatic."

"He almost got you killed while trying to have you kidnapped because he saw us cuddling on the couch. I'm not letting that go."

"Keane—"

"He's right," Rutowski chimed in, and Nelle could hear it. In the female's voice. She was grabbing onto this with both hands, but Nelle didn't know why. What was going on? What was she hiding? She was clearly hiding something! Rutowski should be furious that Jules had betrayed them. That she'd fucked up her little badgers-united plan. But she was only pretending this rage Nelle was witnessing. She knew she was, because she could see it on her face. On the face of her She-badger friends.

Something else was going on. Nelle simply didn't know what yet.

"Can you help us, Elise?" Keane asked.

With a reluctant nod, Elise replied, "Of course. This way, my friends."

The crones began to follow, but Nelle caught Rutowski by the bicep and pulled her close.

"I don't know what you're up to, but I know it's something. And when I find out, chances are . . . I'm going to kill you."

"You know, sometimes, in the right light, you *act* just like your mother."

"Bitch," Nelle snarled as the crone walked away.

It was just starting to get dark when Charlie put out all the baked goods she'd made throughout the day on the outside picnic tables. The waiting bears lumbered over and began feasting while she, unnoticed, walked out the yard gate, past all the cats enjoying a family barbeque, down several blocks into full-human territory, and got into the two-door blue Honda waiting for her.

She had just started the car when the passenger door opened and Stevie got in, a backpack held in her lap.

"What are you doing?" Charlie asked her sister.

"I'm coming with you."

"Okay, you're not—"

"You either bring me," her sister happily threatened, "or I tell the bears their cupcake supplier is about to do something stupid."

"Stevie," Charlie reminded her sister, "you don't fight. I'll spend all my time protecting you."

"You won't. I promise."

"If at any time you freak out and shift—"

"I won't do that at all. I promise. I'm medicated, and I've done all my calming exercises today. But I'm coming. So just deal with that emotionally, and let's go."

Charlie dropped her hands into her lap and debated what to do.

"I'm not letting you handle this alone," Stevie explained. "I know I'm not your go-to girl when shit goes down—"

"That's not it." Charlie scratched her forehead. "I always told Max that if she ever involved you in some crazy shit without my express permission, I would beat her within an inch of her life."

"You've always been a 'do as I say, not as I do' matriarch. I'm sure she'll get over this betrayal."

Her baby sister pointed at the watch on her wrist. The one Tock had picked up for Stevie in Switzerland a couple of years ago. It was a simple device that gave her the time, date, and included a stopwatch. But it was unbelievably precise.

"We are running out of time," she said.

And Stevie was right, so Charlie grudgingly pulled onto the street and headed out.

Chapter 34

After tapping her aunt's knee to get her attention, Dani asked in ASL, "What are you doing?"

"Unlocking a door." Nat frowned and twisted her lips. "Or maybe just a window. . . ."

"I thought Uncle Finn banned you from your laptop after finding out you'd taken money from Gram's account."

"Who says I only have one laptop?"

"You're going to get into trouble. Uncle Mean is going to be Uncle Mad when he finds out."

"Shouldn't you be in bed?" her aunt suddenly demanded.

Dani gestured to the puppy she had resting on her shoulder. "He's hungry, and his mother is sleeping. I didn't want him waking up the other pups. The bears complain when they cry."

Her aunt looked at her with what Dani knew was real concern and asked, "Are you okay staying here with these bears? Do they scare you?"

"Can you keep a secret?"

"You have no idea."

"When Daddy and the uncles aren't around, Auntie Britta lets me ride around on her back like in *The Jungle Book*. It's so much fun!"

Nat smiled and shook her head. "You are your father's child."

Dani finally asked the question she always wanted to ask when she saw her aunt hidden away, working on her laptop, right under everyone's nose. "Are you going to go to prison?"

418 *Shelly Laurenston*

Gazing at her for a long time, Nat finally said, "I hope not. I look like shit in orange."

"Try it again," Analia ordered her sister. She gripped her youngest child against her and watched her sister try to open the kitchen door.

Paolo had set up this "smart" house so that the doors locked through an app on his phone and couldn't be opened without a passcode. Meaning the wives and children could only leave with his express permission. When she had realized it the first time, he'd said it was "for safety." But she knew better.

Swallowing, her sister tried the door for a sixth time, but it still didn't open.

Another She-cat pointed across the kitchen to a dark corner. "I heard a win—"

"What are you doing?"

Analia briefly closed her eyes before facing her brother-in-law. She forced a smile. A smile she'd been using since the day she'd met the de Medicis.

"Going outside for a few minutes. The children need some fresh air."

"At this time of night?"

"It's not that late. We'll be right back. You can come with us if you—"

"No," Silvio said. "You'll stay here. We have much to do, and we can't spend any time worrying about you being away from the house." His gaze moved over the entire group of females and children before adding, "And you're not going anywhere with my sons."

And there it was. *His sons.* He could not care less about his daughters, but his sons meant everything. Did males purposely forget that without females, none of them would exist? Except for a few one-celled beings and perhaps a lizard or two, males were absolutely *nothing* without females. Except males like the de Medicis never saw it that way.

"Silvio—"

"Stop. It's over. I know exactly what you are up to and—"

TO KILL A BADGER   419

Blood splattered across Analia's face, but somehow she managed not to move. Not to roar in surprise and panic. Some of the children gasped, but they'd learned early that quiet around the de Medici males was a smart thing. A safe thing.

She watched her brother-in-law desperately try to speak, but the blade that had entered the side of his neck had cleanly cut his vocal cords. He could do nothing but open and close his mouth and gawk straight ahead.

The blade was yanked out, more blood flying across some of the other She-cats and their progeny. Still, none of them made a sound.

Silvio dropped to the ground, still trying to take a breath. Still trying not to die. And that's when Analia saw her for the first time. She wasn't what she'd been expecting. Not with a name like MacKilligan. She was African-American and tall; wide shoulders; braided and loose hair in a ponytail. With a coldness that made Analia's heart stop, the female hybrid stared at Silvio for a moment before locking that gaze on Analia and the others. She looked them over, and Analia readied her fangs and claws to be unleashed, even while holding her baby.

The MacKilligan, her gaze now locked on Analia, stepped over Silvio's body and walked toward her. Analia didn't look away. She didn't move. She simply waited. It was hard for her. All she wanted to do was protect her offspring, but sudden movements were never a good idea around someone like this. Because once you start moving, you become prey, too.

Now the female was right in front of her, her eyes a disturbing color. Not gold or dark brown, like most shifters. At this moment, they were red. Blood red.

Analia still didn't move.

The female stepped past her, past Analia's sister, and went to the door. She turned the knob, and the door opened. She gestured with the slightest tilt of her head.

Analia motioned to the others. Grabbing the small bags they'd packed just to get them through the night, they all silently hurried out the door. They made it into the hallway and went down the emergency stairs. Paolo's non-blood-related lion males had been protect-

420   *Shelly Laurenston*

ing the building's stairwells. And it was their bodies that now littered those stairs.

The She-cats did what they could to protect their offspring from seeing too much, but they were more interested in getting out rather than worrying about the cubs' mental health at this moment.

Analia heard the kitchen door close behind them and it relocking. Not wanting to think about that too much, she kept everyone moving until they reached the exit.

Once outside, a very tiny blonde was waiting for them. Warmly smiling, she handed over several sets of keys for nearby vehicles.

"The cars are down the block on the left," she said in very precise but non-musical Italian. "The address is already in the GPS. And good luck."

Quietly motioning everyone along and not looking back, Analia knew they would need that good luck.

Travers checked the château doors again and motioned to his fellow badgers to sweep the area.

He should have left when he had the chance, he knew that now. The Von Schäfer-Müllers were not to be trusted. Damn, though, if they didn't pay well. Of course, badgers always paid well. It was the easiest way to buy loyalty.

But now he was in the midst of it, wasn't he?

After jiggling the ornate handles on the massive double doors to ensure they were still locked, Travers turned away to head back deep into the château, but froze when he heard the rev of an engine.

He looked again at the doors over his shoulder and thought, *They couldn't be that crazy—*

Of course, they could be. He knew that not when the truck came crashing through the ornate double doors, knocking some of his team across the hall, pinning others under the wheels, and splattering one slow mover's head into pieces; but when the wall beside those doors was blown apart by an antitank weapon used by crazed, American She-badgers.

The initial explosion sent Travers and another group of his men

TO KILL A BADGER 421

spiraling farther into the house. They hit walls or crashed against the floor, or just kept going until they found themselves in the kitchen.

He only went a few hundred feet before sliding into a wall and stopping.

Sitting up, Travers grabbed both sides of his head and twisted until his neck was again attached to his spine. Thank God he was honey badger.

Once he could feel his legs again, he got to his feet, only to get slammed to the ground once more by the nearly thousand-pound, pissed-off tiger.

The fucking cat grabbed the skin on the back of his neck and took off running, ramming Travers into walls, doors, floors, and other badgers. At one point he simply stood in the middle of the living room and swung him around, tossed him in the air, caught him, and then slapped him against a hard table.

When the cat was done, nearly everything inside Travers was broken or torn. The cat stood over him, bloody drool oozing over his fangs and onto Travers's face. Then he turned and ran away.

As Travers lay there, trying to breathe, he thought, *This will take days to heal.*

But then CeCe Álvarez was kneeling beside him, Stephanie Yoon standing behind her. Lifting her hand, Álvarez gave a little wave and said, "Hi, Travers."

Their past dealings roared up between them, a tidal wave of brutal memories, and Maurice knew he was fucked.

Holding out her hand, Álvarez took the axe Yoon handed to her and stood.

When the blade came down on his neck, severing all but the tiniest bit of sinew between his head and spine, he knew his recovery had just gone from days to absolute *months*.

He walked into the unappealing kitchen of their New Jersey hideaway to get an espresso before the family meeting, but froze in the doorway when he saw his first cousin dead on the floor.

Pulling his gun, he stepped away from the kitchen and back into the hallway. He motioned to his brother, but he just stood there. Then his brother's mouth slowly opened, and blood poured out. When his body dropped, she was standing behind him with a blade in her right hand.

He pointed his gun, but she already had a gun in her left hand. He didn't even know where she got it from, she moved so fast. This gun had a suppressor, and she immediately pulled the trigger twice—

Charlie stepped over the body and stayed in the shadows as she moved down the hallway. Her allergies were acting up again, so she struggled to smell anything. She'd have to rely on all her other instincts to keep herself alive.

As she stared down the hallway, she glanced back and noticed that the cat she'd just shot twitched. It could be a dying twitch or he was still alive. She moved back to stand beside him and put two more bullets in his head.

Satisfied with that, she headed on. But when another cat came charging at her out of the darkness, she realized she should have stuck with just the silent blades. Because even suppressors didn't help with hearing-amplified shifters.

A badger came at him, and Keane slapped it away with his front paw. Another came from behind him, and he slashed it with his back paw.

He didn't have time to deal with all these badgers. They weren't what he wanted. What he was looking for.

Another badger slid to a stop in front of him, slashing at him with a knife, and Keane slapped him down with his paw, held him there, then leaned in so that he crushed the badger's face with his weight.

It was strange, though, hearing the badger still breathing after he'd walked away. Usually when there was spurting, he didn't have to worry about anyone breathing afterward.

He reached the kitchen, but he could see in the darkness that the room was empty. He started to turn around to walk back out when he heard the gallop, spinning to face it when those fifteen-hundred pounds hit him full-on and knocked him deep into the kitchen, right out the back window—glass exploding all around them—and into the garden.

Nelle moved past the battling badgers and went up the stairs to the second floor. She briefly stopped to sniff the air, trying to locate Jules's scent, when Johann's scent suddenly filled her nostrils. He grabbed her from behind before she could react, and a knife swung down. She pushed it before it could hit her in the chest and, instead, it dug into her belly.

She snarled and grabbed his arm. Pulling it away, she twisted until bone broke and Johann screamed.

Still holding the badly damaged arm, she yanked it away from his body, and snapped it at the shoulder, the bone shattering. Shoving him away, she took the blade from her gut.

Using his still-working arm to drag himself to his knees, Johann snarled in direct challenge. But Nelle merely sniffed the air again, and went off in search of Jules.

"Wait!" Johann called out in French. "Where are you going? We are not done here!"

But she ignored him and, as she passed a blood-covered Russian in the tight hallway, snarled, "He's all yours, comrade."

"You wouldn't dare," Johann told the Russian looming over him. "You wouldn't dare kill a Von Schäfer-Müll—"

"In 1766," the psychotic bitch said in flawless Polish, "your ancestor stabbed my ancestor in the back after agreeing to a fair duel over the honor of Catherine the Great. From that day until now . . . blood was owed. And the Lenkovs do *not* forget . . . nor forgive, Comrade Kopanski."

"*Mad cow!*" Johann screamed. "*I will kill you! I will kill you all!*"

Slapping him to the floor with the back of her hand, Ox grabbed the royal badger by the ankle and proceeded to drag him down the hall to where most of the fighting was taking place.

"My friends!" she called out, ignoring his threats. "I need an axe!"

424 *Shelly Laurenston*

★ ★ ★

The lion tackled Charlie to the ground, knocking the gun from her hand, and brought his massive head down to bite off her face.

She slapped her free hand against the cat's jaw and pushed up and away. With her right hand—and the blade it held—pinned under the cat's weight, she continued to push with one hand while trying to pull her legs out from underneath the beast. He slapped at her with his paws, tearing into her tough skin and roaring for the help of his litter mates.

She heard feet—and paws!—running in the floors overhead, and angry Italian being spit out from those still human.

She only had seconds.

Slipping her fingers into the cat's mouth, she started to twist his head away. He bit down on her hand, and she felt fangs hit bone. She growled at the pain, but she kept twisting. The cat tried to turn his head back, but she used all her strength and pushed and pushed, even as she feared her fingers would be chewed off for good, until she saw the muscles in the cat's neck strain against his fur and, finally, burst through to shower her with arterial blood.

The cat slumped down on top of her, and she pulled her mangled fingers out of his mouth. Bullets hit the ground next to her head, and Charlie moved to use the lion's corpse to give her some protection.

Nelle kicked the den door open and found Jules standing by the window that looked out over her territory.

Slowly, the older badger faced her, and the pair stared at each other until, with an instinctual agreement passed down through generations of breeding, they both snarled and charged each other.

When they reached the middle of the room, Jules slashed at Nelle with a tactical blade. Nelle avoided it, but barely. She knew instantly that Jules was as well-trained in combat as she was. Not what she was hoping for with a still-bleeding stomach wound, but what was she going to do?

Jules slashed again, then stabbed for her gut. Nelle caught her hand before it hit her and twisted, slashing with her other hand, which Jules quickly caught. They held onto each other like that, both fighting for dominance, snarling at each other, fangs out.

Nelle twisted Jules's hand hard, and the blade dropped, but now that her hand was free, she yanked it away and used her arm to grab Nelle around the neck. She pulled her close against her chest before releasing her hand. That's when Nelle slammed the blade she still held into Jules's leg, but Jules immediately retaliated by pushing her free hand into the open wound on Nelle's stomach.

She hissed, the pain from that fist digging around inside her, making her think death *had* to be better than this. It had to be!

Nelle jerked her knife from Jules's leg and raised it again, now aiming for the bitch's head, when a hand grabbed her first and held it.

Rutowski stared into Nelle's eyes, a small smirk on the crone's face.

Nelle's lip curled. "You, bitch," she snarled in accusation.

"Know who your friends are, little badger," Rutowski said, before ripping Jules's fist out of Nelle's stomach and throwing the other badger across the room.

"Here," the crone said, while shoving a bottle of glue at her. "Use this on your wound to close it up. Then go help your boyfriend."

"What?"

"He's an eight-hundred-pound cat fighting a fifteen-hundred-pound bear. The odds are about even, but still . . . wouldn't risk it. Now go. But take care of that wound first," she told her before facing a snarling Jules, who'd picked herself up off the ground.

"Hey, old friend," Rutowski said in Polish, pulling a black tactical knife from the sheath on her leg.

"Old friend," Jules said back.

Then the two She-badgers bared fangs and charged each other.

Nelle didn't watch; she simply turned and headed out to find Keane.

Chapter 35

Renzo de Medici pushed his younger brothers aside and stared down at the body of his older brother. Grabbing the corpse by the mane, he pulled it off the female who'd killed him. She was still alive, her left hand nothing but chewed skin and bloody, broken fingers, the middle one nearly falling off.

He motioned to one of his cousins, who had already shifted, and the five-hundred-pound mammoth walked over to the female, slowly opening his maw at the same time. She raised her mangled hand as if to ward him off. It would have been sad if she hadn't killed his brother. But then he heard a *crack* sound. Loud and close by.

Renzo looked down and watched as sinew reattached with sinew, bones snapped back into place, and muscles wrapped around bone, followed by flesh. In seconds, what had been a mangled hand was now just a terribly scarred one with that middle finger slightly off.

The female lifted just her eyes to Renzo and bent those healed fingers into a fist. She pulled back her arm and punched.

Renzo and his brothers reared back from the female when that blood and brain splattered them from the back of his sibling's head. Her arm through his skull, the female stretched her fingers out again, moved them around a little before pulling her arm back out.

When Renzo returned his gaze to hers, she lowered her head and leered up at him with blood-red eyes.

"*Merda,*" he sighed out.

TO KILL A BADGER 427

★ ★ ★

Keane landed on the polar's back, digging his claws in. Zeus reared up on his hind legs, then fell backward. Releasing the bear, Keane rolled out of the way before he was trapped under that weight. They both moved away from each other until they were on their feet and Zeus charged him.

Using his ursine bulk, Zeus rammed Keane into the ground, picked him up by his head, and slammed him into the ground again. Needing to stop the bear's fangs from cracking his skull, Keane wrapped his forearms around Zeus's neck and rolled him onto his back. He opened his jaw and leaned in to clamp down on the bear's throat, but bullets hit him in his side. Startled, Keane lifted his head to roar, and the bear tossed him off, sending him flying across the garden until a tree stopped his momentum.

His Uncle Renzo pushed him out of the way as he ran up the stairs. Hurtful. He thought his uncle had liked him.

But he understood the panic. The assassin who had been sent to kill them was like a machine. No matter what they did to her, how many walls they slammed her into, how many balconies they tossed her over, how many shots they put into her body . . .

She just. Kept. Coming.

He'd seen enough of what his uncles had done over the years to know another predator when he saw one. Whether it was a fellow shifter or the full-humans they made deals with.

But this female . . .

She hadn't even shifted yet. She'd stayed human the whole time, and she didn't relent. Covered in blood from his male kin and her own body, she didn't seem to notice nor care. She was on a mission, and she'd been moving through their house with a brutality he'd only ever seen from his own uncles.

It seemed like every injury, every wound, every defensive attack that harmed her, only made her stronger. Ridiculously strong. And mad. He knew angry females. Saw it in his own mother's eyes when

428   *Shelly Laurenston*

she had to deal with his father. A father whose body had been carelessly tossed onto a coffee table once his massive head had been turned completely around until his massive lion neck had snapped.

Backing up in the hallway toward the bedroom he had shared with a now-dead cousin, he'd almost reached the doorway when his Uncle Renzo charged toward him in his lion form.

At first, he thought Renzo was coming to kill him, but he saw the whites of his eyes and realized it was a panic run. The lion was terrified.

His uncle launched himself up, probably trying to get over him and into his bedroom and maybe out the window, but in midair she caught Renzo's foot and, with two hands, yanked the six-hundred-pound lion back.

He would have laughed at the startled look on his uncle's face, but he couldn't while watching that female push her hands into his uncle's maw and separate his jaws . . . and separate . . . and separate, until there was nothing but the sound of cracking, splitting bone, and his uncle's whimpering. Then, eventually, even that stopped.

With a casual cruelty, she tossed Renzo's body over the balcony, like she'd done to so many other of the males in his family, and then her eyes latched onto him.

Now *he* whimpered, taking a few steps back from her.

She walked toward him until she was no more than three meters from him. Then she stared at him, examining him from head to toe.

Finally, she asked, "Age?"

He blinked. Confused. He'd been learning English, but it was still very foreign to him.

Then she asked, *"Quanti anni hai?"*

He cringed at her awful American accent, but he understood what she was asking.

"I am thirteen," he replied in Italian.

She nodded. "Paolo?"

He looked away from her gaze. He'd heard some of his uncles screaming about her "red eyes," but her eyes were brown. That's all

TO KILL A BADGER 429

he saw. Still, even that was terrifying. He didn't want to challenge this female.

But he also didn't want to say anything about his Uncle Paolo. De Medicis didn't betray their own. It was a death sentence in the coalition. Although, now that he thought about it, there weren't a lot of them left to hand out something like that anymore.

So, he didn't *say* anything. He simply glanced up to the fifth floor and just as quickly looked away.

"Uhhhh . . . *trova tua madre*. . . ?"

Her accent was horrendous, and she was clearly not confident, but he understood what she was telling him. "Go find your mother."

He hadn't been able to spend any time with his mother once he'd turned thirteen. The adult male de Medicis always pulled the sons from their mothers when they turned that age. There was no question and no complaining. But all night, when he was alone and trying not to cry, all he'd wanted was his mamma.

And knowing she was alive somewhere . . .

He nodded at her statement, then watched her examine the ceiling until she spotted a small vent. Launching herself from a nearby table to reach the high ceiling, she used a claw to yank out the grate and then, somehow . . . she crawled into that tiny space without shifting. He couldn't hear her moving around in there, but he could sense it. Could sense she was tracking down his Uncle Paolo.

Should he stay? Should he help?

Before he did anything, he pulled out his phone from his back pocket and texted his mother.

She responded in seconds with an address, a username and password for the car service he could order through his phone, and a sobbing emoji. *I love you, baby. Come. Now.*

He angrily wiped at the tears streaming down his own face—angry because his father had always told him tears were for "females and men with more pussy than cock"—before he charged down the stairs and headed toward the door in the kitchen that would take him to the emergency exit.

430   *Shelly Laurenston*

As he entered the kitchen, he stumbled to a stop when he saw the small female standing there.

When she saw him, she raised her hands as if to ward him off. But then, she looked him over and . . . she smiled. Her smile was so large, he was actually frightened by it. She seemed so ridiculously happy! Why? What was she so happy about in a house of death?

She opened the kitchen door and motioned for him to go, urging him along in very precise and formal Italian. She'd clearly had more Italian lessons than the frightening female hunting down his Uncle Paolo.

He hesitated the briefest second—afraid she'd kill him as he passed her—but then he ran . . . and she let him go, closing the door behind him and sending him off into a future that would no longer be dictated by lion males he loved but hated at the same time.

Something grabbed his back paw and dragged him through several rosebushes, the thorns tearing at his fur-covered flesh before they reached the clearing.

Keane knew it was Zeus who had him. The polar's two-inch fangs digging deep into his muscle.

He rolled Keane onto his back with a hard slap against his side and settled in next to him, Zeus's jaw closing around his throat and tightening until Keane could no longer breathe.

That's when Keane snapped out of his tree-induced confusion and ripped at the bear's face with his claws. When he couldn't move the bear's mouth off him, he went for his eyes, tearing one out of its socket with a single claw.

Zeus lifted his head to roar, and Keane was about to attempt to throw the polar off before he resecured his position on his throat, when she landed on the bear's back.

In silence, Nelle slammed her knife into Zeus's other eye, blinding the animal.

In a rage, Zeus jumped up and shook her off, sending Nelle flipping across the garden. She collided into a nearby ivy-covered wall.

Zeus faced her, hearing her grunt when she slammed against the stone. He was blind, but he could sniff her out.

Keane scrambled to his feet and, over the bear's head, he could see Nelle get to hers.

They stared at each other over the raging bear and, as the polar charged toward her, Keane attacked him from behind while Nelle came at him from the front.

Keane slammed his front paws into Zeus's hind legs, unleashed his claws into the polar's hide, and dragged the beast down. Nelle landed on Zeus's head. Using the blade in her hand, she stabbed at the bear's neck, making sure to rip the wounds open until she could reach those major arteries.

With the bear down, Keane rolled Zeus over onto his back and bit into his groin, digging his three-inch fangs into the flesh and proceeding to pull and tear and rip.

Keane kept going until, finally, he felt Nelle's hand against his neck. He lifted his blood-covered head away from the polar's corpse and nuzzled against her hip before briefly wondering why he smelled the glue he once used to repair Dani's old dollhouse.

A roundhouse kick to the head sent Trace out of the den and into the hallway. Smirking, ready to tear limbs off this bitch, Jules followed, but as soon as she stepped outside her den . . .

She wanted to curse, but she didn't want them to see the weakness.

This was what had kept Trace Rutowski alive all these years, despite so many chances for her to be taken down by entire governments and armies. Her friends. Because wherever she was, they were right behind her.

And this time, her friends were holding Jules's stupid nephew.

Lenkov held an axe, the blade against her battered nephew's throat.

"Kill them!" Johann yelled at her in German. *"Kill them all!"*

So dramatic. Did he forget how hard it was to kill a honey badger? Did he forget the risk they took if they actually killed *all* of these She-badgers? The Van Holtz trouble alone! There were entire nations that

432 Shelly Laurenston

fell when the Van Holtzes got pissed, and this idiot wanted to kill the only badgers who had ever *married* into that Pack?

Then, as if to solidify how lost this particular battle was, Gong Zhao walked in, and she wasn't alone. She had the tiger beside her, in all his black-and-white-striped glory. An eyeless polar bear head hanging from one fang like a well-used chew toy.

Jules blew out an angry breath. "What do you want?" she asked Tracey Rutowski, whose friends had helped her back to her feet. But it was Lenkov who answered.

"I am owed blood!"

"I am not talking to you, Russian!"

Rutowski began to answer, but she stopped, held up a finger to give her a moment as she tried to breathe around cracked ribs.

Jules couldn't help but smile. "You are getting old, my friend."

"*Fuck you!*" Tracey snapped. Always an American first, that one.

"You know what we want," CeCe said, taking over for a now-angry Tracey. "We get what we want, or . . ."

"I," Lenkov said, "or one of my *many* kin, come back for him. And we split him into pieces to send to his dear mother."

"How is she, anyway?" Steph asked. "Still hating you, *old* friend? But absolutely adoring her perfect, perfect son?"

Dammit, they were right. If anything happened to this idiot, her sister would have Jules's skin.

"Fine," Jules agreed. And this time, she meant it. She had to. She knew the damage a Lenkov could do when that particular family decided to restart a blood feud.

CeCe nodded her approval.

It was done. No other words had to be spoken.

But there was still Gong Zhao, who also felt betrayed. *What would she demand?* Jules wondered.

Reaching over to the big cat beside her, she took the polar bear head from his mouth and held it in both hands like a ball.

Waiting for the threats, Jules folded her arms over her chest and let out a long sigh of annoy—

Jules screamed out a long string of curses after that dead bear's

TO KILL A BADGER 433

hard head slammed into her face, breaking not only her nose, but her cheeks and both eye sockets!

Unable to see at the moment, she could still hear Gong Zhao loudly cheer, *"WNBA MVP and still championnnnn!"*

Charlie slid out of the vent and landed on her feet in the middle of what appeared to be a private office. When she turned, Paolo de Medici was waiting for her, a Desert Eagle handgun pointed at her head. Not only was it a .50 caliber, which could actually kill her with a straight headshot, but the gun itself was, of course, gold. Because you couldn't be a tacky mob boss without a tacky gold weapon of some kind.

With a tactical knife in each hand, Charlie readied herself to move. She had one shot at this and—

"Stevie! No!"

But it was too late! Her baby sister charged into the room from the open door and threw herself onto Paolo's back.

Confused by the tiny female on him, he rolled his eyes and reached back to yank her off.

Afraid he would cause Stevie panic—and with panic, came a shift, and with a shift came a possible Godzilla movie storyline—Charlie yelled out, *"No, no, no!"*

But just as Paolo gripped the back of Stevie's adorable sleeveless sundress—the one with little pink hearts all over it—Stevie had one arm around Paolo's throat and was raising her other hand into the air.

Charlie thought her sister was holding a knife, which would be . . . crazy. Her sister didn't really wield knives the way Charlie and Max did. But it wasn't a knife. It was a titanium syringe. And her baby sister slammed that syringe into the cat's jugular vein and pushed the plunger.

Paolo roared and shook Stevie off, sending her into the wall.

Charlie ran across the room and put her body between Paolo and her sister.

Hand against his throat, Paolo's entire body began to shake, the gun falling uselessly from his hand.

"Stevie," Charlie asked her sister without turning around, "what did you do?"

"You know what I did."

Stevie stood behind her now, resting her head on Charlie's shoulder.

Paolo dropped to his knees; then his hands landed on the floor, and he was on all fours. Roaring, the male's body was forced to shift into lion. It wasn't an easy shift, though. The kind every shifter but her would have. The one that only took a second or two for someone to painlessly go from human to powerful beast.

No. This was different.

This shift took time and caused Paolo de Medici great pain. Endless pain as he screamed and roared through every moment of his DNA permanently changing from one thing to another.

When it was done, the lion passed out, his body landing with a crash.

"We have to move," Stevie said. "He won't be out for long."

"What are we supposed to do with him?"

Charlie could, of course, open his veins while he was out cold, but she had the feeling that's not why Stevie had wasted their one chance to deal with their father forever. Her baby sister had something else in mind.

Maybe a zoo or an animal rescue. But that seemed . . . risky, at best. His body and most of his DNA may be lion, but Charlie had the feeling that the appalling human Paolo de Medici still existed inside the powerful jaws and paws of this lion male.

"Don't worry," Stevie said, going over to Paolo's side. "I've got it covered."

"Hello?" a male voice called from a few flights down.

"Up here!" Stevie called back.

A minute or two later, the three older Van Holtz brothers walked into the room. The last time Charlie had seen them, they'd been taking her father away. She hadn't heard from that bastard since. It had been bliss.

"Ladies," one of the handsome wolves greeted them. "We see you've been . . . uh . . ." He looked around and finished with, ". . . busy."

Stevie took off the small backpack she had strapped to her shoulders and dug out a leather case.

"Here," she said, handing the case to Wolf Van Holtz. "These should keep him out until you get him caged and moving."

"Great. Anything else?"

She shook her head. "No. Except thank you for this."

"Our pleasure."

"Uh," another brother asked, "if he does wake up and shifts back to human, what do you want us to do then?"

"He won't shift back."

"How do you know that?"

Stevie didn't answer the wolf's question, simply said, "You better get going. It's Manhattan. It's still early evening. People will wonder what's going on if you're caught carrying a lion around."

She gave a laugh so fake, Charlie had to turn her head before the wolves saw her cringe.

"Okay." Wolf motioned to his brothers. "We've got an ambulance outside and some paramedics from one of our hospitals. We'll cover him up and make it look like a drug overdose or something similar."

The three brothers surrounded the big cat and were about to heave him up, but Charlie wasn't in the mood to witness that pitiful display. Besides, she owed them for giving her a respite from Freddy MacKilligan.

"Hey," she said, stepping between them and the cat. "I've got it."

"I don't think—"

Charlie grabbed the cat by his mane and dragged him out of the room and down the hallway toward the stairs. As she moved, she could hear one of the brothers behind her say, "I see why she plays football."

Chapter 36

"Hi, Daddy."

"Hello, my little crested serpent eagle."

"Daddy."

He smiled at his beautiful daughter. "I'm glad to see you're safe, if a little . . . mauled."

"It's nothing." She wiped at the still-healing wounds on her face. "I'll be fine."

"Yes, but will you be fine by the time of your sister's wedding?"

Through his phone, he watched his daughter's transition from *Happy to see you, Daddy!* to *I hate this family.*

"Daddy," she began, an angry scowl on her face, "you and I both know that this is utter bull—wonderful event!"

Without looking over his shoulder, Arthur knew his wife now stood behind him, and Nelle could see her.

Their daughter forced a smile. "Hello, Mummy."

"Where are you?"

"I'll be home soon."

"Because you promised your sister you would be here for her."

"Yes, ma'am," she said through clenched teeth while still forcing that smile.

"I also have come to learn that Jules something Polish is still alive? Is that true?"

"I don't think 'something Polish' is her surname," Arthur reminded his wife, "and we discussed this, my heart."

TO KILL A BADGER 437

"It doesn't bother you she's taking orders from crazed Americans now?" When he raised a brow, she amended it to, "*Old* crazed Americans."

"Tracey Rutowski made it sound like you two are the best of friends."

"We're not," Lorraine snapped back at their daughter. "I *tolerate* her because she pays very good money for our legitimate shipping services."

"Can we just call it our shipping services?" he asked. No need to explain over the phone how they laundered their money.

"Do whatever you want," Lorraine said to their daughter. "You always do."

Nelle's jaw clenched, and he knew he should get them both off this phone call before things became nasty.

But, unfortunately, his wife was in a mood.

"And is it true you're trying to bring Max MacKilligan to your sister's wedding?"

"She invited her."

"Only to get you to come."

"Max is looking forward to it."

"If she steals one damn thing from our guests . . ."

"It'll be fine, Ma."

"It better be."

"Where are you now?" Arthur asked before things could get worse. "Switzerland."

Confused, Arthur asked, "Why are you in Switzerland?"

"Well, in order to finish the deal with the Von Schäfer-Müllers, I had to get"—she held up a black book with a five-point star on its cover—"this."

"What is that?"

"A waste of my time," she said with an eye roll. "But it was part of the deal, and Tracey Rutowski—"

"Was *lying* to you, foolish child!"

"Lorraine."

"She is foolish! Everyone knows not to listen to Tracey Rutowski

438 Shelly Laurenston

unless they want to be involved in an international incident. Oh, that's right . . . *you already are!*"

"What do you mean she's lying to me?"

Arthur replied, "There's no need for a deal with Jules or anyone. The de Medici Coalition was taken down last night."

Nelle frowned. "What are you talking about?"

"You didn't know?"

"Do you think I would have wasted any of my time getting"—she held up the book again—"*this*, if I'd known?"

Lorraine leaned in, nearly forcing Arthur out of camera frame. "You see? Foolish. If you were home, being a good sister and helping with this wedding, you wouldn't be in this situation. Now you just look—"

"*Lorraine.*"

"—stupid."

Nelle was quiet for a moment before she said, "You're right, Mother."

Lorraine frowned. "I am?"

"You are. You're absolutely right."

And, with that, Nelle leaned back into the cat that had been sitting next to her but out of the phone's camera range. He was mid-bite with what looked to be a waffle topped with a small pile of bacon.

Realizing he could be seen, the cat nearly choked on the food he'd been shoveling into his mouth like the barbarian he appeared to have descended from. He wasn't even dressed! He only wore a thin sheet over his lap, but he was naked otherwise.

"Who is *that*?" Lorraine demanded.

"This is Keane Malone. Keane, this is my mother, Lorraine Ming-Zhao."

The cat forced himself to swallow the food he still had in his mouth and muttered, "Hello, Mrs. Ming-Zhao. Nice to meet you. Hello again, Mr. Zhao."

"Young man."

Arthur did not like to think about his daughter in bed with anyone, but he still felt bad for the cat. He was clearly shocked at being put on camera with Nelle's parents while mostly naked, but the poor boy was trapped between a mother and daughter who had been waging war in the most polite and vicious way since before Nelle's first words.

The cat was simply in over his giant head!

"Malone?" Lorraine repeated. "As in *the* Malones? You and a *Malone*? Are you *trying* to destroy this family?"

"Of course not! But I do hope our wedding is as beautiful as my sister's!"

The cat quickly looked away, and Arthur could do nothing more but blow out a breath and shake his head.

With a startled gasp at that particular blow, Lorraine stormed out of the hotel suite they'd been using for the wedding, slamming the door behind her.

Arthur smiled at his beautiful daughter even while he chided her, "You do insist on playing with your food, my little crested serpent eagle."

"I know, Daddy."

"I wasn't wearing clothes!" Keane yelled when Nelle had disconnected the call.

"Those evil bitches!"

"I did not want to meet your mother for the first time while naked, Nelle!"

"Oh, calm down. She doesn't hate you because you were naked."

"She hates me?"

"She hates you because you're cat."

"But she doesn't even know me. And we're getting married?"

"Not right now."

Nelle got off the bed. She'd been dressed for a while, from what Keane could tell, and had let him sleep until room service had arrived, which Keane had greatly appreciated. He'd needed the sleep. And "those evil bitches," as Nelle was currently calling them, had been pretty brutal when they'd dug out the bullets from his side and

440   *Shelly Laurenston*

back. Not even a local used. Or tools. They'd just used their claws and ignored his roars of pain. But he couldn't complain much . . . he didn't even get a fever, and the wounds were nearly healed.

Nelle stood in front of him in cute denim shorts and a crop top, so he was reaching out to drag her back to bed when she suddenly headed toward the hotel room door.

"Are you going to leave me like this?" he asked, pointing at the tent his cock had created in the sheet.

"You have a hand," she snapped before storming out.

Frustrated, Keane fell back on the bed.

"And if we are going to get married," he said to no one in particular, "she'll have to ask me properly."

Nelle raised her hand to knock on the door of the crone's room, but she decided to kick it in instead.

She was shocked when she got inside. She thought only Rutowski was in here, but Álvarez, half-naked as usual, was passed out on the floor; Yoon, dressed like a bank robber, the hoodie pulled over her head, was snoring on the couch; Rutowski was drooling while splayed out on the king bed; and the Russian came out of the bathroom, a toothbrush in her mouth.

"You do not knock?" the Russian demanded.

"Not when I am this pissed off."

She waved that away. "You are always pissed off. You are never happy. How does anyone tolerate you, little badger?"

"I was happy before you bitches came into my life."

"That is not first time we have heard that . . ."

Fed up, Nelle stomped across the room, grabbed sleeping-Rutowski's foot, and yanked her across the bed.

She woke up swinging, but failed to connect any punches.

"What? What? What's wrong?"

Nelle held up the black book she'd gotten from Lavoie once she'd woken him up in his bed with a gun to his head and Keane roaring beside her in his tiger form. The full-human had handed it to her immediately. And he really was a Satanist. He had his black and red robes professionally cleaned and hung up outside his walk-in closet. Weird. Why not put those *inside* his walk-in closet?

"Why did I get this?" Nelle asked.

Rutowski narrowed her eyes to look at the book. Apparently the older badger needed glasses.

"Oh. That? Wasn't that the deal you made with Jules?"

"What deal? She betrayed us! We forced her to do what you needed by the Russian threatening her nephew with an axe! And I don't know why any of that was necessary, because someone took down the de Medicis last night! While I was wasting my time with Jules and her useless family! And I bet that someone was Charlie!"

"Of course it was Charlie. Who else could do it but Charlie?"

"You unleashed Charlie MacKilligan on the tri-state area without Max or me or anyone else? Are you insane?" She shook her head. "Of course you're insane. You're clinically insane!"

"Stop worrying," the crone said dismissively with that annoying eye roll. "It went perfectly."

"It shouldn't have happened at all!"

"Why are you yelling?" Yoon demanded.

"Because you all lied to me! All this bullshit! You were just distracting me! That's why you wouldn't let us leave! It wasn't for this stupid plan of yours. It was to keep me away from Charlie!"

"That's not true at all," Rutowski said. "Well, mostly not true. We were distracting you, but my plan's a go." And she sounded so ridiculously proud that Nelle realized she wasn't lying. She really thought all of this insanity had been a success!

What was wrong with this female? It couldn't be mental illness. No one mentally ill was this ludicrous!

"What plan?" Nelle demanded. "The de Medicis are done, yes?"

"The de Medicis don't matter. They were just the ones that brought the efforts to wipe us out to light. Now that we know about it, now that we all see it, we can fight it. *Together!*" the woman cheered, her arms in the air and her left leg raised and out to the side. Nelle had

442 *Shelly Laurenston*

been at American-run schools long enough to know what that particular move meant . . . Tracey Rutowski had been a high school cheerleader! Which only made Nelle hate her more.

"Isn't that wonderful?" the crone asked after lowering her arms and legs.

Not knowing what else to say, Nelle finally admitted, "I hate you."

"Oh, sweetie . . . I know. And I really don't care."

Keane had nearly fallen asleep again when Nelle stormed back into the room, slamming the door behind her.

"Oh, good. You're back." Without sitting up, he gestured at her with both hands. "Come over here. Sit on my face."

"We don't have time for any of that. We have to get home. Now."

"Give me what is mine by right!" he roared, then blinked at her startled look. "Sorry about that. There's a thin line of Genghis Khan in my DNA, because my ancestors wanted some powerful shifter babies. It tends to come out sometimes when I'm . . . horny. Again, sorry."

"Let me tell you something," Nelle said, pointing her finger at him, "while I may find that the hottest thing ever, and I *will* be taking full advantage of it the next time we fuck, we don't have time right now. So get up, get in the shower, and let's get to the airport. I've already let Marti know I need a jet—"

"A jet?" Rutowski asked, bursting into their room with a cup of hot coffee in her hand and big smile on her face. "You mean one I don't have to pay for? You don't mind if we catch a ride with you guys, right?"

"Actually, I do mind," Nelle replied. "Find your own way home, crone."

"I could do that. I could also make sure you're interrogated by French and Swiss police for terrorist activities!" Rutowski said, with a big happy smile that didn't feel at all fake, which Keane found extremely disturbing.

"I thought you didn't rat out friends?"

"I don't. And you'll never go to prison. But it will take you *days* to get back to the States. Or, you can just let us travel with you in your family's jet. Your choice."

"But choose wisely!" he heard one of the other crones yell from the hallway. It sounded like Yoon, pretending to be an old man. It was strange.

"Sometimes," Rutowski explained, "Steph likes to quote any and all of the *Raiders of the Lost Ark* movies. Obsessively so. It's gotten worse after menopause."

Then they suddenly heard Yoon yell out, *"Get over here!"*

"She also likes to quote the Mortal Kombat games."

"And that seems normal to you?" Nelle asked.

"I wouldn't say normal. But we're used to it now. It used to be *Star Wars* quotes, but after the prequels in the nineties, she stopped that." Rutowski leaned in and loudly whispered, "If I were you, I wouldn't bring up *Star Wars*. She has *very* strong opinions on all the movies, TV shows, books, cartoons, games, and toys."

Eyes wide in horror, Nelle looked at Keane, but he could only shrug desperately because, seriously, *What the fuck?*

"How old *are* you bitches?" Nelle demanded.

"A rude question, but when it's asked, we say over thirty-five. You know, physically. But emotionally? I still watch *Sixteen Candles* and *Breakfast Club* like it was the first time. So who am I to judge?"

"Get out," Nelle ordered.

"We'll be ready in fifteen! Don't leave without us!"

Nelle faced him. "I hate her."

"I know. But we have fifteen minutes, soooo . . ."

She let out an aggravated sigh and dropped her shorts. "Fine, but you better get me off first!"

"Of course!"

"I'm going to go find Finn and Shay and check on Nat and Dani."

"Okay." Nelle went up on her toes and kissed his cheek—and it was like she'd dropped to her knees and given him a blow job, the way everyone watched them. "I'll see you in a few."

She walked away, staring at the tigers staring at her.

But she lost interest in the nosy cats when she arrived at Charlie's rental house at the same moment Max and her teammates did.

Now the five of them gazed at one another, because they all knew they'd been screwed by those old crones!

"Did Rutowski use *Charlie* to get her shit done?" Max asked, the growl easing out of the back of her throat, which meant she was really angry.

"Yes. Did you four waste your time getting the help from some rando badgers that we don't really need while they forced me and Keane into an international incident that could have sent us to prison for life? The answer to that question is also yes."

"Where. Are. They?"

"Not here. They told me they wanted to check on their children. Then Álvarez asked, 'What children?' And Rutowski was all, 'Your goddamn kids!' And Álvarez was all, 'Oh! That's right! I do have kids!' Then they all laughed and laughed like that was a completely normal conversation and somehow *I* didn't get it because I'm Asian!"

Without another word said between them, they walked up the stairs and over to the front door of the house.

Once inside, they found Berg and his triplets on the couch, eating breakfast. In the dining room were Kyle and Dutch, glaring at Shen, who was happily munching on an enormous amount of bamboo piled high beside his chair. If he noticed the glares because of all the noise he was making, he clearly didn't care. His smile was huge. Almost Zenlike.

But when they arrived in the kitchen, they found Charlie and Stevie bickering. Those two didn't bicker. Not with each other. They bickered with Max. About Max. But never just the two of them.

As soon as Nelle and her teammates walked in, however, they stopped arguing and faced them.

"You're back," Charlie said.

"No," Max shot back. "We're mirages."

"What the fuck is the matter with you? And why do you look like that?"

"Max got beat up by a donkey!" Streep squealed before bursting into hysterical laughter.

"It wasn't like that."

"Yes it was!" Streep, Mads, and Tock crowed together.

Few hours earlier . . .

Streep folded her hands together, placed them on the picnic table, and said in her best "sincere Meryl Streep voice," as Mads called it, "I think combining the forces of the great families, like yours, will only make every honey badger stronger and safer against all enemies out to destroy—"

"Should we get your friend?" Julio Jesús Santiago asked, while pouring Streep more sweet tea.

She glanced behind her and realized that one of the docile donkeys that had nuzzled Streep and Mads until they'd petted her had grabbed Max by the leg and was slamming her into the ground with a viciousness not really seen from donkeys.

"What did you do to that donkey?" Streep called out.

"Nothing! It just attacked me! *Help!*"

Streep waved away Max's call for help and faced Julio again. He was very handsome, and his honey badger family ran an extremely large and successful horse farm. You'd never know that they also brokered in information so they could blackmail mobsters for money that they then used to buy the best dressage horses and to maintain their horse and donkey rescue.

"I haven't seen Joanne go after anything like that since she saw a rattlesnake," Julio said. "Did you guys eat rattlesnake before coming here?"

"No. Not even scorpions. I had chicken salad on the plane."

"Huh. Interesting."

"Not really. Most prey animals see Max MacKilligan as nothing but a predator. Now about that deal . . ."

"Oh. Right. Well, we've already worked something out with Tracey Rutowski. Is there more to do?"

446   *Shelly Laurenston*

★ ★ ★

"You see?" Max said, ignoring the donkey part of that story Streep just told. "Those crones set us up!"

"No, they didn't," Charlie said. "I did."

Keane stood behind Finn and watched him tell their baby sister in ASL that he no longer wanted to discuss it, but she was *never* to tell Keane what she had done.

Then, his hands pausing, he guessed, "He's right behind me . . . isn't he?"

Finn and Shay looked at Keane over their shoulders.

Shay tried to smile, but it failed. Badly. And Finn just said, "Don't be mad. She thought she was helping."

"All you had to do was keep her hands clean," Keane reminded his brothers. "That was it. But I leave for five minutes, and you can't even do that!"

"You were involved in an international incident, and you're coming at *us* right now?"

"That wasn't my fault. But this? This is *your* fault."

"We didn't tell her to do anything but watch Dani."

"What about Dale? Why wasn't Dale also watching her?" When his brothers only stared at him, he said, "Our brother."

"Oh!" Finn shook his head. "Yeah. I don't know where he is, actually."

"I'm sure Mom knows where he is," Shay reasoned.

"Fine. Family meeting in an hour. And," he added in ASL to Nat, "we tell Mom what you've done, and let *her* deal with you."

Nat immediately burst into sobs, but there were no tears. She really should take lessons from Streep.

"Stop," Keane ordered her.

"Fine," she replied verbally before walking away.

Keane gave Finn and Shay one last glare before walking to Charlie's house.

When he had gone inside, Finn said to Shay, "That was a surprisingly calm and rational response from our not-calm-nor-rational brother."

"Yes. I was very impressed."

Finn looked at Shay. "He's fucking Nelle, right?"

"He's absolutely fucking Nelle. And clearly enjoying every second of it."

"Yeah, but he's still going to be a bastard about football."

"He will *always* be a bastard about football."

"Hey, idiots!" Keane called out from Charlie's stoop.

"Don't respond to *that*," Finn told Shay, but the idiot had already turned around.

"Football practice tomorrow! Don't care who you're fucking or where! *We're going!*"

Finn let out a sigh. "Always a bastard about football."

Keane walked into the kitchen, but stopped.

"What?" he asked when Nelle, her teammates, Charlie, and Stevie were just there . . . saying nothing. These females rarely said nothing. Only bad things could come from nothing. "Who was accidentally killed this time?"

Stevie shook her head. "Absolutely no one!" Then she burst into tears and hugged Charlie. "I am so proud of you. So very, very proud."

"I know, sweetie. I know." She awkwardly patted her sister's back until Stevie finally let her go.

"So proud!" the kid cheered with a little fist pump, a big happy smile on her pretty face. He'd never seen her smile like that before. He was so glad for her.

Of course, Max couldn't be.

"Why are you fucking crying?" Max demanded.

"I'll cry if I want to, you mean bitch!"

Then the yelling started, and the two sisters went for each other, Streep and Mads trying to stop them while Tock sipped her coffee and Charlie motioned for him and Nelle to follow her outside into the backyard.

"Hi, Mr. Weber!" Charlie called out to an older bear boar.

"Hello, lovely Charlie. Any baking today?"

"I'll probably start in a little while. You want anything specific?"

"Your brownies are my favorite."

"Nuts or no nuts?"

"Pecans, please. If you can."

"You've got it."

"Marry me, Charlie!"

"You're already married, Mr. Weber."

"She won't mind if you make her those apricot muffins."

Charlie laughed and walked to the other side of the pool Keane loved to lounge in when he was forced to stay in this neighborhood with all these bears. Water always relaxed him.

Well, water and now Nelle. She really relaxed him. He hadn't hit Finn or Shay once! Even when he found out they weren't doing their job! Stop Nat from ending up in prison! How hard was that?

"Charlie—"

"No," Charlie cut Nelle off. "I talk. I know what you did. I know why you did it. And I need you to understand why I did what I did."

"I do. I really do. I hate that it involved"—she closed her eyes, cleared her throat—"Rutowski. *Especially* after I told her to leave you alone. I will not forgive that."

"She's aware. And she doesn't seem to let it bother her. It's okay, though. We get along."

"That's what worries me." Nelle clasped her hands together as if she were pleading for understanding. "I need you to know, Charlie, that I do what I do because you and I are the only ones between the world and absolute chaos."

"Oh, I know. I've always known. We're good. You do your thing and, when necessary, I do mine. But I could no longer wait on dealing with the de Medicis. Not after I got that message asking for my help."

"Your help? From Rutowski?"

"No." She held up her phone, and Nelle read the text.

"Oh," she said, nodding. "Okay. I get it now."

★ ★ ★

TO KILL A BADGER   449

Gio stood by the doorway while his siblings sat on the chairs and couches on one side of the room and the females of the de Medici Coalition sat on the other side, holding onto their cubs like they expected them to be torn from their arms at any moment.

Pina cleared her throat and offered, "We can make some pasta if you're hungry." When they only stared at her, she said it again in Italian. "Or we can order pizza from Pizza Hu— Uh . . . Delminico's down the block."

He almost laughed at his sister's quick save. At least she didn't mention that the pasta she would whip up for everyone included jarred Ragú sauce.

The doorbell rang, and before Gio could go see who it was, one of the She-lions, a blood-related cousin, jumped off the couch and ran toward the door. Not sure what was waiting on the other side, Gio nodded at his brothers, and he unleashed his claws behind his back.

But a few seconds later, his cousin returned with a young male, hugging him and kissing his face as they returned to the room. The boy held her so tight and cried in her arms as they sat down on the couch that Gio put his claws away.

He could already tell the kid had seen too much and may never fully recover. But he also felt he would not be the meanest lion male to ever roam the earth when he became an adult. Not the way he was holding onto his mother right now.

Analia de Medici walked in from the backyard. She motioned to the females she'd brought to the Medici home for safety and recovery. It had been a deal brokered by Charlie MacKilligan, which still fascinated him. He thought for sure she would either kill Antonella when they'd left her alone with his sister, or Antonella would tear the badger hybrid down to the bone. Neither happened. MacKilligan had simply talked and, with a nod from a still-in-her-lion-form Antonella, she'd done the rest until these females and their offspring had shown up at their door in the late evening.

He wasn't sure what was going to happen next. Antonella hadn't told him or Pina anything, but now that he was seeing the boy sob-

450 *Shelly Laurenston*

bing in his mother's arms, he knew. The de Medici Coalition was done. Not all dead, he was sure. If nothing else, there were the older ones living in Italy who could still breed, but they would never be the same. No pride would ever take them in, and any males in those prides would kill them if they tried to force it.

So that had been the deal. Their pride takes in these She-lions and their cubs, and Charlie MacKilligan handled the destruction of the de Medici Coalition.

It was a good deal. One that kept them from losing any of his siblings and made their pride stronger.

Whether Charlie MacKilligan had survived all this, though, he didn't know. It wasn't like they were friends on social media.

Analia motioned to the cubs, and they ran outside to play with their American cousins. She went over and kissed her nephew on the head and wiped his tears, telling him he was safe. Then she faced Pina and said in English, "We will be staying a while."

"Great."

"And we will make food for you. To, uh, celebrate, yes?"

"Oh, are you sure you don't want us to—"

"No!" Analia cleared her throat. "I mean, no thank you. We will do it for you. As gift. And that is not from a jar," she added under her breath, before Bria led the She-lions to their kitchen. He whistled at his baby sister, and she looked at him over her shoulder.

"Let them order what groceries they need and have it delivered."

Because to be honest, all they had were take-out menus and jarred sauce. He didn't even think there was a fresh tomato in this house.

"Are you okay with this?" Pina asked him.

"Very."

With that, he walked over to the boy and sat down beside him.

"Do you normally wear glasses?" he asked the kid in Italian.

Tear-filled eyes focused on him, but he didn't answer, just looked back and forth between Gio and his mother.

"He should be," his mother said.

"You can wear them here. And we'll take you to get new ones tomorrow. I have a great place I go, and they offer lots of frame options. You like books?" he asked the boy.

The kid nodded.

"Great. I'll show you my library. You can take whatever you want." He looked at the boy's mother. "Is that okay with you?"

"I will come?" she asked in English, unwilling to let the son she'd just gotten back out of her sight.

"Of course. This way."

"You have nothing!" Analia suddenly yelled from the kitchen in English. "Nothing! How do you cats eat? Do you all starve? What is *wrong* with all of you?"

Pina looked at him. "Oh, wow. It's like having Mom back from the Bahamas." She let out a small sigh. *"Great."*

Charlie started baking, and the bears lined up outside. The Malone caravan . . . disappeared. Literally. One second they all seemed to be hanging outside, and the next, all the RVs, cars, picnic chairs, and tables were completely gone. The bears were relieved; the Malone brothers were not surprised.

Nelle sat on the porch swing sideways so she could rest her bare feet in Keane's lap. She had been on her phone for at least an hour, and he had been sitting there, staring straight ahead, all that time. He hadn't said a word or seemed annoyed she hadn't really said anything to him. He was just a comfortable cat, staring.

So she was really pissed off when her sister showed up to yell at her.

She just stomped up those porch stairs and started screaming. And, of course, Nelle screamed back. Because she didn't want to hear her bullshit!

It went on for a while because no one intervened. But her sister was the one who stopped first, finally pointing at an oblivious Keane.

"Is he okay?"

Her sister never cared about anyone. Nelle didn't understand why she was asking.

"He's fine."

452   Shelly Laurenston

"He hasn't looked at me once. Everyone looks at me."

Nelle had barely crossed her eyes when the five Belgian Malinois came running up to the porch and ran to the door, scratching at the wood screen. Her sister simply stood there, doing nothing as always!

"Open the door for them!" Nelle ordered.

"Ewwww, no! You do it!"

God, Nelle hated her.

One of the dogs went up on its hind legs, tilted its head to the side, and managed to get the screen door open with its mouth. Then all five dogs scrambled into the house.

"Wow. *Dogs* are smarter than you," Nelle sneered.

The mutual yelling started again until Tracey Rutowski followed her dumb dogs onto the porch.

"Mimi?"

"Tracey!"

Nelle sneered when her sister and Rutowski kissed each other's cheeks like they were all back in Europe. Then her sister hugged Álvarez, ignored Yoon, and air-kissed the Russian.

"All of you are coming to my wedding, yes?"

"Would not miss it, my love. And I have a wonderful present for you."

Her sister clapped her hands together. Nelle hoped whatever Rutowski gave her was a fake.

When Mimi faced Nelle again, her smile flowed away, and she scowled. "You better be available tomorrow."

"I have practice—"

"I don't want to hear it!" she yelled, before hugging Rutowski again and walking down the stairs and back to her waiting car, the driver holding the back door open for her.

"Charlie inside?" Rutowski asked her.

"Am I her party planner? How the fuck should I know?"

"As always, a delight to see you again, too, Nelle Zhao. Although hard to believe you and Mimi are sisters. So different."

"I actually pride myself on that."

The screen door opened, and Keane's baby sister, Nat, walked out.

TO KILL A BADGER 453

Trailing behind her was Kyle. His infatuation with the badger had been obvious from the beginning, and Nelle immediately looked to see what Keane was going to do about it.

He didn't move, but his gaze locked on Kyle the second the poor jackal stepped outside with the tiger's baby sister. A low growl began inching its way up from the back of his throat, and claws slid from his fingers. It all would have been entertaining if she didn't know that Stevie would not appreciate anything happening to her fellow prodigy.

But before she had to intervene, Rutowski said, "Kyle? Kyle Jean-Louis Parker?"

The jackal stopped and stared down at her. He was very tall for a black-backed jackal, and hot. Nelle wasn't surprised that Nat let him follow her around.

Rutowski took a card out of her back pocket. This particular move was not surprising, since she owned and operated fine art galleries all over the world and Kyle was an extremely well-known young artist coming into his own.

"I've been meaning to introduce myself," she said, handing him the card.

"Ms. Rutowski, right?"

"Yes."

He handed the card back to her. "You'll need to talk to my agent. I list him on my website."

Nelle smiled at that particular slap down. Nice!

"Oh, no, I'm sorry," Rutowski said. "The card's not for you. I wanted you to give it to your mother and tell her to call me. I'm interested in her son. I mean your brother. The one who does the realism work. I saw one of his pieces in Seattle, and it was amazing."

"I remember that!" Álvarez chimed in. "He is so good! You must be proud. Little brother pushing you out of the way, huh?"

She slapped a stunned Kyle on the back and walked inside.

"Just have your mom call me, and we can discuss some options. Maybe a show at my Greenwich Village gallery. Or he could be the star of my new London gallery. Ox just hooked me up with a place and, in a few months, it will be ready to open. The event will be fabulous, and it will be a great start for your brother's career."

She returned the card to his limp hand.

"Thanks, kid. Nice to meet you."

Nelle covered her mouth, knowing how brutal that was on a sensitive artist who just got bitch-slapped by badgers. She motioned to Nat with a small jerk of her head.

"It's okay," Nat said to Kyle. "I'm sure she likes your stuff, too."

"Don't coddle me, woman!"

Biting her lip so she didn't laugh, the young She-badger helped the stunned jackal down the porch stairs and away from the house.

"We're going for ice cream," she called back to her brother before he could say anything.

But Keane still hadn't moved.

He was smiling now, though.

"Stop gloating."

Why shouldn't he? The kid got bitch-slapped by the best. Keane couldn't be happier. Especially since the boy had asked Keane and his brothers to pose for him—naked, no less!—more than once. It was weird! He didn't want his sister hanging around such a weird, snobby kid, but he knew that the more he tried to push them apart, the more Nat would cling to that canine. So it was better just to wait for her to get bored. And she would. She always got bored.

Nelle pulled her feet out of his lap, and he was going to complain, but then she replaced those feet with her perfect ass, arms around his neck. She'd even left her phone in her empty spot.

"You're coming with me to this wedding, right?" she asked.

"Is that why you're sitting in my lap? To manipulate me?"

"Yes."

That made him laugh. Her honesty.

"I said I'd go. I'll go. Are you going to meet your sister tomorrow?"

"Fuck no. But she can argue with Mads about that. Because I'll be at practice, and we both know that Mads will not let me leave. Then

TO KILL A BADGER 455

Mads will punch Max in the face for starting this nightmare." Nelle nodded. "It'll be a good day."

Chuckling, Keane wrapped his arms around her and pulled her close, nuzzling her neck and shoulder.

"As much as I like staying at Mads's place now that I've decorated it for her "

"Which still makes her mad."

"—we have to get a place of our own. I can't live with your mother. I might as well live with my own mother."

"Wait." Keane pulled back to see her face. "We're going to be living together?"

"Might as well. After the finals, our coach will be taking over the New York team, and she wants the five of us to go with her."

"So are we moving in together because we're *together,* or because it's convenient for you?"

"Let's not analyze, okay? Things just work out for me. This is working out for me. Why do you have to ruin it with questions and concerns?"

"I'm not trying to ruin anything. I'm just trying to find out if you—"

Streep started squealing as soon as she saw Nelle in his lap, her voice making Rutowski's dogs bark from inside Charlie's house.

"You two are together!" she squealed, before running over. Nelle leaned back against him to avoid her grasping hands. What she wanted to do with those hands, Keane had no idea. *"I'm so happy for you two!"*

"Okay." Mads grabbed Streep's shoulders. "Let's leave them alone."

"Just let me mush their heads together! Just let me mush!"

"No mushing! Tock!"

"Got her!" Mads and Tock each took an arm and had to drag her off like a crazed stalker wanting an autograph.

"She's so strong," Tock complained.

"Has she had her rabies shot? She may need a rabies shot."

Max finally came out of the house as the others took a still-squealing Streep across the street.

456   *Shelly Laurenston*

"Well, well, well," she said, smiling at them. "Look at you two."

"Shut up," Nelle said, even while she rested against him.

"See? *I* made this happen. I got you two together. This was my fine work."

"How is this because of you?"

"Because I exist. If not for me, you'd have never met, and you wouldn't be rubbing your tiny ass on his giant cock at this very moment."

"Go. Away," Keane snarled.

"By the way, did Mimi get in touch with you, Nelle, because—"

Max took off running, laughing the whole way, while Keane barely managed to keep a snarling and snapping Nelle on his lap.

"Let Max go. She's not worth it."

"I thought you were vengeful."

"I am. Very."

"Then you should understand why I need to beat her into oblivion."

"I understand it, but she'll be going to the wedding, too, right? What better revenge than Max MacKilligan at your sister's wedding . . . doing things?"

Nelle's entire body relaxed, and she smiled. "Excellent point."

"I know."

"And it gives me an excellent reason to go shopping."

"Why do you need to go shopping?"

"My teammates can't just wear *anything*, now, can they? I'll have to buy them the appropriate clothes."

"You mean buy *Mads* the appropriate clothes, don't you?"

"Of course I mean that."

"Just to piss her off?"

"Yes."

As if knowing they were talking about her, Mads screeched from the front of her house across the street, "*Nelle!* We've gotta talk strategy. Get in here!"

Nelle stood. "Want to come?" she asked. "I'm sure your brothers will be there. And there will be food."

"Yeah, okay."

She took several steps away from him, but before Keane could get up, she faced him, cupping his jaw in her hands and leaning in close.

"And we'll be living together," she told him, "because I love you. And if you ever try to leave me, I'll hunt down the slut you left me for and make sure she pays for it with *your* life. Get me?"

Keane grinned. "Perfectly."

"Good!" She kissed him. It was quick, but powerful. Then she strutted off as only Nelle Zhao could in tiny shorts and a tight white tee. As confident as any woman he'd ever known.

His niece, who'd been coming from the back of the house, ran over to the porch and climbed up onto the banister behind the swing. Wrapping her arms around his neck, she asked, "Is my Uncle Mean in love?"

"Yes. He is."

"Will my Uncle Mean become Uncle Nice now?"

"Not in this lifetime."

"Good. I'm not sure I could handle that." She kissed him on the cheek before climbing over him and skipping her way across the porch.

"Besides," she added before disappearing into the house with Charlie, "I'm sure Nelle wouldn't like Uncle Nice, anyway."

Yeah, he knew that, too.

Chapter 37

Paolo woke up slowly. He remembered being caged. He remembered being shoved out of a plane in that cage. Now he was on the ground, but he wasn't dead. Strange. The fall should have killed him. Then he saw the material covering his cage. A parachute, he guessed.

He stood and quickly realized he was lion. He tried to shift to human, but nothing he did . . .

Drugs must still be in his system.

He tried again. And again. Waited an hour, then tried again.

He couldn't shift back to human.

What the fuck?

He remembered someone landing on his back and plunging a needle into his neck. He thought it was to knock him out, but he remembered his body being forced to change, despite him trying to stop it. Now he couldn't change back.

He wasn't sure, but he felt like this was . . . permanent? No. It couldn't be.

Paolo walked toward the cage door, and with one push, he was outside of it. He padded a few feet away and realized they'd dropped him in the middle of Africa.

Fucking wolves. Fucking wolves!

When he saw them again, he'd kill them all! And when he tracked down the MacKilligans . . .

Until then, he would stay here. He could make a life here until whatever they'd used on him wore off and he was able to shift back to human. He was among his own kind, wasn't he?

Deciding to find water and hunt down some food—he was famished—he started walking but came face-to-face with a . . . man? He sniffed. No. A shifter. Honey badger. As if life wasn't bad enough right now.

With wide eyes, the badger looked at Paolo, then his cage. His eyes narrowed, and he started to say something, but his entire body jerked, and he ran off into the bush.

Paolo didn't know why until he heard a small roar.

It was a pride, walking toward him. Three males and a large number of females.

Perfect. He could make this work. They weren't smarter than he was. They were just animals. He was a shifter. Far superior.

He walked toward the pride, ready to become one of them, when he saw two of the females run back to protect the cubs following behind. This pride had cubs. *Shit.*

The males roared, and the females began to circle around him.

Paolo roared back, not sure how to communicate with them. Not sure how to tell them he was one of them. He just wanted—

A male jumped on his back, and Paolo threw him off. But a female attacked his hind legs, dragging him to the ground. More females attacked; the males charged, going for his neck, slashing paws against his spine and face.

He fought back, kicking off the female who held his leg and running off into the bush where he'd seen the badger go.

Paolo neared a body of water that the badger was currently trying to get through. He thought if he could get through it, too, he might get the pride off his scent. But a massive female tackled him from the side, taking him down before he ever reached the water, and the males joined in, grabbing him around the throat, the groin, and the gut.

The last thing he saw as he felt fangs and claws tear his body apart was that fucking badger fighting off a crocodile that had sprung at him from the water.

The badger was kind of winning, too . . .

460   *Shelly Laurenston*

* * *

Keane had just lined up all the champagne glasses and was about to send them flying across the room with a twitch of his claw when Nelle's mother barked, "No! Bad!" at him like he was a cat she'd found in her backyard trash cans. Then she snapped at the all-Asian waitstaff and motioned for them to clean up all the glassware.

"Stop *doing* that!" she ordered him before swan-ing away to greet people at other tables with a fabulous smile and a charming laugh.

A few minutes later, Nelle dropped into a chair next to him.

"You doing all right?" she asked.

"Your mother hates me."

"And I *love* you for that."

She motioned to a waiter, and two glasses of champagne were placed on the table. But the waiter said something to Nelle in Chinese before quickly walking away.

Nelle laughed. "My mom told the staff to take any plates or glasses away as soon as you're done with them and *before* you shot-put them across the room." She laughed harder.

Seeing her laugh, though, absolutely made his day. She had not been happy since she'd been forced to spend the night in her sister's suite with all the other "idiots," as she had called the bridal party. She had texted him selfies the entire evening of her unhappy face in different situations with the bride and her bridesmaids in the background. He had wanted to rescue her, but she'd insisted it wasn't necessary. But to have "bail money ready in case I kill every one of these pple in the nxt 3 hrs." He was beginning to learn some of her weirdly worded texts, although she kept more of the seriously coded words to a minimum once she had realized he'd had to ask his baby sister what the hell she was talking about.

It had been a nice wedding service, though. A seamless combination of two very different cultures. Although Keane could see why Nelle didn't understand what her sister was doing. It wasn't simply because her sister's new husband was a full-human, or because he had to be the whitest white man alive, or even because he was an annoying

TO KILL A BADGER 461

billionaire tech bro who thought his money had made him a "man of the people"—actual idiot words spoken by an actual idiot at one point during the evening—but because the man was, in fact, monumentally *stupid*.

Keane had been forced to overhear a conversation between the man and some of his friends, and it had been so painful that Keane had finally lobbed a plate of food in their direction just to shut them the fuck up. He'd lost a lovely bit of half-eaten prime rib, but it had been worth it. And the staff had immediately replaced his food without question with some Kobe beef.

One of the dude-bros had come over to challenge Keane for his "outrageous asshole-ness," but as soon as Keane stood up and scowled, the six-foot-two, former NFL player had slunk back to his friends, and they had ignored him the rest of the night.

Keane had to admit it . . . he *loved* bullying full-human males. It had to be the most non-Nelle-involved fun he'd had in a long time. They were just so *stupid*.

Then again, Nelle's sister was incredibly vapid. Maybe this really was the best she could do.

"Uh . . . Nelle?"

"Yeah?"

"Do you have a black eye?"

Grinning, she nodded. "And so does my sister!"

"So your mom hates you, too?"

"Probably, but I don't even know if my mother has heard about it yet. But my sister started it."

"You sound like Max."

"I know."

He pointed across the enormous room that held more than five hundred guests—this event was absolutely *insane*—and asked, "You do know your friends are stealing, right?"

Nelle glanced over at her teammates. Somehow those four badgers had gotten an entire dance floor full of people to polka. Keane didn't know how, but he admired the skill required.

462   *Shelly Laurenston*

"No. They're not stealing."

"I'm a Malone, Nelle. I know when I see pickpocketing. For some of my cousins, it's the first thing they learn after using the potty."

"Yes, they're stealing, per se. But they're not *taking* anything. They're just"—she waved her hands around—"mixing things up a little."

"What?"

She gestured to a woman speaking to her mother. "That's Dame Lora Norris-Brunwich. The necklace she's wearing is costume jewelry. It wasn't when she arrived, though. What she was wearing was *that*." She pointed at another female. "That's Jenny D'Bomb. DJ and social media influencer, who is now wearing a one-point-five-million-dollar necklace made from the finest jewels of India. The question is, will anyone notice before either woman leaves?"

"Everyone's pretty well drunk, so probably not. But your friends are weird."

"They are. And they're my 'teammates,'" she said with air quotes, "when Streep's around."

"Got it."

Nelle suddenly crawled into his lap and rested her head against his shoulder.

"Thanks for coming to this shit show," she sighed out.

"Thanks for not forcing me into a tux."

"I told you I wouldn't."

"You ever see a big-chested guy in a tux? No matter how good the tailoring, we always end up looking like the Hulk tearing out of his clothes. It's not attractive."

"You look perfect in your all-black, 'I'm just secret security' outfit."

"I borrowed the jacket from Berg. Or his sister. Or his other brother. I really don't know which one."

"It *is* hard to tell those three apart."

She lifted her chin to look at him. "I was wondering—"

"If we could have sex in the bathroom? The answer's yes."

"No. Yes . . . later. But no, I was wondering if you're okay with how things worked out?"

"With what? This wedding? Because I don't care. Wait . . . am I supposed to care?"

"No, no. Not the wedding." She chuckled a little. "Look, I know you're very particular about your vengeance."

"I am."

"And that things didn't work out, recently, the way any of us expected."

It took Keane a second to realize what she was talking about, but once he did . . .

"Oh. That. Uh. Yeah, I'm fine with how it all went down. In the end."

"You are?"

"Yes. Um . . ." He took a moment to look all around him before continuing with his reply in a low voice. "I didn't care if it was me or Finn or Shay or even my mom who took care of . . . those things. I just wanted it done by family. It was owed to us. And, between you and me . . . I do feel that Charlie MacKilligan is, truly, family."

"Awwwwww!" that voice said from behind him and Nelle, before Streep wrapped her arms around them from behind and continued saying "awww" in the most annoying way possible.

"I am so happy you two are in love!" she loudly cheered. "And that you finally see the MacKilligan sisters as family, Keane! Because they love you, too!"

"Where did you even come from?" Keane snarled. "I looked for you!"

She squeezed them tighter, making Keane again wonder how strong these badgers actually were.

"Mads," Nelle called out, "you better come get your girl."

"Oh?" Mads said, standing on the other side of the table and clearly not helping, "is she doing something you didn't ask her to do? Like decorate your house or buy a dress and shoes that fit perfectly? Does her doing that bother you?"

"Get Streep, or I'm breaking *both* my hands before the champion—"

"Fine!"

Mads walked quickly around the table and pulled Streep's arms away from Keane and Nelle.

464   Shelly Laurenston

"But I just want to smoosh their faces together!" Streep begged.

"Not today. Maybe some other time. Now," Mads suddenly called out to anyone in earshot, "let's all *polka!*"

"No, no!" Nelle's mother said, quickly coming over. "No more of that." She forced a smile before turning on her daughter, fangs out, and snarled, "Get your friends out of here this *minute!*"

"Are you sure? I thought you wanted me to stay until the very—"

"Do it!"

"Yes, ma'am."

Slipping off his lap, Nelle waved at her teammates. "Let's go. Right now."

Mads dragged a still-grasping Streep toward the exit. She really wanted to "smoosh" their heads together. Keane just didn't know why.

Tock was right behind them, her gaze on her watch. Max caught up a few seconds later and, as she passed Nelle, said, "Probably a good idea to go. Someone just realized she wasn't wearing that eighty-thousand-dollar tennis bracelet she had on when she walked in."

Once the others were clear, Nelle took his hand, and they began to weave their way through the enormous crowd and toward the exit he'd been looking at with longing all night.

Nelle waved at her father just before they walked out. He gave her a warm smile before returning to the conversation he'd been having with some prime minister from somewhere important and, before Keane knew it, they were outside and free.

He stopped to take in a breath of fresh New York City air . . . well, it was summertime. So "fresh" was relative. But still. It felt like freedom!

"Hey!" Max called to them from a few feet ahead. "We're starving. You guys up for diner food?"

"Yes!" Nelle replied. "I'm assuming you're hungry," she said to him in a quieter tone.

"I'm a tiger. I'm always hungry."

"You don't mind eating with my teammates?"

"Will Streep keep trying to smoosh our heads together?"

"She will, but I'll beat that out of her before the entrees come."

TO KILL A BADGER 465

"Then it's fine."

"I'm texting Keane's brothers and my man to meet us," Max announced.

Those lucky bastards hadn't been invited since the Zhaos hadn't authorized any "plus ones" to Nelle's teammates.

Nelle released his hand to wrap her arms around his waist, leaning into him as they followed behind the others.

"I love you, Nelle," he told her, unable to stop himself.

"I love you, too." She squeezed him a little tighter. "And I love you even more because my mother absolutely *hates* you now."

"That should bother me," he admitted, hugging her close. "But you know what, beautiful? It really doesn't."

Epilogue

They were on her. Wouldn't let her get past. All of them huge and pissed. Of course, most of them were covered in ripening bruises and still-open wounds. But Nelle was fast. She dribbled under one bear, around a cheetah, and barely avoided a She-lion's big hands.

Then she spotted Max all the way across the court. Closest to the basket. Nelle faked a shot to her, sent it to Tock instead. Tock dribbled forward, head-faked, then sent the ball to Streep. Streep immediately shot it to Max. She caught it, but the other team was already on her. So she bounced it between a She-bear's incredibly long legs, and Mads got the ball. With the timer ticking down, Mads took two big steps and went up in the air, one hand high, the ball in her palm . . .

She dunked that bitch into the basket as the final whistle blew! And it was done.

They'd gotten that last basket in, and they'd beaten the other team by a mere two points after three overtimes.

Mads landed hard on the ground, dropped to her knees, and screamed. The entire team was off the bench and on the court, tackling her to the ground. A big pile of happy female predators cheering, screaming, and roaring. Except the cheetahs. They happily chirped instead.

The crowd roared along with them, and music began to play. People ran down to the court, and suddenly Keane was hugging her and lifting her up onto his shoulders. As proud of her as if it were an American football game and not a game he liked to call "stupid."

It was actually quite wonderful. Shay and Finn were there to support Tock and Mads. Zé was there for Max, along with Max's sisters. And Streep's fiancée, Ashley, was there, and Max still didn't seem to remember her despite knowing the female since high school!

In time, the entire team was all on the stage when the trophy was given out. Well, first they got caps with the year and CHAMPIONS written on the front and white T-shirts with the same. Then the trophy was awarded . . . to the team owners. Millionaire hyena females that giggled and held up the trophy, even though Nelle didn't think they'd spent a second playing on a court in their entire lives. Then the MVP award was given out, and it went to Max MacKilligan, which made even Mads happy.

If that had been the end, it would have been perfect. But when Nelle saw her father politely applauding from the stands . . .

She jumped off the stage and ran to him, throwing her arms around his neck and hugging him tight.

"What are you doing here?" she asked loudly, so as to be heard over the still-cheering crowd and the music.

"You made your sister's wedding, only punched her in the face once, and didn't make your mother tell me she wanted you disowned. So how could I miss this momentous occasion for my little girl?" He motioned to the court. "You were amazing out there, my little crested serpent eagle."

"Daddy."

He hugged her again.

"He's very proud of you," he said to her. "Your big kitty."

Nelle knew that. Keane was still on the stage with the team, Dani on his shoulders, her little fists in the air, cheering louder than anyone.

"I'm glad," her father continued. "I would never want you with a man who couldn't handle your success." He leaned in and whispered, "I hear his football team is not very good."

"He's whipping them into shape, though, Daddy."

"Good."

"Want to come with us to dinner?"

"No, no. Your mother is waiting. But a family dinner invite will be on its way soon. You and your tiger will come, yes?"

"Of course."

"Good. And one other thing before I go . . ."

"Yes?"

"It's being said that Paolo de Medici is dead. His remains found somewhere in Africa."

Nelle stared at her father a moment before replying, "Good."

"My feelings exactly . . . my little crested serpent eagle."

"*Daddy.*"

Charlie watched her sister and her teammates head to Mads's house for a late-night party. Doing something at a club had been discussed, but no one was in the mood for that. They wanted some time with just the team and their partners. There'd be a barbeque the next day in Charlie's yard for the entire team, the owners, and everyone's family and friends. It would be huge.

And Charlie was actually looking forward to it, which was strange. Usually parties made her anxious, but she was so proud of her sister and her friends, she couldn't wait to host something for them. Especially since Nelle would be doing most of the work. That girl did love to organize and decorate. Apparently a "staff" and "professional party planner" had already been hired and had been to her yard to "measure the space."

Whatever. Charlie was sure it would all go fine.

She whistled, and her dogs came running, coming to a dead stop at her feet. They gazed up at her and fell in step as soon as she started walking. She forgot their leashes again. Not that she used them, but she liked to have them in her hand in case cops drove by.

It didn't matter, though. She had no intention of going for a long walk with the dogs. They just needed a break before she went in for the night. Berg was waiting for her with cheese and wine and Chips Ahoys. Her favorite chocolate chip cookies, much to his fascination, since his neighbors had been offering her money if she'd bake more of *her* from-scratch chocolate chip cookies.

As she and the dogs turned the corner, she realized she now had ten dogs instead of five, because five Belgian Malinois and Tracey Rutowski settled in next to her.

"People find sneaking up on me is not a wise move," she reminded Rutowski.

"Well, Giuseppe de Medici learned that the hard way, didn't he?"

Charlie stopped and faced the She-badger. She was in too good a mood to play games with Tracey Rutowski. So she cut right to it.

"What do ya want?"

"To hire you."

"Forget it. I don't steal for others, and I don't care how great the take will be—"

"I'm not talking about stealing. I'm talking about an organization to protect honey badgers. And I want you to run it. It'll be *my* deal. Me and my friends, I mean. We'll make sure you get what you need, including money, papers, weapons, whatever. We'll bring in the assignments and make sure they're legitimate. You and whoever you hire make sure our kind stays safe. That's the deal."

"You want *me* in charge of protecting honey badgers . . . worldwide?"

"Yes. You. I can't imagine anyone else. And everyone agrees with me."

"Everyone? Who's everyone?"

"The Santiagos, the Davises, the Von Schäfer-Müllers, the Zhaos, the Mings. As well as the Akinyi from Kenya and the Osondu out of Nigeria. We've got their support and their financial backing."

Charlie studied the She-badger in front of her. One of the Malinois went up on its hind legs and, while meeting Charlie's gaze, Rutowski petted it on the neck and head. The dog nuzzled her arm with true affection, and the way she looked down at the canine . . .

"You tricky bitch," Charlie said.

Rutowski blinked at her in feigned surprise. "What?"

"You weren't trying to get the families together to fight the de Medicis. You were getting them together to back your little protection agency."

470 *Shelly Laurenston*

"I knew you could have handled those lions without any help. But they were an excellent catalyst to prompt the others to get involved."

"Over the years, we've had others try to wipe out our kind. You've had more than enough catalysts. So . . ." Charlie closed her eyes in exasperation and let out a long sigh. "Oh, my God. You could have started a group like this at any time, but . . . you just didn't want to pay for it yourself, did you?"

She shrugged. "I never pay retail."

"Wow . . . I see why Edgar Van Holtz hates you."

"Ugggggh!" she said, head dropping back. "He is *still* such a whiny bitch!"

"And *you* are a cheap ass!"

"I am budget *conscious!*" She smirked. "Soon, you'll appreciate that. When we're working together."

"After the way you used Nelle? And those badger families? What makes you think I'd ever trust *you?*"

Tracey Rutowski took a step so they were close; face-to-face and, keeping her voice low, said, "Because, Charlie MacKilligan, what you're about to learn about me . . . I *never* let down my friends."

Sometime in the eighties . . .

"Leave us."

There was the slightest of hesitation, but his men walked out. They were Stasi. If they knew anything, they knew to follow orders.

But the American, Manse, lingered. "What are you going to do?" he asked in German.

There was no reply, though, for such a stupid American question. Just waited for him to go, which he did.

Once alone with the prisoner, he stared down at her.

She was young. Maybe fifteen? But for someone so young, she had quite the history. And strength!

The little Russian still hadn't given up her contacts in East Germany. He needed those names. And he was going to get them.

Standing in front of her, making sure she saw his size and scars, so she would understand *exactly* what she was dealing with, he began, "Now, my sweet—"

A strange sound had him turning, but before he could really look, he realized what he'd just seen right in front of him.

Snapping back around, he stared at her.

She was tied to the chair, arms locked behind her back and her ankles secured to the chair legs. He'd taken off her blindfold but had left her gagged so she could do nothing but scream and cry.

In other words, he'd made her as vulnerable as he could.

So why was she so calm?

"I can call my men back in," he threatened her in Russian. "Would you like that, my sweet?" He smiled. "I think you would like that."

He heard a thump from overhead and briefly glanced up, but saw nothing but the stone ceiling.

Returning his focus to the girl, he stared. Confused. Something had changed.

She still seemed so calm. Her gaze direct, almost bold. Her legs crossed at the knees . . .

Wait. Her legs had been secured to the chair, yes?

Another thump. This one under his feet.

He didn't like this at all. He started to call out to his team, but that's when he saw the girl scratch a spot on her face with a free hand and no gag blocking her finger.

"What the—"

Something landed on his back; a small hand wrapped around his mouth to silence him, while the other hand buried a blade into his shoulder muscle. He reached back, grabbed, and threw. A different girl from the prisoner spun across the room and slammed into the wall.

He reached for his gun, but the holster was empty. Then the gun was slammed into his face, and he stumbled to the side. A wooden stool slammed into his back and knocked him to the ground.

Three girls in denim jeans and T-shirts and American sneakers stood in front of him, staring down at him.

He didn't understand. What was happening? *How* was this happening? How did they get in here?

"My friend," his prisoner, no longer secured to the chair at all, said to a brown-haired girl. And she spoke English. Excellent English.

"Oksana. I am so glad to finally meet you!" An American? How did an American *child* get into East Germany, much less a secret Stasi facility?

How . . . when . . .

What was happening?

Knowing he needed to warn his superiors, he began to drag himself toward the door, but a small hand grabbed his foot, yanked him back.

"And where are *you* going, Mr. Pervy?" the American asked.

With those four girls staring down at him, the American handed the blood-covered blade she'd stabbed him with to the Russian.

"Would you like to do the honors, my friend?" the American asked.

"I would, comrade. Thank you." His prisoner crouched so she was close to him and said, "Would you like that, my sweet?" She smiled, and that's when he saw nothing but rows of small, white fangs. "I think you would like that . . ."